PRAISE FOR Steve Piacente's

BOOTLICKER

stevepiacente.com

"Piacente's tenure as Washington correspondent for the *Post and Courier* gave him an insider's view of South Carolina politics, racial issues and backroom shenanigans that helped make his second novel ... an intriguing, suspenseful political thriller."

— *Larry Tarleton, retired publisher, The Post and Courier*

"A fascinating read about the threads of power between Washington and South Carolina."

— *Professor J. David Woodard, Clemson University, author of, The New Southern Politics, and, The America that Reagan Built.*

"Piacente ... takes us into the mind of aspiring news reporter Dan Patragno and political rising star Big Ike, bringing new meaning to the term 'political lynching.' Intrigue, race crimes, a hidden past and retribution take the reader on one thriller of a journey. Piacente nails it."

— *Melanie Saxton, book editor and reviewer, Houston, TX*

"A haunted politician and an ambitious reporter collide on a story that promises not to disappoint. Piacente sets the tone for terrible secrets to be revealed in such a masterful way that you are hooked from the opening sentence."

— Collette Scott, Phoenix, AZ

"Authentic and exciting from page one! *Bootlicker* captures the inside stories from a reporter's point of view."

— Candy O'Donnell's Blogspot, Orangevale, CA

"Piacente is clearly a Washington D.C. insider, well versed in how newspaper reporters and newspapers work. Well done."

— Skip Stern, NY Goodreads reviewer

"A tightly wound and seductive tale ... I was hooked from the start."

— Marsha Pesavento, owner, Artisanal Wilmette, Wilmette, IL

"Suspense never felt so good."

— Susan Chiellini, Tampa, FL

"It's not easy to write the next great story. Piacente does it and does it to perfection."

Barbara Briggs Ward, Author/Allustrator, Ogdensburg, NY

BOOTLICKER

A Novel by Steve Piacente

For My Wife Felicia,

And our Children,

Danielle, Ali and Nick

Some pursue happiness; others create it

… Anonymous

BOOTLICKER

A Novel by Steve Piacente

1   *Dan*

D an Patragno opened the front door to a smell that made him
shudder. Couldn't be from the bodies, he thought. Too soon to
start rotting, or was it?

He breathed through his mouth and tiptoed past the threshold of the
shabby little house as if live mines hid within the scruffy shag carpet. He
sniffed the odor of rancid food, dirty laundry, sweat, mildew, and yes,
maybe the beginning of decaying bodies.

Three cops and a plain-clothes detective huddled in a back bedroom
talking to a young woman, but Dan didn't want to join them just yet. He
detoured to the kitchen, pulled a skinny pad from his back pocket, and
flipped to an empty page. "Murder-suicide: 8/2/92," he wrote.

The sink was stained, chipped and crammed with dishes, some clean,
some crusted with spaghetti sauce from what he figured was a happier
night, maybe last night. Dan barely moved. He closed his eyes a second
and tried to imagine the husband and wife sitting at the sad, four-legged
table with its pale blue vinyl tablecloth and folding card chairs. Did they
laugh as they ate their spaghetti? He felt sure they called it spaghetti, not
pasta. Did the man smile as he stabbed a fork-full and twirled it against

his spoon? Did he listen as his wife talked about her day?

He opened his eyes to the kitchen mess. Half an iceberg lettuce sat on the counter, the outer leaves brown and sagging. An empty box of apple cinnamon *Pop Tarts* topped the stuffed trash pail. His eye followed a wall that was standard landlord white to a clock with Roman numerals and a long, stuttering second hand that told him this miserable Saturday wouldn't be over for another two hours.

Got to hustle to make the final. He reached for the door of the humming refrigerator, and, knowing better after eight-and-a-half months on the night cop beat, pulled it open. The bulb was out, but there was enough light to see three tall-necked bottles of beer, a half-empty plastic jug of milk, several small jars of baby food, butter, pancake syrup, a few dimpled red apples, and a Styrofoam container from a fast food restaurant. A line of dirt ringed the vegetable drawer, and the freezer compartment was caked with ice. He put his finger on the frosty door to feel the cold.

"*Patragno*, what the fuck are you doing?"

He slammed the fridge shut. Something plastic and colorful flew to the floor, bounced on the linoleum and skidded to a corner by the garbage pail. The brown and yellow object was a fridge magnet shaped like a hotdog splashed with mustard. He picked it up and handed it to Berkeley County Detective Stan LeTourge.

"Looking for clues, Stan."

"Jesus, you're not even supposed to be in here. I told you to keep your hands to yourself. You're a reporter, not a detective. You mess up a crime scene and it's my ass."

"Sorry Stan, you're right."

LeTourge shook his head. "This isn't Thursday hoops, Danny. This guy killed his daughter, then did himself with a shotgun."

The detective loosened his tie and paced to the other side of the kitchen. "You begged me to let you in. Said you wouldn't touch anything. Right. None of you guys care about anything but the story. I turn my back to talk to the mother—she's got a cut over her black eye that took twelve stitches—and find you in here looking for a snack."

Dan bowed his head and snuck a look at his watch. One hour, fifty minutes to deadline.

"You're right. I got carried away. I was trying to find something, I don't know what. A reason. Something to explain it."

They both glanced up as pebbles of hail began tapping the kitchen window and a streak of lightning lit the yard. Dan caught a glimpse of a metal clothes tree and tried to focus on a pair of jeans and several tiny T-shirts fastened to the line by wooden clothespins that were holding firm against the summer storm.

"Okay," LeTourge said. "Just keep your mitts off everything and get lost before the TV guys show up, or they're going to want to come in too."

"Couple of questions?"

"Yeah, don't use my name. We haven't notified next of kin. Say 'a Berkeley County Sheriff's Department source.'"

Dan nodded. "What do you know for sure?"

"It's a domestic. He—name's Willie Agee, spelled like it sounds, A-g-double-e—beat her, probably not the first time. She, Clarissa—C-l-a-r-i-s-s-a—Agee, drove to her mother's apartment in Goose Creek, twenty-five minutes north. She left the kid with him. He called, told her to get home. She said no, and he started shooting. That's it."

"Was the guy mental?"

"Yup. No details yet. Definitely spent time at the county hospital. Grew up in foster homes, quit high school. No blood relatives we know about in the area. No close friends."

"What did he do for work?"

"Part-time garbage man for the county. He worked today and yesterday."

"Age?"

"Twenty-three. She's twenty. The baby … " Stan exhaled. "Baby's name was Monique—M-o-n-i-q-u-e. Nine months."

"Did Willie Agee have a record?"

"One drug bust and some kid stuff. Stolen cars. Fighting. Public nuisance."

"Hold on. My pen." He shook it, tapped it on the pad, licked its needle point, coaxed some ink into place.

"Ready?" Stan said. "Or would you like to borrow my pen? Maybe you just take *my* notes."

"Sarcasm's not your strong suit, Stan."

"Okay, a neighbor said he came over after the first blast. The houses out here are a hundred, a hundred-fifty yards from each other. The door was locked. He looks in the baby's bedroom window, sees the butt of the firearm on the floor and the barrel in Agee's mouth. Neighbor started hitting on the window, but Agee ignored him."

"Did he live after … "

Stan snorted. "Shotgun was a big one, Danny. Mr. Agee was a dead sumbitch before his brains splashed the wall. Don't print that. Oh, yeah, he was loaded on crack and we found a nice stash of powder in his bedroom. Print *that*."

Dan finished scribbling and looked up, waiting politely before springing his last question. LeTourge yawned and rubbed his eyes. "Gotta wrap up. See you later."

"Stan, can I talk to the wife?"

"Nope, she's a mess."

"Three questions."

"You're taking advantage of our friendship."

"Three, that's it. I'll be gentle."

The detective shook his head disgustedly, but pointed to the living room, where Clarissa Agee sat in a tattered green paisley rocker. Dan glanced through the doorway and rubbed behind his left ear, where a deadline headache was gathering force. The tough part was trying to respect her privacy (impossible, but he would be sympathetic) while mining for a nugget that would make his story better than anyone else's. He needed some piece that would add depth, or drama, or even, hope of hopes, help others spot warning signs in people like Willie Agee. Maybe head off another tragedy somewhere else. And maybe get him off the night cop beat. Dan watched a moment as the toes of the woman's sneakers rose and fell, pushing the rocker back and forth over and over.

"She grabbed what was left of that baby up in her arms before we could stop her," LeTourge said, his explanation for why blood stained Mrs. Agee's gray T-shirt.

Dan took one of the folding kitchen chairs and planted it in front of the woman. Two tan-uniformed sheriff's deputies glanced at LeTourge, who signaled his okay for the interview. Dan felt one of the cops look at him like he was puke.

"Mrs. Agee, I'm Daniel Patragno from the *Charleston Herald-Leader*. Could you tell me what happened?"

Clarissa Agee stared straight ahead, rocking in steady rhythm. Her elbows rested on the arms of the chair, her hands formed a triangle over her mouth. A tiny gold bracelet circled two fingers and she looked deep in thought, like someone searching for the word that unlocks the Sunday crossword. Dan saw her tongue move tentatively and stop under the front teeth on the right side of her mouth. As she pushed gently, three teeth wiggled in their sockets and watery blood oozed up.

"Didn't believe him," she said softly, rocking more quickly.

"Mrs. Agee?"

She put her middle finger to her teeth, pulled it away and looked at the blood.

"Didn't believe him," she whispered again.

"What didn't you believe, Mrs. Agee? That he would use the gun?"

One of the deputies put his hand on the reporter's shoulder. Dan threw it off.

"That's it," the deputy said, thumb hooked in his thick leather belt. "Leave her alone."

Clarissa Agee put her heels down and stopped rocking. Dan and the deputy forgot each other as she started speaking in a slow, quiet monotone, eyes half shut and unfocused.

"Said if I didn't get back right away, he'd kill Monique. Said if I didn't come back, he'd shoot the baby and then himself. Said he loved me, said he was sorry he hurt me."

She wiped her tears on her shirt and brought back blood-smeared fingers. The bracelet slid to her lap, then to the floor. She left it.

"Why didn't you take Monique with you when you left?" Dan said.

Clarissa Agee pushed her toes and the chair started rocking. She looked at him for the first time and touched her stitches. "He beat me. Hard. His fists … had to run."

"Why didn't you come back when he made the threat? Wouldn't that have stopped him long enough to get help?"

The deputy shifted and scowled.

"Didn't believe him," she said. "Didn't think he could do it. Didn't think no man could kill his own like that."

"Mrs. Agee, did your mother come back to the house here with you?"

"Mama's hip … She's in a wheelchair."

Dan closed his notebook and stood, aware there were fifty minutes to deadline. He turned to leave and pivoted back. "I'm sorry for your loss, Mrs. Agee."

"I heard the shots," she murmured.

"What?"

"I heard the shots. He never hung up the phone. Screamed loud after he shot Monique. I heard him. Like an animal." Clarissa Agee slumped forward. "I heard the second shot. Then I didn't hear nothin' more."

The last wrenching quotes made his handwriting sloppy as a second-grader's. This was the piece that would catapult him to the front page and raise his stock in the newsroom. His pen grew hard to control; he could only fit a few of her words on a page before having to flip to another, and was still writing long seconds after she'd stopped speaking. In that space, he heard the rain beating the roof and the cop's impatient breathing. Finally, he finished, forced out a thank-you and condolences that drew no response from the blank-faced woman, and raced for the door. Before it slammed shut, he heard one cop say to his partner, "Prick reporters."

2   *Ike and Ezra*

Big Ike is tumbling through dreams of poverty and palaces when he feels the room shudder.

"Ike."

The voice is young … old … new … *familiar*. Ike tries to will the quiet to return. He rolls over and is frozen by words he has heard before and knows well.

"Need to talk, Ike."

"Again?"

He groans and rubs his eyes with the soft heels of his big hands.

"Ok, ok, gimme a second."

He draws his legs around wearily and sits up on the side of the bed facing the window. His striped pajama shirt has ridden up his barrel chest. He doesn't straighten it. The room is black save for a blade of moonlight that has pierced the curtains. He peers through the window, sees a tree across the street and a swing blowing back and forth in the breeze. *That swing.* It is as familiar and disturbing as the voice.

"You, me, we got to get this straight."

"Of course, of course."

This time the voice is laced with anger.

"I never did nothin' man, least nothin' to deserve what I got."

"I know. God I know, Ezra."

"You know. Course you know. You Ike Washington. Big Ike. Big man."

Ike brushes sweat from his forehead with two slow, windshield wiper swipes and cleans his hands on his pajamas. Ezra is not done.

"I didn't do nothin' wrong. You knew it. Why'd you run?"

"Scared."

"Me too. More scared than you."

Ike snakes his tongue along the back of his front teeth. No fillings, no jagged crevices. He has always had good dentists, white dentists. Not like those he came up with. *Most of them boys never saw a doctor, never mind a dentist.* An image rises from the distant past, of Ezra cleaning the storefront glass of McCauley's Drugstore. Squeegee in one hand, soft white rag in the other. Oh, how he would check from each angle to make sure he didn't leave smudges. And oh, how Old Man McCauley always found something wrong anyway. Ike says,

"I was just a boy. I didn't have a chance."

"That's the best you got?"

"It's the truth, damn it. I would have been dead."

"Like me."

"I'm sorry."

"You're sorry. Good word. That's you: Sorry Ike."

3   *Dan*

The drive from rural Berkeley County to the newsroom in downtown Charleston would take fifteen minutes, maybe twenty in the storm. Dan wiped the foggy windshield with his shirtsleeve and shut the radio, composing as he drove. He tried hard for the *lede*, knowing if he could get the first sentence—one that told the whole sordid story in twenty-five words or less—the rest would drop into place. He considered writing it straight, in bulletin fashion: *A twenty-one-year-old Berkeley County sanitation worker killed his infant daughter, then committed suicide after a domestic dispute Saturday night, police said.* Thing was, TV and radio would tell it that way a hundred times between now and tomorrow morning, the earliest most would read the paper. He decided instead to begin with the survivor.

Up ahead, he could make out a sharp bend to the left that signaled the end of I-26 and the beginning of downtown Charleston. He ignored the flashing red light at the end of the exit ramp and pulled onto East Bay Street. Three long blocks and two more lights to the paper. He glanced right, noticed the rain had driven off the usual crowd in front of the chicken joint. He pulled out his ID, set it on the dash, and wiped again at the windshield.

Even after business hours, management made employees use IDs to open the parking lot gate. Dan parked in the closest space to the building and raced across Bull Street to the double glass doors in front of the building, where he had to flash his card to the night security guard.

"Dan, you're sweating!"

"You're not gonna believe this one, Amos." He popped his ID into a narrow silver slot that opened another glass door that led to a hallway and two creaky elevators. The *Herald-Leader*, the "South's Oldest Newspaper," was pieced together each night in a 90-year-old, three-floor building that blended New South technology and Old South charm at the corner of Bull (an endless source of amusement to critics), and Columbus streets. Circulation, personnel and the printing presses were on the first floor. Advertising, a small lunchroom, and a rooftop eating area with white wrought-iron furniture took up the third. The newsroom, including sports, features and graphics, was on the second.

Dan was about to bolt up the stairs when one of the elevators arrived. He entered and tap-tapped number two seven times before the doors would close. A pair of steel cables groaned and he glanced up, vowing for the hundredth time to investigate precisely how the city public works department inspected elevators.

He checked his watch: 11:45. The most he could hope for was thirty minutes writing time. A half-hour to turn nine pages of sloppy notes into what he hoped would be front-page material. He pounded the elevator door like a slumlord. "*Come on.*" He looked at a page of notes and imagined Willie Agee at this very moment, hurtling toward Hell, half his head blown away. Christ, he was only a year older than that psycho. And Clarissa, left to clean up the mess when she was done rocking.

He was thankful the bodies were gone by the time he had gotten there.

Now the job was to get it all in one story, and fast. So far, he hadn't screwed up in eight months of covering the seediest beat at the paper. He had become expert on rapes, gang fights, arsons, even one high school gym teacher who was arrested for banging a student. Most of it seemed to break on his watch, and right near deadline. Tonight would be no different. He ran a hand through his wet hair and was through the doors as soon as they cracked open.

"Patragno, you got thirty minutes, not a second more. Tell me what this story's gonna say."

Dan didn't bother looking up. The voice, he knew, belonged to Lee Cohen, night city editor and the Southern newsroom's only other Long Islander.

"Young guy, crackhead who's been in and out of mental hospitals, killed his kid and himself while his wife was on the line listening to the whole thing."

The editor's eyes narrowed. "Yeah?"

"Yeah."

"Okay, we'll take it out front. Give me fourteen inches, no more."

"You got it."

The long, rectangular newsroom was packed with six-desk cubicles separated by lightly smoked Plexiglas and soft gray partitions. A bone-colored computer linked to the paper's in-house network sat on each steel-gray modular desk. Reporters had twelve-inch monochrome monitors with dark screens and bright green characters; editors got sixteen-inch color monitors. All had access to the same electronic warehouses— called "baskets"—that were loaded with the day's international, national, sports, business, and state news and provided by the *Associated Press*, *Knight-Ridder*, and the *New York Times News Service*. The network allowed users to send and receive messages, and for reporters to route stories to the proper editors. Since such transfers took only seconds, it was possible for a completed story to be edited, sent back to the reporter for minor adjustments, then routed back to the editor within minutes.

Dan saw the light on his phone flashing and tried to resist checking his messages. He could do it later; every second was precious now. The light glowed orange, then went dark. Orange, dark, orange, dark. He grabbed the phone and punched in Star 7. Wrong number. He slid his chair in front of the computer, typed "Patragno" on the login line, and "WAPO" for his password. The secret code word was a daily reminder that his destination was the *Washington Post*, not the *Charleston Herald-Leader*. Summoning the lead still bouncing through his head, he typed:

HANAHAN—Clarissa Agee listened on the telephone in horror Saturday night as her distraught husband killed their infant daughter, then turned a .22 gauge shotgun on himself. He died instantly.

He read and re-read it, closed his eyes, and read it again. The words felt good to his ear. Now he needed a quote, some words to get across the mother's state of mind, something that would give the sense of the story in one or two more lines. He flipped pages in his pad until he came to the quote he knew no other reporter would have. And typed:

"I heard the shots," the 19-year-old Berkeley County housewife told the *Herald-Leader* in an exclusive interview. "He never hung up the phone. Screamed loud after he shot Monique. I heard him. Sounded like an animal."

Next came a summary paragraph and attribution. He tried several combinations before settling on:

The tragedy began early Saturday evening as a domestic dispute. Mrs. Agee fled to her mother's house in Monck's

Corner after she was beaten by 23-year-old Willie Agee, a part-time sanitation worker with a history of mental illness and drug abuse, according to a Berkeley County Sheriff's Department source.

Dan wrapped up twenty-four minutes later. He glanced around to make sure no one was looking, then held out his hand to see if he had the deadline trembles. Pleased when his fingers held steady, he punched a key that transferred the story to the city desk. "All yours, Ron." He sat back and relaxed. A few more of these, he figured, and he'd be packing for D.C.

Eighteen months ago, he was sitting pretty: top five percent at Georgetown, editor of the college paper and an intern at the *Post*. Seemed like an express lane to permanent employment at 15th and L, where he would begin work at the Metro desk, move up to, say, state politics, then try for an assignment abroad. Maybe something in Europe. He would find relatives in Italy. His aunt would have wavy black hair, smell of sweet plum tomatoes, and have him to dinner often.

Turned out the *Post* had a hundred better-qualified applicants and only a handful of openings. Start someplace smaller, they said. So he flooded the nation's top papers with his resume and wound up with two crappy offers, eventually choosing the Deep South over the Far West, spending a year as a high school sportswriter in Naples, Florida, before landing in Charleston. Dan waited to see if there were questions from Cohen or either of the two other editors who would read his story. Once everyone was happy, the piece would wind up on the front page of the city edition, the final version of the day's paper and the one read by the cream of the newspaper's readership, everyone who lived and worked downtown.

Production-wise, every night was pretty much the same. After each of four editions of the next day's paper was printed, an intern, most likely from the College of Charleston, brought several copies to the newsroom. Dan decided to wait for the final. He liked the feel of a paper fresh off the giant Goss Metroliner presses. The words seemed cleaner, the pictures sharper, the ink more pungent.

He thought about a follow-up for Sunday and began sorting through some possibilities. There was the neighbor he didn't have time to interview, and the funeral arrangements. Would Clarissa Agee let the baby be buried next to the father? What would the young widow have inscribed on her child's tombstone?

Or her husband's? And what would she do now? Dan cleared a spot on his desk and put his feet up. He considered addressing domestic violence in a longer piece for next weekend. Detective Stan LeTourge would help with local stats, and he could check with the attorney general's office for state figures.

"Patragno, in here a minute."

Dan kicked over half a cup of old coffee as he swung around. Lem Butcher was usually gone by 8:30, after the first edition was out on the white and orange *Herald-Leader* trucks and headed for points north, south and west. A sturdy boat would be needed to deliver east, where Charlestonians liked to say the Ashley and Cooper Rivers met to form the Atlantic Ocean.

Lem Butcher was probably the only city editor in America who doubled as a newspaper romance advisor. But, "*Ask Lem*" was one of the paper's most popular features, and Lem's logo, in bold, ten-inch Times New Roman with a heart-shaped exclamation point at the end, was plastered on billboards, bus panels, and newspaper racks all over town. His face was not, however, for Lem, though savvy as Ann or Abby, had bulldog cheeks and a gold-plated front tooth that some advertising hotshot decided would turn off women readers. Lem mocked the strategy by hanging one of the posters on his office wall. Taped below "Ask Lem" was a photo of himself wearing a silk shirt unbuttoned to his hairy belly button and a dirty, open-mouthed sneer through which poked an inch of his pink, pointy tongue.

Though unendingly patient with his lovelorn fans, Butcher spoke a clipped shorthand in the newsroom. It was, "Whatcha got?" or, "You call this a *lede*?" Or the one everyone mimicked: "Move! We work for a *daily* paper." Butcher wanted at least two front-page quality stories each day from his stable of twenty-two reporters.

Dan mopped up some of the cold coffee, though most had already seeped into the papers, notebooks, and old police reports piled on his desk. "Right there," he called over. "Ron, need anything else?"

"Nah, you did good. Guy was a sick bastard."

Dan threw out the wad of soggy paper towels and found Butcher pondering a letter handwritten on loose-leaf paper. "Be right with you, Patragno." He held up the stack of pages. "This one's from Darlene. The dear girl has a sister-in-law coming on to her husband. The husband's flirting back, right in front of the family. The sister-in-law's ten years younger than the wife and used to flash her legs in TV commercials for a local car dealer. Darlene wants to know how to handle it without making a scene."

Dan flashed on Willie Agee, considered a joke, and decided against it. Too raw.

Butcher turned to his computer. Unlike many of the middle-aged managers, he was a good typist and rapped out several quick paragraphs. He pushed his glasses to his forehead, moved closer to the screen and re-read his work, making small revisions.

"Okay, that takes care of her. How you doing, Patragno? Tough night?"

"Sort of. Seems there's been a lot of … "

"How'd you get into that house and talk to the mother?" Butcher interrupted, pushing his chair out from his desk so that their knees were only a foot apart.

"I knew the detective working the case. We play basketball on open gym night at The Citadel."

Butcher locked his hands behind his head and leaned back. "And this jocko detective simply let you into a fresh crime scene? And talk to a woman whose baby was just shot dead?"

Dan didn't know if he was in trouble. This kind of crap never came up when he was covering sports.

"Relax," Butcher smiled. "You did great. Real enterprise. In fact, that's why I called you in. Boot camp's over. As of now, you're off night cops. I'm putting you on day cops."

Dan fought for self-control. Butcher laughed.

"I'm kidding, Patragno. Your writing is good, your instincts are good for a Yankee, and you've been reliable so far. What I'm doing, at least through November, is moving you up, putting you on politics. Ever cover politics?"

The answer was no. He felt suddenly small and inconsequential. How could he have been in Washington four years and never covered anything that qualified as politics?

"A little," he answered. "Some campus stuff at Georgetown. Faculty versus administration stuff, and there was a student protest against apartheid in South Africa."

"Good. 'Politicians are the same all over. They promise to build a bridge even where there is no river.' That's from Nikita Khrushchev. Know who Khrushchev was?"

"Didn't he run Russia during the Bay of Pigs?"

"Good, they taught you some history. We've got our own history in the making this year. There hasn't been a black congressman from South Carolina since the Civil War, what some still call the *War of Northern Aggression*."

Dan hoped Butcher wasn't headed into a rant about Lee, Grant and what might have been if a different flag was flying when the dust cleared at Gettysburg.

"Last year, the United States Justice Department told our state legislature to draw a new congressional district with a black majority in time for the November election. The idea was to tilt the odds so that a black candidate would almost surely win. That would end the record of no black congressman in ninety-eight years. Any of this ring a bell?"

"Sure. The favorite is Ike Washington, mayor of one of those little towns in the—what do they call that rural, middle part of the state—the PeeDee, right?"

"Right. The town is Kilgo. Know anything else about Ike Washington?"

"Not really."

"Washington works backstage for Senator Lander McCauley. Most call him 'Mac;' we're more formal at the paper and usually use 'Lander.' It's pretty well known that if anyone in a black community wants something from Lander McCauley, Ike Washington is the guy to see. First thing I want you to do is start working on a profile of Washington. Read the clips in the library. Talk to some of the politicos around Charleston. Then go up there, meet him, find out what he's about."

Dan rose, a little dizzy, aware suddenly that his headache was gone. At the door, he paused. "You want me to handle the follow-up on this murder-suicide?"

"Who's on day cops tomorrow?"

"Baxter."

"Let him do it. Leave him a note. A suicide note. Ha!"

Dan nodded, turned, then looked back. "What'd you tell her, by the way?"

Butcher squinted.

"Darlene. The one with the sister-in-law."

"Oh," Butcher smiled, glancing at the letter atop his pile. "I told her to get right in that woman's face and not worry about making a scene. You remember that advice, hear?"

4

He awoke happy Sunday morning. He'd slept alone, but front-pagers were almost as good as sex. He used the bathroom, slugged down OJ from the carton, and trudged to the small patio of his second-floor apartment, running shoes in one hand, a pair of not-too-dirty sweat socks in the other. All was quiet for as far as he could see, from the maze of downtown shops, restaurants and municipal buildings whose exteriors were monitored by the pinch-nosed, eagle-eyed historic preservation crowd, to his favorite house across the way, the beige *Italiante* with round head arches and a chocolate balustrade that wrapped around the second floor, pretty as a doll house. In colonial times, Charleston was the nation's fourth-largest city. Today, it was a small town with a big attitude.

History in the *Holy City*, where churches claimed nearly as much real estate as high schools, was more than a string of events that ran from past to present. Tradition and heritage were worn like jewels, revered like religion. The Civil War was not fought so the South could keep slaves, many Charlestonians had patiently explained to him, but to stop Washington from snatching up rights that belonged to the states. Rights guaranteed in the Constitution. *And yes, young man, the Confederate flag still flies proudly over the Statehouse in Columbia and aboard the pick-ups of many a patriotic, God-fearing South Carolinian. It flies to honor a way of life and the thousands who died defending their Southern heritage, not to irritate the civil rights crowd,* they said as if discussing canker sores. *Where is it you said you're from, boy? Dee-Cee? Tell you what. We'll take down the flag the day they let girls into the Citadel.*

Such remarks would end with a cocked eyebrow that said, "Patragno. Hmmm. Pa-trah-no. Spell that, please, sir, and if you plan to reside in our fair city, kindly speak in a manner we can understand."

Christ, what was he doing here? A New York liberal in the Court of Sir John Calhoun. Dan told himself again and again he was building a resume.

He laced up, slid some Sinatra into the Walkman and left his rented one-bedroom on Montagu Court early enough to see last night's rain burn off the streets in a steamy mist. Jogging in August was torture after nine, and he had stirred awake with the need for a long, hard run. Lanky palms stood frozen in the hot, still air and giant C-17s rumbled in and out of Charleston Air Force Base as he looped around Colonial Lake, turned east on Broad and south on Meeting Street toward the Battery.

Dan knew more than most about the city's history, having done a fair bit of homework before arriving on the advice of a Georgetown journalism professor. This was the town where people sick of Washington long ago set a standard for complaining that has never been matched. Astounding, that a piece of parchment signed in anger by men with bushy sideburns could send American boys with different accents into mortal combat. But the Ordinance of Secession stuffed gunpowder down those skinny, old muskets, and it wasn't long before the fight was on.

More recently, there was Hugo the hurricane, whose cruel winds ripped the giant steeple from St. Matthew's and the twin spires from

Blessed Sacrament, tossed shrimp boats into streets where African slaves were once paraded to auction, and overturned statues, gravestones and monuments that had sat on the city's most sacred ground. Hugo snuffed out Charleston's lights, shut her schools and phones, and snapped trees that stood since horses were used to get from here to there, not to haul huge wooden carriages full of wide-eyed tourists from Lansing and Toronto.

Dan was a sophomore at Georgetown and rookie reporter at *The Hoya* when Hugo hit. He remembered a few fleeting TV images—the usual assortment of shredded rooftops and vacant-eyed townsfolk huddled in high school cafeterias—but never gave it much thought.

Later, perusing the newspaper clips, he'd learned Hugo was an assassin who left a heartbeat. In the eerie calm and rubble and floods that follow a killer storm, the city blinked, shook itself off, and threw the finger to Hugo, by then turned north and headed for Charlotte. Local pride flared and led to the kind of rebuilding that hadn't been seen since proud Lee swallowed hard and handed his saber to Grant in a cheerless little corner of the Virginia countryside.

Now, as Dan jogged past the gleaming white Four Corners of Law and down to the Battery, where gulls squawked and a few downtowners strolled with their kids or dogs, he decided South Carolina's Charleston was a genteel city with brass knuckles always tucked one pocket away. At White Point Garden, a water's edge park once literally awash in oyster shells, he jogged in place to read the inscription on a tall, stone monument: "To the Confederate Defenders of Charleston." The Southern commitment to order and violence, when necessary, was written without words in unnaturally straight lines of giant oaks cloaked in Spanish moss, and in ancient black and gray cannons, some bearing faded brass plaques, others adorned with menacing piles of dull, black cannon balls.

Bootlicker

Out in the harbor, sturdy Fort Sumter sat much as it must have looked in the spring of 1861, when it was crammed with anxious Union troops waiting for the testy Rebs to make their move.

He circled the Battery, running along the raised pavement adjacent to Charleston Harbor. Small, inky waves lapped the shore; giant, green-stemmed oleander bushes, azaleas and dogwoods bloomed forth in bursts of rose and plum. *NationsBank* put the temperature at 81 degrees. On the horizon, old Sumter seemed undeserving of the daylong invasion of tour boats that would begin within the hour. To his left, the colorful mansions of *Rainbow Row*, among Hugo's most ravaged victims, sparkled in the morning sun. An elderly couple dressed in milk-white linen sat on a long, shaded piazza and sipped coffee as they shared the morning paper. *His* paper, he reminded himself, with *his* story splashed out front.

A half-mile down East Bay, Dan felt a cramp poke his empty stomach. He rubbed his side and pushed on, ignoring the pain and sweat dripping from his chin and wrists. He wondered fleetingly about Clarissa Agee, but decided she was no longer his problem. He tried to focus on Ike Washington and the old senator, but the cramp nagged and he had to slow to a fast walk. The streets, some blacktop, some narrow cobblestone, were mostly empty. A gull swooped into a dumpster and flew off with a hunk of hamburger roll.

At the next intersection, Dan turned left and came to a familiar outdoor restaurant with cedar picnic tables, yellow umbrellas and a grinning, four-foot wooden pelican. The bird's long, narrow beak held a sign: *Bernie's Broad Street Bistro*. Dan leaned against one of the tables, pulled the plug on Sinatra, and stretched his calf muscles.

"Hey kid, you're dripping."

Dan kept stretching, this time balancing himself on the pelican. He put his mouth near the bird's weathered ear. "Tell me something," he said. "How does anyone get the nerve to call this pile of yard-sale left-overs a *bistro*?"

Snickering, Dan turned just in time to dodge the holding end of Bernie Weinstock's sidewalk broom. He sidestepped behind a table and slipped a second and third playful thrust, but the fourth found its mark. He took the blow but grabbed the broom, shoving it back into Bernie's yellowed apron. They glared at each other a moment and broke out laughing.

"Truce?"

"Truce."

Dan let go and Bernie tossed him a dishtowel.

"You're a weird kid, know that? *Sinatra*. No wonder you never have any dates."

Dan laughed. "I date plenty."

Bernie Weinstock, one of the first locals he'd met when he moved to Charleston, knew what was happening on the street because that's where he spent most of his time. Tourists were drawn to the cafe's umbrellas and goofy pelican. Natives liked that Bernie, after fourteen years on Broad Street, listened to their peeves and opinions with a bartender's attentiveness, and served big mugs of hot, strong coffee that wasn't named, flavored, or over-priced. Dan liked Bernie right off. The first morning he stopped in the cafe seven months ago, Bernie spent an hour explaining the city's different neighborhoods, political factions, and blue-blood families. Since then, Dan had heard many of his friend's stories about quirky Charleston.

"You're still sweating. Hang on, I'll get juice."

In another life, Bernie had toiled more than a decade for the *Philadelphia Inquirer*, racking up a crate full of journalism awards. Investigative pieces about corrupt councilmen, illegal campaign contributions, and rampant nepotism in state government all ran under the by-line: Bernard S. Weinstock. In time, Bernie got to feeling everyone hated him: the people he wrote about and those who worked for them; his wife, because of the hours he put in; the younger reporters at the *Inquirer*, due to the bar of self-expectations he kept raising higher and higher. Ascending into management wasn't even a consideration—he wouldn't spend his time cleaning other people's crap. After the divorce, he sat in his half-empty apartment and took stock, pausing when he came to three file cabinets stuffed with every article he'd ever written. Sipping *Grand Marnier* from an orange juice tumbler, it occurred to him that those stories were really the guts of much bigger stories, books even. The real-life characters he wrote about were just as alive as any on the best-seller lists, their tales just as sordid. Bernie decided to quit the paper, find a quiet place where he could support himself in a job that had nothing to do with journalism, and devote his talent to writing novels. By mid-1978, he was a Charlestonian. He used his prize money and savings to buy and jazz up the *Broad Street Bistro* with a beach motif that included the pelican. Bernie stuck his name on the sign, worked like a beast, and made the restaurant a hit in less than two years.

Dan occasionally asked about his writing, but it was rare these days for Bernie to think about the two unpublished novels that sat in his waterfront home on Isle of Palms.

"Here you go," Bernie said, planting a pitcher of pulpy juice and two glasses with ice on the table.

Dan sat and toyed with a small vase of yellow Jessamine. The cramp was gone and he felt good. He gazed at the street, playing a game that only worked early, before traffic and tourists got their chokehold on the Historic District. He liked to imagine Charleston's streets as they were in the crazy days before the Civil War: the quiet trampled by rebellious South Carolinians who quit the nation rather than deal with Lincoln; the spirited Southern boys headed for war instead of work; the slaves, who would soon pack the little they had and walk freely off the plantations, perhaps passing and looking in the eyes of their former masters.

"Saw your story today."

Dan stiffened. Bernie always backed into some analysis of his stories with an off-hand remark. But his friend was busy buffing a butter knife with the end of his apron. Thin white threads of hair stuck to his nearly bald head like the strands of a janitor's mop. His shiny, freckled pate coupled with a gray moustache pomaded into two neat handlebars gave him the look of an Old West saloonkeeper.

"Good by-line for you," Bernie said. "Nice clip to have in the file. Deadline pressure and all."

"Thanks." He felt the "but" coming.

"But I'm wondering, because it used to get me sometimes when I was in the business, what do you do with your personal feelings when you cover that kind of story? Would you ever call a few weeks later to see how the woman is doing? Not for another story, just to find out what's up?"

Bernie still had the reporter's irritating instinct to drill for the *why* of things. "I'm like a surgeon, Bern. They pay me for operations, not house calls. Besides, I'm off cops. Boss has me covering the race for that new congressional seat."

Bernie put the knife down and went to work polishing a fork. "A surgeon. Their training includes medical school and a residency afterwards."

"My line of work you learn on the job. You can't kill anyone writing stories."

"But you can still do damage."

26

Bootlicker

Dan tapped the table and moved his foot to cut off an ant darting under the table. Bernie polished another knife. A church bell announced ten a.m. Dan looked around to find the church; Bernie used the gleaming knife to check his teeth and fiddle with his moustache.

A couple walked up with a young boy. All wore starchy, new souvenir tee shirts. Bernie rose. "Gotta work. Stick around and don't be pissed."

He attended to his customers while Dan sipped the orange juice, then sat back down. Neither spoke until Bernie told his manager to watch the restaurant. "Let's walk. I want to show you something."

They cut back to East Bay. Bernie put his arm on Dan's shoulder, squeezed it, let go. "You need thicker skin." They walked past a new restaurant that claimed to serve "the old city's freshest seafood."

"Over-rated," Bernie said. "Fancy furniture, crappy food." Dan looked into the smoky glass and saw their Laurel and Hardy reflection. Crappy food was among Bernie's vices.

When they reached the Old Exchange and Provost Dungeon, Bernie motioned to the elegant brick building that was once Charleston's social, political and economic center. "During the Revolution, patriots in Boston dumped tea in the Harbor. Here, they did it different. They stole tea from the Brits and stashed it right here. When the coast cleared, they sold it to help pay for the war."

"So?"

Bernie laughed. "Even guys on the same side don't always agree a hundred percent. There's a dozen ways to reach the finish line. I know a few things about where you're at right now. I point 'em out, you take what you like and dump the rest." He pivoted and started mock jogging, gorilla arms pumping. "I gotta get back. One day we'll race."

"Right." Dan watched Bernie jog toward the restaurant, then walked past the giant Customs Building. He cut left on North Market Street and watched as dozens of flea marketers set up for the crowds that scoured the aisles each day for a piece of the city they could wear on their backs, nail to their walls, or set on their tables. Most of it was crap: shorts, tank-tops and tee-shirts that said *Charleston* and fell apart in the first wash; wooden ocean critters pasted together by bored sixty-year-olds who thought it would be fun to move south, live on the beach and give up shaving; and outdated posters from last year's *Spoleto* arts festival. One guy still sold shirts that said, *I Survived Hugo!* Hidden in the garbage were a few gems: pre-mixed packages of *Edna's Lowcountry Red Rice*, a sizzling-hot Cajun barbecue sauce that Dan used on burgers and chicken, and sturdy sweetgrass baskets made by solemn black women who sat in small groups practicing the old craft brought to South Carolina by slaves from West Africa.

Dan tried talking to one of the basket makers once. She was old, with deft leathery fingers that stitched as she spoke.

"Slave days everyone used these baskets," she said, moist eyes fixed on her work. "Here, smell."

She held out her unfinished work. He closed his eyes and breathed deeply. The raw material had a sweet, morning farm smell. "Nice."

The woman laughed. "That's why they call it sweetgrass, honey."

The basket makers weren't out yet. Dan kept walking down North Market, pausing once to pat the head of a Clydesdale hitched to a heavy tour carriage. "Slavery's still alive, huh, Trigger?" he whispered, roughing the horse's thick mane.

The afternoon was free, so he decided to read all that the newspaper morgue had on Ike Washington and Senator McCauley, then drive to Kilgo and start scouting around Monday morning. He put his earphones back on and jogged the rest of the way back to his apartment at three-quarter speed. At the corner of Montagu and Rutledge, he stopped to again admire his story, which was prominently displayed in all the *Herald-Leader* racks. His sweet fifteen minutes of local fame would last until about midnight, when Monday's paper would replace Sunday's. Any leftovers would be carted to the recycling bin along with his moment of stardom.

Only Lem Butcher's faceless, cardboard promo remained day after day, urging Charleston's miserable couples to spill their lovesick guts and give everyone else a cheap little breakfast thrill to get the day started.

5

The only road into Kilgo was a two-lane, third-rate stretch of black-top that felt squishy hot under the '89 *Prelude's* steel-belted radials. Were S.C. 128 a face, sensitive people would say it had character.

But it was just a road, and repairs probably weren't in the next few rounds of cards. Everyone knew Kilgo had no clout in the Statehouse, where lawmakers with an eye on something bigger, or even a few more terms in the same cozy office, routinely passed the biggest chunk of high-way funds to cities that could return the favor, like Charleston, Green-ville, and Columbia, the noble capital burned to ash during Sherman's 1865 Southern Glory Tour.

There were a hundred towns like Kilgo scattered along the two near-ly straight highways that ran from stately Charleston in the southeast, through busy Columbia in the center, and on to Greenville in the state's thriving northwest corner. Dan imagined each with a bar, breakfast joint, or perhaps both, where local experts sat facing the backs of their chairs, elbows slung over the tops, and argued about sports, politics and current affairs of one sort or another.

He held his Coke against the dash and thought of the Honda's tired shocks as a small sign welcomed him to "Historic Kilgo." He saw plenty old, nothing historic. A gray barn beside an enormous weeping willow caught his eye just as rubber, pothole and gravity found each other in a jarring crunch. Coke splashed his shirt. He wiped it with his hand, then put his hand on the wheel, realizing too late he'd made both sticky. The state highway map at his side, already folded against its manufactured creases so he could see the center of the state, flopped to the floor. "IKE's PLACE," described by campaign manager Ruthie Baines as a brick, can't-miss-it diner in the center of town, was nowhere in sight.

Dan shaded his eyes and peered to the right. Nothing met the campaign manager's description. He crept past a drugstore, the *Cat's Cradle Arcade*, some dreary municipal buildings, a lonely car wash, *Evan's Barber Shop*, where an old-fashioned pole swirled red, white and blue in the afternoon heat, and a hardware store with rakes and a used lawnmower out front for twenty bucks "as is." *Piggly Wiggly* was getting most of the afternoon action.

Before long, three traffic lights went by and there was another sign: "Thanks for visiting Historic Kilgo!" He cursed, checked for on-coming traffic, and U-turned back to town, where Route 128 was called Union Street.

Two young men were out on a corner. One wore a faded white tank top, black pants, and tan sandals. The other was bare-chested with baggy shorts and untied sneakers. Dan pulled up for directions.

"'Lo," he said, making quick eye contact. "I'm looking for Ike's place?"

"What you want with Big Ike?" The man who spoke, more with curiosity than attitude, leaned toward the open window. Dan followed his gaze. Beside the map on the front seat were a reporter's notebook, a laptop, and a half-empty bag of trail mix. Dan hoped his Washington, D.C. tag wouldn't raise suspicions as the guy walked around back like an insurance inspector.

"You government?"

He kept the D.C. plate—first in Florida, now in South Carolina—for the same reason he used the WAPO password. They were reminders. His goal each day was to add to his stack of clips, convince the *Post* or someplace like it they couldn't live without him, and haul ass out of the Palmetto State before the DMV came calling. None of that mattered now.

"Government?" he said, reaching for his *Herald-Leader* ID. "No, I'm a reporter. From Charleston. They told me Mayor Washington knows all there is to know about politics around here."

"How 'bout that plate?"

"Just moved from D.C. Haven't changed 'em yet."

The bare-chested man drained the last of a jumbo drink, set his feet and arms like Magic Johnson, and fired a graceful free throw at a metal garbage can. Score. "That the truth 'bout Ike."

Both men were about thirty and smelled like they'd been working hard. Or maybe not. Kilgo was in Cady County, where jobs, his research had shown, were scarce as BMWs. Most men like these worked on small tobacco farms, textile mills, at the rubber plant just outside town, for the county, or not at all. Average Kilgo families lived on less than sixteen grand a year, about half his salary.

"Ike's is a mile up Union, then left on Arnold," tank top said. "But he ain't there now."

"Thanks." Dan lingered, feeling the need to make some departing gesture, not wanting the men to laugh when he drove off. Should he nod, wave, salute? The men looked at him. He was far from Georgetown, M Street, the shops and bars, always bustling with the well dressed and well educated. "Thanks." They stared a moment and walked off.

When Dan found the restaurant, he saw why he flew by on the first pass. The diner sat two blocks in from Union Street and was small out front as a dry cleaners. Instead of a sign or banner, "IKE's PLACE" was painted in sloppy olive cursive on the front window. The diner was made of brick—she was right after all—but years of scorching sun had bleached the red to a mucky white.

Several middle-aged and a few very old black men were hanging out front. Some sat on the cracked concrete curb, others stood in a small patch of shade cast by a faded canvas awning. A few shifted when he pulled up. Bits of conversation carried through the window.

"Got my ten?"

"Check's in the mail."

"God, it's hot."

"You want hot, wait 'til you see the scatback they got at Clemson this year."

"Boy can run! He from Summerville?"

"Lexington."

"How come he didn't go to USC?"

"Musta' gave him a faster car at Clemson. Ha."

"Nope, faster women!"

As prep, Dan had quickly reviewed the library clips, which named Mayor Ike Washington of Kilgo as the favorite among several men and one woman hungry for the new congressional seat. The stories also affirmed Butcher's analysis, quoting insiders as saying Ike was the man blacks always saw if they wanted help from U.S. Senator Lander McCauley.

Though Ike and the old, white conservative were an unlikely team, Dan understood each got something in the bargain. McCauley got a liaison to black voters. Ike got a job, prestige and his own power base. Plus, McCauley was raised in Kilgo at a time when the town was more white than black. Ike and McCauley probably met before the senator moved on.

Dan grabbed a pen, notebook and pocket recorder from his briefcase. He slid out of the car and hesitated, concerned suddenly that the men would be insulted if he locked the door in front of them. He put the rubber-handled key in and turned; the push-button locks sank with a soft click. He dared a look up and was relieved that no one seemed offended.

The men cleared a path to the door as he approached. "How'd ya do? young man?" one said. "Warm one, ain't it?"

Dan smiled but focused on another man, not more than forty, sitting *Thinker*-like on the sidewalk with his back against the brick. His chin sat on his palm, his elbow, on a bent knee. The other leg stuck straight out, forcing Dan to step over to get to the screen door. He stopped. "Excuse me." The man rubbed his fingers back and forth along the sidewalk as if trying to sand down his fingerprints. The leg stayed. Dan cursed himself for locking his car doors.

"Thomas Lee, move that leg 'fore I move it for you," one of the others said. Thomas glared in Dan's direction and muttered, "When I'm ready," but pulled in his leg. Dan nodded his thanks and reached for the door. He didn't unclench his fist until his fingers found the rusty handle.

Inside, two of a dozen high-backed booths were taken, one by a waitress and dishwasher gazing at each other like new lovers. Dan stood self-consciously a moment, watching as she slipped off a peep toe sandal and danced her bare foot up the dishwasher's leg. Despite a large AC unit in the back window, the diner was musty. He brushed his chest, still damp from the spilled soft drink, and cleared his throat. The dishwasher nodded to the waitress. She craned her neck around, held her eyes for a second on his wet shirt.

"Need another drink, hon?" she said straight-faced from the table. The dishwasher snickered and tied his soiled apron in back. He walked through a pair of swinging doors through which Dan could see another man in a white chef's hat tacking colored toothpicks into the top of a triple-decker club.

"I'm Dan Patragno, ma'am. From the *Charleston Herald-Leader*. I was supposed to meet Ike at four-thirty. I'm a little early."

He felt the waitress take him in and spit him out. Neatly pressed brown pants, beige polo, medium-length sandy hair. Early twenties, clean-cut, no wedding band. He half-expected to hear, "Hold tight, Gomer, I'll get him."

Before she could, a back door opened and another woman entered. Unlike the waitress, she walked up like he'd won the lottery, arms outstretched, smile blazing.

"Dan," she said, taking his hand in both of hers and squeezing. "I'm Ruthie Baines."

As their hands touched, his, white as soy milk, hers, a soft butternut, he realized he had never been more grateful to see a smiling face. Especially after that asshole on the sidewalk and the smartass waitress.

"How were my directions?"

He thought about spilling his Coke, overshooting the diner, the guys who mistook him for a Fed, the gauntlet outside the diner.

"Perfect."

The back door opened and the mayor, blustery as a ringmaster, joined them. "Welcome to Kilgo, Mister *Charleston Herald*. How y'all doing down there in the Holy City?"

"Dan Patragno, Mayor. Call me Dan. Glad to meet you."

"Folks call me Big Ike."

At maybe 5-9, 190, Ike didn't much live up to his nickname. Dan, taller, saw that the mayor's oval head was topped with wisps of tightly wound gray and black hair. He had ears too small for his short haircut, and a full moustache that moved like a black caterpillar when he smiled. What *was* big were his gut and the sweat stains that bled through his ivy green dress shirt.

"Let's you and me go in my office. Yvonne," he said to the waitress still seated at the table, "bring some Cokes. Ruthie, we'll see you later."

Ruthie made a small bow, took a few bird-steps backwards, and caught Dan's eye. "Coffee when you're finished?"

"Sure," he said, and followed Ike Washington, Jr. into a cramped, wood-paneled office cold enough to store meat. He saw why—a second, smaller air conditioner working hard in a corner window. The walls were crammed with cheaply framed photos of the mayor with various politicians and other local celebs. Dan recognized a few VIPs, including Senator McCauley. He jotted a note about the last photo, which showed the mayor and senator shaking hands at a ribbon-cutting ceremony at the opening of a new elementary school somewhere in Cady County.

Ike settled into a black leather rocker ridiculously large for the cramped office and leaned forward. "Lord, it's hot. I'm always hot. Can't crank the AC up high enough for me."

Ike patted the unit like a faithful retriever; Dan struggled to keep his face even. The room couldn't have been more than 68 degrees.

"Well, *Charleston*, you didn't come all this way to yak about the price of tobacco. What can I do for you?"

"It's election time," he shrugged. "That means candidate profiles. I drew your name."

"Lucky you."

"I need the usual. Your stand on some issues, some background info. I've also got a few questions about your work for Senator McCauley."

Ike pressed down on the desk and the rocker started moving. "What about the Senator?"

"Well, one of the things we're curious about is how he's managed to patch relations with black voters over the years."

"Hold on. This is a story about me or another racial thing about the Senator? I've had enough of all that."

Dan cursed himself for not sticking with his usual interview strategy: Get a few runners on before going for extra bases.

"No, no, it's about you, of course. But I don't have to tell you all the things McCauley used to say before desegregation, how he acted, what he believed. History says McCauley was the guy who came down on civil rights marchers. He didn't want to integrate schools, fought for separate restrooms, said it was okay for restaurants not to serve black customers."

Dan realized he was talking instead of asking questions. He stopped, snorted a breath of air-conditioned air, let it out through his mouth. For some reason, the thought occurred that he'd never had a close friend, man or woman, who was black. Not in New York, not in Washington. He breathed again.

"McCauley overcame that," Ike said. "Even later, when African Americans became a force, he got reelected."

The Cokes arrived and Ike downed half his bottle in one swig. As the drink vanished, so did Ike's country accent.

"I'll give it a shot." Ike took another long drink and put the bottle down empty. He folded his arms across his chest, rocked back and stayed there, holding his position by wedging a knee against the desk.

"When I was a boy in this town, Lander McCauley—Mac, that's when people started calling him Mac—represented everything I hated. 'States' rights. We knew what that meant. It meant the state had all the rights. Black people didn't have squat."

Dan pressed hard and wrote fast. The muscles between his thumb and trigger finger started to ache.

"See, I'm mayor now. I have a nice house and a nice car. My wife has a nice car. My son has a master's from Clemson and a beautiful family up in Charlotte. My granddaughter Marva, bless that girl, will go to a nice university. That child is something and she's going to be *some-body*."

Ike slid closer to the air conditioner and wiped a row of sweat beads from his upper lip. "When I was a boy, I went to Anderson Elementary, where my mother taught, and to St. James High. Those were the colored schools. St. James stopped at tenth grade. White folks didn't treat us second-class. They treated us Third World. There wasn't any Kiwanis or Rotary. There were White Citizens Councils and the Klan."

He paused to rub the slightly misshaped pinky on his left hand. Dan stopped scribbling. Ike studied his crooked finger, held it up, seemed fascinated when it twitched on its own.

"This is the stuff you want, right?"

Dan nodded, hoping Ike would stay on track. This was more profile material than he expected. He glanced at his recorder to make sure there was plenty of tape.

"Mac McCauley was just beginning his career then. He was a city judge. He wasn't a friend of the Negro, but he wasn't the worst. Not hardly. Otherwise he wouldn't have been senator all my adult life. That's longer than you've been alive. Right?"

"Why didn't blacks do more to strip McCauley of his power?"

Ike tapped his Coke bottle and threw a foot up on the desk. New Cordovan loafers, no tassels. He seemed irritated.

"Study your history, young man. Integration did not come easy here, but it came easier than in Mississippi and Alabama. Mac McCauley did not sic police dogs on us. He never blocked the doorway of USC. Later, he hired black folk to work in his Washington office. That sort of thing helped. If you told me in '56, when our folks in Montgomery got their seats up front on the buses, that Mac McCauley would vote one day to make Dr. King's birthday a holiday ... " He wagged his head, laced his fingers. "I would have said you were crazy. But he did."

"A lot of people say the senator did those things to keep his career going, not because of any heartfelt changes. What about it?"

Ike picked up a soft brown leather key case embossed with the words "Lincoln Town Car." He dangled the keys in front of his eyes and seemed to enjoy the sound they made as they clinked together. "I don't know the answer to that one, Charleston. You want to know what's in the Senator's heart, better ask him."

Dan considered pressing, but decided Ike was right and steered toward the mayor's personal history. Ike told it in dispassionate fashion. His father, Isaac, Sr., died young. Ike and his brother were raised in Kilgo by their mother, who taught at the black public school, and, later, at the integrated middle school, for thirty-seven years. She died several years ago after a stroke. Ike's brother was killed in Vietnam. Ike's wife was Cynthia. Their only child, a son, lived with his family in North Carolina.

"So why do you want this new job in Washington? You tired of being mayor? Aren't you afraid of Potomac Fever?"

Ike leaned forward so that both elbows were on the desk. "Ever heard of George Washington Murray, Mr. Patragno?"

He had not.

"Mr. Murray was the last African American congressman from South Carolina. He wrote books on race relations. Eighteen ninety-seven was his final year in office. The white powers at the time trumped up some charges. He was convicted of forgery in 1905 and ran off to Illinois. George Washington Murray is buried in an unmarked grave outside Chicago. There is no monument to him in this state. I think it's wrong that we haven't had a black in Congress in nearly one hundred years. This state is one-third black."

Dan jotted a note—Ike had shifted to full campaign mode. "I'm not saying whites can't do a good job of representing blacks. But if that's true, so's the other. Blacks can do just as good a job representing whites."

Ike stopped and opened the door. His voice returned to normal. "Yvonne, another Coke. How 'bout you, Dan?"

"I'm fine. You would have to give up your work for Senator McCauley if you win?"

"Yes, sir. That job ends the day I am elected."

"You sound pretty confident."

"Oh, I'm going to win," Ike said, toasting the world with his fresh Coke. "You go on and tell everyone down in Charleston. Ike Washington will be this state's next black congressman. First in a hundred years. No doubt about it."

6

Ruthie intercepted them as they left the office. "We leave for Columbia tomorrow at noon," she told Ike. "Dan, you in a rush?"

"Nope."

The diner was three-quarters full and Yvonne was working the floor alone, hustling as much as she'd been slacking before. Ike spotted an open table. "Why don't you two sit down and I'll get Yvonne to bring the coffee?"

Ruthie nudged Dan to signal she preferred someplace new. He looked a moment longer than necessary at her khaki shorts and sleeve-less, white cotton top. Her arms were so lean, he could see her triceps wink. He asked if Ruthie could show him around town instead and Ike said, "Sure. Not that she knows much. Ruthie's from Florence. But go on; she knows enough not to get lost."

Dan shook his hand. "I'll be covering your race from now on. Tomorrow's the Rotary Club?"

"Masons. You get to see all of us in action."

Ruthie took his arm and tugged him toward the door. "Back in awhile," she said.

Outside, all but three of the sidewalk group had wandered off. "'Lo, Miss Baines," one said. The orange sun was sinking, though no street-lights had come on. Downtown Kilgo looked deserted and old enough to die in its sleep.

"Hey, boys, how you doing? Best get home in time for supper."

"This one," Dan said, but Ruthie was already walking to the Honda. Of course—she'd seen the D.C. plates. He opened her door first, reaching in to put his laptop in the backseat. He was embarrassed about the trail mix and tried to stash it under the computer. When he leaned out of the car and straightened up, she was directly in front of him. Their hips brushed.

"Sorry," he said, feeling the open door behind him, edging around it as if he were on a ledge seven floors up. She put a hand to her mouth to hide a smile.

"Where to?" He worried that some indefinable momentum would be lost if they didn't start moving. He gunned the engine and it returned a street-racing wail that was loud and inappropriate. He looked over and saw the bemused bums watching like chaperones.

Ruthie slipped off her mahogany flats and put her feet on the glove compartment. Even pretzeled up, her legs were long and elegant, ending in toenails the color of dark grapes. She crooked her elbow and pointed toward town. "Thataway."

Ruthie sank into her seat and gazed toward a pet store as he turned right on Union and drove slowly past the barber shop, drugstore and *Piggly Wiggly*. All were closed but the supermarket, where two women were chatting over their grocery carts. Three scruffy boys tore through the parking lot on skateboards.

Navigating carefully past a police station not much bigger than Ike's diner, Dan pushed on a cassette sticking out of the tape deck. Mechanical fingers pulled it in and gave back more Sinatra, cockier-sounding this time and bolstered by Count Basie and all that brass.

Ruthie pulled down the visor, checked her plum lipstick in the lighted mirror, and flattened her top lip against the bottom one. "That's what you listen to?" They were at the sign at the edge of town inviting them to return to Kilgo.

"Sorry," he said, wishing he'd chosen rap, soul, gospel, blues, or whatever it was she liked. A blush rose and he saw in the rearview that his ears had turned cartoon pink. He wondered where the color went when black people blushed. He wondered why he was wondering such things. What spell had she placed on him? "I like Sinatra on long drives. My dad used to play it around the house." He ejected the tape and invited her to choose. She hit the seek button, listened to a second's worth from one station after another until classical music filled the car. Piano, fast, almost manic.

"You play?" he said the instant the thought occurred.

"Would that surprise you?"

"No, course not." Christ, now she thought he was a dope *and* a bigot. His hands tightened on the wheel. She waited another moment, then leaned against her door, facing him, forcing him to look and see her laughing. "Just funnin' you, Yankee."

"I know," he grinned, knowing very little.

They reached an intersection with a row of country mailboxes and a graying wooden fence that marked the far edge of a nearby farm. Nestled on another corner sat what looked to be the first Texaco station built in North America, replete with two pumps sporting the old rolling readout instead of digital numbers. "Stay north on 52. We'll go to the pride of Lake City, the *Squat and Gobble*."

He looked at her, saw she was serious, heard her laugh again when he turned back to the road. Dan put his window down, checked the side-view. Nothing behind, nothing ahead except a small, Dodge flat-bed loaded with peach baskets and moving slow enough for the dusty shepherd standing in back to sniff all that rushed his way. A bumper sticker read, *She's A Child, Not A Choice.*

Ruthie jabbed his shoulder. "Really," she said. "The *Squat and Gobble.* Good food, cold beer. And yes, I'm a pianist. I play classical and some jazz."

"Play for me sometime?"

"We'll see."

Ruthie leaned back and closed her eyes, fingers tapping silent notes against her thigh. Dan passed the pick-up on a long straightaway and forced himself to concentrate on the countryside. They were in the center of the new congressional district, the largest and poorest of the state's six seats. People here had the least education of any South Carolinians and led all the wrong categories: unemployment, infant mortality, high school dropouts, teen crime rates, and single-mother households.

But they sure were believers, he thought, as they passed Mount Zion AME. A splintered sign beside the single-room, whitewashed barn of a church advised, "DON'T LOOK BACK. KEEP GOING FORWARD TO GOD." Underneath, a flyer announced Pastor Jimmy Brown's next service would be Sunday at 8:30. "All" were invited to attend, though the place looked like it would burst if more than thirty parishioners happened to show up.

Churches easily outnumbered mom-and-pops in the district, though the rundown, little houses of worship bore little resemblance to the religious palaces in Charleston. He thought of Charleston's Circular Congregational Church, where the city's first settlers sat down in 1681 to sharpen their knives for war with the Church of England. And to give famed Meeting Street its name. Beside the church and within its imperious black, iron gates lay the oldest graves in Charleston.

He lowered the radio. "This term, 'dark-meat' precincts. What's it mean?"

"There weren't enough black voters in the old Sixth to create a majority, so black precincts had to be carved out of the other five districts. That's the dark meat." She said it cool as an almanac.

"If you take all those black voters out of the other districts, doesn't it make the remaining seats more conservative, more Republican?"

Ruthie sighed. "Ike says sometimes you've got to give a little to get some."

They drove the next several minutes without speaking. The road narrowed to one lane in each direction as they passed long stands of pointy pines, a small cemetery with weathered headstones, and then a clearing where a straw-hatted farmer worked his field with a mule-drawn plow. It could have been 1940.

"One more thing." They were stopped at a light. The log cabin restaurant lay dead ahead, forty yards on the right, its gravel parking lot nearly filled with aging pick-ups, station wagons and one candy-apple red Firebird whose license plate was framed in a gold-colored link chain. "Everyone calls you Ruthie. Okay to call you Ruth?"

She crossed her arms, assessing, appraising, and deciding in an instant. "Sure," she said.

Inside, he noticed small piles of trash beside each table. The *Squat* had the dirtiest floor he'd ever seen in a restaurant. "Look at this place."

"They're peanut shells," she laughed. "Everyone gets a bucket. You're *supposed* to throw the shells on the floor."

The clientele seemed fifty-fifty black and white, but Dan didn't spot another interracial couple. The Firebird stuck in his mind. He pictured the owner as a white redneck or black bigot just itching to roll up his greasy sleeves and start trouble. "Hey, boy, whatchu doin' with her?" either might say. And he would answer, what? Doing business? Talking politics? What *were* they doing out together? Yes, she was beguiling, but race aside, he was a journalist and she was a source. The code of ethics said to keep her at arm's length, the opposite of what he'd been thinking since they left the diner.

No one looked up when they walked in. Dan asked for a booth near the back and, when they were seated, sipping longnecks and eating peanuts, could not bring himself to throw the shells on the floor. Ruthie took his arm with her right hand and made him sweep the tabletop. "Loosen up," she laughed. He stuck a shoe into the pile and felt the shells crunch. It reminded him of the ballpark.

"Tell me about the others running against Ike," he said.

"There's no one else, only Ike."

"I'll respect you more if you're honest, Ruth."

She smacked his forearm and placed her hands down as if addressing a piano. "You first. Who is Daniel Patragno?"

"That's fair. *In The Beginning*," he said, drawing a pretty smile. "I grew up on Long Island. Valley Stream. No valley, no streams. Dad and Uncle Sal wore silver chains with little horns and owned Patragno Bros. Moving and Storage in Brooklyn. Mom kept the books. Anthony Patragno, Sr. wanted me in the family business. Right. Break my back hauling other people's crap, trucks that stunk like mildew. No thanks. He made me work summers in the warehouse and we had lots of fights. Especially when I told him I wanted to go into newspapers. And when he heard I was moving south."

Dan turned his collar up and whispered like an angry Mafioso. "'Carolina? Whata you gonna do down there? Ain't nothing. No pizza, no Mets, no Yankees. Grits'll give you the shits. What are they going to pay you? I'll double it.'"

"Was he right? Are you miserable?"

"Nope, I'm having fun. I'm not going to stay my whole life, but it's okay for now. How about you?"

She brushed another mess from the table. She wore a thin, gold bracelet on her right wrist and two delicate gold rings on her left hand. "Well, I'm twenty-six, an only child, but not spoiled. No way. My father's a preacher in Florence, my mother teaches piano."

Dan fought to pay attention, but was more interested in how the light from a slowly swaying lantern above played off her neck, smooth and, he knew intuitively, delicious.

"I interned for a state legislator while I got my B.A. in political science at USC," she said. "When Ike decided to run, I interviewed and got campaign manager. When he wins, I'll go to D.C. as chief of staff."

"You're cocky, too. Tell me about the other candidates."

She held up finger number one and said, "Cady Owens, III, the elder statesman. Eighty years old, state legislator, funeral home owner."

Dan knew about Owens. Most of the press had written him off as too old. That might prove a mistake. Owens, never without a black suit, stiff white shirt and skinny black tie, had a following. His supporters, huddled outside Charleston in Owens's hometown of Walterboro, respected the years in the trenches he put in when social change was slow in coming. Owens had earned a trip to Washington, they argued. If he didn't think he was too old, well, they didn't either.

"Two," Ruthie said, her fingers a scissors. "The jock."

That was Derrick Maussipant, a six-four, 31-year-old Lowcountry lawyer and former College of Charleston hoops star. Maussipant worked in the public defender's office and walked with the swagger of a man who could dunk a basketball without a running start. "Hasn't paid his dues," Ruthie said. "Let him spend some years on City Council. Let him win a few in Columbia, see if he can't get that damned Confederate flag torn down, then he can think about Washington."

She stopped. "Hey, this is background, right? You're not going to quote any of this."

"Deal. Just so you know, though, you're supposed to set the rules before you start gabbing."

"You won't burn me," she said, sharp as a beat cop. "You like me."

"We'll see."

She flicked a shell at him and sipped her beer. Someone somewhere fed the jukebox, and the *Temptations* were with them, not too loud, just enough to get her shoulders moving.

"Dianna Harley's the one we're watching. Fifty-two, state NAACP chair, sells real estate in Columbia. I don't think she can beat Ike, but we need her if he doesn't win the primary and there's a runoff. She doesn't like Ike working for Senator McCauley. In her math, compromise equals sell-out."

Their ribs arrived with two more beers. Ruth brought her fingers to her temples and combed her soft, chestnut hair behind her ears. She wore penny-sized hoop earrings thin as paper clips. "Don't watch me when I eat," she said. "And hurry, he wants me back in a little while."

Ike's decision to work into the night was no surprise. The August 25th Democratic primary, just seven weeks off, was the real contest. A white Republican waited in the general election, but Justice Department gerrymandering all but ensured the district's new congressman would be a black Democrat.

Dan was about to ask another question when a woman stopped at their table. He knew her face.

"You're Dan, the reporter from Charleston?" Her voice jogged his memory and he quickly stood. "Clarissa Agee." She looked different from the woman who rocked like a mental patient and told how her husband killed himself and their baby girl. "Clarissa, this is Ruth." As the women shook hands, Dan saw that Clarissa's face, though carefully made up, was still bruised. Her eyes were swollen and looked dry, as if drained of tears. He asked how she was doing.

"Trying to get along. This is the first time I've been out in awhile. Mama and me are visiting some family and we got hungry." She paused. "The funeral was hard. That little coffin."

Dan put his arms around her. He was wrong; she had more tears in there. He remembered Bernie's advice and was ashamed he hadn't called the woman.

"I'm sorry," she said, pushing away and drawing a breath. "Just wanted to say I thought you did an honest job. You told it true. I cut out that story and saved it."

He nodded. Clarissa Agee waved half-heartedly to Ruthie and went back to her table.

"Sorry," he said.

"What for?"

He liked that she didn't ask for an explanation. It made him want to talk.

"I just switched to the political beat," he said. "Until a week ago, I was on night cops. I had to interview that woman after her husband shot her daughter, then killed himself."

"I heard about it."

"I'm more glad to be off cops than you could ever know. Politicians may be sleazy, but at least they don't shoot each other up."

"Not usually."

Dan ordered another beer and drank it quickly. Ruth finished off a rib and picked at the curly fries. Looking at him closely, she said, "You don't fit in here."

He took it as he thought she intended, as a compliment. The brief melancholy spurred by Clarissa Agee was gone. She pointed to his face, said, "You have … No, there." He wiped the wrong side, then the right side, but missed the spot of barbecue sauce. She leaned across and did it for him.

"You don't fit in either," he said. The numbness in his feet reminded him he wasn't much of a drinker.

"So let's go," she said, her eyes daring him to look away.

It was 9:15. He put a twenty on the table and followed her to the parking lot. The night was moist and filled with the chatter of crickets, pond frogs and night birds. Gray clouds hid the moon, yet the stars were close. Dan opened her door first like before, knowing she'd be right behind him when he turned around.

His mind ticked off a dozen reasons why he shouldn't bring his face close to hers: They just met. His mother would clutch her rosary beads and scream for Jesus if he brought home a black girlfriend. Ruth worked for the politician he was writing about. She might be trying to use him.

Dan turned and leaned in anyway, glad that all it took was three beers to invest himself with the reckless confidence of a seasoned drunk. So be it.

She touched his chin. "We shouldn't."

"I'm sorry, you're right. I'm writing about your boss. It's too soon. We're so different. Shit, I'm sorry, Ruth."

"You didn't do anything wrong."

He turned away, face burning, intending to get in the car and drive them back. Something stopped him and he turned back. She hadn't moved. Her hands were at her sides. He took a halting step forward and she matched him, face tilted up, big brown eyes open. "We may regret this," she said. The distance between them vanished. This time when he leaned in, he felt her hands, one around his back, the other on his neck, gently pulling him in. She smelled sweet, like honeysuckle.

•••••

His head was clear by the time he got back to Charleston and bee-lined to the cafe. Bernie stayed open until midnight during the summer, and there was a good crowd enjoying his coffee and homemade straw-berry cheesecake.

"The mayor's campaign aide, you say?"

"Top aide."

Bernie whistled. "You ought to write *Dear Lem*. Tell him you want to hit the sheets with the top aide to a candidate you're writing about, a guy who's running in one of the most important elections this state has ever seen."

"I know, I know. And don't forget my parents. The only black person I ever saw in our house was a moving man's helper."

"It doesn't matter what color your new girlfriend is. Here's what mat-ters. You write a good story, people will say it's because you're sleeping with her. Write a bad story, Ike will say the reason is 'cause you two had a fight. And how do you think the others are going to feel, Owens, Maussi-pant, Dianna Harley? Think they're going to treat you like an objective reporter?"

"It won't affect my work."

Bernie's face said he didn't believe it.

"It *won't*." He cracked his knuckles. "I'm too hyped up to go home. Ike gave me some great profile stuff. I'm going to go in and write it up."

Bernie leaned back in his chair and lit a thin cigar. "Sure you want to do that now? Maybe you should wait, let things settle."

"Christ, Bernie, the issue is how it looks, not that it's actually going to influence me. Nothing's even happened yet. One kiss." He smiled. "A very good kiss."

Dan toyed with the handle on the aluminum umbrella pole that rose out of the center of the table. The umbrella collapsed a few inches, and he cranked it back up. "I can separate personal and professional, and this is going to be a great story. This is going to get me noticed."

"*That* I believe," Bernie said.

7   *Ike*

Ike slid behind the leather steering wheel and reached for his seat-belt. The silver buckle was hot; he had to maneuver to avoid burning himself as he pressed it into the receiving end. He stole a look at Ruthie Baines and exhaled. Ruthie was smart and worked hard, but sometimes he didn't get what set her off, like now.

"What's wrong?"

"Nothing."

"How can I fix it if you won't tell me?"

"Ike." She crossed her arms, measured her words. "You're running for a district where people live paycheck to paycheck. They drive the cars they bought ten years ago. And you buy a *Lincoln Town Car*. You think that sends the right message? We talked about this."

"You talked. I think people *like* seeing me in this car. Plus, I've worked hard, I deserve it."

"How much?"

"How much do I deserve it?"

She didn't smile. "How much was it?"

"Forty-six, nine," he muttered, then added hopefully, "but it's the

Cartier series; glacier blue, 210 horses, 4.6-liter engine."

"Forty-seven thousand? It takes people in this district *four years* to make that much."

Ike studied the Lincoln's high-tech control deck. When Ruthie went off like this, the smartest thing was to let her go until she ran out of air. He braked lightly and eased into drive. As they turned onto Union Street, the AC blew like a front from Canada until the temp fell to 68 degrees. Ruthie pulled the halves of her sweater around and fastened a button. Ike shifted and the leather captain's chair moved in exquisite response. He imagined the seat as a living servant. *Whatever your big ass wants, I will deliver.*

He slid in a CD as they cruised out of Kilgo. The disc vanished and an orchestra appeared led by his favorite, Ray Charles. Ike sang with enthusiasm, *"Still crazy after all these years."*

"Goddamn!" he shouted, startling Ruth, who was studying the day's schedule: morning fundraiser in Manning, lunch with the Masons in Columbia, and an afternoon tour of Colonial Rubber back in Kilgo. "You tell me old' Ray and the boys don't sound like they're right in the backseat."

Ruthie started mouthing one to ten.

"Eight speakers, Ruthie. JBL, 145 watts, digital signal processing."

She reached six and slammed her clipboard. "I don't know why you hired me. Don't you see? You flash through poor neighborhoods in this thing—through the country where they don't even have a health clinic – and folks will think you're a pimp."

"Or an athlete." He grinned, puffing his forty-inch waist.

"Look, you want to lose this election, do it without me. When I signed on, you agreed we'd consult on big decisions."

"It's a car, no big deal."

"It's not just a car. Everything is more than what it seems right now. A car is about who's behind the wheel, whether he's got the heart to stand up in Washington. Don't you take anything lightly, Ike. People are looking for symbols and heroes more than they're looking for a congressman."

That was too much. He slapped the dash and pulled onto the shoulder. "You questioning my stripes, Ruthie?"

"It's got to go back. Get yourself something more appropriate. Pick out a glacier blue *Taurus*."

Ike leaned forward slowly and put his forehead on the wheel. The leather felt good and smelled rich, but he wasn't thinking about the car anymore. "Call Dr. Greene in Manning. Tell him we can't make the breakfast."

"He's got fifteen doctors and dentists waiting to put campaign checks in your hand."

"Reschedule it. Now."

While Ruthie called on her cell, Ike turned back toward town. Just before they reached the southern city limit, he turned onto Ascension. The road was only wide enough for one car at a time, and cluttered on both sides with mostly small, wood-frame houses set close enough for neighbors to open their windows and trade recipes. For every three houses in good repair, there was one with blistered paint, tangled weeds, and corroded shingles that sagged under the weight of poverty that ran in a tortuous line back to the days of LBJ.

Half a mile from Union, Ascension Road wandered like a lost traveler, jogging right, looping left, then running straight a bit before another quick right. Finally, the pavement quit and the road turned to a grayish mix of tightly packed gravel and white rock.

They crunched over rusty railroad tracks that had no crossing gates and a rickety, one-lane bridge, and were suddenly at the edge of a swamp thick with loblolly pines that blocked the glare of the morning sun. Ike pulled over and shut the ignition. Ruthie waited. "C'mon," he said. "I'm going to tell you a story."

"Here?"

"Here."

"We're not really dressed for a picnic."

They got out and she followed him to a small clearing, where he hitched up the pants of his pinstriped suit and sat on a tree stump more than thirty inches around. Ruthie stood before him. "Grab a tree," he smiled, his anger nearly gone.

She tugged her skirt down and sat on the smooth-topped stump next to his. The dirt under their dress shoes was tea-colored and showed their footprints.

"You're important to me, Ruthie, you know that. You've done excellent work so far. We're ahead, and you're a big reason. You've got good instincts, great timing. You go home late and come in early. I need you with me to win this race."

She adjusted a trio of silver bracelets that slid too far down her wrist.

"Thing is, sometimes your angle on all this is ... well, it's *limited*. Ike Washington didn't show up in 1992 and decide to run for Congress. You have to understand my past. This"—he opened his arms wide to indicate the world of his childhood—"is where I grew up. You never even knew there was a community back here, did you?"

"No, but I ... "

"You remember I had a brother."

"Jerome. He died in Vietnam."

Ike nodded. He tossed a rock down the unmarked road, which opened to overgrown forest and abandoned farmland for as far as they could see. "Nothing here now, but this place was alive when I was a boy. We played in Sampson's Creek, hunted rabbits in that forest."

He watched her look side to side, then behind. There was nothing but trees with branches big enough to be trees themselves, and dense, green underbrush that had yet to meet a Cady County chainsaw.

"One day—I'm just a kid—I'm digging for worms. Jerome goes flying by. He takes the old steps to our little house in one jump. Colonel—half lab, half god-knows what—starts barking like crazy and Mama comes running out. She had one of those old, metal watering cans in her hands."

"Jerome's so excited, all he can say is, 'Mama, Mama.'"

Ike pulled on the knot of his tie and opened his top button, rotating his liberated neck in slow circles. He reached back and massaged a stiff spot, then looked at the back of his right hand as his bad pinky began its jig.

"*And?*" Ruthie said. Ike laughed at her impatience and sank back to his story.

"It was summer," he said, "the summer of 1959."

·····

Marva Washington put down the watering can, grabbed her older son by the shoulders. She had to reach up because he'd grown taller than she over the winter.

"What's the trouble?"

"No trouble, Mama. Just figured out what I want for my birthday."

"Your birthday? You come racing up here like a bear after you, and it's about your birthday? You six or sixteen?"

Jerome lowered his chin. Mrs. Washington crossed her arms, and Ike saw her eyes soften a stitch. "Alright, alright. What's your heart set on, birthday boy?"

Jerome shot back to life. "I was just down Union Street. They got big signs posted on light poles, in store windows. Signs everywhere."

"Signs? What signs?"

"Circus comin' tomorrow to the Armory. Elephants, trapeze, bearded lady. Mama, that's what I want, for you, me, and Ike to go to the circus."

Her smile faded and Ike knew the answer.

"Jerome, the circus came through Cady County one time before. You're right, they have it at the Armory. And only whites are allowed in the Armory."

Ike went to the colored school where his mother taught fourth grade, played at the colored park, and used the colored restrooms and water fountains. He never considered the circus would only be for whites. Jerome, either, from his expression.

"Maybe there's a colored section," he said.

"No colored section. Now you forget the circus. Pick something practical, like the fishing pole Ike got last year."

Jerome went down the stoop one slow step at a time. He picked up a rock at the bottom and flung it hard into the woods. Then he went off, with Ike close behind. "Let me be."

Next morning, Ike woke to his brother's hand on his mouth. And to Jerome's new plan.

"Get dressed. If we can't go to the circus, we'll least go to the parade."

Ike yawned. "Man, there's no parade. Still dark."

Jerome held up a finger. "We get there early, we'll get a good seat. Now get dressed, don't wake Mama."

Ike pulled on an outfit that matched Jerome's—dungaree cutoffs, clean, white T-shirt, and low-cut canvas sneakers without socks.

When they tiptoed to the kitchen for a glass of milk, Marva Washington was waiting.

"You two best never go in for bank robbing. You'd be the loudest crooks in the business. Where you think you're going?"

Ike looked at Jerome.

"Downtown to watch the circus parade. If we can't see the circus, we can see the parade. Ain't a law against that, is there?"

Ike watched his mother's face. She'd been judge and jury since the boys' father died ten years ago. Every so often, one of the adults would talk about how Isaac Washington, Sr. might have lived if there'd been a doctor nearby. Mama wouldn't talk about it.

"Your father was a hard-working, honest man who loved you. That's all that's important," she would say.

Ike waited for a sign. "No, there *isn't* a law," she said finally. "Not *ain't*. You can go. After breakfast."

"Thanks, Mama," Jerome said, grabbing Ike by the arm and yanking him out the screen door. The spring was broken and, as usual, the door flew open, bounced off the side of the house, and slammed shut. The rebound jarred a black frying pan off its hook on the wall. It clanged loudly on the floor, and Ike was suddenly afraid their pass would be revoked.

"We'll eat later," Jerome said, out-running any chance of penalty.

As he struggled to catch up, Ike heard his mother speak to the only one left to listen. "Good boy, Colonel. You stay here where you belong."

"Wait up," Ike yelled as Jerome sprinted past old Mr. Autrey's and onto the dirt road that led past a half-dozen shacks and tenant farms. From there, the rocky trail led to the new, one-lane bridge that crossed Sampson's Creek, past the railroad tracks, and on to town. Jerome sang *Railroad Bill* in time with his long strides. Ike tried to keep pace.

Off to the east, the sun broke out and the sky changed from misty gray to a blue so pale, it was nearly white. Ike saw a column of baby wood ducks trailing their mother and two squirrels race through the branches of a moss-draped oak. The boys stopped when they came to a giant tortoise inching toward the creek. "Take him all day to reach the water," Ike said.

Jerome bumped him. "Race you to the church."

Cross Keys Baptist was sixty yards ahead. Jerome won easily, but Ike was struck more by how lonely the church looked on Saturday morning. Tomorrow, it would be filled with most of the black families that lived in Kilgo and Cady County. The men were farmers and had one church outfit: black suit and stiff, black shoes, a white shirt, and a long tie or bow-tie. Some wore black hats that they took off and held on their laps for services.

Most women worked at the sewing factory in town or as housekeepers. They worried about their looks more than the men. Ike could remember many Sundays when he and Jerome had to wait while their mother fussed with her hair or the sash on her black cloth dress. The boys knew she was ready when she called for help with her necklace.

Marva Washington owned one strand of pea-sized silver pearls, an anniversary present one year from her husband. Ike thought the necklace made her look like a queen.

As the boys caught their breath by the church, Rev. Roscoe Haney appeared with a straw broom. He took the unlit pipe from his mouth and said, "Morning, Mr. Washington and Mr. Washington. Where you goin' so early?"

Jerome answered. "Morning, Reverend. We're headed to town for the circus parade."

The pastor looked at his watch, puzzled. Ike laughed. The reverend could sermonize the paint off walls, but simple matters threw him.

Jerome explained, "We get there early, we get good seats."

"I see. Well, be careful, don't get in no trouble."

Jerome hooked Ike around the neck as Rev. Haney turned to his sweeping. "Let's go."

There was one more bend and a long, open space in the woods before town. As the boys moved into the final turn, Ike wrinkled his nose at a heavy, unfamiliar odor. "What is *that*?"

They looked at each other.

"Elephants!"

They ran to a thick tree and peeked into the clearing. "Oh, gosh," Ike said, his face mashed against the rough-edged bark. Before them was a small tent city with at least sixty men and women, and a mass of elephants, lions, and tigers tethered to trees or stakes, or locked in heavy metal cages with iron bars and padlocks big as a second baseman's glove. Ike inched closer and saw some of the people sitting around small campfires while they cooked breakfast or drank coffee from metal cups. Off to one side, two boys that looked about his age threw glittery bowling pins back and forth. The pins spun and landed perfectly in each boy's hand, narrow end first.

"When did they get here?" Ike said.

"Musta' been last night."

"Think we should go closer?"

Instead of answering, Jerome pointed nervously back to the tent city. Ike turned and saw a six-foot, three-inch monster with great tufts of blue hair and a giant red nose bearing down on them. He inched back to Jerome.

"Hi-ya, fellas," the clown said as he hooked his thumbs in the brass snaps of his blue-and-white striped overalls. "I'm Marty. Come on down, meet my friends. I'll feed you to the lions. I mean, ha-ha, I'll let you feed the lions." He smacked his knee, honked a hidden horn, laughed again like a lunatic.

Ike moved shoulder to shoulder with Jerome. "I don't know."

"Aw, come on." Marty swept aside a low branch and led Ike and Jerome into his world of acrobats, trained horses, strongmen, sword swallowers and wild animals. Everyone greeted them as they passed, even little *Rubberhead*, the human cannonball.

"Would you believe I've never, ever had a headache in my life?" he said, rapping on his head like it was a door.

Most surprising to Ike was the mix of black skin and white, of dark, almond-shaped eyes and round, pale ones, of American voices and foreign. He watched, amazed, as black men played poker with white men *and* white women. He passed a troupe of Chinese acrobats eating eggs fried by a tall man with a thick, black moustache and Spanish accent.

"*Buenos días, muchachos.* Some breakfast? Coffee, maybe?"

"Thank you, sir. We already ate," Ike said.

When they reached the animals, Jerome stopped. "They can't get out," Ike said as a yellow-eyed circus cat paced in his narrow cell.

"I'm not taking any chances."

Marty asked if they were coming to the show. "Going to be a good one. We got a new high-wire artist from Russia. Walks ninety feet across a rope thin as your little Johnson. (*Honk*) And she's eighteen feet in the air."

Ike tried to imagine the tightrope and the terror of being up that high. "There a net underneath?"

"A net?" The clown was incredulous. "This ain't some two-bit sideshow from Topeka."

Jerome stepped up. "They don't let colored in the Armory."

Marty frowned, his made up face twisting into a funny mask. "Shame. You come anyway. We'll find a spot. Anybody says anything, you tell 'em you're Marty's guests. Can you remember that?"

"Sure, thanks," Jerome said. "C'mon Ike, let's go so we can still get good parade seats."

The boys clambered back to the trail, turned the last corner and emerged at the south end of Union Street. Up ahead, several families with small children were already waiting for some action. City, county and some state and federal officials were milling around. Kilgo High, the white high school, had donated its navy and gold-clad marching band, which was assembled on a special VIP platform in front of City Hall.

"Looks like they're expecting Eisenhower himself," Ike said.

The boys drifted up Union Street, trying to melt into the growing crowd. Though excited, neither forgot Mrs. Washington's standing warning: "Don't never draw attention to yourself 'mongst white folk." The boys moved to an area where most Negroes had gathered, and where the view was not as good.

"Let's get closer," Ike said after they claimed space near McCauley's Drugstore.

"This is fine," Jerome said, a warning in his voice. "Don't forget. We're going to the real show this afternoon."

Ike didn't believe it, Marty or no Marty.

"Excuse me, boys." Ezra James, a few years older than Jerome, appeared with a bucket and rubber squeegee attached to a long broom handle. He wore a short-sleeved white shirt and tie, neatly pressed blue jeans, and black canvas sneakers. His pants were held in place by a brown leather belt with an oversized silver buckle that gleamed in the sun. Engraved in the silver were the letters *EJ*, his initials and nickname. The back of his shirt said *McCauley's Drugstore* in neat, red letters.

"Hey, EJ, gettin' ready for the show?" Jerome said.

"Yeah, got to give these windows another going over before the elephants ride in."

Ike watched as Ezra—he did not know him well enough to use *EJ*—wet a section of glass with the soapy water in his bucket. He used a fat, yellow sponge to scrub, pouring on extra elbow grease to loosen several spots soiled by the birds. Ike admired the muscles that bulged in Ezra's arms; he looked powerful as the circus strongman. For the last step, Ezra got the black rubber squeegee, pressed it against the glass, and pulled down in long, even strokes. After finishing a section, he shifted a bit to the side to check his work from a different angle. The artist and his canvas. Most times the glass sparkled and Ezra moved to the next pane.

"Lookin' good," Jerome said.

EJ nodded. "Mr. McCauley said it best shine like diamonds. Lots of big folks going to be through here today. Even got his son in to help run the store."

"The judge?" Jerome said.

"The one and only."

From what Ike had heard about Judge Mac McCauley, blacks would do near anything to stay out of his courtroom. But wait, something was going on down the street. Using his palm against the sun, Ike tried to see what was causing the commotion. He looked past the anxious faces in the clarinet section of the Kilgo High band, beyond dozens of little girls and boys squirming on their daddies' shoulders, and down the smooth stretch of road that ran between the stores and municipal offices that were the heart of downtown Kilgo.

Somewhere a signal was given and received. The band struck up "Stars and Stripes Forever," and people started cheering. American flags flew everywhere. Ike strained to see farther than his eyes were able. Someone got in his way and he elbowed for better position. No one would give ground and the crowd by *McCauley's* was now six deep. Ike found a fire hydrant and stepped up, balancing on the stubby cap.

When he looked again, an elephant with a red satin crest on his chest was leading the caravan up Union Street. A dark-skinned boy with silky pants and golden turban rode the giant beast and waved happily. Ike felt the wave was for him and returned it, forfeiting his shade.

Behind the elephant were three more. They traveled heavy trunk to skinny tail with giant placards on their sides. *Circus today! 4 p.m.* the signs screamed in red and blue.

Next came the clowns, eight of them, in four golf cart-sized yellow cars. Some got out and chased each other with water pistols and buckets of confetti. Ike saw Marty and tried to get his attention, but the leggy clown was too busy returning water gun fire at a pink-shoed partner in a billowing pink dress with white polka dots.

After the clowns were jugglers in blue tights. Ike saw the boys from the tent city and their bowling pins, as well as a man who kept two plates spinning on top of long bamboo poles held in each hand. Ike imagined the man tripping and getting trampled by several small trucks that were next in line.

The trucks towed cages that looked like the skeletons of railroad cars. Instead of seats and windows, the cars had thick iron bars on top and on both sides. Some were divided so that each could carry up to three animals, mostly lions and tigers. Ike focused on the second of three cars, where a rough-looking man in blue jeans and brown derby kept poking his cane at a tiger. The man sat on top of the car and teased the edgy cat, which swiped angrily at the cane.

As the car reached McCauley's, the band began *Dixie*. Ike saw the man remove his derby and bow gravely to the officials on the viewing stand. As he did, the tiger threw himself against the cage. The man jerked back, lost his footing and fell to the ground. People laughed as he stood and dusted himself off, trying to pretend the fall didn't hurt. Ike was glad, but wondered what the tiger was in for after the caravan moved out of sight.

After acrobats, cowboys on trick ponies and a flat, padded trailer featuring Madame Vacheska, whose gold-spangled leotard flashed brilliantly as she flipped and tumbled effortlessly, the parade was nearly over. Kilgo's mayor officially welcomed the circus to town, and Judge McCauley followed by urging everyone to attend the afternoon show.

"Everyone who's white, he means," Jerome whispered as he helped Ike from the hydrant. The boys watched as the parade wound toward the Armory just north of town. Madame Vacheska was still waving and blowing kisses.

The Cady County Armory, built to host 4-H conventions, agricultural fairs, and an occasional rodeo, was perfect for the circus. The horseshoe-shaped building was big enough to handle two rings of action, an elephant "dance," the high-wire apparatus, *Rubberhead's* cannon and cargo net, and eight hundred spectators. More than nine hundred crammed in for the opening show late Saturday afternoon.

Jerome tapped his foot as he watched the line. The longer he watched, the faster he tapped. Then he stopped. "I'm goin' to that circus. You come if you want to." Ike followed.

The brothers walked in the performers' entrance at the far end of the arena, where their nervous fidgeting caught the eye of a circus bouncer and some white boys with slicked back hair rolling dice. The bouncer asked the brothers for their tickets.

"Don't have none," Jerome said. "Our invite's from Marty the Clown."

The bouncer eyed the gang and told the brothers to wait in a small office inside the back door checkpoint.

"Told you this was trouble," Ike said. "Those guys know we're here."

Jerome opened his mouth to speak and the door swung open. "Fellas! You're not going to be able to see much from here."

Marty steered them through a maze of corridors until they emerged near a scaffolding behind the main stage. A small part in the purple curtain separating the audience from the performers gave the boys a perfect view.

"Your seats," Marty said grandly, producing two metal folding chairs. "Not front and center, but close."

Jerome gave Ike an "told-you-so" smirk and shook the clown's hand. "Thanks, Marty, this is the best." Marty bowed and waved with a royal flourish. "Gotta go. We open the show."

Minutes later, Ike heard a sound that made his heart lurch. It started small, but kept building. He peered into the orchestra pit and found the source: six soft-felt mallets on three gold-bottomed kettledrums. A man in a black tuxedo and top hat stepped on-stage.

"LADIES AND GENTLEMEN … "

Ike could not pull his eyes from the ringmaster. He was suddenly overcome with affection for his brother, whose determination got them into the forbidden circus. This was a day he'd always remember. He reached over to give Jerome a playful slap on the knee and misjudged the distance. As he glanced over, he saw a fist fly into Jerome's back.

Jerome opened his mouth and no sound came out; the punch had knocked him breathless. Ike tried to stand, but someone had his shoulders. "You next, boy," whispered a voice that smelled of beer and tobacco. He watched helplessly as the boys from outside the arena stood Jerome up and took turns beating his stomach. "Move 'em back here," the leader said, motioning to a darkened area away from the stage curtain. "Hurry up."

Ike counted six. He didn't know names; the faces were familiar. All went to Kilgo High. One was a wrestler. A hard-pack of *Luckies* bulged from his shirtsleeve.

"Hold this one," the leader said, pointing at Jerome. "Uppity niggers. Think they can go anywhere they want. Next place they're goin' is the nigger hospital."

The wrestler kept Jerome's arms pinned behind his back. Ike started to cry. Someone slapped his face. "Shut the fuck up."

The leader turned back to the wrestler, who was still holding Jerome. "Got him?"

"Ain't goin' nowhere."

Ike saw Jerome's face. His eyes were squeezed shut, but he wasn't crying. Ike could see the veins in his brother's temples throbbing as he fought for air.

"Gonna mess up you up good, mother-fucker. You're going to be a circus freak yourself when I'm done."

As the leader drew his arm back, fist clenched and fitted now with brass knuckles, a man with a straw-colored crew cut stepped into the light.

"Whoa," he said, his voice a soft command. Everyone froze. "What's going on here, boys?"

Ike blinked through his tears and gasped – Judge Lander McCauley.

"We got an invite, Judge," Ike blurted. "Marty the Clown."

"Shut-up," one of the boys said, twisting Ike's arm.

The judge stroked his smooth-shaven chin and strolled forward a few steps, hands deep in the pockets of his gray dress trousers. "Boys," he said, addressing the gang, ignoring Ike and Jerome, "today's a happy day for our little town. What say we be generous and let these two get on to where they belong?"

"But Judge."

McCauley's cold eyes ended it. Ike and Jerome were released and stood in place. A moment passed. Ike held slim hope that they would be allowed to return to their seats. "Well, get!" the judge snarled. "'Fore I change my mind, feed you back to these here lions." The gang laughed.

As the boys scrambled out, Ike heard the ringmaster's booming voice. "AND NOW, ALL THE WAY FROM RUSSIA, THE FANTASTIC, UNCOMPARABLE MADAME VACHESKA!"

•••••

Ruthie touched Ike's cheek. Unlike hers, it was dry.

"How did you ever start working for that man?"

No answer. "Ike, how did you go to work for McCauley?"

He tilted his head back, breathed in the humid air, blew it out at the branches swaying gently high above. "I'll tell you that another time. We need to get to Columbia. Lot of media going to be there."

As they stood in the soft dirt, she said, "I'm sorry for the things you went through, Ike, that you had to grow up in those times, but the car's still no good. Please take it back."

"No. I work hard. I've earned that car."

8

"Make sure to talk up your experience and contacts," Ruthie said as they pulled into the back of the Masons' lot on James Street and Ike helped himself to two parking spots. "You know this district best because you've been up and down a thousand times. Be respectful of Owens and Harley. Don't hit Maussipant too hard."

"Ruthie, relax." Ike licked two fingers on each hand and mashed down the tight, black-gray curls that already lay flat along his temples.

Ruthie scouted the back window. "Crap. Leigh Sanderson from the *Statesman*. Careful with her."

Ike cracked the door and felt a rush of hot air. "Why don't you take that woman out for dinner some time, like you did that Patragno kid. Get a few drinks in her, get her to open up a little. We … "

"Need the media to work for us, not against us," Ruthie finished.

"Right. And that means … "

"Doing whatever it takes," she said without enthusiasm.

"Good girl. Now do your job. Give me twenty seconds lead."

Ike walked briskly to Leigh Sanderson and fought not to show his distaste for her get-up: hiking boots under a loose beige skirt, white cotton tank with spaghetti straps and an old brown backpack. Whatever happened to dressing like a professional? The *Statesman* was the largest paper in Columbia and known for its aggressive coverage of the state legislature. He threw a smile and buried her pasty hand in both of his. When the reporter tried to ask a question, he apologized and nodded toward the lodge.

"Have to catch you after, Leigh, I'm late."

Ruthie washed up in his wake. "You need interview time with Ike, Leigh?"

"Not really. It's kind of stuffy in there," she said off-handedly. "I was just waiting around, saw you guys pull up in 'man-of-the-people' Ike Washington's brand new—now, just what *is* that thing?"

The reporter took several reconnaissance steps to the car and read the silver script nameplate that was plainly visible from where they stood. "Ah, Ike's new *Lincoln Town Car.*"

"That's not ours."

"No?" She spit her gum into the bushes.

"I mean, it's going back."

"Tell me about it," Sanderson said, swinging her ratty backpack around and reaching for a pen and pad.

•••••

The Masons' idea of lunch was barbecue sandwiches, sweet corn drenched in butter sauce, iced sweet tea, peach cobbler for dessert and a blizzard of announcements about new Masons, old Masons, dead Masons, honorary Masons, and visiting Masons.

"What *is* a Mason, anyway?"

Dan, already inside, had waited until Ruth was away from the other reporters before getting near.

"A craftsman," she said, her nose in a leather folder that bulged with

Ike's schedule and talking points. "Brick, stonework, that sort of thing."

"Hey, listen."

"Can't now." She moved off, all business, toward the gang of reporters massed in the back of the room.

In front, the candidates waited at a gardenia-topped table reserved for spouses. Ike sat between his wife, Cynthia, and Abraham Harley, husband of Dianna Harley. Cady Owens, III was a widower, Derrick Maussipant was single. Though famished, Ike did not eat. Senator McCauley, the most reelected man in state history, once told him that voters were repulsed by the sight of politicians "shovin' biscuits and gravy down their yaps." He also didn't want to risk barbecue in his teeth.

"Have something, dear," Cynthia Washington said. "You left before breakfast. I can hear your stomach."

"Yes, more grumbling than usual," Abe Harley chuckled. Harley was a Columbia proctologist who bought three suits each year when the Harleys made their annual trip to Manhattan.

Ike considered asking if he ate with the same hands he used at work, but instead clapped him gently on the back. "I like being a little hungry before I go to work, Abe. Gives me an edge."

Twenty minutes later, the four congressional candidates were summoned to the raised dais, introduced, and asked to keep their opening remarks brief.

"No offense. We want to hear all you've got," the emcee apologized, "but most of us have real jobs and have to get back to work." He smiled and fifty Masons laughed with him.

The order was left to the candidates, who quickly agreed Cady Owens could lead off. Owens carried a small, wooden box to speaking events because most podiums were too tall. He reached for his stand, hoisted it to waist level, and shuffled to the microphone.

"Looks like every step hurts 'im," a Mason whispered.

Owens rearranged his tie and pulled out a short stack of three-by-fives. He looked thoughtfully at the cards and stuffed them back in his suit pocket. He cleared his throat and began, "Friends, there is no sense reading my credits. You've known me for years. You knew me in the fifties when I was locked up at the sit-in at McCauley's Drugstore over in Kilgo."

He waited, letting the image do its work: menacing whites standing over passive blacks hunched on plastic swivel seats at the whites-only lunch counter, taunting, spitting, and worse while the Kilgo cops looked on, tapping billy clubs against their legs.

"You knew me when I ran for the state legislature the first time twenty-two years ago, and when I marched with Dr. King. That was a long time ago." He paused again, shook his head as if it were impossible nearly thirty years had passed.

"Much has changed, much remains to be done. You know me, and I know you. I know your mamas and daddies and some of *their* mamas and daddies."

Owens ran a bony hand through his coarse white hair and removed his glasses. "That's what this new seat needs—someone who's been through the fire. I've been through so many times, I should be nothing but ashes." People laughed. Owens' warm smile thanked them for understanding. "Please give us your support."

Ike made sure he clapped the loudest. His latest poll of district voters said people considered Owens a wise elder. They would not vote for him because of his age, but he deserved respect. Ike considered a moment, then stood as he pounded his hands together.

When the applause ran out, Derrick Maussipant slid his chair back and stood. But he miscalculated. Owens was still returning to his seat and there was only enough room in the narrow aisle behind their chairs for one to pass. Maussipant leaned back, balancing precariously on the edge of the four-foot dais. As he did, Owens slipped by. For a moment, it looked like the old gentleman had bulldozed the young athlete.

"Now that's a man whose path you don't want to block," Maussipant kidded when he reached the podium.

The crowd liked his style, Ike saw. "Nice-lookin' boy," an elderly woman near the front told her neighbor. "Polite, too."

Derrick nudged Owens' small platform aside with his foot and straightened the silver arm of the microphone to its tallest position. "Thank you all. I'm Derrick Maussipant. I'm an attorney in the Lowcountry, but got my law degree here at USC. I did my undergraduate work at the College of Charleston and played a little ball for the *Cougars.* Some say thirty-one is too young for Congress; I say it means I have a lot of energy. And I'm not ashamed to say I'm ambitious. I think my energy and ambition will serve you well in Washington."

Ike watched the audience, saw they wanted to like the kid but that he was going too fast, trying too hard. Running out of breath and words. Painful memories flooded back. *Pace yourself, boy.* He shuddered. He could see himself giving a practice speech years earlier, nervous, racing, and Lander McCauley's disgusted face. *Pace yourself. You're like a bee in a bottle.* Constant practice, ceaseless criticism.

Maussipant sensed the problem. "Sorry, I'm new at this. Here's what I'll say: We are a small state and a poor district. We need someone who will work long and hard in Congress to make sure we get our fair share. Please give us a look before you make a choice."

Ike rose from the other side of the dais and was at the mike before Maussipant sat down.

"Whew, that boy does have energy," he admitted, feigning fear and mopping his forehead. "He'll make a fine legislative assistant when I get to Washington."

Maussipant saluted sheepishly. The crowd laughed and Ike joined them, giving reporters just enough time to jot down his one-liner. His smug expression said that if the hall were a pet store and the Masons a family in for a puppy, he'd be the one.

"Folks, I'm not about putting others down. But I'm really the only one here today who understands how Washington works." He caught Cady Owens writing something on a legal pad, but charged ahead with remarks that had already been approved by McCauley's people.

"I know some of you don't like Senator McCauley, haven't ever forgiven him for things he said back in the old days. That was his daddy owned the drugstore, by the way, not him. I'm not here to defend the senator, even though he's changed plenty over the years. I'm here to assure you I'm my own man." He repeated slowly, "My own man."

"Have I learned anything working all this time for Mac McCauley? You bet. I've learned how sewer projects get funded and how to get more money for roads and bridges and schools. I know which people to call when a Social Security check doesn't come; I know which agencies to bring in if a person is denied a job because his skin is black." Ike paused and sipped his water. The room was so quiet, heads turned when Dan flipped a page in his notepad.

"My daddy died when I was a boy," Ike said. "I never really knew him. Mama's gone too, and my only brother gave his life for this country. Vietnam." Ike let the word sink in. "After all these years, my son Jerome—Sorry, I mean *our* son—" he waved to Cynthia, who nodded to the audience and blew a small kiss—"is grown and blessed with his own family. Jerome was named for my brother. He and his wife and our granddaughter live up in Charlotte. That means I am at last in a position to make a difference. Let me make a difference for you."

He had taken more time than the others. No one seemed to notice except Dianna Harley, who left her seat and began walking to the podium. The Masons were standing as they clapped.

Some, planted volunteers already committed to the campaign, chanted, "IKE FOR YOU IN '92, IKE FOR YOU IN '92." Owens and Maussipant shifted uneasily. Ike bowed deeply, as if to say he didn't deserve such acclaim but would strive to be worthy.

Dianna Harley pulled the microphone down and began. Ike grinned as he held a finger to his lips and urged the crowd to hush and be seated.

"I don't have any amusing stories," she began sternly. "I'm here because I want you to consider how long we have waited for a person of color to represent us in Washington. I look at this crowd, at the oldest among you, and it makes me sad. You have lived all your life in this state and never had a black congressman. That is about to change, and we can't just hand the job to anyone. It must be someone with experience, but with strength and vigor. It must be someone strong, but someone who also possesses the right experience."

Dianna Harley paused and everyone seemed to feel the weight of what was coming.

Ike kept his breathing steady, forced a casual grin that said the woman was well intended, but just didn't get it.

"Tough customer," Dan nudged Ruth, who blew at her forehead and didn't answer.

Dianna tapped a long, cream-colored fingernail three times on the podium. The mike picked up the sound, sent it ricocheting through the hall. Her next words started soft as a prayer. Several Masons leaned forward, then back as she gathered force.

"Most important, our emissary *must not* be someone with divided loyalties and a lot of debts, especially to a man who tried so hard through the years to hold us down. This job is too important to go to any old bootlicker."

Cynthia Washington put her hands over her mouth.

Ike shot up. "Now hold on."

Abe Harley rose halfway in his seat, a man ready to defend his wife.

Dianna Harley glared at Ike. "Excuse me," she said. "You had your time. This is mine."

Cady Owens sat back in his chair and lit a cigarette. Derrick Maussipant's broad shoulders slumped.

Ike was still on his feet. "You sell fancy houses to rich folk and you're questioning my credentials?"

"I make sure black folk don't get cheated when they try to buy a home. And I run the state NAACP. Are you even a member?"

The reporters scribbled furiously. TV crews kept their cameras trained on the dais.

Ike kicked Cady Owens' wooden stand off the dais and walked out. Dianna finished to stunned silence and was quickly engulfed by reporters. Owens and Maussipant watched a moment, then left in the other direction. Cynthia Washington remained with her elbows on the table, fingers locked, eyes closed.

Ruthie followed Ike to the back parking lot, where he was pacing beside the glacier blue *Lincoln*.

"How did you let that happen?" he demanded.

"How did I *what*?"

"You heard me."

Ruthie pinched the bridge of her nose, kept her voice controlled. "How was that *my* fault?"

"You're the campaign manager. I told you I don't like surprises."

"Dianna Harley doesn't share strategy with me."

"Don't be a smartass. You worry about the wrong shit. You worry about what kind of goddamned car I drive. You should have worried about getting me ready for that bitch."

She walked to the *Town Car*, caressed its shimmering roof with a hand that trembled in anger. She turned to him with her hand still rubbing. "Speaking of cars and bitches, Leigh Sanderson is doing a story about your new *Cartier-series Lincoln*."

Ike looked long at Ruthie, saw her eyes narrow like she was ready to squeeze off a shot. The fingers of her other hand were pale from clutching the leather folder. "Get back in there and try to contain the damage," he said. "Tell those damned reporters I'll talk to them out here in ten minutes."

She contemplated the words through her rage. "Put this in the car," she answered finally, thrusting the folder at him. He took it; she turned and waded back into the battle.

When she was gone, Ike threw the burgundy folder in the backseat, fired up the AC, and placed a call to Washington. A receptionist answered and patched him through to a personal secretary, who asked him to hold. Ike wiped his face with a handkerchief. After a moment, an old, raspy voice said, "McCauley."

"Senator, we've, um, I mean, there's been ... What? Yes, I know. I'm sorry to bother ... Yes, sir. Well, we've got a small problem. I'm in Columbia, outside the Masons' lodge. All the candidates got to speak. I did fine, sir. Lots of applause." A sudden enthusiasm seized his voice and then vanished when McCauley told him to "get to it." Ike loosened his belt a notch, saw his belly and shirt lurch forward.

"It was that damned Dianna Harley, Senator. She said if they sent me to Congress, I'd still be working for you." Ike touched the windshield and studied his oily fingerprint. "She spoke last, so I didn't get a chance to answer."

McCauley's voice was low. "Those reporters still there?" "Yes, sir." Ike held the small phone to his ear.

It was as if the pilot were dead, he thought. Instructions were being issued from ground control in Washington; he'd have to land the plane. "Yes, sir," he said again.

When Ike hung up, he was still alone. His head hurt, his knees were stiff, and his crooked pinky ached. The finger was bent at a slight angle that made the knuckle look deformed. He inspected the digit and watched as it began to twitch. Ike tried to loosen his tie and broke the top button off his shirt. He looked at it and saw two, tiny white threads still attached. He felt a trembling begin somewhere deep in his belly. He closed his eyes and a small tear squeezed out, though he was fighting, not crying. Fighting to hold down a memory.

The terse order.

The waiting, his arms pinned, his pulse banging.

Tyler Hawke's crazy laughter.

The pain, sharp and sudden.

And then the end. And the beginning. Of his servitude.

•••••

"Ike. Ike, you okay?"

He saw Ruthie's face through the tinted window. Her mouth was moving, but he couldn't hear a word over the hum of the AC and Ray on the stereo. She looked worried as she shaded her eyes and peered down at him.

"Open up."

He found a small knob on the side of his seat and brought himself back to a sitting position. As he clicked the door lock button, she yanked his side open.

"They're coming. You want them to find you here and start asking questions about the car, stay where you are. Otherwise, come with me."

Ike hauled himself out and, collecting himself along the way, walked with Ruthie to the back door of the Masons' lodge.

In a moment, the reporters—four print, though no Leigh Sanderson—an AP radio man, and two TV crews filed out. All wanted more reaction to Dianna Harley's attack.

"Desperate people say desperate things," he said, composed and confident. "Our polls—and I'm sure hers, if she's run any—show no one knows Dianna Harley. I guess she figures the only way to build herself up is tear me down. That's not the kind of person who ought to represent this district."

Dan stepped forward. "Why should voters believe you won't keep working for McCauley if you make it to Washington?"

"That's fair, Mr. Patragno, even though you and I have had that discussion. My work for the senator ends with my election, and he knows that. Neither of us would have it any other way. Now, if that's all, I've got another event and we need to get moving. Ruthie?"

Ruthie moved to his side as the reporters rushed off to start filing their stories.

"Excellent," she said as they walked slowly back to the car.

"Want to drive?"

"Not funny, Ike. Not funny at all."

9   *Dan*

He chose not to write his story in the paper's one-room Columbia bureau. With no traffic, the straight shot from Columbia to Charleston down I-26 would take ninety minutes so long as the troopers keep their radar guns holstered. He composed as he drove, visualizing the *lede* and opening grafs as the monotonous miles, one-mall towns and Civil War battle sites disappeared in the rearview.

He was in the newsroom by four, a half-hour ahead of the daily budget meeting where editorial chieftains plotted the next day's paper.

"Patragno, whatcha got?"

"Dianna Harley beat up Ike Washington at the Masons."

Lem Butcher looked up from his list. "Talk to me."

"She said Ike's in Senator McCauley's back pocket. Wouldn't be independent in Washington. Called him a *bootlicker*."

Butcher said the word aloud. "I like it. Sounds like porn. Give me twelve to fifteen inches. Write tight and slug it 'Masons.'"

He nodded as Butcher made the addition to his list and darted for the conference room.

Dan saw the red light on his phone flashing and punched Star 7.

Three messages, nothing important. He slid his chair in front of the computer, typed "Patragno" and his password to sign on.

Looking at his notebook, he set his fingers on the computer keyboard and typed:

COLUMBIA—Kilgo Mayor Ike Washington, considered a leading contender to become South Carolina's first black congressman since Reconstruction, is a pawn of one-time segregationist U.S. Sen. Lander McCauley, one of Washington's rivals charged Monday.

Dan read and re-read several times, making minor adjustments. He would have to try for a comment from McCauley's office. He looked at his watch, saved the story—he saved every three paragraphs lest he lose everything if the mainframe crashed—and pushed Star 9 for a long-distance line.

"Sen. McCauley's press office, Jane Peeples speaking."

"Jane, Dan Patragno at the *Herald-Leader*. I'm wondering if the senator would have any comment on a remark made today by Dianna Harley about McCauley and Ike Washington."

"What remark?"

Intuition told him she'd already heard, but he played along. "Quoting from my notes, Harley said black voters shouldn't support a candidate with debts to a man 'who tried so hard through the years to hold us down.'"

Dan imagined her silent curses: *Late afternoon and he's bothering me with this crap.*

"Jane?"

"We'll have to get back to you," she answered. "Number?"

Dan gave it and said, "ASAP. *Please.*"

"I'll do my best. The senator's stuck in an Energy Committee hearing."

Dan wrapped up, leaving the third graf open for McCauley's quote, and joined the editors after a signal from Butcher. The summons was no surprise; Butcher liked his reporters to understand how decisions were made on story placement and on ethical questions.

The budget meeting, two parts business, one part horseplay, lasted each day from 4:30 to about 5:15. Editors from different sections sat at a round oak table in a wood-paneled, smoke-free room without windows and a few *Holiday Inn* paintings. Each got a few minutes to run down what his shop had for the next day's paper. The ideal—rarely achieved because the daily news was a messy work in progress, not a tidy, corporate report—was a quick huddle that got everyone up to speed and back to work. Overtime was routine because some stories were still developing. Other stories would fall through, while some had reached editors, but needed work.

"Okay. National, what's up?"

The meeting was run by Managing Editor Marshall Ryder, a gray-haired, soft-spoken ex-Navy man who switched from learned elder to ruthless despot if warring factions around the table couldn't reach quick agreement. Deadline allowed only so much time for debate.

"Nothing much," said the national editor. "Congress is still out for the summer; Republicans will re-nominate Bush and Quayle at their convention in a couple of weeks."

"Sports?" Ryder said.

"City tennis championship. One of our guys did a nice feature tying how locals get ready to how the pros are preparing for the U.S. Open."

"Got art?"

"Yeah, good action stuff."

"Give that nice display with a three-column photo," Ryder said. "People will enjoy that."

"On it."

"City Desk? Lem?"

Butcher glanced at his list. "Two strong ones for 1A. We've got a new wrinkle in the Greenville girl trying to get into The Citadel, and we've got one of the rivals in the Sixth District race—Dianna Harley—needling Ike Washington pretty good."

"Needling" wasn't the word Dan would have chosen.

"What's the wrinkle?" someone asked.

"The girl's got herself a hotshot woman attorney from the ACLU who's making a stink," Butcher said. "The Citadel's getting defensive."

"I'm sick of the first-girl-at-the-Citadel thing," said the sports editor, drawing glares from his female colleagues.

"What did Harley say about Ike Washington?" asked features editor Nina Stapleton, a Charleston belle whose refined manner made her a target for all who didn't appreciate the importance of a proper Southern upbringing. Which was nearly everyone in the newsroom.

"Said he's McCauley's little lapdog." Butcher dragged out the syllables, stuck his tongue out at Nina and wagged it obscenely.

"Lovely," she said. "Our romance columnist and his filthy tongue."

Ryder clapped his hands. "I like the Ike piece better for the front." No one disagreed, which meant Washington would land on the front page and the Citadel piece would lead Metro.

Dan gave silent thanks. He also caught Nina Stapleton frown at Lem Butcher. "Bastard," she mouthed. He winked.

"Alright, who's left? Style? International?"

"I'll go," said the foreign affairs editor. "More fighting in the Gaza."

"There's a surprise."

Fifteen minutes later, Dan was back at his screen when the phone rang. He saved his work. "Newsroom. Patragno."

"Dan, Jane Peeples."

Dan swiveled and grabbed his pen and notebook. Some reporters took notes on their computer; Dan felt sources got nervous when they heard the click of a keyboard.

"Here's our comment. Ready?"

"Go."

"Ike Washington has been an exemplary employee for more than three decades."

"Slow down. I'm not a stenographer."

"Sorry. Ready? Here's more: Mr. Washington has never worked against the interest of African Americans in South Carolina. Rather, he has brought to my attention and helped me address special concerns in black communities throughout the state on transportation, education, employment and health issues."

"That's it?"

"That's our statement."

"Great, Jane. Want to tell me what McCauley really said when you told him about this?"

"That's what he said. Sorry it's not what you wanted."

"Right. Anything else?"

"That's it. So long."

He returned to his screen and started typing in McCauley's remarks. Bullshit or not, the senator got his say. Let the readers sort out who was right and wrong.

"Patragno, you forget this is a *daily* paper?"

"Three minutes."

Butcher walked to his desk and sat on a corner. "After we finish with this, I want to talk about your Ike profile. That's going to need work."

Dan nodded. When Butcher said a piece needed work, it usually meant major rewrite. Extra work didn't worry him; failing to meet Butcher's standards was different.

He put the thought aside and ground out the last few paragraphs. He finished with a short recap of how and why the new black-majority seat was created, stuck a -30- at the bottom to denote the end of the story, and shipped it.

"You've got 'Masons' in the Metro Basket," he messaged.

"Got it," Butcher yelled back.

Dan stretched, checked his watch, and took the elevator to the third-floor cafeteria for a dinner of vanilla yogurt, cookies and coffee. No one else was around, so he ate and read a week-old copy of *Sports Illustrated* someone left behind. When he returned to the newsroom, most reporters were gone and the night editors were busy tidying up copy, headlines and cutlines for the first edition. Butcher, on the phone in his office, motioned for him to come in and shut the door.

Dan tried and failed to remember the last time he'd seen Butcher's door shut. He cracked his knuckles.

Butcher walked to the window that overlooked King Street, stretching the coiled beige telephone cord into a straight line. "Yeah, alright, kill the photo, add the story. The page'll look gray, but I don't see a choice. The story's more important than the picture." He hung up, sat at his desk and faced Dan.

"Good job today."

"Thanks."

"Not so good on the Washington profile."

"Oh?"

"Come 'round."

Dan pulled his chair to the side of the desk as Butcher called up the profile. For a moment, the monitor screen was blank. Then the story appeared. On top, Dan saw the dreaded word HOLD in bold letters followed by Butcher's initials.

"This is a rehash of everything everyone else has written about Ike: humble start, put himself through school, blah, blah. Thirty-five inches of fluff. We used to call this kind of story a wet kiss."

Dan felt nauseous. His palms moved from his thighs to his knees and back again, as if he were trying to shine his pants. He glared at the computer screen and saw the pale green cursor blinking impatiently, taunting him. "I interviewed more than a dozen people. This is the kind of stuff they said. What am I supposed to do, make up things that are unflattering?"

"What dozen? Ike's fan club?"

Dan slid his chair back from the desk and crossed his arms.

"Look, Patragno, you haven't done any digging. Doesn't what Dianna Harley said today bother you a little? Aren't you more curious about the connection between Washington and McCauley? If Ike Washington was some ordinary black kid out in the sticks, why in the name of the Good Lord Jesus would he have caught the attention of Lander McCauley?"

The questions hit like darts. "What was Washington before McCauley?" Butcher demanded. "Was he a welfare kid? A hoodlum? Christ, this relationship has been going on longer than most marriages. Do Washington and McCauley even like each other? Do they hang together? If so, where? Who else is part of the crowd?"

Dan didn't answer. The questions were obvious and he'd missed them all. Worse, he'd written a story as if he were head of Ike's public relations firm.

"Alright, quit feeling sorry for yourself. Here's what you do."

Dan took out pad and pen.

"Put that away and listen. It's very simple. Go back and bang on a lot more doors. If you talked to a dozen people the first time, talk to three dozen this time. And forget about the ones we always quote, the party officials and committee chairmen and all that. Talk to people who grew up with Ike Washington. Find the ones who knew him before he became successful. Dianna Harley put her finger on something today. She probably doesn't even know what it is, but she hit a nerve."

Dan flipped absently through his notebook, but the words he saw weren't on the page. *Wet Kiss. Big, Wet One. Smoocherama.* No *Washington Post* for you, sucker.

Butcher said, "I want more. I'll give you three weeks. No other assignments, just this." And don't forget *Dear Lem's* advice: *Get in their faces; don't be afraid to make a scene."*

· · · · ·

"Two ways to look at it," Bernie Weinstock said next morning at the Broad Street Cafe. "First, he thinks you're good enough to get better. That's not true of everyone at that rag. Second, you're goddamned lucky he doesn't know you're hot for the campaign manager. What's her name?"

"Ruthie Baines."

Dan rested his arm on the pelican and lifted his gaze to a distant church steeple. "She wouldn't even talk to me yesterday."

"She was busy."

"I know."

"I don't think you do, but you're about to learn why she was busy."

Dan looked at him cock-eyed. Bernie rose and got a paper from the table by his cash register. He returned and tossed the *Statesman's* A-section in front of him. What was in the competition? Even upside down, Dan could see there were two front-page stories by Leigh Sanderson.

He turned the paper right side up and saw the first was the same as his, about Dianna Harley laying into Ike. The second, accompanied by a three-column, five-inch deep color photo, was about Ike campaigning for the state's poorest district in a $47,000 Lincoln Town Car. *A $47,000 Lincoln Town Car!*

"Stumping in Style," the headline said.

Terrific. Now there was a missed story to go with the wet kiss.

10   *Mac*

As he stood shaving with a straight-edged razor, Mac McCauley saw his silver blade catch a ray of light from the row of naked bulbs over the bathroom mirror. He tilted the razor experimentally, watching the beam race along the wall as he shifted his wrist, then he bit his thin, lower lip.

"Jesus H, that boy's tongue is long enough to cut his throat."

"Who, senator?" Auralee stood behind him, head on his back, bare arms easily circling his flat, naked belly. He saw her hands touch and recalled his last birthday, seventy-four candles, by God, when he slipped alone into the dusty attic of his home in South Carolina, found the trunk where he kept the pants from his old Army uniform and slipped them on. They fit as if newly issued.

McCauley smiled, then blew at some sugar-white curls that were itching his forehead. He put down his razor, massaged a dollop of *Old School* pomade into his scalp, and combed his thick hair. Auralee gave a final hug, ending with a quiet kiss on the back of his neck. She stepped back and fastened the leather eyes of his suspenders to the two buttons inside his trousers.

"Never mind, little girl. Talkin' to myself. You hit my age, you get a little touched." He looked past his foam-covered face in the gilded mirror and saw her pouting with lips too pink and glossy for someone who worked in a Senate office. Her lavender dress fit too snugly over her hips and bosom, and she wore too much rose-smelling perfume.

He felt himself stir and thought seriously about a desk-top rematch. She'd be game, he knew; she was always game. A knock at the door shook him back. "Get that."

Auralee shrugged and walked off, unlocking the deadbolt. As the door opened, Carter Strickland brushed past with faxed copies of articles from three different South Carolina newspapers. "Senator, you seen these?"

McCauley opened his mouth and cocked his head to the left, forcing a patch of white stubble into the path of his blade. He stroked twice and dunked the razor in the stoppered, pedestal sink. "You did not say good morning to Miss Auralee, Carter."

Strickland clutched the articles and rolled his eyes at the cathedral ceiling. Auralee did not mix much with McCauley's other staffers. Her job was to answer rare calls here in the senator's private Capitol office— he called it the *Roost*, everyone else called it the *Hideout*—and to keep the liquor cabinet stocked with *Jack Daniels*.

"Jack home?" McCauley would say when he wanted a drink.

Auralee DeMossier also spent a good part of each day indulging her unlikely passion for the bassoon. When McCauley was out and the office quiet, she'd unpack the long-throated instrument she was assigned as a child because the band teacher had too many clarinets, fit its complex sections together, and play until her lips ached. At first, security was startled by the low, mournful melodies Auralee produced. Opinions varied on her talent; no one really knew much about the bassoon. Most were happy enough that the instrument did not shriek or whistle. McCauley said it was okay for her to play, which was enough for staff and security.

Carter Strickland reached under his pants leg and hitched up a sock. "Morning, Auralee."

"Good morning, Mr. Strickland."

Both men looked at her. Auralee sounded like *Tweetie* when she tried to put on a business voice.

McCauley let the water down and wiped his face with a fresh towel that bore his initials. Taking the clips from Strickland, he fastened his suspenders in front and reached for his glasses. "You know I don't like to be bothered here, Carter."

"Sorry, sir, thought you'd want to see these."

The articles, all front-pagers, recounted Dianna Harley's assault on Ike Washington. Details varied, but each told the same story: that, to her thinking, Ike was McCauley's little doggy and would continue fetching his slippers if voters sent him to Washington. McCauley frowned slightly as he read.

"What are we going to do about this?" Strickland said. "We've got to start thinking about '94."

McCauley held up a hand that silenced his chief aide. "Auralee, run along and take your coffee break. Carter and I have business."

Auralee grabbed a beaded purse and walked as quickly to the door as her three-inch heels would allow. The scent of artificial roses followed her and made Carter Strickland wrinkle his nose. "Smells like a funeral home in here."

McCauley again held up his deeply-lined palm. His eyes narrowed on a fourth article, from the *Columbia Statesman*, that said Ike was running around the state in a *Lincoln Town Car*.

"Carter, get that dumb sumbitch up here. *Today.* I want his fat ass in that chair by five o'clock." Strickland reached for the phone and punched a number on the speed dial while McCauley kept up a rambling monologue.

"Taught that boy all he knows. Set him up, took care 'a his family, positioned him to win this race. He ain't goin' sour on me now, damn it. I need him in the House."

Strickland cupped his hand over his ear so he could hear Ruthie Baines. "That's right, Senator wants him on the next plane to Washington."

"Ungrateful bastard," McCauley said. "Wasn't nothin' but a bare-foot lint head guzzlin' beer in the woods when I came along."

"What?" Strickland said angrily into the phone. "Senator don't care about any campaign speeches. He wants him here today. Tell him, damn it."

Turning, Strickland said, "Please sir, I can't hear."

McCauley looked up, his freshly-shaved face red with rage. "I want her, too."

This time it was Strickland who held up a hand. And said into the phone, "Good. Make sure he's on it. You, too. The Senator wants both-a-you."

He hung up without saying good-bye and turned to his boss. "There's a 3:20 from Columbia. They'll be here before 5:00."

"That chair," McCauley said, pointing to a colonial Windsor made of hickory and fitted with a generous seat pad of red satin. "I want him in that chair."

McCauley slapped on some cologne, finished knotting his bowtie and yanked his pocket watch up like a yo-yo. "Jesus H, I'm s'posed to be at a hearing started ten minutes ago."

Strickland yawned. "Haven't seen no hearing start on time since I got here."

"It's *my* hearing, Carter, Energy Committee. We're working that bill that'll stop the damned D-O-E from dumping nuclear waste at Savannah River."

"Yes, sir, of course."

McCauley took a long look at his aide. "You know what the Savannah River Site is, right Carter?"

Strickland pushed out his chest like his job was at stake. "SRS is an old nuclear weapons plant near Aiken, Senator. It helped the nation win the Cold War by producing a radioactive gas called tritium. It's owned by the U.S. Department of Energy, but is South Carolina's largest industrial employer. There were twenty-five thousand jobs once, but that's shrunk to fifteen thousand. And the Aiken area is important to our reelection chances two years from now."

McCauley pulled the ends of his bowtie a final time and shook his head in a way that said he was still disgusted Carter didn't know the morning schedule.

"Call over there. Let 'em know I'm comin'."

•••••

When he arrived on the Hill at six each morning, Mac McCauley paused to gaze a moment at the Statue of Freedom atop the Capitol dome. It was a silent salute, and his dark blue eyes would fill with love and reverence so fierce, he could have been a man jailed abroad looking at a five-by-seven of his wife and children.

In a town where years on the job counted as much as stripes on a uniform, McCauley long ago seized quarters on the first floor of the Russell Building, the closest to the Capitol of three Senate office buildings. The clubhouse where lawmakers did their business and played to *C-SPAN* was a block away, reached underground by subway. Most days, a zombie-eyed driver named Willie worked the single subway car, which sat twelve on four pairs of padded bench seats that faced each other. Willie took the trouble to learn each senator's name—even the new ones—but was surly to everyone else he ferried back and forth beneath Constitution Avenue.

Of course, one could walk to the Senate chamber and back to the buildings that housed the senators' offices and committee rooms, which was how Mac McCauley took his exercise.

His private office was tucked away on the second floor of the Capitol near the Rotunda. No one was allowed to pester him there, not staff, colleagues, constituents, contributors, not even Sarah McCauley, his wife. The *Roost* consisted of a large ante-room with a camel-colored couch that converted to a double bed, a conference room with a low-hanging crystal chandelier and knotted pine table once used by Henry Clay, and a bathroom larger than the living room in the senator's boyhood home in Kilgo.

The corridor that led to his private sanctuary was not on any tourist map, and protected by a heavily lacquered, unmarked pair of oak doors with brass push plates. If a family from Des Moines or pair of union reps from Detroit happened to swing through, two blue-billed Capitol Hill cops chosen personally by McCauley for their respectful manner would gently steer them back to their tour guide.

"Hello, Senator, need anything this morning?" one of the cops said as he left for the committee hearing.

"Gotta lock up a few bureaucrats, boys. Cover my flanks."

Standard question, typical response. The cops laughed anyway. McCauley jabbed one in the shoulder and continued, the rubber-souled *L.L. Beans* his wife ordered each year by catalogue squeaking softly along the tiled floor. The senator's day was but a few hours old, but God, he felt alive.

Asses needed kicking.

•••••

When he returned at 4:45 p.m., Auralee was filing her nails in the ante-room. She did not stop when he entered. Ike Washington was already inside on the designated chair, and Ruthie Baines sat near Auralee on the camel couch.

"Hello, senator," Ruthie said, rising and offering her hand.

McCauley took it and looked at her hard. "You're the gal runnin' that campaign?"

"Yes, sir."

"Well you ain't runnin' it so good."

Ruthie's dark curls were all piled on her head except for one on each side that dangled down her cheeks. She found the left one and tugged. "We were doing okay until yesterday."

"Looks like you're circlin' the drain today."

His eyes, like his hands, still held hers. "I'm gonna go in there, get things back on track with your boy. You make sure they stay there, else our next meeting won't be this pleasant."

Ruthie pulled her hand back, nodding that she understood. Auralee, as was her habit when she was bored or nervous, took a reed from the bassoon case and wet it with her pink lips as if a performance were about to begin.

When McCauley opened the door to the inner office, Ike was fanning his face with *Time* magazine. A defensive-looking Bush graced the cover.

The old senator walked in, closed the door gently, and they were alone. A brass pole lamp buzzed in the corner, and a poster-sized, metal-framed photo of Mac McCauley, Sr. standing out front of McCauley's Pharmaceutical in Kilgo stared down from the near wall.

Ike stopped fanning and laid Bush on a small end table. "'Lo, Senator. Been awhile."

McCauley didn't answer or look at Ike. He removed his suit jacket and draped it over a brass music stand. His white shirt was starched so stiff, it showed no wrinkles even after a full day's use. McCauley poured himself a shot of *Jack*, downed it in a gulp, and poured another.

Ike wiped the sweat off his forehead. When he reached again for *Time*, McCauley's hand somehow beat his to the magazine.

"You wanted your ass in a fancy seat. Now it's there. Enjoy it a minute."

Ike tensed. "What do you want me to do?"

McCauley sipped his second shot. "Isaac," he said thoughtfully. "You know what your name means, Ike? It's origin?"

Ike's eyes opened like a child's.

"It's from our good friends the Jews," McCauley said, twisting one of his gold, American eagle cuff links. "Means 'laughter.' You Jewish, Ike?"

"No, sir."

"Well then, are you laughin' at me?"

"No, sir. I … " Ike's pinky started twitching. He grabbed it with his other hand, forced it to stay still. "Everything was going great, Senator. Money was coming in, new poll showed us way up, we've got solid chairmen helping us in every county."

McCauley pulled up a plain black chair, planted it in front of Ike's knees, and sat down so they were nearly face to face. McCauley was the smaller by far, but his intensity made the other man shrink back.

"What'd I teach you to do when you're way ahead?"

Ike wiped his forehead. "Play like you're behind."

"What about showing' your hand?"

"Don't do it."

"What'd I tell you to say when they start that hooey about you being my boy?"

"I'm my own man."

"Your own man," McCauley mocked and drained his shot. He put the small, thick glass down with a crack that was loud enough to summon Auralee. She entered silently, refilled his glass, left without a word.

Ike let his trembling pinky loose and turned his hands to fists. He started to rise. McCauley stared him back into the chair.

"This feel finished to you?"

"No, sir."

"Now then, first thing we're gonna do is find something on that woman, what's her name?"

"Harley. Dianna Harley."

"Yep, I'll put someone on that. Whatever dirt we find, we'll feed you. You save it til the next time she opens her yap. Anyone else causing trouble?"

"Nah. Owens, Maussipant, they're nothing."

"I remember that boy Cady Owens," McCauley said. "Used to be a troublemaker. Now he's a grave digger."

"He owns a mortuary in Walterboro."

McCauley's smirk said it was the same to him. "Who's the other one running?"

"An attorney from Charleston named Derrick Maussipant. Just a kid."

McCauley sat back and loosened his bowtie. "Next thing is you get rid of that fancy car. Last thing we need is bad stories in the *Statesman* newspaper that get picked up by the AP and run in every goddamned shopper paper in the state."

Ike was silent.

"You're gonna fight me on this?"

Ike rested his hands on his thighs. He looked toward the picture of

Mac McCauley Sr. and sighed. "Guess I made a bad call on the car."

"Damn straight."

"I'll get something else. *Taurus* maybe?"

"*Taurus* is fine. Good boy."

McCauley went to the liquor cabinet, poured himself a fourth drink, and brought a shot back for Ike, who swallowed it in a gulp.

"One last thing before you get your ass back to the great state of South Carolina."

Ike shifted and the red satin pad slid out toward his knees.

"Get rid of that Baines girl. I'll get you someone can manage a campaign. Should-a done that from the get-go."

"Senator, 'scuse me." Ike stood and walked behind his chair so he was looking down at McCauley. "Respectfully, I think that's a mistake. Ruthie's good, she has contacts everywhere. People like her, reporters like her. Please."

McCauley snorted. "I saw how much that reporter from Columbia liked her, the one wrote about you and your *Town Car*."

"Senator, truth is ... " Ike looked out the second-story window, where the tops of hundred-year-old oaks stretched toward the walls of the Capitol. "Truth is, Ruthie told me bring the car back. I was the one wanted to keep it."

McCauley plucked a thread from his trouser leg. "That so?"

"Yes, sir. She knows her business."

McCauley fell quiet. Ike waited. The lamp buzzed. "Okay, she stays for now." He paused. "Jesus H, if she's so damned smart, try listening to her once in a while."

McCauley rose and held the door open. Ike walked through. Ruthie took his arm as if he'd had a hernia repaired. Auralee smiled sweetly.

"Are y'all staying the night?"

"No," Ruthie said. "We've got a seven-thirty flight back to Columbia and three campaign events tomorrow morning."

"Well, have a nice flight. There's cabs right across Constitution. Know your way?"

"Yes, Auralee, thank you."

"C'mon. I'll walk along with you." McCauley opened the outer office door and led the trio into the hallway.

"How's it going, boys?" he said when they reached the officers.

Both cops stood. "All's quiet, Senator."

McCauley walked briskly, bypassing a bank of elevators in favor of a wide, polished staircase with a brown-and-beige marble banister that wound down to the basement. Many nodded to him or said hello, and he returned each greeting with enthusiasm. Near the escalator that led to Willie's subway, a portly woman approached with a fine-tipped black marker and small album that said, *Precious Moments.*

"Senator McCauley?"

"Yes, lovely lady."

"We're from Laurens, Senator. Me, my husband, we been voting for you for years. Would you sign my book and let my husband take a picture?"

"Why, Laurens is one of my favorite towns, darlin'. You know the Marcus family down there? Textile folks, good people."

McCauley took the pen, found an open page. "What's your name, dear?"

"Beverly. Beverly Darwin. This is my husband, Thomas."

Thomas Darwin waved sheepishly. McCauley took his hand and shook it. "Glad to meet you, son."

In the book, he wrote, "For my old friends Thomas and Beverly Darwin. Sincerely, Mac McCauley." He signed at the bottom, leaving plenty of space above for the photo.

As the husband started fidgeting with his camera, McCauley said, "No, no. Ike here'll shoot it. You get in with us."

The husband handed Ike the camera and moved beside his wife. McCauley moved him to the other side so that he was between the couple.

"Everyone say, 'FED-RAL DEFICIT,'" McCauley said. Beverly and Thomas Darwin laughed, and Ike snapped a frame. The flash echoed and several people turned. "One more, Ike. Make sure you don't move that camera. Honey, do something to make us smile."

Ruthie made herself disappear behind Ike's bulk and started flapping her arms. From where McCauley and the Darwins stood, it looked like Ike had four arms, two thick and heavy, two thin and spastic. The effect made everyone laugh, and McCauley was pleased.

"Safe home," he told the couple.

"Bless you, sir."

McCauley pointed them toward the Capitol, then turned and led Ike and Ruthie in the opposite direction toward the escalator down to the subway. At the last moment, he veered right and took the adjacent stairs. They followed.

"You're in good shape," Ruthie said.

McCauley didn't answer. When they reached the subway car, Willie was waiting, a rumpled copy of the *Post* sports section under his arm.

"Afternoon, Senator," he yelled over the electronic hum of the newer, automatic cars with sliding doors that traveled on a nearby track between the Capitol and the farther Senate office buildings, Dirksen and Hart. "How 'bout a ride, sir?"

"Hah, you know better than that, Willie." McCauley waved him off and started pounding down the walkway that ran alongside the subway track and toward the Russell building. Ruthie kept pace, Ike fell a few steps behind.

Twenty-five yards in, Willie rode by with a carload of self-important aides and wide-eyed Indian tourists. He slowed as he approached McCauley and his companions. "Older you get, faster you go, Senator," Willie said with admiration.

McCauley stopped to bow and a black-haired woman in a gold sari reached across her companion to take his picture.

"This is what it's about," he whispered in Ike's ear as the subway car made a sound like grinding metal and whisked off. "Be smart and stick to the play book. One day they'll be falling all over you, too, snappin' your picture and asking for autographs."

Ike nodded like a son receiving wisdom from his father. Then his eyes fluttered as if he were trying to blink out a gnat.

"What's wrong with you, boy?"

Ike blinked again and his eyes stayed shut. He clutched the left side of his chest under his arm and pitched forward. McCauley stepped back and let him fall. "Jesus H, get a doctor," he yelled at Ruthie.

11   *Ike and Ezra*

He is in a small, brick building the size of a one-room schoolhouse. There is no roof and patches of reedy grass have sprung up where the floor should be. The spiny, green blades tickle his bare feet. Outside, twelve-foot steel poles spaced five feet apart are propped against the walls to keep them stable and aligned. Without these polls, the structure would collapse. Ike looks around, disoriented, through mist thick as truck exhaust.

"Hey, boy, c'mere, take a picture. Hey, boy, don't say nothin' 'less I say it's okay. Hey, boy. Hey, boy. Hey, boy."

Ike follows the mocking voice, waving his hands and fanning a path through the mist.

"You."

"Me."

"Is this heaven?"

"You think you earned heaven? Earned your stripes. Shee-it!"

Ike peers around. They seem to be amid the ruins of an ancient temple. The idea that something so old could remain solid and standing gives him courage.

"I did my part. Coming up, I helped lots of my people."

He quickly realizes his error.

"Our people, I mean. I meant our people. I did what I could."

"Reason I'm here is 'cause you did 'xactly nothing.'"

"What you're talking about was different."

"You let yourself off easy, Ike."

"I don't, Ezra."

"You see what you want, no more. Like you got your own fog machine inside your head. Just turn it on when you need some."

"You're wrong. You don't know ... "

He tries not to stare at Ezra's collar of ugly scars. Somewhere in the mist, he sees the present: McCauley, the Capitol subway tunnel, the fawning woman with the camera.

"Am I dead? Tell me!"

But Ezra has gone.

12   Ike

Someone had his hand. He felt pressure, soft and steady, followed by the point of a woman's fingernail.

"Still with us?"

Ruthie, with worry in her voice. Good, let her worry. Then he remembered: McCauley, the subway, so dizzy. He opened his eyes slowly to fluorescent light and felt his nose twitch at a pungent smell from childhood. It was a cleaner his mother used to scrub the linoleum, *Pine Sol*, *Lestoil*, one of those. He moved a leg and a paper blanket crinkled beneath him.

Ruthie squeezed his hand. "Slow, Ike. You're okay, but take it slow. We've been in the Attending Physician's Office in the Senate twenty minutes. They checked you out. No heart attack; they think it was exhaustion or anxiety. When was the last time you ate?" Hypnotic classical music flowed from a wall-mounted TV tuned to *C-Span*, which was broadcasting a vote from the Senate.

Ike pulled his hand back from Ruthie's and massaged his Adam's apple. "Thirsty." Ruthie gave him a paper cup with water and ice chips. He sipped and pulled his lips away. "Cynthia."

"She wanted to come. I told her I'd have you home before she could get here. We're on the last flight, 10:55." Ike wagged his head to shake off the brain fuzz. The door squeaked open and a middle-aged man entered, eyes on his clipboard, pen scribbling. He looked up and pushed gold-rimmed glasses to his forehead.

"Well, Mr. Washington. Trying to scare the tourists? I'm Dr. Thom."

"Don't know what happened. Saw that subway train coming."

"Yes, well, let's have a listen." He plugged the ends of a stethoscope in his ears and placed the metal oval on Ike's chest. Ike looked for trouble in the man's eyes, prayed for him to come up smiling. He didn't smile, and the only thing his gray eyes said was that he was in a hurry.

Dr. Thom removed the stethoscope and let it hang loosely around his own neck. "Any history of heart problems?"

"No."

"Ever fainted before? Any seizures?"

"Nope."

"Any chest pain right now?"

"No."

"Good. When you get home, have your doctor arrange a chest X-ray, blood work, and a few other tests I'll write down. The EKG says your heart's fine. Our paramedic found low blood sugar, which is probably why you passed out. Did you eat breakfast or lunch?"

Ike finished buttoning his shirt. "Just a jelly doughnut this morning."

Dr. Thom frowned. "You seem like a busy man. Lot of activity, this kind of heat, you have to keep fuel in your system."

"Thank you," Ike said.

The doctor nodded and dashed off a few more lines on his clipboard. "I've got a nurse bringing you food—sandwich, orange juice, chocolate chip cookies. Eat and you can go."

"I'm not really hungry."

Another frown, and Ike said, "Okay, I'll have something."

Dr. Thom put his clipboard on the end of the bed. "You could stay overnight and let us run those tests at Walter Reed. Senator McCauley said to take good care of you. You two must be good friends, he was very concerned."

"No, no, I'm fine. I'll eat and be on my way."

"Suit yourself. I've got other patients, so I'll be off."

"Kind of cold," Ruthie said after the doctor left and Ike was eating. He had almost forgotten her. She sat on a small, stool, knees touching, delicate chin perched in her hands. Ruthie was smart and beautiful enough to do anything, yet she stuck with him. He wanted to kiss her. On the cheek.

Both looked up at a knock at the door. It opened before they could answer, admitting a heavy-set woman in a beige suit and clunky gold bracelets on each wrist. She held out a hand. "Mayor Washington, Jane Peeples, Senator McCauley's press secretary. He asked me to check on you."

"Everything's great," Ruthie said with an edge. Jane Peeples turned. Ike threw a glance. "This is my campaign manager, Ruthie Baines."

"As you can see," Jane said to Ike with a gesture toward the TV, "the Senator had to return to the chamber. He's presiding over debate on the transportation bill."

Ike looked at the set. Whatever the Senate had been doing a moment ago was over. Now the camera was fixed on McCauley, who sat in the president's chair trying to restore order on the floor. His colleagues ignored him. Ike found the remote by his bed and punched up the volume.

"Senators, we need to move on," McCauley said. "The senator from Colorado has an amendment—an important amendment—and deserves our attention. Kindly take your conversations outside the chamber." No one looked up. The talking continued.

Ike felt his heart fly as McCauley found his gavel and tapped it three times. "We will not proceed until there is order," he said. The senators ignored him as they would a sidewalk musician. McCauley suddenly pounded his gavel two times. The crack was startling. *"Order in the Senate!"*

Ike found his hands numb from gripping the side railings attached to his bed. He saw Ruthie staring and forced himself to relax.

Up on screen, several clusters of lawmakers dispersed and the Senate returned to order. "Thank you, friends and countrymen," McCauley said, once again the Southern gentleman. "The senator from Colorado may continue."

Jane Peeples smiled with pride. "One thing Mac McCauley likes is order. I've got to get back to my office. Safe trip."

Ike didn't answer. Ruthie rose and said good-bye. Once McCauley's aide was gone, Ike began a deep breath and stopped mid-way. "I can't stand the smell of this place. We've got time, let's walk." He took one of the cookies and left the rest of the food uneaten.

·····

Capitol Hill was still overrun with sweaty tourists, self-important aides in khaki pants and navy blazers and an occasional lawmaker when they walked out of the Russell Building and crossed back over Constitution Avenue. They aimed for the north side of the Capitol, toward the massive marble archways and columns that made the place look like a Greek temple, but took a wide sidewalk that cut to the right through the trees Ike had seen from McCauley's window. Ruthie read aloud a few of the labels tacked to the rough-edged bark: *"Scarlet Oak, Red-Flowering Dogwood, Japanese Pagodatree, Fernleaf Maple."* He wasn't interested.

Bootlicker

The sidewalk, adorned with old-fashioned, gray-green lamp posts and wrought-iron benches with smooth wooden slats, curved in front of the Capitol. They crossed through a parking lot reserved for congressional staff and paused in front of the Reflecting Pool. Ike glanced up at stone-faced Ulysses S. Grant, flanked by two lions and looking cold and weary enough to tell Lincoln to get himself a new general, then leaned forward, putting both hands on a thick border of white granite that ringed the pool.

"Ike, you okay?"

Gulls bobbed up and down as the wind kicked up small waves that rippled from east to west. Nearby, two boys whirled a Frisbee back and forth, trying to see who could throw closest to the pool without dunking it in the shallow water.

Ruthie touched his neck softly for a moment and backed up. He looked over and saw in her face that she'd reached some sort of limit. He waited. She looked like a wife who's found a shade of lipstick she doesn't own on her man's collar.

"Ike, what are we doing here?"

He searched for an answer, said nothing.

"What does McCauley have on you?"

He looked at his shoes. Brown wing-tips, size eleven-and-a-half. Scuffed by the toes, still shiny on the sides.

"I don't go one more step with you—here or anywhere—until you talk to me."

The Frisbee glided into the pool and splashed his pants. Ike fished it out and handed it to one of the boys.

"Sorry, mister."

Ruthie waited. He returned her glance, looked away, and began walking toward the House side of the Capitol. Ruthie watched him go, then hustled to catch up.

"*Ike.*"

"C'mon, sit in the shade." They picked up the sidewalk trail and found a bench under a willow oak that cast a forty-foot shadow. It was less busy here, almost secluded. Ike sat and looked up at the Capitol. Was there a place for him inside? Would he become the first black man from his state this century to serve in Congress? Did he deserve it?

Ruthie circled the base of the oak, one foot in front of another, counting softly. "Thirty-one steps around," she said, joining him.

He knew she was trying to give him time. And that she would leave if he didn't explain himself. He couldn't let that happen. Ruthie could be maddening, but she always had one eye on him, the other on the goal line. McCauley could take his Town Car, but not his partner. She was nothing less, despite her age.

"I told you," he said slowly, still looking at the pristine Dome, "about the first time I met Mac McCauley. At the circus with Jerome."

Ruthie nodded. "When you were kids."

"The second time I met him was a little later. Another accident."

Ike could see she expected the worst, perhaps that he had committed some heinous crime and gotten caught by McCauley, then a municipal judge.

"Ruthie, Cynthia doesn't know any of this. That's the way it stays."

"You're married all these years and she doesn't know?"

A squirrel wandered by. They watched as it walked up to them, curious and unafraid. "Not Cynthia, not anybody. Just me and McCauley. A few others knew, but they're gone. Jerome knew. And Mama, at the end."

Ruthie considered. "Maybe you shouldn't tell me. Maybe it's better I don't know. Then I won't have to lie to the press."

Ike reached down to pet the squirrel. It scampered away and shot up the tree. Ike looked at his palms, pressed them together, closed his eyes. Then he hugged himself, gently at first, then hard enough to pull his suit jacket taut. He rocked slowly, unconcerned about whether anyone was watching. Then his arms went limp.

"I need to tell it. It's time."

Ruthie put her eyes on the Washington Monument. "Alright then, go on."

As the words began gushing out, he nearly laughed at himself. The seasoned politician stammering like a frightened child.

"Saw him do it. He was there, the leader. Should've run right away, but I didn't, and he caught me watching."

"I don't understand."

"I tried to be still. Ricky Lee ran off right away, but I was scared. Tried to stay still, but I stepped on something. Branch, leaves, something. Made 'em all look around. Judge saw me."

Ruthie took his chin, steered his face around to hers. "Who's Ricky Lee? What judge? McCauley?"

Ike pulled away and fell silent. Sweat slid from his temples and past his round, brown cheeks. He moved back and forth as if on an aged rocker, staring dead ahead and seeing himself in the forest as McCauley and the other, Tyler Hawke, took the life of Ezra James.

"Ike, please." Ruthie took his elbow, shook him back.

He continued to stare ahead and began speaking again, this time in a low monotone.

"Ezra James was a boy worked at old man McCauley's drugstore. They called him EJ."

"I remember from your story. He was there the day of the circus parade."

"Ezra—EJ—never got in trouble. But things were different then, change was coming. Everyone felt it. 'Lotta crackers were scared. Fear bred violence. It was four years after Rosa Parks and four before Dr. King's march here in D.C., down there beside old Abe Lincoln, 250,000 people. Things went back and forth, gains and setbacks. In '59, four black men were lynched in the South. At least that's the official count."

"How did McCauley fit in?"

Ike nodded. "McCauley." A droplet of sweat fell to his pants. He rubbed it in to a spot that was already damp. "He was county judge, husband, father, town councilman. Only a few knew what happened nights; he traded that black robe for a white one."

Ruthie's eyes widened. "I never read anything about McCauley and the Klan."

"Small-town paper wasn't going to tell, and by the time bigger papers and TV started paying attention, he was out."

"I interrupted you. I'm sorry."

He shrugged. "Ezra was a boy did what he was told. Got to work on time and stayed late whenever Old Man McCauley—the judge's father— asked him. Summer of '59, there were others in town, college kids from up north, some black, some white, trying to get folks registered. People were scared at first, wouldn't have nothing to do with them. Ezra was like that, wouldn't even talk to them. Said he didn't care about voting."

Ike looked down. The squirrel was back. He was a fat one, gray with a white belly and full tail. The summer had been kind. He stood on his back legs and darted his head back and forth like a jaywalker. "Old Man McCauley had another kid working at the drugstore with EJ, a boy named Lionel. Lionel Daniel. Lionel liked those college kids, they pumped him up. He started helping them register folks. Old Man McCauley warned him to stick to washing the floor and carrying groceries. Lionel didn't listen. White folks in Kilgo—especially the old man—decided to make an example."

"And picked Lionel," Ruthie said softly. Ike stroked his chin and spoke with more control. "I found out later it was young McCauley made the mistake. He intercepted Ezra instead of Lionel. Stopped his car out on Highway 33, took him in a truck to Marion Forest. They wound up right near where me and Ricky Lee were playing hooky. Wrong place, wrong time."

Ruthie glanced toward the Bush White House. "They kidnapped him in the daytime?"

"It was just getting dark. There were two of them, McCauley and another, a skinny guy, Tyler Hawke. No one ever called that man anything but Tyler Hawke. Hawke was drunk and still drinking. The two of them wore regular clothes and Klan masks. They dragged Ezra out and put him on his knees in the dirt. Hands were tied behind his back. When they pushed his head down, I saw they used his own belt to tie his hands. Had a silver buckle, said *EJ*."

Ike covered his eyes. Long moments passed. "Ezra said he never did nothing wrong, they were making a mistake. Didn't care about votin' or civil rights or none a that. Old Man McCauley would vouch for him, he said. The old man—his boss—would tell them he was a good worker, minded his manners.

"That's when Judge took off his mask. Said, 'shut your mouth, you lying black bastard. My daddy told me you been running around with them college punks, tryin' to stir up our niggers. You were warned.' Ezra said it wasn't him, it was the other boy who worked at the drugstore. Lionel. *Lionel*. His belt had *EJ* on it. They wanted Lionel, not EJ. McCauley slapped him and Tyler Hawke laughed."

Ike rubbed his hands together fast. "Was a crazy laugh, Ruthie, something that'd scare you if you heard it." Ruthie, face graven, touched the strand of pearls around her neck. It was loose enough for her to loop a finger underneath and touch her thumb on the other side.

"Trees were thick like these," Ike said, lifting his eyes to the branches above. "They hid me. Ricky Lee already took off. Don't know why I didn't run, too. Something held me there. I wanted to help Ezra, but those men were crazy. Tyler Hawke drank his booze through a hole in his hood. McCauley got down on his knees nose to nose with Ezra. Said they were going to show what happened to niggers who crossed the line. Ezra stopped crying and dropped his head like he was praying. McCauley grabbed his throat, screamed, 'Look at me when I'm talkin' to you.' Ezra looked up like he was told, then ... "

"What?" she demanded. "What did that poor boy do?"

"Spit hard in Mac McCauley's face."

Ruthie's shoulders went slack; now she knew the end.

"They beat him. When he fell and couldn't yell no more, they took turns kicking him. Both of them were wearing leather shoes, Ruthie. I remember. Black leather shoes with pointed tips. After awhile, Ezra didn't even try to protect himself."

Tears mixed with Ike's sweat as he finished. "McCauley took out a handkerchief real calm, wiped his face. He was smiling. He said, 'Get that bastard back up and get the rope from the truck.' It was quiet. Both of 'em were out of breath; Ezra had nothing left. Hands were still tied behind his back with that belt. McCauley found a high branch, said, 'This'll do.' Ezra's eyes were closed and his lips were moving. He was praying, I think. 'Bring him here,' the Judge said. That's when I must have moved. Stick broke. 'What's that?' Judge looked around and saw me. I started to run and heard him laugh. 'Let him go. I know that boy. We'll get him later; he won't get far way out here. Finish this first.'"

Ruthie stood and made a slow circle around the bench. Ike wiped his face. He stood and she pressed into him, resting her head on his chest. His hands stayed by his sides. When he began again, his voice wasn't much more than a whisper.

"I ran and ran, must have been two miles. Couldn't go home. That's where they'd look first. I didn't want to get Mama and Jerome into it. I might have gone to Ricky Lee's, but I didn't think of it. I got so tired, I stopped running and walked. Walked for hours. Felt like I saw all Cady County that night. My clothes were wet and God I was thirsty."

Ike patted Ruthie on the back and stepped back. He sat down on the bench, put an elbow on the top rail and rested his head on his hand. His control was returning. Ruthie sat in front of him on a patch of grass. She looked dazed and unable to absorb much more, but he continued.

"I needed a plan, decided to wait 'til dark and try 'n slip home. I'd tell Mama and Jerome what happened, then pack a bag and leave Kilgo. I waited 'til after midnight. It was a quiet night. I heard crickets and frogs and dogs, but I didn't hear no sirens." Ike rubbed his knees, pulled absently at his calf-length black socks. "Weren't no sirens for Ezra."

"I guess it was about one in the morning—didn't have a watch, so I'm not sure—I snuck through the orange trees we had in back. I looked and didn't see anything. I kept creeping toward the house. When I stepped out of the trees, Tyler Hawke was there. Had a baseball cap and a small pistol. I was going to make a break, but he saw it in my face, said, 'I wouldn't.' He came closer, grabbed my collar, said, 'C'mon. Judge wants you.' He took me to the same truck from the woods and tied my hands in back. Put a blindfold on me and pushed me in the back seat. I thought he was taking me back to the woods, but the drive was too short. When he took me out, the blindfold slipped. We were at a white house. He took me down a brick path to a door to an office in the basement. The door opened and there he was. Had that crew cut made him look like a Marine. Judge McCauley."

"Were any others around?" Ruthie said.

"No one. The Judge took a seat at his desk. They put me in a chair on the other side, like I was applying for work. 'Get him a drink,' Judge said. He was wearing a short-sleeve white shirt and had cleaned up since the afternoon. Tyler Hawke brought a pop and I drank it."

"I said, 'Your honor, you don't need to hurt me, I promise … ' " He cut me off. Walked around slow, stopped behind my chair. I waited; time was movin' slow. He put his hands on my shoulders, kind of squeezed them. He leaned down and put his mouth by my ear. I felt his lips. Said soft, 'You think you're gonna join that boy Ezra in the graveyard. You're not. You're gonna join me.'

"I didn't understand the man. I was seventeen, scared, cold, poor, no daddy. I thought he was crazy. What was he talking about, join *him*?

"McCauley walked back around the desk. Said, 'First, anyone asks, you didn't see nothing at the woods today and don't know nothin' about it. Got it?' I shook my head fast. He said, 'second thing, Ike, is you and I are going to become friends. You're gonna help me and I'm gonna help you.' I looked at him. He laughed.

"He said, 'It's like this, Ike. I'm a judge, but I want more. Gonna run for the state legislature from this county. Thing is, I ain't the only one. Three others want the same job. Four of us are going to split up the white vote, but if I can get all the niggers with me, I'll win. That's where you come in.'"

For a moment, Ike was back in the basement office. He smelled the still, musty air and the judge's cigar. He felt his sweaty clothes glued to his body, the desperation of knowing he could bolt for the door, and yet never escape. He saw himself running from the woods as they tightened the noose on Ezra. He shivered and Ruthie made a move toward him. He accepted her hand.

"McCauley said, 'See, Ike, I've been on the look-out for one-a-your people. I might not have picked you, but this is how things worked out. Everything happens for a reason. Yessir, I believe that. After I win this seat, I'm runnin' for higher office. I need to know what's going on in every nigra town in this state. You're going to tell me who's screwin' who, who's broke, who's a drunk, who can be bought, and how much it'll cost.'"

Ruthie pulled back. The picture was taking shape. "They taught you, gave you money, made you powerful?"

"That was the deal."

"And you worked black precincts because McCauley couldn't campaign openly for black votes without pissing off the whites."

Ike nodded.

"McCauley said he'd kill you if you turned him down?"

"Said I could go with him or go with Ezra. I didn't have a choice, did I, Ruthie?"

She brushed the back of her skirt, sat back down. After the briefest hesitation, she said, "No, Ike. There was no choice. I'm trying to understand the irony. He lynched one boy he thought was trying to register voters. And then he coerced another boy into building support among blacks."

Ike looked at his left hand. "One more thing."

"What?"

"After I said I'd go along, the Judge said to me, 'Ike, my boy, you know what insurance is?' I didn't know. He said, 'Insurance is protection against the unexpected. Yessir, protection against the unexpected. I need to know that you're never going to go back on the deal we're making here tonight. I mean, you're saying one thing now, but you might wake up tomorrow and feel different.'"

"Tyler Hawke moved behind me. He got some kind of fat hammer from somewhere and handed it to the Judge. McCauley said, 'You might wake up and start feeling bad over what happened to that uppity bastard.' Tyler grabbed me, held me down in the chair. I tried to fight him. Too strong. Judge said, 'If you feel like that, you need to remember what could still happen, Ike.' I told him I wouldn't, not ever. Tyler Hawke forced my arm out on the desk.

"Judge laughed. Pulled up that big, wooden mallet. I saw him play with it a second, test the heft, smooth the end a few times with his fingers.

"Then he said, 'I know you won't, Ike. I know you won't.'"

Ruthie's hands pulled at the grass around her. Several blades broke loose and she rubbed them around in her fingers. Ike hardly recognized his own voice when he spoke again.

"He crashed it down on my hand. Tyler Hawke was laughing like crazy, Ruthie. I heard him. Laughing and screaming something over and over."

"Oh, Ike."

"Even afterwards, Tyler Hawke kept on screamin' it. Crazy loud, like a lunatic.

'*Order in the court,*' he was saying. '*Order in the fuckin' court.*'

"Judge turned his back and didn't pay no attention. Hung up his mallet and didn't say no more."

•••••

It took some time to gather himself. Ruthie let him lean his thick shoulder against her as the past and pain slowly receded. Evening was on them, but the sinking sun had splashed the clouds with red and orange, and the sky remained alive. "We need to get to the airport."

She stood and pulled his hand. Ike rose, rubbed his bloodshot eyes, and took a few unsteady steps, nearly tripping on a tangle of ancient tree

118

roots that were thick as mature branches. He shook his head. History was always getting in his way.

"I need to ask," Ruthie said as they traced their earlier steps back toward Constitution Avenue to look for a cab. He was silent. She said, "What happened after that night? How did you start working for them? What happened to your finger?"

Ike held his hands out, palms away, like a man checking his manicure. It wasn't until years later that he discovered the human hand has twenty-seven bones, including three in each finger. He learned from a medical book that he'd suffered a "displaced and angulated fracture of the proximal phalynx" in his pinky. Such injuries heal poorly unless straightened in the early stages of healing. That much he knew without the book.

"They brought me home, left me alone a week. I told Mama and Jerome I fell on my hand playing football. She made me ice it, but I never saw a doctor."

He shuffled a few more steps. They were near a guard booth on the East side of the Capitol, where a zigzag line of concrete barriers shaped like enormous flower pots stood between the politicians and the suicide car-bombers.

"You know the road that runs back into the old, black part of Kilgo, Ruthie? Where I took you that day, told you about the circus?"

"I remember."

"Wasn't nothin' but brown dirt in 1959," Ike said. "It washed out after every hard rain. You'd ruin your shoes just walking home from town. McCauley had me talk to the folks back in there. At first, they thought I was crazy—a colored, high school kid promising that Judge Lander McCauley would get their road paved after he got into the state legislature. I told them all they had to do was vote for him."

Ike gazed straight ahead. "They'd look at me, these folks who were still nervous about registering, but McCauley expected it. He had me ready with a little speech. I'd say the choice was him or a few others who weren't promising anything in return for their vote. Give it a try. Nothing to lose, and there won't be no more violence. And you might get yourselves a new street—Judge even said you could pick the name."

"Who picked 'Ascension Road?'"

"That was Rev. Haney's little joke. Roscoe Haney was pastor at Cross Keys Baptist. Died years ago."

Ruthie touched her necklace again. "So that was your first test. They drilled you on what to say. Wait, where did they work with you?"

"McCauley had two sidemen. Tyler Hawke was the muscle, a tobacco farmer named Bunk Meacham handled the politics." Ike shook his head. "Never saw Bunk Meacham in anything but baggy blue jeans and a straw cowboy hat. Sides of his hat were rotted through. He wore it anyway, all the time."

Ike flagged a Capitol Taxi. The driver pulled over and stopped ten feet ahead. Ruthie opened the door for Ike and joined him in the back seat. "National Airport." Ike looked at the driver's photo. Chaim Lev had a thick, black beard and wore a white, V-necked T-shirt. He didn't seem a bit interested in his passengers. Still, Ike lowered his voice.

"Bunk Meacham didn't smoke the tobacco he grew, he chewed it. Always had a lump in his cheek. I'd go to his farmhouse once, twice a week. Sometimes McCauley was there, sometimes not. I was scared in the beginning; thought maybe they'd changed their minds about me. But they never hurt me again. Maybe I was a good student. Maybe it was because everything went right that first election."

They turned left on 14th Street, saw a crowd waiting for turns to see town from atop the Washington Monument.

"Was pretty simple, Ruthie. The state House seat that includes Kilgo was open; McCauley was one of four Democrats. Everyone figured it'd be close. By grabbing up the blacks, he won by almost two hundred votes. No one even knew what he was up to 'cause I was the messenger. What we call a 'surrogate' today."

"No one was suspicious when all those blacks started registering?" Ruthie said.

"Sure." Ike laughed and shook his head at McCauley's evil genius. "But the man had both ends covered. One part of town, he'd yell about keeping black and white separate. But he was careful, didn't say 'nigger this, nigger that' like the others. In our end of Kilgo and Cady County, I slipped around telling people like Pastor Haney not to mind all the talk, that once McCauley was elected, the car at the front of the victory parade would be a bulldozer, and they would get their new road. McCauley never committed any more violence that I know of."

Ike saw the cab driver's eyes glance in the rear-view and return to the highway. They were exiting 395 for the George Washington Parkway. Planes roared by every minute or so.

"What about Ezra James' family?"

"He didn't have any family in town. The cops made a little show of investigating Ezra's murder, but it went down as unsolved. By Thanksgiving, no one even remembered Ezra James."

"Which airline?"

Ike was startled by the cab driver's voice. Ruthie answered.

They rode another mile, passing joggers and roller-bladers clipping along paths and parks that fronted the Potomac, then took the exit for National Airport. The driver weaved in and out of traffic and had them at *USAir* moments later.

"What you told the reporters—that all this with McCauley ends when you get elected—you really stand by that, don't you?" Ruthie said as they got out.

Ike reached in his pocket and pulled out a twenty. "Of course." Their eyes locked a moment, then Ike shut the back door, stood, and passed the twenty to the driver through the passenger door window. "Keep it."

The driver took the bill and turned toward him, revealing a gap between his front teeth that made it hard to tell if he was smiling.

It reminded Ike of the heady day after that first election, when McCauley took him outside Bunk Meacham's farmhouse, cuffed him gently behind his head, and handed him a hundred-dollar bill.

"You did good," McCauley said, still a little drunk from his victory party. He pinned a "Mac in '59" campaign button on Ike's chest and said, "*We* did good."

Ike remembered looking at the hundred. It was the first time he'd seen a bill that large. It was crisp and smelled new.

Did he smile when he took the money? No, he didn't, he was certain of it.

Bootlicker

13

Ten p.m., Washington to Columbia. No surprise that the DC-9 was nearly empty. Ike took the right side of row seven for himself, Ruthie took the left. He pushed the armrests back and slid into the window seat, hoping to nap during the hour-and-change flight. He didn't like flying, didn't like it from the moment he walked into the plane: the plastic smell of the cabin air, the narrow aisle that forced him to walk sideways, the loud and rapid climb into the clouds that always made his ears ache. Deep down, he worried that flying was unnatural and even foolish—arrogant man messing with forces he didn't really understand and in places he certainly didn't belong. Crashes never surprised him. One cough from God was all it took.

The thought jolted away any hope of sleep. He reached into the elastic pocket under his folding tray and fished out *Attaché*, *USAir's* travel magazine. A cover story on Christmas getaways. He considered the several weeks that lay ahead and realized that by Christmas, he would either be a congressman or a loser in need of a holiday far from home. Maybe he would visit an island in the Caribbean, enjoy some white sand beaches and women with bright smiles and vacation morals, not that he'd ever cheat on Cynthia. Anyplace would do, so long as the natives didn't care about overnight polls or his position on affirmative action and welfare reform.

He tried to thumb to the feature and found the magazine was new and its glossy pages stuck. Ike licked his fingers, skipped past some ads, and found himself staring at a story about Charleston. "Thanksgiving in the Holy City" was printed in Old English black type over a photo of stately St. Michael's Church. The church, white, stiff and arrogant as Ralph Reed and the Christian Coalition, stood tall against a sky as blue as the sea in his Caribbean getaway. *"The steeple atop St. Michael's rises 182 feet from the ground. The church's four-faced clock has been a Charleston landmark since 1764."*

He narrowed his gaze to the four clocks. Each pointed in a different direction and had a round, black face with white Roman numerals. He would have expected the opposite scheme, white face set off by black numbers. On closer study, he realized that white was the color of choice for James Gibbs, the 18th-Century architect. The massive, square base of the church was white. So were the second, third and fourth levels, which rose into Charleston's skyline like a slender wedding cake. The lattice-work around the church bell was white, as was the handsome woodwork around the windows. Those clock faces, though, they were black—black icing on a white cake. It was a clever choice; the contrast was striking and completed the grand design. Lander McCauley was the only other man he could think of who used the two colors with as much finesse.

Nothing said Charleston more than St. Michael's. Old, proud, confident, aristocratic, certain of its standing—that was Charleston. So different from Kilgo, he thought. So different from the country barn where he learned his craft.

What he told Ruthie was true. After the night they smashed his hand, McCauley left him alone for two weeks. Ike walked home from the colored high school the same way each day—one block down Union Street, back through the quiet dirt roads that led to Sampson's Creek, and then through a short stretch of woods until he reached the cluster of shacks and small houses that included his home. Usually he walked with Jerome, but that fall his brother was running cross country for St. James High.

One afternoon, Tyler Hawke was waiting. Ike didn't say a word, just threw his book-bag in the truck and got in. If any neighbors noticed him driving off, they didn't say anything. People in his part of town were used to keeping their heads down and minding their business. Though blindfolded the last time he was in the truck, he remembered its smoky smell and the feel of cracked vinyl beneath his legs.

Tyler drove with a silver flask between his knees and didn't say a thing. There was no conference table in tobacco farmer Bunk Meacham's barn north of town. There were no textbooks, no lectern, no neat rows of chairs or desks, and no chalkboard. The barn did not have a telephone, air conditioning or plumbing. If Ike got thirsty, there was a barrel of well-water and a rusty ladle. If he had to piss, he'd go outside in yellow and pink-flowered bushes that grew wild among the trees. The barn had a base of cut logs, wood-slat sides that rose at both ends into a pair of upside-down V's, and a steep, tin roof the color of dull iron. It was bigger than his house and quiet enough to hear the flies buzz around the filmy eyes of Bunk's old sorrel and a gray-muzzled coonhound named *Cody*. Though clean of clutter and cobwebs, the faintly sweet smell of tobacco leaves curing in the rafters mixed with that morning's horse dung made Ike twitch his nose and breathe through his mouth.

He had no classmates and only one instructor in the early days. His professor was prompt, demanding, and, at times, surprisingly encouraging.

At first, Ike could not look at Lander McCauley. The judge would talk about how important the upcoming Democratic primary was because there "ain't no Republicans in South Carolina. This first lap is the whole sha-bang," he'd say.

Ike, eyes unfocused, hands trembling, would see Ezra, weak at first, strong enough at the end to spit at the white men with the rope.

He tried hard to look like he was paying attention. Inside, he was afraid they'd hurt him again and claim they needed more insurance. *Know what insurance is, Ike?* When enough time passed to realize he was no longer in danger, resentment slowly overtook fear. How long would he have to keep coming to this place? What did they want from him? When would it be over? It was punishment not for committing a crime, but for witnessing one.

McCauley, so intense Ike could make out lean, ropy muscles under his checkered shirt, diagramed his campaign strategy on the dirt floor. He used a crooked hickory branch to make marks signifying himself, his two opponents, and the white voters of Cady County. "Three of us gonna split up these folks," he'd say, pointing to the uneven circle that represented the whites. "None is gonna get enough to win the race outright."

Ike, though unconfined, would remember the feel of being held down, arm pinned, his hand awaiting the blow from the mallet. There had been a moment before the pain registered, an instant when he thought McCauley struck the table instead of his fingers. Maybe Tyler Hawke's crazy laughing is what made him think that.

Now McCauley looked at the end of his stick, walked over to the black anvil Bunk Meacham used to repair horseshoes, and filed it to a point more suitable for campaign maneuvers. "Over here," he said, scratching a second, smaller circle into the brown dirt, "is my ace. Ace 'a spades, right Bunk?" Bunk winked. "These are your people, Ike. This is how I'm going to leave those boys running against me in the dust." McCauley kicked the ground with the toe of his boot. The 1959 campaign strategy plan flew at *Cody* the coonhound, which lifted his tired head and wagged his tail warily. Bunk Meacham leaned against the wall on two legs of a frayed wicker chair, an unlit, half-smoked cigar wedged into his back teeth. "Simple right?" McCauley said after back teeth.

"Yessir," Ike said, eyes down.

McCauley slid his hand along the hickory stick, stopping when he reached a bump in the thin, supple wood. He looked at the rough spot and picked at it with his fingernails until it was smooth. "'splain it back to me, then."

An image of the circus flew into his mind. He heard the long, black whip crack, saw the tiger do its tricks.

"I said run it back to me."

Ike poked a finger around the hole in the knee of his patched dungarees. Blue threads gave way and the hole got bigger. McCauley tapped Ike's wrist with his stick. "Were you payin' attention?" In the corner, Bunk Meacham fired a match and lit his cigar.

"Yessir, I ... "

McCauley watched him intently. Bunk puffed out white circles that rose lazily to a loft filled with giant cubes of yellow hay. *Cody's* ears flinched at the sudden quiet.

Ike rubbed his eyes with his thumbs and forced himself to concentrate. At St. James, he was considered a smart student who only made average grades. His mother would look at his report card and shake her head. *You're too smart for Cs, Ike.*

He felt sick, but forced himself to whisper the words: "Colored folk go with you, you win that election."

McCauley looked at Bunk, then smiled and struck the ground excitedly with his stick. Dirt flew up. "Jesus H," he said. "That's it 'xactly."

They fell into a routine: Monday, Wednesday and Thursday, three o'clock to four-thirty. Since Jerome was at practice and Mrs. Washington didn't get home until five-thirty, Ike didn't even have to account for his absence. Tyler had taken to meeting him at the edge of town to avoid any questions from neighbors.

On many afternoons, McCauley would come in with a newspaper, either the *Columbia Statesman* or *Kilgo Gazette*. He'd sit in a chair, elbows on knees, the paper down before him, reading until he spotted some item he wanted to discuss. Sometimes it would be local news about the campaign. Other times, he would talk about national events: Ford finally dropping its big flop, the *Edsel*; the runaway success of "that chariot movie with the guy who played Moses;" how a white fighter from Sweden named Ingemar Johansson "beat the bejesus out of Floyd Patterson" to win the world heavyweight champion.

"Guess he showed your boy, eh?"

Ike had never heard of either fighter.

McCauley flipped the sports page and Ike saw the handsome black Patterson on his knees, right glove clutching the rope as he struggled to get up. The fierce-eyed Swede stalked him, hoping, it seemed, that his foe would rise so he could knock him down again. As his hand healed and the election drew closer, Ike found himself drawn to the political game. Though he had no name or reference point for what was happening and didn't understand the nuances about which McCauley and Bunk Meacham got so excited (the reserved farmer, McCauley's ally for years, would hitch his overalls, gather a wad of tobacco-colored phlegm, and fire it across the barn when the campaign news was especially good), there was a momentum that pulled him along. This much he knew:

only one could win, and there were no rules, at least the way McCauley played. It was a slowed-down version of the frantic roller derby matches he'd once seen on TV. Claw your way through the pack. Train one eye on the short straightaway and banked turns ahead, the other on those trying to take the lead. Anyone gets close, use hands, hips or shoulders to slam them over the side rail. Hit hard enough to make sure they don't want to come back, and don't forget to wave on the next lap. Rubbing it in was a big part of the fun.

"I'm sending you out to talk to some folks," McCauley said one day. "You need some new clothes, you can't go looking like that."

He looked down and was ashamed. His mother had sewn a second patch on the knee of his blue dungarees. He wore a plain red T-shirt and black PF Flyer sneakers made of canvas. He was 5-8, 142 pounds with short, tightly wired black hair. Next month he would turn eighteen. "I got a church suit," he said, too embarrassed to look at McCauley.

"Naw, I'm going to give you a man's name, my personal tailor. Tyler Hawke'll take you. He'll fix you up."

Ike rubbed the toe of one PF Flyer against the other. "I don't have no money."

"What? Boy, you've got to learn to talk up if you want people to hear—"

"*Said I don't got no money.*"

McCauley, rarely interrupted and never shouted at, walked to Ike and put his hand on the teenager's shoulder. Ike recoiled. McCauley held him firmly and patted him on the back.

"That's more like it. Don't worry about no money. The new clothes will be your pay for the work you've done so far."

"Who you want me to talk to?"

"That preacher, Reverend Haney over at Cross Keys Baptist."

Ike looked away quickly. Reverend Roscoe Haney was his preacher; Cross Keys was the church he'd gone to his whole life.

"Judge," he said quietly, "you want the Reverend to help you in the election? You want him to get black folks to go your way, help you beat those other guys?"

"That's it. Here's the deal, and it's mighty fair. They vote for me, I'm gonna get some crews out there and pave the road that goes ... "

"Judge, you still gonna be runnin' with the Klan nights?"

McCauley stopped cold. Ike had not planned the audacious question, didn't know how he'd react to whatever the judge said. It was possible, he felt deep down, that he would walk out and take the consequences if McCauley refused to quit the Klan. Ike had been careful to keep his voice neutral a moment ago, but knew he'd placed himself in danger. Mc-Cauley glanced at Bunk's wicker chair. He seemed glad that his top aide was not present. "I ought to clean your plow, asking me something like that," he said quietly. McCauley walked slowly to the anvil, swept some dust off the rough, metal surface. He touched its iron-headed hammer, but didn't pick it up. Instead, he went to the old dog, took a slack cheek in each hand, and lifted its face off the barn floor.

"Boy's got a pair of balls on him, eh?" he said into *Cody's* snout. The dog licked his face. The judge let him. Then he returned.

"What I'm sayin' is 'tween you and me, and it don't have nothing to do with anything you want or don't want. Has to do with politics, and the future."

The judge went on awhile about changes that were coming, something about new attitudes he saw gaining speed in South Carolina and in the country. Anyone who wanted to be governor or senator or a congressman would have to pay attention, reach out, make friends, build co-alitions. The old way would not work anymore. A *New South* was rising.

"Look at this," he said, reaching with unsteady hands for a pile of newspaper articles he'd clipped. "May 25, 1959: U.S. Supreme Court said it was illegal for Louisiana to ban fights between white and colored boxers. Imagine that. June 22: Four white kids got life terms for raping some black gal in Tallahassee. Later this summer, they're gonna mix black and white kids at some high school up in Little Rock. Integration, hah! They got a governor up in Arkansas named Orval Faubus. Orval will never—*never*—go for no mixed-race classrooms."

McCauley closed his eyes and peered into a place Ike couldn't see. "And Governor Faubus is gonna lose. Not me. I'm not going to be a loser."

"Now, Knights of the Ku Klux Klan is full a good men, lot of them are my friends, one of them's my daddy," he said. "But he—they—they don't see it the way I do. I've been thinking about that business in the woods. Thinkin' a lot. Anyway, I'm leaving that bunch. You don't say word one about it, got me?"

"Yessir." Ike raised his eyes, saw McCauley looking hard for any sign of gloating or disrespect. There was none.

"Let's talk more about those new clothes. Tyler Hawke is gonna take you to Mr. Lee, my tailor in Columbia. You've got to look right if you're gonna be working for me."

·····

The plane's intercom squawked. "Ah, folks, First Officer Bentley from the flight deck. We're going to hit a few bumps heading down into Columbia tonight. Storm moved through a little while ago. Please fasten your seatbelts. We'll do the best we can to keep you comfortable."

Ike checked to make sure he had a barf bag. He looked across the aisle at Ruthie and found her smiling at him.

"You okay?"

He nodded as the plane bounced, shivered and recovered. He felt

God's breath at play, saw at once how small and insignificant they all were. The plane dropped as if through a trap door, then leveled off. He hunkered down, braced his feet against the legs of the seat in front, clutched at his arm rests, and waited for the next bump.

·····

McCauley had bragged about Benny Lee, tailor to the best-known politicians in South Carolina. The inside of his small shop on Mary Street was filled with a sports bar's worth of autographed photos of himself with governors, senators and lesser VIPs. Benny was the son of industrious Korean immigrants who endured twenty-seven New York City winters before deciding to sell all they could, pack the rest in a beat-up blue Mercury, and move to Miami. Little Benny was asleep in the backseat when the engine block cracked about halfway through the trip, in Columbia. Mr. Lee, squinting at a crumpled map with a thin, gray line drawn in number two pencil that ran from Manhattan to Miami, reasoned that since it was September, still 90 degrees, and that the beach wasn't all that far away, South Carolina would do as well as Florida. Thirty-four years had passed. Benny's parents were gone, but he was among the most successful small businessmen in town.

"That Benny—he tries to sound like a cracker, even plays country music on the radio," McCauley had laughed.

Ike quickly noticed the small man's arched eyebrow when he walked through the front door of the shop on Mary Street, setting off a set of silver door chimes. Hawke stayed in the truck, just like he did when Ike took his lessons at Bunk Meacham's barn. There was one other customer in Benny Lee's store, a white woman with long, silver earrings and frosted blonde hair piled high on her head.

Ike felt their eyes boring in. "What is it, boy?" Benny said, one hand slipping into a drawer beneath the cash register.

"Excuse me." He felt dirty and out of place under the woman's gaze. His face burned. "Excuse me, Judge McCauley, he said … "

Mention of his sponsor prompted the tailor to withdraw his hand from the drawer. "Yes, yes, Judge McCauley. Come with me, young man."

Benny Lee settled with the woman and joined Ike in back. He produced a withered, yellow tape measure and told Ike to strip to his underwear. Then he flicked his wrist and the tape measure shot forward.

"Waist, twenty-nine. Too skinny," Benny said, jotting the measurement on a notepad. "Leg, thirty." He put the yellow tape around Ike's neck. "Hmm, fourteen-and-a-half, but a little more. We make fifteen. Sleeve, thirty-three. Good. Now step with right foot," he said, indicating a metal plate shaped like a foot. Ike stepped on and Benny slid a small silver bar from the top of the plate until it was snug with his big toe. "Shoes, ten-and-a-half. Black trouser, white shirt, black tie, black shoes, black socks. Ready one week. You come back."

Ike hadn't moved or said a word.

"You get dressed now. Come back one week for clothes."

When he returned to the car, Tyler was laying across the front seat, flask on his chest, straw hat over his eyes and bare feet dangling out the driver's side window.

"What the hell took so long?"

Ike shrugged. "I just did what he told me."

"Where's them clothes?"

"He said we have to come back in a week."

Tyler sucked the last of his cigarette and replaced it with a toothpick from behind his ear. When he started the engine, the radio volume was too high and the dial was between stations. He fiddled with the cracked silver knob, and a black bar moved a fraction to the left. *Love Me Tender* pierced the static. Tyler Hawke joined with Elvis, adding his raspy, off-key tenor to the King's sweet baritone.

As they pulled out of town, Tyler took a sidelong glance at Ike and shook his head. "I swear I don't know why we're wastin' so much time and money on your black ass."

•••••

Ike stared desperately at the little curtain that separated cockpit from cabin. Someone once told him that fixing his gaze on a point on the horizon would quell nausea. Since it was too dark to see outside the plane, he chose the curtain.

It wasn't working. His stomach was rising; he could taste its bitter edge. In his peripheral vision, he saw Ruthie dozing peacefully and, for a moment, hated her. His head buzzed and his palms were sweaty. Fight it, got to fight. Oh Lord, why did he eat the peanuts? He felt a piece of crushed nut in his back tooth, but didn't dare try to retrieve it, afraid that even the motion of his tongue would push him over the edge.

The plane dipped. He cursed the pilot and prayed to God. Let us pass, he prayed, let us pass. He pulled out the barf bag and hid it in the pages of the magazine.

•••••

They let him dress in private and the clothes fit perfectly. Ike admired himself in a door-length mirror that Bunk Meacham dragged out to the barn long ago because of a crack that ran north to southeast in the upper right-hand corner. Ike ducked below the jagged line and worked his tie, pushing it deep into the sharply pressed collar of his new white shirt.

"That Benny Lee, he's slick," McCauley said.

Ike saw him in the mirror. He'd come in quietly without Bunk. "Time's come to stop hiding this from your family, Ike. I want to go out to your house tonight, tell your Mama I gave you a job, that you're gonna be working for me from now on."

Ike's hands were still at his tie. He watched McCauley in the mirror. "Well? What's she gonna say?"

"Don't know."

"You just let me do the talking, hear?"

"Yessir."

"Tell her I'll be around after dinnertime."

The judge arrived alone at seven in his four-door sedan. Ike knew the car and was watching from the window of the tiny living room. There was still plenty of light, and the children of Sampsonville, as both races knew black Kilgo, were out playing. They stopped their games, street stickball for the boys, sidewalk jump rope for the girls, when the enormous, black Chevy with county license plates snaked over the dirt road, paused, and stopped in front of the Washington house. A small crowd gathered and watched as Lander McCauley looked at himself in the rearview mirror, touched his tongue, and smoothed each side of his blonde crew cut. "The judge," one of the children whispered. Word that McCauley was at the home of Marva Washington raced through the neighborhood, with speculation following that Ike or Jerome must have killed someone or robbed First Federal. Before he could get to the front steps, several adults were among the gaping children. The less bold, like Ike, peeped from their windows.

McCauley, carrying a gallon jug of apple cider, turned and unfastened the top button of his suit jacket. "Just a social call, folks. Y'all go home. Nothin' ta see."

The children turned and went back to their games. The adults watched a second longer, not convinced. Defiance flashed in the eyes of one woman who stood with her arms crossed. "Them boys in trouble? I've known them boys since they was babies. Used to baby-sit 'em. They in trouble?"

McCauley laughed. "No one's in trouble, ma'am. Like I said, just a social call."

Marva Washington stepped out on the porch, arms crossed. Ike, watching closely from his window, saw she had her church face on. At the back of the crowd, he also noticed Ricky Lee Bishop peeking through a crowd of adults.

McCauley turned and took her hand.

"Pleasure to meet you, Mrs. Washington. Been trying to explain to your neighbors that this is a friendly visit."

"Pleasure to meet you, sir," she said formally. Her tone changed as she took a few steps toward her friends. "Thank you for your concern," she said, shooing with her hands. "Everything's just fine. Get on home."

The crowd broke up. The woman who spoke to McCauley took a last look at his car. "Call if you need me, Marva." Mrs. Washington nodded and held the screen door open for McCauley. He stepped behind her and pulled the door back a little further. "After you, please," he said. "This here's for you." She took the cider and walked inside.

They went into the narrow, L-shaped room that served as kitchen and living room, where a pot of coffee sat steaming on a plain oak table that had been in the Washington family for three generations. Ike and Jerome were waiting, and rose when their mother and the judge entered.

"Hello, Ike, hello, Jerome," McCauley said, shaking hands and looking each boy in the eye. Ike watched Jerome. He'd warned his brother not to mention the fight at the circus. Though McCauley saved them from a beating, Ike never forgot the nasty ring of his last words: *Well get, or I might change my mind.*

McCauley sat at the table, hands clasped.

"May I be excused?" Jerome said.

"Why don't both you boys go on," Mrs. Washington said, then looked quickly at McCauley. "That's okay with you, your honor?"

"Fine, fine." The boys slipped out, stepping lightly as prison escapees. Jerome went outside; Ike went to their bedroom, leaving the door open.

Marva Washington brought out a silver tray with mismatched cups, a creamer, two teaspoons, a small sugar bowl, and a plate of bakery cookies, crunchy vanilla topped with chocolate buttons.

"You didn't have to go to all this trouble," McCauley said.

"No trouble, sir."

"Everyone calls me Judge, Mrs. Washington. Wish you'd do the same." Ike peeked and saw his mother smile and nod. "Well, then, what I wanted to tell you is that I've hired your boy Ike to come work in my campaign for the state legislature. He's a bright boy, as you know, I'm sure, and I need someone to help me get the colored around here and all over the county registered and votin' for Lander McCauley."

Marva Washington sipped her coffee like she was weighing the first taste of a new wine. McCauley waited. Ike, hidden, held his breath.

"Seems like you should have made this visit 'fore you hired him, not after," she said, pointedly adding, "Judge."

McCauley was unfazed. "No disrespect, ma'am. Just needed to see if he could handle the job before I bothered you."

"Why did you pick my Ike? Must be thirty older colored men in town who know more about politics than him."

"No offense, m'am, but I wanted someone young, someone I could train my own way."

Marva Washington continued as if reading off a list. "How did you find my boy?"

"One of the people who work for me recommended him," McCauley lied.

"But there's lots of young colored boys round here."

McCauley's voice was even. "And we chose yours."

"But ... "

"Ma'am, respectfully, sometimes it's a mistake to question good fortune too hard."

McCauley's tone seemed to shake her confidence. Ike knew the judge was trying to be polite, but in the end he'd get what he wanted.

"What's he going to be doing?" his mother asked quietly.

"Lots a things," McCauley said. "And he's going to learn a bunch, too. Gonna teach him about plans I have for some projects back up here—some road and sewer projects. He's going to talk to people, tell them what they need to know and do to get registered and vote."

"For you," Mrs. Washington said.

McCauley watched her. "Well, yes, ma'am, that's the idea. He's working for me to help me get elected."

"How much is his salary?"

"He's going to work four hours a day, three days a week. He'll make thirty-five dollars a week. That's a little better than two dollars an hour."

In his room, Ike's eyes widened. It was the first he'd heard about a salary.

Marva Washington fell silent, then said, "Ike, come out here, I know you're listening."

Ike came, head bowed.

"This is what you want to do, work for the judge?"

In his moment of hesitation, he saw the dead boy, Ezra. But it had been weeks, and the scene in the woods felt unreal, dreamlike. The investigation was long over; outsiders had been blamed. Since Ezra was an orphan, there were no relatives around town to remind him of the lynching or press for further action. Ike remembered his pinky, which had healed crookedly, and which twitched on its own every so often. But his heart also beat on its own. So what? In that moment of hesitation, he felt his feet sliding into the new leather shoes, his legs, into the soft, black pants Benny Lee cut and sewed and hemmed to fit Ike Washington, and Ike Washington only. There was no other pair of pants like that in the world. And then there was the new-found money. Thirty-five dollars a week. Still.

"Yes, m'am. I want the job."

Mrs. Washington looked at McCauley. "My boys are all I have, Judge."

"Don't you worry," he answered. "I'll take good care of him."

A half-hour after McCauley left, Ike was summoned again by his mother. "There's something someone's not telling me."

Ike stiffened. Her intuition made clear that his old life ended with what he saw in the woods. Before, he was the same as every other Negro country boy in South Carolina—safe, but struggling, happy, but only so long as his ambition wasn't too strong or his vision too grand. His would be another life of used cars and street stickball.

"Well?" she said.

And what if he told her? Going to the cops would put all three of them in danger. Changing her mind on McCauley would tell him she knew and produce the same result. Do what's right and pray for help? That would be her way, but he didn't have as much faith. If it turned out wrong, he'd pray for forgiveness. He made himself look puzzled.

"Nothing else, Mama."

She took his chin, raised his face, handed him the toughest question of his young life. "Isaac Washington Junior, did you do something wrong?"

He forced himself not to blink. "No, ma'am."

"That judge catch you at something wrong? Is he holding it over you?"

"I didn't do anything wrong, Mama."

·····

"Ah, folks, First Officer Bentley from the flight deck again. Sorry about the bumps going down to Columbia. The good news is we're through the worst of it and about thirty miles from the airport. We should have you down on the ground in eight to ten minutes. Sorry again, and thanks for flying with us."

Ike saw the stewardess coming to make sure the seat backs were straight and tray tables upright. When she reached his row, he kept his eyes lowered and passed her his barf bag.

"Poor thing," she said. "Can I get you something?"

Get me on the fucking ground, he thought. Make that asshole hold this crate steady.

"I'm fine now."

"Well, just tap that white button over your head if you need me," the stewardess said sweetly. "That was a little rough coming down."

"Yes."

"Sure you don't want a cup of Coke? Might settle your stomach."

"Nothing, thanks."

When she moved on, Ike looked at Ruthie, who glanced down quickly and pretended she was reading. In a moment, she met his eyes.

"Get a good night's sleep," she said. "We start early tomorrow and it's going to be a busy day. Three events and four interviews."

"And a car to sell," he added miserably.

14   *Dan*

Dan followed the waist of the ball-handler, intent on stopping a drive or an easy jumper. He watched the waist so he wouldn't be fooled by the eyes, which can say left when the mind has already chosen right, or pass when a decision has been made to shoot. The waist cannot lie like the eyes. Not even the mouth can lie like the eyes.

The kid was three inches taller and a step quicker, but he wasn't going anywhere without his belly button. He feinted right and drove hard left; Dan stuck close. They were step for step and the kid was getting frustrated. He was new to the Thursday night crowd and had a purple tattoo burned into his right bicep that said, "Cherry." When the muscle was flexed, like now, the letters got big. Force it up, Dan thought, seeing himself smack the basketball back in the kid's face.

What he didn't see was the screen. Cherry's biggest teammate set a block that erased him like a wrong answer. One second he was running to his right, the next he lay in a heap. The wicked witch after her bath, he thought as the kid sank an easy lay-up. "Stan, call the picks?" Dan said, rubbing his shoulder.

"That's the fourth basket for your man," LeTourge answered. "Fight through and quit whining."

"I'll fight through, just let me know it's coming. Screen left, screen right. You're a cop. You're supposed to know how to direct traffic."

"I'm a *detective*, sonny. I don't do traffic."

Dan took the out-of-bounds pass and dribbled up court. When he reached the top of the key, Cherry went for a steal. Dan switched hands, keeping his body between ball and defender.

The kid wound up with an elbow in the chest. Action stopped. "Offensive foul, man!"

"My ass. You're reachin' in, *Cherry*." He said it in a mincing voice that made the kid square off and take a few steps forward and call Dan a punk.

"*Punk*?"

"S'right."

Teammates corralled the two before it went further. Dan caught Stan smiling. The intensity nosed up as the score hit seven-six, eight-eight, ten-nine, and then, ten all. The kid called for the ball and, with Dan up close enough to count his fillings, said, "Game-time, chump." He rocked back and faked a shot from the foul line. Dan nearly went airborne, but recovered in time to flick the ball from behind. Stan snatched it and hit Dan streaking to the opposite basket.

"Kid was right," he said as they aimed for the locker room. "It *was* game-time."

"You picked it up down the stretch. What got into you?"

He threw a hand across Stan's chest. "Did you let me crash into that guy on purpose?"

"You needed a wake-up call."

"Man."

"I'll make it up—beer's on me. Where to?"

"Let's scoop Bernie and hit someplace downtown."

"Deal."

They covered the quick hop from The Citadel to Broad Street in minutes. Stan drove with a hairy elbow hanging out the window of his Berkeley County-issued sedan. It was a warm, quiet night lit by a three-quarter moon. Clever street lamps with fixtures shaped like carriage lanterns marked the way for tourists enjoying the shirtsleeve weather and downtown Charleston's grab-bag of bars, restaurants and shops. On one corner, a candle store where rapt Midwesterners, their minds far from icy gusts howling down from Canada, watched craftsmen drip, shape and carve wax into green and red Christmas trees. Across the way, a tiny storefront opened into a vast showroom where two women in jade scarves sold hand-made necklaces, tapestries, African face masks, bracelets, and leather pouches of marbles.

Great item, those marbles: twelve for two bucks. Dan remembered being in the store one day looking for a gift for his mother. Kids sank their hands into the barrels of hard, smooth pearls like they were digging in sand, enjoying the feel before having to make the hard choices. Solid, see-through, small, fat, flecked … Lime, lavender, silver, ruby, black-and-white. Mom and Dad would have to go for two dozen if they wanted to get out of there.

Stan double-parked beside a convertible in front of the Broad Street Cafe. Dan cut through customers waiting to be seated and found his friend talking to three couples in Reebok-crested tennis outfits squeezed around a table for four. The smell of grilling burgers made him swallow. He jabbed a finger in Bernie's ribs, whispered, "Cop outside named Le-Tourge wants to see you."

"Scram, I'll catch up. Where?" Bernie whispered back.

"*Hydrant.*"

"See you in thirty."

·····

Stan said, "You handled the cop beat almost a year. You know how to find information. Arrest record, civil, criminal judgments—stuff like that is all in the public domain."

Dan slid his empty mug along a fat knot in the lacquered bar table. "Done, Stan. I've been through court records, police records, and three different newspaper libraries. Nothing."

"Ever consider that Big Ike Washington, Jr. is a straight-up guy?"

"Could be, but, Yo, Bernie."

Bernie Weinstock maneuvered through a large weeknight crowd hovering around the bar. "Hey, glad you two came by, I needed a break."

Dan signaled for another round. "Beer's on me tonight, Bernie. My reward for Stan's advice."

"What's up? Not Big Ike again."

Dan ran his thumb along his mug. "I've also been to that crappy town three times. Either no one knows how Ike and Lander McCauley hooked up, or they aren't saying. Blacks and whites in Kilgo love Ike like James Brown and won't say anything bad about the senator. Nearly everyone has his own story about McCauley: he tracks down lost Social Security checks; he sends cards when their kids graduate, get married, and have their own kids; he wears a cowboy hat and rides a horse in their 4th of July parade. I've been knocking on doors at random. Nice houses, falling-down houses, it's all the same. One old guy—it was 94 degrees and he's got on a flannel shirt—he threw me off his porch after two questions. Said Ike was the best mayor Kilgo's ever had."

"It's simple," Bernie said. "If you think there's something there, you have to keep going back."

"That's your advice?"

"That's it."

"Then you're paying for your own beer."

Bernie said, "Maybe you're going at it wrong. Maybe you ought to corner McCauley, see what he's got to say. Or maybe the other candidates? Seems like that Dianna Harley's worth a try."

Stan leaned in. "I think it's bigger than that." He took a long swallow and belched. "It's like B-ball tonight, Dan. You got knocked down. When you got up, you were tougher. That geezer? He's the pick. Fight through. Quit whining."

Bernie added, "If you act like you think their town is small and crappy, if they even get a whiff of that, you're dead. They won't give you shit."

Dan felt the red rush his cheeks. They were piling on, didn't know how hard it was to find the guts of this story. No bodies, no guns, no fingerprints. He remembered Lem Butcher's criticism and the vow he took not to present his editor with another wet-kiss story on Ike.

"Gotta start early," he said, dropping a twenty on the table.

•••••

Another morning rush hour in August. Sitting in the still of Kilgo, he pictured Washington. The Beltway, Metro and bus stops, all jammed. The paper, delivered, read and now full of old news. Fresh stories taking shape. Life. Action. It might smell bad, it might be aggravating, it might be loathsome as the crud lurking in Chesapeake Bay, but there was *life*.

Not in historic Kilgo, not unless you're talking still life, he thought as he sat on the hood sipping coffee near the corner of Union and Main. He looked at his watch: 9:12 a.m. A vegetable truck passed, only the third vehicle in twenty minutes. Now what?

He had no plan. All he knew was that his story was in Kilgo. He'd risen early to reach town by rush hour, but the effort hadn't yielded anything but a cup of gas station coffee. He finished it, squashed the cup and threw it down in disgust.

"That can cost you fifty dollars in this town, young man."

Dan hadn't seen the cop come up. Sneaky old bastard wore a khaki uniform with a short-sleeved open shirt and navy kerchief tied loosely around his neck. His skin was leathery and only a shade lighter than the nightstick hanging alongside his holstered revolver.

"Sorry, officer." Dan found the cop's ID badge. "Officer Edward Bishop. I'll pick it up."

"Yes, you will."

Dan retrieved the cup and looked for a trash can as Officer Bishop watched with his arms folded. There was none around.

"Behind you."

Dan turned around again and saw the faded green pail behind a mailbox. "What's your business here?"

That was sticky. As mayor, Ike Washington was this guy's boss. It wouldn't do to say he was investigating the town's top politician. Plus, he hadn't been exonerated of a possible fifty-buck fine for littering.

"I'm on business, sir."

The cop moved his hands to his hips. Edward Bishop was a small, well-built man who could have passed for forty-five had it not been for a full, gray beard and the receding hairline that pushed back into a *Brillo* patch of short gray curls.

"What kind of business?" The cop pulled out a pad. "And is this your car?" The *Prelude* was three steps from a fire hydrant.

Dan stammered and began pleading, hating that he couldn't find any escape route but the naked truth.

"Wait. I'm a reporter with the *Herald-Leader* in Charleston. I'm working on a story about Ike Washington. I was just standing here trying to figure out where I was headed next. Please, no ticket. I picked up the cup and I'll move the car."

Officer Bishop nearly smiled. "I wasn't giving you a ticket, son. This is my personal log. I keep little notes on everything I do each day. Helps pass time. Show me your ID."

Dan produced his press pass. The cop returned it and steered him to a pair of wrought-iron benches that faced each other in a small park back from Union Street.

Officer Bishop winced as he sat. "These knees. Body gets like an old car; parts wear out, break down."

Dan pointed to his car. "Um, is it okay to leave … "

"Shee-it," the cop chuckled. "No one's turned that hydrant on in thirty-four years. I know cause that's how long I been on the job, since 1958. First black man in the department. Three months, I'll be done, retired. Living off my pension and fishing Lake Marion 'til I empty her out."

Dan relaxed. "Kilgo's sure quiet."

"This gun." He patted his holster. "Never been out 'cept for training."

"Ike runs a peaceful town."

Officer Bishop looked up. Dan cursed himself for going too fast, but the cop was just looking at a garbage truck turning into the Post Office lot.

"Big Ike's a good man, treats cops square. I don't know him much myself. Had a nephew used to run around with him. Ricky Lee Bishop, my big sister's boy."

"Think Ricky Lee would talk to me? I'm looking for folks who knew Ike when he was younger."

"Ricky Lee passed. Prostate cancer got him a few years ago."

Dan cracked his knuckles. Another hard pick. He was on his ass again.

"My sister's still around, though."

Big deal. Another old woman who loved Ike. Plus, he said *big* sister. That would probably put her around seventy. Still, the cop was trying to be nice.

"What's her name?"

"Jenny. Jenny Bishop."

"Live nearby?"

"Nope. She's down your way. Makes those straw baskets someplace, what are they called?"

"Sweetgrass."

"Yup. Makes sweetgrass baskets down in Charleston."

Dan jotted, *Jenny Bishop, basket maker, Chas.*, in his notebook and thanked Officer Bishop.

"Good luck in your fishing."

"Same to you, young man. You run into Jenny, tell her Hey. Don't see her much anymore. We lost touch."

"Got a number?"

"Nope, no phone."

Naturally.

They shook hands. The cop held on and looked into his face. "You don't sound like you're from Charleston."

Dan smiled as if it were a compliment. "I'm not. Temporary duty. I'll be moving back North pretty soon."

The stocky cop looked like he might say something else. His lips tightened and his dark brows lifted a little and drew together, but all he did was nod and release Dan's hand.

He returned to the car and swore when he saw all the windows closed. He braced himself for stifling heat and got in, reaching for the morning *Herald-Leader* that sat in the passenger seat in a plastic driveway wrapper. His mission today was to talk to real people, not insiders, but that wasn't going so well. The daily political calendar would tell him if any of the congressional candidates were due in Kilgo or at least in nearby towns. Car door open, he paused to read about the grief Ross Perot was causing Bush on the campaign trail, and *Dear Lem's* terse advice to a guy whose wife had, like the Reagan and Bush administrations, become a rabid fan of deficit spending.

Read my lips, Lem wrote to the distraught husband. *Find purse, take plastic, slice and dice with nearest scissors.*

The calendar put Ike in Columbia, Cady Owens in Sumter and Derrick Maussipant down in Charleston. Dianna Harley was going to a lunch in Cady County. A plant visit on Ike's home turf had possibilities. He put the paper down and started the car. The steering wheel was so hot, he had to drive one-handed, switching every few seconds until it cooled. He had two hours to kill before noon and headed for the part of town where Ike had grown up.

He'd been to the neighborhood before and wasn't surprised this time at the odd mix of graceful little houses with fenced-in vegetable gardens that stood shoulder to shoulder with clapboard shacks propped up on naked cinder blocks. Many roofs were capped with smoke-colored shingles that gave the neighborhood a feeling of middle-class sturdiness. Other houses sagged in the middle like the backs of old trail horses. There was much more here now than forty years ago when Ike was growing up. More houses, more people, less open space. Yet the street and nearly every yard was empty due to the heat.

Dan slowed to watch a fenced-in mixed breed bark and snarl at the mailman, who seemed used to the routine. He studied the names on his envelopes and magazines and paid no attention as the frantic beast raced up and down the yard, drool flying. The mailman wore his summer uniform: dark shorts, light blue shirt, and black shoes with tire tread soles. The dog looked like he would gladly take a bullet in his blocky head if he could just get hold of the mailman's bare thigh for one violent moment.

Dan stopped suddenly and turned back to town. Ricky Lee Bishop might be dead, but there had to be others from Ike's high school class still around. The black high school was replaced by an integrated middle school long ago; the library might have old yearbooks. He checked his watch again: 10:25 a.m. The library ahead on Union Street was open.

And attended, he saw when he entered several minutes later, by a small, white-haired woman who, hearing his request, pushed her glasses down on her nose and peered at him like he'd asked for a copy of *Hustler*. "We don't have anything like that here, young man. Try the county historical society."

"Where's that?"

Her glasses slipped, but landed safely thanks to a beaded string attached to both ends and fastened around her neck. "Out the library lot, turn right, one-point-seven miles north on Union. It'll be on the left."

"Thanks." Dan wanted to see the woman smile. A wooden name plate with small brass letters identified her as Cornelia Hobbes—Head Librarian. "You have a nice day, Mrs. Hobbes."

"Thank you," she said, replacing her glasses and shuffling some papers on her desk. "Tell Iris I sent you. She once taught at that school."

"Thank you, again, ma'am." She did not look up or smile.

If the library was the smallest he'd ever seen, the historical society was barely more than a garage with a three-step walk-up. A paper taped to the door said, "Back in twenty." Great. Twenty minutes from when?

He walked around the little building. Nothing but trees, bushes and some crows on a telephone wire. *Ca-Caww, Ca-Caww.* "Who asked you?" Dan answered. He walked back around front and sat on the steps, wondering for the first time whether the Washington-McCauley story was more than he could handle. The concrete was hard and he reached around to rub the muscles in his lower back.

A moment later, a portly black woman pulled up in an old station wagon. She looked surprised to have a visitor.

"You must be Iris," he said as she gathered some packages from the backseat and walked toward him.

"Who wants to know?"

Gee, did everyone here go to the same charm school?

"Dan Patragno, ma'am, from the *Charleston Herald-Leader*. Can I get those for you?"

"You may back off the step so I can open the door."

"Oh, sure."

Inside, it was cool, with a hint of a mildew smell that he knew would swell and blossom without the AC. Heavy gold curtains with navy sashes covered the windows. The walls were busy with framed maps, historic county documents, and black-and-white photos of local figures. An old-world globe rotated to North America sat in one corner.

Iris put her packages down. "There. Now, what can I do for you?"

Dan explained, mentioning that he knew she once taught at St. James. He finished with his question about the yearbooks.

"Yearbooks?" She laughed. "We were lucky if we had enough text-books. Colored people then didn't have no money for yearbooks."

His disappointment must have been obvious.

"Look, you want to find some folks who came up with Mayor Ike. I'm sixty-seven years old and lucky to find my way to this little building three days a week. I don't remember who that boy's friends were. Why don't you just ask him?"

He looked at the globe, imagined he could see Pennsylvania Avenue and himself at a White House press conference. *Yes, Mr. Patragno, your information is correct. President Bush would like to discuss that with you privately. This way to the Oval Office.*

"Oh, I see. You're going behind Ike's back. He don't know about it.

That it?"

"Not exactly."

"Well, good luck to you." She leaned forward on her desk and looked at him until he left.

•••••

Kentland Mills opened its doors north of town in Cady County in 1905. The old yarn plant still had its enchanting, turn-of-the-century wooden floors, but had been refitted with high-tech spinning machines from Kyoto, Japan, that increased efficiency and allowed the Kent family to cut its staff in half. Business was good, despite stiff competition from overseas factories that paid slave wages or ran on child labor.

Today's Kents had a hundred or so employees and, thanks to clear sailing whenever utilities or zoning issues arose, an unwavering loyalty to Mayor Ike Washington. Which was why Dianna Harley was not invited inside. To cover his butt in case of an upset, Dan found out later that current owner Edison Kent had granted her permission to greet workers at the front gate. It was less efficient than speaking to a larger audience, but better than nothing.

Unlike some pols, he saw quickly that Dianna Harley knew how to knock on a door without barging into the living room. She took care of business—a quick handshake, a warm smile, a simple request that the voter consider her—and let the Kentland mill workers enjoy their lunch hour. If someone wanted more, to hear her stand on NAFTA or gun control, she managed it without ignoring the next person in line, supplementing her answer with a blue and white pamphlet that she pressed into the worker's hand.

"Checking out the competition?"

He spun around, tried to look unfazed.

"I could ask you the same."

Ruthie laughed. They were fifteen feet from where Dianna Harley continued to greet the mill workers. "A little reconnaissance never hurts. We heard she was here and Ike sent me over."

"And?"

She put her arm around him, turning them away from the other candidate. "She can talk to these guys 'til she turns blue. Edison Kent is with us, and where he goes, his workers go."

Dan removed her arm. She looked like she expected it.

"You mad at me?"

He looked down, then into her eyes. Soft, brown cashmere, set off by a liquid white unspoiled by the tiny red lines he got when he was tired or stressed. But she went from hard to soft too easily and it made him uneasy. "At the Masons ... "

"I know, I was a bitch."

He felt the air go out of his anger. She wore a skin-tight emerald shirt under a summer slate jacket, and short black skirt with black half-heels. Her dark hair was pulled back and her neck was bare, save for the spot of perfume he imagined her dabbing on that morning. He wanted nothing more than to taste that spot.

She misinterpreted his silence. "I get uptight at big events. He likes everything to run smooth. I was *working*."

"Like I'm working now."

She bit her lower lip lightly, weighing something. "We're both working. Why don't we get together later when we're both *not* working?"

"Where?"

"Where else?"

"Ike's? I'll pick you up at seven," he said, putting on his best Southern accent. "But no more *Squat and Gobble*."

"We'll go to my place." She lowered her chin as she said it, smiling just enough to show the top row of her white teeth. Her eyes were bright and hinted at mischief.

He nodded, trying to keep his pulse in place. Did she just say they were going to have sex, or that she'd make him an omelet? Shit, was Dianna Harley getting ready to leave?

He turned to catch Dianna, then back to say good-bye. Ruthie was already off to the parking lot, black skirt swaying east and west with each step. Her walk was like her smile—soft, easy, natural. He would have to tell her.

Dianna Harley wasn't in the mood to talk about Ike. She wanted to talk about herself—her qualifications, her vision, her achievements. "My campaign is not about putting him down," she said, conveniently forgetting the charge she made at the Masons. He reminded her.

"That had to be said; it doesn't have to be repeated."

Then she repeated it and he scribbled it down.

"Everyone knows McCauley tells him what to do, will *keep* telling him what to do if Ike wins this election."

"Do you know anything about how Ike started working for Senator McCauley?"

Dianna Harley had stiff, black hair with a streak of gray in front and a heavily sprayed roll on the side tapered to a point that reached just below her chin. She touched the side, careful not to brush against any of the caky makeup on her cheek.

"We've looked into that, it's very murky." She waited while he peered with her into the murkiness. "There's no record. There was nothing in the papers. We're not even sure when he started working for him. I didn't grow up here; I don't know the background."

An aide appeared. It was time for Dianna Harley to move on.

"If you find anything interesting, give me a call," she said, extending her hand. "I'd like the chance to comment."

"Sure."

•••••

Three members of the vagabond sidewalk crowd were hanging outside Ike's Place when Dan pulled up and parked next to a new, beige *Taurus* with temporary tags. He was less self-conscious this time, and locked his doors without a thought for what the gesture might signal.

"Hello, young man."

"Evening." He walked with purpose to the front door, nearly barreling into Ike, who was on his way out, and in a hurry.

"Patragno, did we have an appointment?"

"No, Ike, this is social."

"Social." Ike smiled like he'd walked into the kitchen and found them naked. "Well, have fun. I'm off to Sumter County. Sleeping over a friend's. Early start there tomorrow."

"Campaign stuff?"

Ike nodded and pressed a button on his key chain. The *Taurus'* lights came on and the door locks popped up.

"Where's the *Lincoln*?"

Ike shook his head as if to say he was fed up with reporters not paying attention. "We told you guys that *Towncar* wasn't ours. Always looking for dirt. This here's my car." Ike looked like he expected the *Taurus* to jump up and lick his face. "Fine American car. Sturdy. Dependable. Economical."

Ruthie pushed through the door and filled the void that threatened to develop into breaking news. "Don't forget we added the community center in Sumter tomorrow," she told Ike. "Meet you a little before six."

Ike got in and powered down his window, watching her the whole time. He reached out and tapped the side-view mirror, then shined off the smudge with his jacket sleeve. "I need you fresh tomorrow; get some sleep."

She waved him off and led Dan to his car. "Away! Before I scream!"

He felt like he'd been handled, led away from a possible story, but in truth didn't really care much about Ike's new ride. It was the guy's attitude that irritated him, the way he steered simple chit-chat into a tug of war.

Ruthie sensed his thoughts. "Look, we sold the *Lincoln* and bought a *Taurus*. You're the first to know. If you think it's such a big deal, you can write a story tomorrow. But how about we just relax tonight? No more business 'til morning."

He wanted nothing more, but stayed quiet and pretended otherwise.

"Don't make me get tough with you," she said, clenching a fist.

"Now I'm worried."

Ruthie lived about an hour away in Florence, but was staying in Kilgo until Election Day in a house rented by the campaign. She directed him to a cozy, heavily wooded North Kilgo neighborhood called Shemp's Landing.

"Shemp's Landing," he said. "Where do Moe and Larry live?"

"Think I don't know the Stooges, wise guy?"

Good, he thought, they were back on solid ground, flirting easily as the setting sun fought the dark, streaking the evening sky with wispy red trails and heavenly orange peaks that held the stars backstage.

The development was built around a small lake and waterway that fed into Lake Marion, Ruthie explained, pointing out several Sunfish and motorboats that bounced with the small waves that lapped their fiberglass bottoms.

"Next right, second house on the left," she said, guiding them to Azalea Court and a small, light-colored bungalow that had a driveway but no garage. A sapling oak tethered to two stakes, plus sod so fresh he could see the seams between pieces told him the house was less than a year old. Ruthie let them in, and he indeed smelled a house that was not yet a home. Fresh, almond paint, new, Berber carpets a shade darker than the walls, no cooking smells, no clothes tossed on the couch, paintings and knickknacks that were already in place when she moved in. "I'm not here much," she said. "It came furnished."

The only personal touch was a stark, black upright that sat opposite the couch and arched brick fireplace in the living room. An eight-by-ten in a beveled glass frame sat on top. The photo showed Ruthie between Ike and another man roughly the same age that Dan took for her father. The three had their arms around each other and were smiling like a trio of drunks trying to pass for sober.

Ruthie saw his interest. "Dad and Ike surprised me. They shipped my piano down from Florence. We've always had it; my mother learned to play on that piano."

"You promised to play for me."

"I said we'd see."

"C'mon."

"Let me start dinner."

"I'll help."

"You relax."

He reached up to see if he could touch the thick wooden beams that ran across the ceiling. They were too high, even when he crouched and jumped. He wandered to the piano and thumbed through a music book while she worked in the kitchen. "There's no Sinatra in there," she called over the sound of rushing sink water. He didn't answer. She came out and said it again.

"Funny." He walked to her, hands at his sides. She stood still, a small question in her eyes as he came closer. "I need to do this before I can relax," he whispered.

She smiled. He looked into her eyes until they closed, softly, with anticipation. Her lips bore just a trace of pink gloss and were parted slightly. He didn't want this kiss to be too hungry, like last time outside the diner; he just wanted the feel of her lips, to enjoy them without rushing. Both were full; the bottom pouted a little. A gift from God, incredibly sexy. She'd taken off her jacket and her shoulders were bare and creamy brown against the sleeveless green top. He did not touch them, didn't touch any part of her with his hands. Instead, he leaned from the waist and pressed his mouth on hers, moving gently until the fit was just right. He knew in a moment that she was a woman he'd never tire of kissing.

"So soft," she whispered, eyes still closed. His hands moved as if on their own, first to her slender waist, then up and down her back, exploring, caressing. He had been with other women, but had never felt such an ache. He wondered what she was thinking. Funny that you could be so close to someone, so physically close, and not know their thoughts. Or sleep next to someone for years—his parents came to mind—and never share the same dream. He pulled back a few inches and waited for her eyes to open, the sage old adage about playing defense appearing uninvited in his mind, like a first wife at her ex-husband's second wedding. *Watch the eyes—they can lie better than the mouth.*

He tensed a bit. Her eyes opened, deep brown, full of sudden concern. "What's wrong?"

"Play for me," he said, not knowing why it was suddenly so important. "Not now," she murmured, putting her hands behind his neck and nuzzling his cheek.

He took her wrists and slid from under her grasp. "One song. Anything, I don't care."

"But the dinner."

"One song."

She put her hands on his chest and gently pushed him to arm's length.

Ruthie opened the black-padded piano bench and took out a music book with a white binder. She flipped through several dog-eared pages until she found the piece she wanted. He sat on the floor and leaned on the couch as she slid the bench closer to the piano and took off her rings, placing them on the small, wooden dock that bordered the instrument's highest notes, the place where a nightclub pianist would stick his ashtray.

The piece started so softly, it reminded him of their recent kiss. The music was slow and wistful and a little dreamy. He thought of lying on hot sand after diving into the cold surf. He admired her fingers, which struck the keys and returned to ready position like game, little soldiers, and her back, straight in a way that suggested strength, not stiffness.

Her left hand was efficient and talented as her right, a claim not many of his basketball buddies could make. After awhile, he stopped analyzing and let himself go with the music. She had reached a critical moment when her left hand was playing quick counterpoint to a slow, mournful melody played by her right. Her face was tight with concentration. He could see pencil marks on the sheet music where a piano teacher, perhaps her mother, at some point drilled her hard through this section of the music.

The end came several minutes later with a return to the slow, expressive tempo that introduced the piece. She knew this part well, he saw, for her eyes closed and her shoulders and neck swayed slightly. The last chord required all ten fingers, but Ruthie didn't look at the music or her fingers.

When she was finished and the echo faded to silence, he got up and sat next to her, but in the opposite direction, with his back to the black and white keys. He held her and she held him back, and the quiet felt so good, he didn't say a word.

15   *Ike and Ezra*

Why you alone here?

Oh, God, not now. Not when he was so tired, not with tomorrow racing at him like a bullet.

Up, up, time to visit! Why you alone, I said?

Ike's eyes are closed, but he is awake, trying to orient himself. Ezra has come to this unfamiliar room with the small, single bed and sheets that smell of lilac. Ike has been dreaming of himself as a boy. He and his father were tracking a wild dog—no, a fox. A fox had been in the chickens again. They walked through the woods, his father carrying an old shotgun and kneeling to check the ground every few yards for clues. As he kneeled one time, Ike looked into the trees in the opposite direction. The fox lay on the ground, flat as he could make his small, scrawny body. His brown and white muzzle was smudged with red and he licked the sides of his mouth while staring intensely at the man and boy. Ike watched a second longer, then turned and walked off with his father.

The forest dissolves and he remembers. He is staying overnight with Agnes Stono, a friend and the most popular politician in Sumter. She'd said they needed to talk about something important in the morning. He peeks and sees the sun is still asleep. The moon is full and Ezra sits in its brightness on a desk by the window. The milky light makes a shadowy silhouette of his head and shoulders, which turn toward him.

I know you ain't sleeping.

No.

You're alone tonight.

Cynthia gets tired of politics.

Maybe that's it, maybe not.

She knows winning this race is what matters, that going to the Congress is what I've wanted all along. She knew it from the beginning. So pretty, she was, so smart.

Smart enough to know you got secrets.

I don't have any secrets from Cynthia.

You're a liar. You know, I know, she knows.

Ike touches his chest at the once-hard V of flesh above the top button of his pajama shirt. He sits up and pads around until he finds his terry cloth slippers. Even on overnight trips, he likes having his slippers. He locates the left, fingers the opening, slips it on.

She loves me, trusts me. My son, what he would think? He would hate me, be ashamed. I couldn't take it. His wife, and my little granddaughter ... Marva. It would tear us apart.

Everyone's gonna know soon.

You're going to tell, now, after all this time?

Nope, you're going to tell it.

No.

I'll be watchin'. Do a good job. When you do it, make sure you do a good job. Don't leave nothin' out.

16   *Ike*

He woke suddenly, as if to a fire engine in full flight. His eyes popped open; there was no alarm, just quiet. He knew before he felt around with his hand that his pajama shirt was plastered to his back with sweat. A bad dream, that's all it was, another nightmare. He got up, walked to the window, touched the desk. Nothing. What was he looking for, evidence of sanity? He rubbed his eyes too hard and saw a kaleidoscope of flashing gold and white against the blackness of his lids. Bad dream, he told himself—too much stress, working too hard. Everything will settle down once the race is over and people start calling him *Mr. Congressman.*

He repeated the salutation in his head for the millionth time and pictured himself on the U.S. House floor with one of those old-time, pot-bellied lawmakers he saw all the time on *C-SPAN* tugging at his elbow. "We need your vote on this one. You with us, Big Ike?"

Oh, he'd be a player alright, and when he left the chamber, there'd be a pimply-faced page from Des Moines, Iowa, or Idalou, Texas, in a navy blazer holding an elevator. "This way, Mr. Congressman," the kid would say. And he would return, "Thank you, Billy," remembering to say the boy's name.

Ike started for the bathroom attached to his bedroom. There was a knock at the outer door. "It's nearly seven. We start in a half-hour."

"I'm up," he said, moving to the bathroom.

"This is going to be a good day, Ike."

He looked in the mirror, saw in his watery eyes the type of weariness that follows a long day, not a night's sleep. "I could use one, Agnes," he said, reaching into the shower for the hot water so the bathroom would fill with thick, hot steam. He turned the knob and paused to look at the small finger on his left hand, which had begun to dance, kicking to the side and lurching back. Kick out, lurch back. He stared at his pinky, thinking that he might—just this once—be able to will it to stay still. The brown digit was thick for a pinky and dusted with coarse, black hairs below the middle knuckle. It stayed in place three seconds, then took a spastic jump left. Ezra's words came to him. *You're the one going to tell it. Do a good job.*

He smothered the pinky with his other hand. He squeezed so hard, both hands began to feel cold despite the rising steam from the shower. *I'm not telling anything.* There'd been times over the years when he'd considered revealing what happened to Ezra James, times when the guilt and shame he'd managed to cage broke loose and tore at his insides.

The closest he'd come was at the dentist. Ike laughed ruefully at the image of himself lying back in the chair, nitrous oxide flooding his nostrils, Dr. William Steigner's surgical-gloved fingers pressing the screaming drill bun so far into his molar, he thought it would surely burst through his jawbone. Even through the gas, he could smell the drill burning away years of rot and decay that had grown beneath his silver filling. "This one's a goner without endodontic treatment—root canal," Dr. Steigner had said.

Billy Steigner. Ike remembered a shy young man with a medium Afro who could never muster the nerve to approach a woman in a bar. Billy had been with him in Columbia the night he met Cynthia at a softly-lit Negro blues club called the *Red Rooster*. When Ike returned to his table after one of several dances with Cynthia, Billy was gone.

Time passed and the two men, never that close to begin with, lost touch. Ike got serious with Cynthia and Billy rode off to dental school to become Dr. William Steigner.

Ike tried to see through plastic goggles designed to protect his eyes from flying tooth debris. As the dentist worked, a buxom, white-bloused assistant prowled around his mouth with a little, straw-shaped vacuum that sucked up everything that broke free of the excavation site. When she nodded all was clear, Billy began probing deep into the tooth's narrow, curving roots with a reamer, the dental equivalent of a metal push-pin. Uncomfortable, Ike thought, trying to keep his tongue out of the way, but it didn't hurt. He was too juiced up on laughing gas and *Lidocaine.*

"You okay?"

He nodded. Billy had some sort of magnifying lenses and a fiber optic light attached to his regular glasses that made his eyes look like tiny marbles. He put the pin down and reached for the drill. He revved it a few times like a kid guns his car at a light, then went back in. Ike was scared when he first sat down for the procedure, but the gas had given him a new perspective. *Save the tooth.* That's what Billy had declared most important.

Now they were allies. Ike's job was to stay still and give his friend a clear shot at the battlefield. Billy would drill, scrape and pick his way through the advancing army of bacteria marching slowly through his once-pure enamel until he reached the core. The core, the essence, was still good. Billy would strip away all that had been spoiled, cleanse the roots, seal the holes with cement, and protect his work for the rest of time with a porcelain crown.

Ike opened a fraction wider. He liked having Billy on his side. When his friend was through, Ike decided he would share the thoughts that were swirling through his mind. The drill made its high-pitched scream, then lowered a tone as it pressed into another cache of silver. The assistant made a cat-like swipe with her vacuum. Ike sighed. Yes, Billy was someone he could talk to. He would understand; they were allies.

Forty-five minutes later, the gas was off and a temporary cap was seated on the tooth stump. Ike felt it with his tongue and rubbed his forehead. "You okay?" Billy said again. He nodded. "Sit in the waiting room 'til your head clears. We'll wrap this up in one more visit." Ike made another appointment and left the office.

Usually, it was fear that stopped him. Fear of McCauley; fear that he'd be hated by his own people for waiting so long to tell; fear of losing the standing he'd worked so hard to build; fear of the look he knew would be in Cynthia's eyes; fear of the way he knew his son would turn away. *Oreo.* That's how they would think of him. He couldn't bear it. There had been only one moment open to him, and he hadn't seen it. Right after. He should've told right after. Told all he'd seen and hoped people would take his word over the word of a county judge. Hoped they could've found evidence linking McCauley and Tyler Hawke to the crime. Instead, he'd closed himself in his room and wrote all he could remember on three pages of his mother's unlined stationery. He dated the pages and hid them away.

Now, alone and rushing in Agnes Stono's cream-colored bathroom, he let his hands separate. The crooked pinky behaved a moment and began twitching again. He returned to the sink and stared into the mirror until his face disappeared in the humid fog.

Agnes was 52 years old and the most popular member of the Sumter County Council. Two years ago, her husband, one of several men who supervised prison work gangs sent into the county to pick up garbage from the sides of local roads and highways, had a weak moment and let his boys stop off for a game of pick-up softball at an overgrown field far from town. The spirited game led to a raging thirst and Alvin Stono's second moment of weakness—three six packs of Budweiser purchased from a rural mom and pop near the county line. Nothing happened—no drunken crime spree, no rapes, no attempted escapes—but the deed was discovered and Alvin Stono was peeled from the county payroll like a dirty Band-Aid.

Agnes thought the punishment too severe and said so. Compounding her rage was Alvin's constant presence at home, she told Ike one day when he was sounding out possible county chairmen for his campaign. Alvin slept late, wore sloppy gym clothes every day, and was often asleep and snoring on the couch when she came home at night. He stopped shaving. He watched hours of television each day, and started shouting out the answers when his favorite game shows came on. His answers were never correct, giving Agnes even more reason to argue for Alvin's reinstatement to the Corrections Department at the outset of each council meeting.

"Mr. Chairman," she would say as eyes rolled from one end of the C-shaped table to the other. "A point of personal privilege, please. This is about a case of injustice, of a punishment far outweighing the crime, that I feel must be taken up by this council."

Marital ties notwithstanding, the other board members were outraged that Agnes would stick up for "this criminal who endangered the entire community," as one put it, and eventually voted her off the board, an action permitted by the county charter. The same charter did not prohibit her from running the following year, which she did, easily earning a spot back among the same council members who threw her out.

People didn't care much about Alvin, who landed in the county rec department with a better-looking uniform and a slight salary hike, but they loved Agnes Stono. She was a large woman with a small, devoted dog named *J.R.*, after the handsome villain in *Dallas,* her all-time favorite TV show. J.R. Stono was fawn-colored with a black mask and lustrous black eyes that bulged out of his 14-pound frame, which stood just 10 inches off the ground. Like his namesake, he was a bit of a rogue. Once, when the Stonos were out, J.R. found and burrowed his way into a nearly-full box of chocolate-covered cherries. After devouring every piece and licking the cherry goo off his dark muzzle, he plopped down on their eggshell-white leather couch and promptly got ill. "J.R. Stono, what did you do!" Agnes said when they returned. "That's a bad boy. Baaad boy."

Still, her voice was soft, not harsh. Agnes had a weakness for the dog's wise, wrinkled brow and corkscrew tail, and was hardly ever seen in public or private without J.R.

Agnes' second, more serious passion was helping the quiet, simple folks who lived by choice or circumstance in rural Sumter County. They were people who lived country miles from jobs and doctors, people who too often shook their heads and went back to their chores after hearing that a child had to repeat a grade, or, later, earned barrel-bottom SAT scores. They were the people who got passed over—or who more likely never were considered—when government grants filtered down from Washington.

Agnes was also the aunt of congressional candidate Derrick Maussipant of Charleston. Dashing as he was, everyone knew her tall, athletic nephew didn't have a chance against Ike, or even against Cady Owens or Dianna Harley. But he did have a small following that mirrored his youth, eagerness and attractiveness, and which he could bring to the negotiating table.

When Ike came downstairs, Agnes' table was in fact the first thing he saw. Piles of pancakes and Belgian waffles filled two white, leaf-shaped platters that sat in the middle of an all-you-can-eat buffet jazzed up with a rose-colored tablecloth and two slender, crystal vases overflowing with fresh jessamine. Red-eye gravy, thick and brown, bubbled in a flame-heated ceramic boat, waiting for the biscuits that were rising in the oven. Beside the gravy was a family-sized orange-and-white bowl with grits that were laced with butter *and* cheddar cheese. The coffee brewing was strong, Ike guessed Colombian. Other platters were heaped high with scrambled eggs, bacon, sausage, and fruit salad.

"Quite a spread, Agnes."

She smiled and lit two soft-pink candles, even though the sun was already so bright, the living room shades were drawn.

"I want to help you, Ike, you know that. We've been friends a while and I'd like you to succeed."

He heard a car pull into the driveway and turned his head, but Agnes Stono kept talking.

"You're going to need some help, not just the kind you can get from Lander McCauley. After breakfast, we're going on a field trip. It'll help you understand this district a little better."

Derrick Maussipant appeared at the front door with two aides. He was taller than the doorway and had to duck to be seen by the people inside.

Ike looked at Agnes, but she walked past him. "Hello, nephew, come in. We were just sitting here talking about life's curious twists and turns." J.R. kept a respectful distance from Derrick's size fourteen penny loafers.

"Hey, Ike."

"Derrick," he said, trying to look as if he'd been expecting the younger man.

"My campaign manager, Janet Herman, and my scheduler, Robert Bocci."

Ike shook everyone's hand, making sure to repeat each name, but kept looking to Agnes. She caught his eye, but apparently wasn't ready to deal. "No one talks business until all this food is gone. That includes you, Alvin Stono," she said to her husband, who was walking downstairs in the smart, sky blue pants and shirt worn by employees of the county rec department. Alvin froze mid-stair and saluted. Derrick laughed and accepted a plate from Agnes. The others fell in behind him.

Chairs with trays had been set up in the living room because Agnes' breakfast feast took up the entire kitchen. Ike sat next to Derrick and tried talking basketball. "Heard there's some hotshot in Williamsburg scoring twenty a game," he said, all the while thinking how nice it would be to add Williamsburg and other Maussipant strongholds to his own electoral column.

Derrick nodded. "Todd Jamison. The real thing. Six-three, two-thirty, can shoot, drive, and handle the ball. Everyone's after him—Duke, Maryland, UNLV, Arizona, North Carolina. I heard he's leaning to the Tar Heels." Agnes jumped in. "I know the Jamisons. What that boy needs is a team with a deep bench. Lots of good teams make the NCAA tournament, but the ones that advance are the ones with more than five or six good players."

Neither man could disagree.

"Which gets me nicely to why we're here." Ike put down his plate and wiped his mouth with a napkin. Derrick and his aides did the same. Alvin Stono kept eating. J.R. worked his way to Ike's plate, stood on his stubby back legs, and began helping himself.

"I don't BS around, Ike, I'm not going to start now. Derrick here is doing nicely for his first time out. He's built up some support in the Lowcountry and around Columbia. But we all know he doesn't have the resources to keep going, and no one's stepped forward to bankroll the rest of his campaign. He and I have discussed it, and he wants to throw in with you."

"Why, I'd be delighted."

"Let me finish. He's not coming empty-handed and he doesn't want to leave that way. Derrick?"

Derrick Maussipant leaned forward, hands on his knees like he was going to rise from his chair, but stayed seated. "It's simple, Ike. If I work for you now, I want to keep working for you after you're elected. I want to be your legislative director in Washington."

"But I've already got … "

"I know Ruthie Baines. The job she wants is chief of staff. That's fine. I'm a lawyer; I want to focus on legislation, not administrative stuff. Actually, I think we'd make a good team, which would reflect well on you. One more thing." Gesturing to his aides, he said, "Janet and Robert want in too. They'll need full-time staff jobs in D.C. or here in the state after the election."

Ike knew he should discuss it with Ruthie first, and maybe even McCauley, but the deal was too tempting. Maussipant's crowd would add a mid-season spark and deliver hundreds, maybe thousands of voters in areas where he, Ike, was weakest. He looked to Agnes, who narrowed her eyes and nodded that he should go for it.

Ike stood and shook hands before Derrick could get up, ensuring he wouldn't have to look up at the much taller man.

"Should I announce a press conference?" Derrick said.

"Sure, but hold off one day. There's a reporter I'd like to leak this to. His editors have him nosing around, looking for dirt or controversy—anything to sell newspapers. This is just the thing to throw him off."

"Fine by me," Derrick said. "Aunt Agnes?"

"Yes, do it."

Ike rubbed his hands together briskly. "I'll make sure the Charleston paper gets it first, then we'll do a joint press conference. Where do you want to meet up, Columbia?"

"Columbia it is," Derrick said. "Tomorrow, let's say 10 a.m. The news won't have gotten around that early, even if it's already been in the *Herald-Leader*."

Derrick and his aides took off after breakfast. Alvin Stono pecked his wife's cheek and left for work. Agnes began to clear the dishes and Ike went upstairs to call Ruthie.

"You still in bed?" It was hard to keep the excitement from his voice. "Listen up. Wait, don't get up yet. Better if you're laying down. Maussipant just dropped out. He's coming to work for us."

Ike decided he could wait to tell her the rest of the deal.

Ruthie tried to talk. He cut her off. "Gotta go. Agnes has something to show me; I don't know what it's about. She knows everyone around here and it could mean votes. I'll meet you later. Shhh, listen. I want you to leak the news about Derrick to Patragno when you see him. Let him use it for tomorrow's paper. We'll—Derrick and me—we'll make it official tomorrow at a joint press conference in Columbia. That's it."

Agnes called from the kitchen. "Ike, you ready?"

"Pumped and primed, Agnes. Let's go."

"J.R., come to mommy, we're going for a ride." She kneeled and the dog jumped into her arms. She held her face out and he licked it with a pink tongue not much wider than a postage stamp. "Good baby, good boy."

On the way out of town, Agnes took him down the 100 block of Church Street, where century-and-a-half-old Victorian homes made of stately red brick and fitted with wrap-around porches made Ike wonder if there was a better place to live than South Carolina. Nearly all the homes had long, swaying trails of lavender and white Japanese irises that looked like fancy gift-wrapping. Out on West Liberty Street was Swan Lake Iris Gardens. The name was clunky but accurate, for, Agnes said, seven of the eight known varieties of swan lived in the park and fished its lake amid ancient stands of cypress, oaks, pines, and iris gardens bursting with color.

Out on the main drag, the ambience was less inspiring: the usual strip malls, a few dominated by an occasional *Super K* or *Home Depot*; more than enough fast food joints to keep the local cardiologists busy; a few beat up-looking motels and hotels, and a clutch of gas stations whose location at the edge of town suggested the end of civilization and the beginning of a hard, lonely wilderness that did not embrace strangers foolish enough to run out of fuel.

Ike soon saw this wilderness was precisely where Agnes Stono was headed.

"I know you didn't grow up in no three-story brick mansion, Ike, but you didn't have to grow up like this neither. That people still have to live like this in 1992"—she shook her head and made sounds of disgust—"well, you'll see."

She didn't say anything else, just kept driving down the winding, two-lane country road until they hit a green and white sign marked *Crayesville*. Agnes turned right at the sign, drove another half-mile, then took another right at an unmarked dirt road. Ike remembered Ascension Road in Kilgo and knew that even a mid-sized storm would make this hilly trail impassable.

"Keep in mind we're less than three miles from city limits," she said. Agnes followed a pair of grooves in the light brown earth etched by what Ike figured were truck tires until they reached a one-story wood frame house with a pitched roof made of rectangular slabs of tin held in place by three, perilously thin wood posts. The porch floor sat two feet off the ground, propped up by grayish cinder blocks that had been placed vertically, rather than flat, for a bit more height. There was an ancient wicker rocker on the porch and, beside it on the floor, two, old green plastic bowls, one empty, one half-filled with water. Ike noticed J.R. staring as if the bowls might hold treats laid out for him.

An elderly black woman, very small with pearl-framed glasses too big for her tiny face and a faded, plaid shawl around her shoulders despite the heat, stepped into the doorway as they got out of the car and walked toward the concrete stairs.

"Hello, Miss Josephine."

Miss Josephine pulled at the ends of her shawl. "You here to see my toilet again?"

Ike looked at Agnes. He'd expected a tour of rundown homes, some perhaps with teen-age mothers and shabbily-dressed children. There would be an old bike with flat tires and a rusty basket, a burned out pickup in back that the kids used for rock-throwing practice, wet clothes pinned to a line that fit every size except the absent father. He'd seen it all before. But toilets?

"Yes, ma'am," Agnes said to the wary woman. "This is Isaac Washington, going to be our next congressman. I wanted him to have a look, explain the situation out here."

The woman looked skeptical. If she'd had a rifle, it would still be trained on them, Ike thought. Miss Josephine weighed things a moment more and waved them up the steps and into her home. J.R. came too.

"Best watch that little thing," Miss Josephine said. "Shamus in here'll swalla' him whole. He's been ornery lately. Belly's hurtin'."

Agnes bent over to scoop up J.R., but he slipped past her and beelined straight to Shamus. Agnes stood ramrod straight and screamed,

"J.R. Stono!" Her tone froze the little dog, but too late. Shamus, a cocktail of pit bull and shepherd, met him in the center of the living room with teeth bared. Ike and Agnes stared at the standoff—it looked like snack time for Shamus. Miss Josephine moved with surprising agility. She snatched a cherry-wood cane with a bone-colored, fist-shaped handle and gave Shamus a rap on the snout. The dog yelped and slithered to a back bedroom, long skinny tail hanging low between his legs. J.R. did a victory prance back to Agnes, who seemed unable to decide whether to kiss or scold.

"What did you do!" Kiss, kiss. "Bad, boy, scaring mommy." Kiss, kiss. "Don't you ever … " Kiss, kiss.

Miss Josephine looked at Ike. "Told you ta watch that thing. Toilet's over there."

The bathroom to which she pointed appeared ordinary enough, though the toilet looked considerably newer than the other fixtures. When Ike flushed, nothing happened. He lifted the seat and saw there was no water. He removed the top of the tank and saw that it, too, was dry.

He replaced the tank top and closed the plastic lid. "Well, it's sure not going to work without any water."

Miss Josephine made a tsk-tsk sound, pressed her lips together, shook her head. "Our next congressman," she said, arms crossed.

"That's the point, Ike," Agnes said. "The folks out here—there are 34 homes—aren't connected to the city sewer lines because they live just outside city limits."

"Simple," he said, taking a seat on the throne as if he were king and had divined the answer. "Septic tanks."

"Our next congressman," Miss Josephine repeated, removing her shawl and wrapping it around her hands. Her shoulders were barely wider than a wire clothes hanger.

"They can't get permits from the county, Ike," Agnes said. "Ground's too muddy."

Ike crossed his legs. "Ground's too soft for septic tanks and they can't get hooked up to the city sewers." He couldn't quite grasp it. "Why is it that they can't get tied into the sewer system?"

Miss Josephine clicked her tongue and walked out, leaving Agnes and Ike alone in the dysfunctional bathroom. "Four million reasons, Ike."

"Huh?"

"That's what it will cost—four million bucks to connect these *country* folks to Sumter's sewer system." Agnes' voice dropped a bit. She hugged J.R. close to her bosom. "That's also what it'll cost for Agnes Stono to deliver Sumter County to Ike Washington in November."

Ike exhaled and made a whistling sound.

"I don't want a thing for myself," Agnes said quickly, putting J.R. down and warning him to stay put. "But it's outrageous that this poor old woman has to use an out-house. An *out-house*, Ike. In nineteen hundred and ninety-two. You figure out a way to make this happen, and I'll work hard enough to make folks think I'm the one running for Congress. Once we get Sumter wrapped up, I'll get up to Kershaw, Lee, and Darlington counties."

Ike was still thinking about the toilet. "You don't care if I ask for the senator's help on this." It was a question, even though his voice didn't rise at the end.

"I'll be straight, Ike. I don't like that man, never have. Don't want a thing to do with him. Mac McCauley was a racist in the old days, and if he changed, he changed to hold on to his job. I myself don't think he's changed a bit. But no, I don't care where the money comes from. This job is long overdue. If these folks were white and the community was called

Sumter Estates instead of Crayesville, it would have been done a long time ago."

"I'm thinking the senator could shake some money loose from the Department of Housing and Urban Development. You know, HUD."

Agnes laughed. "Don't talk like a bureaucrat, Ike. Doesn't impress me. Bring me a check with one four and a lot of zeroes."

Ike wasn't certain he could deliver, but stood and shook hands, sealing his second deal of the morning.

Agnes looked him over and glanced slyly at her watch. "Eleven-thirty and you've already wrapped up maybe half-a-dozen counties," she said. "Told you this was going to be a good day."

Miss Josephine reappeared. Her shawl was back on, and the cherry-wood cane was in her hand. "What on earth are you two still doing in here?"

"Just leaving, ma'am," Ike answered, gently touching the woman's bony elbow. "That's a beautiful shawl. Did you make it?"

The woman pulled away. "Watch your little dog on the way out. I let Shamus out the bedroom and his mood ain't much improved."

Agnes gathered J.R. in her arms. "Thank you Miss Josephine; we'll be in touch. Mr. Washington's going to get something done about the sewer situation."

Agnes and J.R. went first. Ike followed, walking sideways as he kept a watchful eye on Shamus. He felt like more like he was escaping than leaving. As he inched along, he backed into a round coffee table, jarring a stocky lamp crowned with a shade of blue and green stained glass. The lamp pitched forward, then back, then forward again.

Ike, still unwilling to turn his back on the guard dog, shot a hand out and made a lucky, blind save. He righted the lamp and hurried for the door.

Shamus growled. Miss Josephine smiled for the first time.

"Our next congressman," she said.

17   *Dan*

He pushed back from the desk and read his first four grafs, the guts of the story.

Former College of Charleston basketball star Derrick Maussipant will abandon his congressional campaign today to support rival Ike Washington, Jr., informed sources have told the *Herald-Leader*.

Washington and Maussipant would not confirm the rumor, but have scheduled a joint press conference for this morning in Columbia.

Maussipant's exit leaves Washington, funeral home owner Cady Owens, and state NAACP Director Dianna Harley as the remaining Democratic candidates vying for the 6th Congressional District. Less than a month remains before the Aug. 25 primary election.

He ran his fingers lightly around the keyboard re-reading, tinkering and considering what should come next. He tapped the dark and light gray rows of letters, numbers and program commands hard enough to create click chatter, and soft enough to keep anything unwanted from appearing on his screen. Typing made him think of Ruth at the piano. "So soft," she'd said. And then—his eyes wandered past the computer screen and became unfocused—and then holding her, breathing her in, the feel of her legs against his as they slept. Okay, as *she* slept. Truth was, he'd been too excited to keep his eyes closed, too amazed at the past few hours, too thrilled to learn that she slept naked. In the morning, still lying with her back to his chest, he'd lifted the covers slightly to look down at their bodies. He thought he was tan from being outside so much, but his legs were pale next to Ruth's dark skin. He stared a moment longer and pulled the blanket back up. Was race part of the attraction? Was it for her? He didn't think so and hoped not. He remembered pulling her closer and kissing her sweet neck over and over. She snuggled against him and they made love again, more slowly this time, the bedroom swirling with triangles of warm sunlight carved by a glass prism suspended from the cathedral ceiling.

Afterward, they made blueberry pancakes. They ate and shared the newspaper. He liked that the first section she reached for was sports, and that she seemed to like reading quietly as much as him. Later, when he cleared the dishes, she surprised him, spraying him with a burst of lukewarm water from the sink hose. They'd wrestled and somehow wound up back in the bedroom. She was strong. He liked that, too.

"PATRAGNO!"

He stiffened and pulled his eyes back to the screen.

"Do I get that story sometime tonight?"

"Ten minutes, Lem."

Butcher looked at his watch, shook his head. "See me when you're done."

"Sure," he answered, though he couldn't imagine what *that* was about. He pushed the city editor from his mind and forced himself to stop thinking of Ruth. What else did people need to know about Derrick supporting Ike? That's all that mattered for the story. There were a few questions he couldn't answer. Like, why was this happening now?

Derrick was low on campaign cash, but could have hung on through the primary. And, what was Maussipant getting out of the deal? No answers at the moment. He wrote it the best he could, using phrases like, "It's unclear why Maussipant dropped out so close to the election;" and, "Some speculated that Maussipant will land a top staff job if Washington wins the race."

He saved, spell-checked, and shipped it to the Metro desk. "All yours: Twelve inches, slugged, *Derrick.*"

"Where can I find you, Dan?"

"In with Butcher."

Night editor Lee Cohen rolled his eyes. "He's on the rag big-time today."

The city editor who doubled as romance columnist had his shirt sleeves unbuttoned and rolled back twice. His wrists and forearms were meaty enough to hide the veins beneath the putty-colored flesh. Butcher closed the door, a bad sign.

"This wasn't the assignment."

It took a second to understand his boss's shorthand. Butcher spoke the way reporters were supposed to write: inverted pyramid; news first, background second. He realized Butcher was criticizing him for bringing back a story other than the one he was assigned several days ago in this very office. "I'm not done with the big profile," Dan said. "This came up and I thought we should have it in the paper. No one else has this story for tomorrow. We beat everyone."

"Where'd it come from?"

Dan laced his fingers, put them behind his head. "A credible source."

"It came from Ike Washington's camp, right?"

"What's it matter? It's accurate and it's news."

Lem Butcher rose from the corner of his desk. He walked to the window and stared down for a moment at the newspaper's parking lot. This late, the lot was usually empty. "Don't you see, kid? They fed you this. They're making nice with you. You took it like a trained pup."

Dan re-tied his right moccasin. Too tight. He did it again. "That story is news no matter where it came from," he said. "Besides, I can take a good story without losing sight of the bigger piece. You know I can." He let his chin drop and clasped his hands between his knees, trying to think it through. He flexed his toes in the re-tied moccasins, looked back up. "What's this really about, Lem?"

"Where'd you get the story?"

"I told you."

"Specifically."

"Ruth Baines, Ike's campaign manager." It came out more quietly than he intended.

Lem looked in his eyes. "You sleeping with her?"

"How's that your business?"

"It's my business 'cause I'm your editor. If you're involved with a source on an important story, I need to know."

"How about you judge my work on its merits, and if I have a romance problem, I'll write *Dear Lem*."

The hint of a smile appeared on Butcher's thin lips. He played his thighs like bongos, then looked out the window again and glanced up, as if searching for the thunderstorms that were supposed to roll through before midnight. "You've got balls, Patragno. Here barely more than a year, talking to me like that. I like it." Butcher returned to the corner of his desk and hitched his pants before sitting down. "But I still need to know. Are you seeing that woman?"

That woman. He fought to keep his voice even. "Yeah, I'm seeing her. But it hasn't affected one word I've written. And it won't."

"No, it sure won't."

Dan waited. Butcher was looking at him dead on again.

"You're off Ike Washington. Until I say different, you're on general assignment. Ask Cohen what he wants you to cover tomorrow."

"You can't do that. I've got … "

"You've got a vested interest in the goddamn outcome of this election."

Dan stood. Butcher, smaller by two inches, older by two decades, faced him. They were close enough to trade uppercuts. Dan could see a faint line of dirt around the inside ring of his boss's white shirt collar. The guy was screwing with his career. He fought an impulse to grab Butcher's loosened tie and plaster him against the office door.

"I don't have any vested interest. I couldn't care less if he wins or not."

Butcher shook his head to say he'd heard the same arguments before in other battles with other reporters, battles he'd apparently won without exception. His response, quick, harsh, trampled the end of Dan's last sentence.

"Tell it to Dianna Harley and Cady Owens. Tell it to the hundreds— what am I saying—the *thousands* of people who are voting for them and who read this newspaper. Tell all those people you're not going to slant your reporting to help your new girlfriend."

"I would, but it's nobody's business."

"It doesn't matter. You're off the race."

Dan glanced toward the newsroom. The shouting match had drawn attention. He caught Lee Cohen looking directly at him, but *everyone* was watching. Reporters, copy kids, and the rest of the night crew—even Cyril and Fabian, the two old brothers who wore color-splotched guaya-bera shirts each night as they swept up the trash—were enjoying the un-expected break in their dreary routine.

Yelling wasn't going to work, that was plain. He backed off and took a turn at the window. When he spoke again, his voice was calm. "Dear Lem," he said, as if reading from a letter. Butcher watched him suspiciously.

Dan picked up a leaf of paper off Butcher's desk and began again. "Dear Lem, I have accidentally fallen for a client of the firm where I work. My boss wants to take me off the case because he says my objectivity has been compromised. I say I can separate personal and professional. Plus, no one at the firm knows this case better than me. Any advice?"

"Cute," Butcher said. "No dice. You don't work for some private firm, you work for a newspaper read every day by the public. Our credibility is all we've got."

"C'mon Lem, meet me halfway."

"There's no halfway, kid. You're either dating this woman or you're not. I can't have you covering Ike Washington if you're involved with his top aide."

"So that's it?"

"That's it."

Dan rummaged through a list of crappy options, rejecting the first outright. He would not break up with Ruth. He could quit; he could go over Butcher's head to Marshall Ryder, the executive editor; or he could lie. Quitting would wreck his resume, going to Ryder would ruin his life at the *Herald-Leader,* even if Ryder were to take his side, which was unlikely; and lying would probably get him fired, which was a blacker mark than quitting.

He rubbed a sore spot on the back of his neck. For a moment, there was silence. He saw Butcher check his watch. Wait, there was another way.

"The election is less than a month away," he said, suddenly excited.

"If Ike wins, he goes to Washington; I won't be covering him anyway. If he loses, he won't be news anymore and nobody will be covering him. I don't want to do this, I don't think it's necessary, but, what if I put the relationship on hold until after the election?"

Butcher held up a finger, opened his door and snarled at the newsroom audience. "If you people don't have any work to do, get the hell outa' here."

Eyes cut back to computer screens, hands reached for telephones, enthusiastic sweeping commenced.

Butcher closed the door and faced him. "You'd agree to that."

"Yes."

"I'd have your word."

"I swear it."

"How 'bout her?"

"She'll understand. She doesn't want to screw this up either."

"One a.m., Friday night, you're alone, she wants you to come over. She's panting in the phone."

"I can resist for three-and-a-half weeks."

Butcher looked at him squarely. "I'd be reading every word of your copy myself. One thing looks out of whack—just one thing—and you'll be on night cops until the next century."

"I'd agree to that."

Butcher put his hands on Dan's shoulders. "I'm not kidding. I'd probably have to fire you."

"I know."

Butcher turned and leaned against the door. Still facing away, he sighed and said, "Okay. Don't mess up."

"Thanks, Lem."

"Don't thank me; just don't make me sorry. Now let's get a beer."

When they were seated at the *Hydrant*, tall, iced glasses of Heineken half drained, Butcher told him why the first few days would be easy to stay away from Ruth.

"I want you to go to D.C., interview Senator McCauley about Ike."

"When?"

"Soon as you can set it up. Tomorrow, if he'll see you."

Dan took a long drink. Bernie had suggested an interview with McCauley the night they were here with Stan. "Good idea."

"Let's talk about what you're going to ask him," Butcher said. "Get your pad."

•••••

Jane Peeples, the press secretary, was surprisingly agreeable the following morning. After checking with McCauley, she phoned back and said that If Dan could get himself to D.C., the senator would see him at 4 p.m. "Come to my office when you get to the Hill," she said. "I'll take you over."

Washington was so different from Charleston, it always surprised him that the flight was barely over an hour. He landed at National just after three, and, after a brief mix-up over arrival gates—all of *USAir's* bays were occupied, which resulted in a ten-minute delay and muttered curses from a group of South Carolina businessmen—grabbed a black and yellow city cab. At the Russell Building, Dan looked at his watch and saw he was a half-hour early. He wound up talking with a cute, strawberry blonde receptionist with apple-red lips who manned the senator's phone lines and front office. Her name was Lila and she spoke in a Southern drawl undiluted by her time in Washington. After a few minutes of chit-chat and mild flirting, she got to what was bothering her. "How come you work for Charleston and talk like a Yankee?" she said.

"I work for a South Carolina paper, but I'm from up north."

She looked confused, so he put on a McCauley-like accent and said sweetly, "But I surely love your be-yoo-ti-ful state."

Fifteen painful minutes passed before Jane Peeples emerged. He noted the press secretary rated an office with a door and window that looked toward the Capitol; most of the other staffers labored in cubicles separated by long rectangular blocks covered in soft blue cloth.

He'd spoken to Jane Peeples by phone, but had never seen her. She was a slightly heavy woman of about forty who struck him as someone constantly on the lookout for ways to get two, maybe three, things done at the same time. He could see her driving one-handed, the other five fingers wrapped around a cup of coffee, a cell phone, or maybe the morning paper. Indeed, when she came out, Jane Peeples was still wearing a telephone headset that kept her hands free. The coiled, connecting wire dangled down her back. She put one hand in his to shake hello and used the other to sweep back a nest of wavy brown hair that had broken free of the morning mousse. Her fingers knocked the headset to the floor. He moved to pick it up, but she beat him, talking all the while.

"Dan, it's been crazy around here today. He might be a little late for your appointment."

"No problem," he said, thinking, *There goes the 6:30 back to Charleston.*

The near-secret trail that coiled around to Senator Lander McCauley's private office in the Capitol was predictable: polished marble floor, large paintings in heavy, gold frames that depicted momentous events in American history, and two clean-shaven cops stationed midway between the office door and an adjoining corridor. What surprised him was that no one seemed to notice the somber, mellifluous music that filled this tiny alcove in the Capitol. It was a reedy sound that made him think of an Irish funeral, though he'd never been to one.

"That's Auralee," Jane Peeples said. "She's our receptionist, and a part-time musician. When there's down time, she practices her bassoon."

Dan nodded. He'd heard life inside the Beltway was a different animal.

"Do all senators have private offices in the Capitol?"

"Nope," she said with a toss of her hair. The answer didn't tell him much, but he recognized the tone. Trash talk. As in, *My boss rates.*

Jane opened the door to an empty office with an antique desk, two chairs and a couch, and a narrow, yellow-and-white-curtained window that stretched from floor to ceiling. Auralee was apparently practicing inside McCauley's inner sanctum.

"Auralee, yoo-hoo," Jane called toward another door. "Miss DeMossier."

The music continued, sad and plodding. Now the melancholy strains made Dan think of the Saturday-morning cartoons of his youth: hulking, patch-eyed pirates, vanquished rivals forced to walk the plank, a treasure map scrawled on crinkly parchment … Jane Peeples opened the inner door and hissed, "*Auralee.*" Dan peered in and saw Auralee pull a cane-colored mouthpiece from her lips. Her cheeks were pink and swollen, as though ready to blow into the next passage.

"Dan Patragno is here from the *Herald-Leader.* He has an appointment with the senator at four. I need to get back to my office. Please come take charge."

The breath that would have formed a flurry of notes came out of Auralee's mouth as an exasperated whistle. "Right there," she said.

Jane Peeples raised her eyebrows and left, waving briskly as she departed. Dan sat on one of the high-backed, black leather chairs in the outer office. Auralee joined him and began dismantling her instrument. The inside of the fake alligator bassoon case was lined with plush, blue felt.

"You play very well."

"Thanks, hon." The bassoon was made of reddish-brown wood and had silver keys. She wiped each section with a gray cloth before placing it in the proper compartment in the case.

"What was that you were working on?"

"You know Mozart?"

"Not really."

"That was Wolfgang's concerto in B flat."

"You play in a symphony?"

Auralee snorted. "No, just a community orchestra. And here," she said, her eyes circling the private office of Senator Lander McCauley." Dan made a mental note to find out how much the taxpayers were laying out per annum for Mac McCauley to keep the bassoon-playing Auralee DeMossier tucked away in a secret office. God knows what else she was playing up here.

"So, have you heard from the senator?"

"He doesn't tell me his schedule." She looked at the clock above her desk. It was already 4:15. "I don't know what to tell you. You can wait if you want. I'm here 'til six. Coffee?"

"Sure." Dan kept his pad in his pocket, but stored away the information Auralee seemed only too happy to impart. She seemed sad and lonely, all dressed up and smelling like rosy car deodorizer. He wanted her to leave the room, go to the bathroom or something, so he could write it all down.

At 4:45, their conversation exhausted, Mac McCauley burst into the office.

"You Patragno?" he said, mispronouncing his name with a hard g.

"Pa-*trano*," Dan corrected. He rose to shake hands, but McCauley never fully entered the room.

"I apologize, son, but we got a committee mark-up going on, and if I'm not there, those sharks are going to gobble up all the bacon I got marked for the great state of South Carolina. Be back soon as I can."

With that, he left and Dan found himself alone again with Auralee. "That's the boss."

"Know when the last flight back to Charleston leaves?"

"We can check." She pulled out a laminated sheet of paper. The top third, he could see, was filled with a carefully-drawn picture of a house key and the numeral symbol followed by an "s" to make it plural. He puzzled over the meaning for a second, then realized: *Key Numbers.* Yes, Auralee was surely servicing more than the taxpayers in Mac McCauley's hideout.

She ran a pink fingernail down the left side of the page. "*USAir?*" She found it, dialed, and used the airlines' automated system to get the information without speaking to a single person. "Plenty of time," she said. "Last one leaves at 9:30."

It was twenty minutes before Auralee's quitting time when McCauley returned.

"I apologize again, young man," he said, ignoring Dan's response and turning to Auralee. "Anyone on my trail, Miss DeMossier?"

"No, sir."

Dan thought he saw the senator frown at Auralee as she gathered her things—the day was not quite over, after all—but if he did, she pretended not to notice. "It was nice talking to you, Mr. Patragno. Senator, I'll see you in the morning."

"Enjoy your evening," McCauley said a little too formally. He motioned Dan into the inner office and followed him through the door. When they were inside, he said, "Gal's the best secretary I've ever had.

Knows where I'm supposed to be better than I do. Musician, too. Plays a big, old bassoon."

"I heard."

McCauley shucked off his charcoal suit jacket and hung it neatly in a closet. "Oh?"

"She was finishing up when I got here with Jane."

"Ah, well, if she's caught up with her work, I don't mind her practicing. Adds some class to the place."

Dan took out his pad and flipped past three pages of notes he'd scribbled earlier when Auralee took a bathroom break. Though anxious to begin, McCauley's confidence—or was it arrogance, given how he'd casually blown off the earlier appointment—made him nervous. "Senator, you know I'm here to talk about Mayor Ike Washington of Kilgo."

"Good man."

"Yes, well the first thing is, could you tell me how he came to work for you? How long has it been? (*Christ, stop rushing. Let him answer.*) How did you first meet Ike?"

McCauley laughed. "That's three questions in one." He squeezed his cheeks thoughtfully between thumb and index finger, then let the digits slide to his chin. "Don't remember the year, it was a long time ago. I think I was in the Statehouse, that would have been around the early Sixties, when this place"—he gestured out the window to indicate the nation's capitol—"was overrun with draft-dodgers and hippies and pot and women who wouldn't wear bras and men who wouldn't get haircuts. Jesus H."

"You were saying about Ike … "

"What? Oh. Ike was just a kid."

A light within the phone on a coffee table began to blink and he picked it up. "McCauley." Dan shut his tape recorder. McCauley swung around in his chair, showing Dan his back, and threw his feet up on his desk. "Teach his Texas ass to mess with me," he said into the receiver. "My people need that money. That bridge is so decrepit, I make Mrs. McCauley take another route to town. He wants his project, he better back mine." McCauley listened a moment and started punching his finger into the air. The angrier he got, the more pronounced his Southern drawl became. "No suh, that ain't goin' ta happen. Your boy must need ta sneeze, cause his brains are all fulla dust." Another silence while he listened. Then, "Nope. No, that ain't happenin.' *No*."

Dan began to wonder if McCauley'd forgotten him. He cleared his throat, loud enough to be heard, not so loud that it would come off rude. The senator remained on the phone. At least three minutes had passed. What should he do? What *could* he do? Dan looked around the room, his patience gone. He'd flown all this way, put up with airport hassles, parochial secretaries and an hour of the rose-scented Miss Auralee DeMossier, and now the guy he came to interview was ignoring him.

He stood and walked to a spot where McCauley would have to see him. He feigned interest in a large black-and-white photo of downtown Kilgo taken on—he scanned the corners and found the date penned in black marker in the upper right side—8/1/59. Closer inspection showed it was Mac McCauley, Sr. standing in front of *McCauley's Drugstore* in a striped shirt and pants with suspenders. He was a husky, proud-looking man with straight hair slicked back with whatever tonic passed for gel in those days. The glass in the storefront behind him was so clean, Dan could see that the photographer had captured some sort of parade in the reflection. Most people in the crowd were watching a caravan of—what was it, a marching band, some kind of floats, a caravan of animal cages—crawling down the street. Two young black men were the exception. They were facing the store, watching McCauley get his picture taken. Though small and in the background, Dan could see that one wore a white apron and was leaning against a broom. Half a toothpick stuck out from his mouth. The other was simply observing, arms at his sides, as Mac McCauley senior half-smiled for the camera.

"That there was my daddy."

McCauley's voice startled him.

"Nice photograph," Dan said. "I wasn't even born in 1959. What was going on that day? Looks like a parade."

"Circus came to Cady County for the very first time. A grand day."

"Who are these two guys?" he said, pointing at the two black men.

McCauley rose and joined him in front of the photo. "Damned if I know. Might have worked at the store."

Dan looked another moment, then returned to business. "You were telling me about Ike."

"Ike's going to make a great congressman. He knows that new district, knows the people, knows the problems."

"Yes, sir, but I was asking about how the two of you met."

"Not much to tell. I was county judge and planning my first run for the Statehouse. Handful of us Democrats were running in the primary; figured if I could get the blacks to vote for me, I'd have an edge. I hired Ike to help me win those black voters."

"But Ike was just a kid, then. What did he know about politics?"

McCauley laughed bitterly. "Son, you think politics has always been what it is today? Polls, consultants, TV ads—sellin' candidates like laundry soap? Winning an election Tuesday and startin' out Wednesday raisin' money for the next race? We weren't slaves to surveys or focus groups back then. We went to a neighborhood, found out what was on folks' minds, where they needed help. No pollster politics. If they liked you and you got things done, you got the votes. Man, I used to wear out two pairs of leather shoes every time I ran a race."

"Were you the first to court black voters in Kilgo?"

"Surely one of them."

"That must have been an odd feeling."

"Meaning what?"

"Just that growing up in the segregated South, it must have been hard to suddenly go with hat in hand to the people who were considered second-class citizens."

"I never considered anyone second class, Mr. Patragno. The doctrine was 'separate but equal,' and I didn't make it up. That was the law and I lived by it."

Horseshit, Dan thought. But he was getting off track. "So Ike, a kid ..."

"A kid who was sharp and willing to learn what needed learning."

"Yes, a kid who was sharp and willing to be trained, became your liaison to the black community."

"Liaison's your word, son. Ike Washington was a smart kid with a lot of ambition. He had a good mama—his daddy died young—and he wasn't afraid of gettin' in the trenches and working hard. He learned his job fast and moved up. And that's why he's going to become a congressman, and why me and him are going to be working together again real soon."

"Working together is not the same as him working for you."

"That's why I said it the way I did."

Dan locked eyes with the senator and was surprised when McCauley looked away first. The old man sucked at something in his back teeth and shook his head.

"I'll let you in on something" he said. "You can write it or save it, I don't care. But this is why Ike's going to be good up here. Just today he called about a problem down in Sumter. Now he ain't even the congressman yet, but he saw something wrong, something unfair, and wants to get it fixed. There's a small part of town outside the city sewer system. Bunch of houses there—think he said forty of 'em—don't have no sewers and the folks can't get permits for septic tanks 'cause the ground ain't just so. You're a smart reporter. You want to know why they can't just tie 'em into the sewer line. They can't do it 'cause no one's got the four million bucks it's going to cost to do the job."

McCauley bit the end off a cigar and fired it up with a silver lighter. Dan scribbled. His mind was racing. Was this political sleight of hand or the type material that makes great profiles? Was McCauley leading him away from the real story, or making the story more real with an inside look at how things actually get done in D.C.? Cracker frankness or city smarts?

"Tell you something, Dan," McCauley said with a conspiratorial nod. "I haven't seen any of this first-hand, but Big Ike convinced this senator with one phone call. I'm going to do all I can to get a chunk of the money Sumter needs to get those poor bastards some toilets. That's just plain fair."

Dan wrote furiously.

"Jesus H, don't write that I said 'bastards;' use some other word."

Dan kept his eyes low as he wrote, but nodded yes, sure, no trouble, happy to oblige. He'd decide later whether to quote him precisely.

McCauley checked the time. "You get one more question, son. I got places to be. A senator's day doesn't end when the sun goes down, like some around here."

Dan considered calling him Mac. After all, the senator had called him Dan, and everything seemed so nice and friendly. He found he couldn't summon the nerve.

"Senator, are you going to campaign for Ike down in the state?"

McCauley looked him up and down. "You mean, would an outright endorsement help or hurt Ike with the blacks? Why don't you say it straight? I don't mind answering."

Dan knew his cheeks and ears were getting dark. He saw McCauley staring and felt like a red-eared fool. He forced himself to say it:

"Would your campaigning with Ike help or hurt him with black voters?"

"Damned if I know, son, and I'm leaving it up to Ike. If he wants me, I'm there. If not, there's plenty to do around here. Look around." He stood, dismissing the young reporter. "Now, you say 'hey' to the big bosses down in the Holy City. Tell 'em I'll be in to see 'em next time I'm down."

18   Ruthie

"Are you Ms. Baines?"

Ruthie swung around, chin down, clipboard with the evening's itinerary wedged between hands and elbows. She wore a sleeveless apricot
dress with round sepia and bone earrings and a matching necklace. The
air-conditioned room was too cold—at least for now, since no one had
yet arrived for Ike's speech at the Old Sumter Community Center—and
her arms were dotted with goose bumps. "That's me," she smiled. She put
the clipboard down and rubbed her forearms as if it were winter instead
of 84 degrees outside.

"Agnes Stono," the woman said, hand extended.

"Agnes!" Ruthie brushed past the hand and hugged the older woman, who hugged her back. They stepped apart without quite releasing
each other and began to laugh. "Agnes, Agnes," Ruthie said, looking like
she might start another round of hugging. "You're all Ike's talked about
for two days. You've helped us so much. And now." Her wire-thin gold
bracelets glimmered in the beam of a TV camera light as she reached out
toward the community center and its rows of still-empty seats. "And now
all this. Unbelievable."

Agnes shushed her. "Don't kid yourself, child. Free food is why folks
are coming tonight." She looked Ruthie up and down. "Skin and bones.
Ike ever give you time for a real meal?" Agnes led her along the long wall

on one side of the center. More than a dozen silver casserole trays with *Sterno* lamps had been set in a horseshoe pattern and were crammed with barbecued beef, mashed potatoes, fried chicken, country ham, macaroni and cheese, and banana pudding. Eight plastic pitchers of iced tea, three rows of canned soft drinks, and a rubber bucket of ice cubes filled the last table. "I want to see your plate heaped high later. Make sure you try some of these," she said, steering Ruthie to a platter that made the younger woman pause.

"My mom makes snap beans too," Ruthie said, trying to muster enthusiasm for the slimy-looking green beans.

"Not like mine." Agnes' voice dropped low enough to pass on state secrets. "Onions, salt, pepper, hot sauce and fatback. Makes 'em nice and slippery."

Ruthie laughed. "Snap beans with fatback. Just what the surgeon general ordered."

Agnes led her to the ham, which was sliced and coated with gluey sauce. "Send your surgeon general my recipe for milk gravy. Fry the ham in an iron skillet, brown some flour in the droppings, then pour milk in the pan and stir 'til it's nice and thick."

Ruthie's eyes widened. "*That's* what's on that ham?"

Agnes squeezed her elbow. "You'll love it." People were starting to wander in. Some were still dressed in the day's work outfit: shirt and tie, simple dresses, a variety of blue-collar uniforms. Some had changed to tees and sandals. Ruthie watched as the Sumter neighbors greeted each other with hugs and handshakes. Those who kissed cheeks made sure their lips met flesh. The event was already feeling more like a picnic or family reunion than a political event.

"Those your snap beans, Agnes?" asked a balding, middle-aged man in a tan shirt that said, "Sumter County Fire and Rescue."

"Yep." Agnes wagged a finger. "Hands off 'til after the speech."

By 6:30, the room was so full, three men were sent to a storage room for more folding chairs. Agnes went to a microphone set up on a small stage, welcomed the crowd, and asked everyone to take a seat. "We'll be starting shortly."

Ruthie looked from her watch to the small hallway that led to the community center's front entrance and back to her watch. No Ike. She spotted and hurried over to Cynthia Washington, who had come in with some friends. "Do you know where Ike is?" Ruthie whispered.

Mrs. Washington, dressed more for an evening on the town than a stump speech in the country, touched a gold hoop earring hanging from a delicate, two-inch gold chain and gave Ruthie an appraising look. "That man goes to a hundred events a week. I can't possibly keep track of all his comings and goings. Don't you keep the daily schedule?"

"Yes, but."

"Well, then."

Cynthia Washington turned back to her friends. A few minutes passed. At first, the people were quiet, but then a buzz started. Ruthie felt it. *They got us seated, shut us up—and for what? Why couldn't we eat first? Why can't we eat now?* At 6:45, Agnes shot a look. *Well?* Ruthie walked briskly through the crowd to the front of the building, barely noticing its cinder block and siding construction. She swung open the heavy glass door and was hit by a rush of hot air that made her nose itch and triggered a sneeze. She scanned the gravel parking lot. No *Taurus*, no Ike. The schedule had him at a private fundraiser in nearby Rembert from 5:00 to 6:00. That left plenty of time to get to the center, so where was he? She returned to find Agnes back at the microphone, trying to kill time. People were hungry and getting restless. The aromas wafting over from the casserole trays weren't helping matters.

Agnes' eyes brightened when she spotted Ruthie. "I'm sure Ike—I mean, *the congressman*—will be here any minute," she said playfully, the mike a little too close to her mouth. "For now, I'm going to let you get acquainted with Ms. Ruthie Baines."

Agnes put a hand on her hip, turned sideways, and looked back at the audience over her shoulder. She waved the other hand dismissively and said in a sultry voice, "Ruthie's the one really runs things, anyway. C'mon up here, child."

Ruthie hesitated, pleading with her eyes. "She needs to feel welcome," Agnes said. The crowd was eager for any action and clapped with abandon. Ruthie was trapped. Hands over her mouth, pulse thrumming— this was a first—she walked to the podium and took the mike. Agnes embraced her briefly, whispering, "Talk to them. Tell them about yourself."

Ruthie closed her eyes, as if by doing so she might blink away the now-hushed crowd. It didn't work. She felt Cynthia Washington's hard gaze from a seat near the front and knew Ike's wife was enjoying her discomfort. She said a silent, forceful prayer for Ike to appear that went unanswered. "Hello," she said haltingly. The mike screeched; children clasped their ears. Ruthie moved back a few inches. "Sorry. I said, Hello to y'all."

"'Lo, sister," an old man said, lifting a worn, brown derby as he spoke.

Ruthie flushed. She hadn't expected a response. "Like Agnes said, I'm Ruthie Baines. I'm Ike Washington's campaign manager. I'm twenty-six years old and, well, to tell the truth, this is my first big political campaign."

"Baines," another man said thoughtfully. "There's Pastor Baines up in Florence. You a relation?"

"That's my father," Ruthie said.

"There you go."

A woman in a silky brown-and-black-flowered dress jabbed the man. "Let the girl talk, Cyrus."

Cyrus leaned to the side and cocked his head at the woman. "Just tryin' to make her comfortable."

Ruthie watched the couple and glanced at Agnes, who had taken a seat by the silver platter of country ham. Agnes waved with the back of her hands, urging her to keep going.

"Yes, I grew up in Florence. I'm an only child. My father is Pastor Baines of Union Baptist Church, my mother teaches piano. Ike and my daddy go way back."

"Do you play too, honey?" It was a large, short-haired woman that Ruthie knew to be Mattie Williams, the center's director.

"Why, yes. I double-majored in music performance and political science at USC."

"Play for us, child," the woman said. Ruthie looked around. No piano. Mattie Williams signaled to two men, who disappeared into a storage room and wheeled out a padded dolly that held a new, flat-black spinet. The men rolled the dolly before her. One hit a lever that lowered the piano to the linoleum. The other returned to the storage room for a matching bench.

"You're one of the first to play our new piano," Mattie Williams said proudly.

Ruthie sat and touched the keys experimentally, hoping to get a feel for the instrument before she started playing. She felt the tension ease from her shoulders; this was easier than talking. She glanced back to the director, who nodded. "Go right ahead, hon."

Ruthie put her hands in place and took one more quick look at the audience. The piano had been placed catty-corner to the crowd, so the people could see her face. She began with a long arpeggio that began down in the lowest register and ended on high F, then played the opening refrain of *America the Beautiful* in slow, languorous phrases without any tempo, like a vocalist introducing a song before the orchestra joins in. She didn't know why she chose the patriotic hymn. It felt right and was the first thing to pop into her head.

A good choice, she realized. All talking ceased, and some started humming along. Ruthie ended the first stanza nearly as quietly as she began, stopped for the briefest of moments, then played and held the opening chord. Eyes closed, lips rounded to a perfect circle, she sang, *Oh, beautiful, for spacious skies …*

Voices spoke to her from the audience.

"Yeessss, ma'am."

"Sing, child, sing out." Ike and the food were forgotten. Ruthie's neck and shoulders began to sway as she fell into 6/8 time, the bone centerpiece of her necklace moving to and fro like a hypnotist's medallion. A TV cameraman took interest and began filming. By the time she reached the chorus, people were clapping in rhythm and singing along. Ruthie's voice rang out loudest. She'd started out sweet as summer dew, but her singing now had a bluesy, almost dirty feel. *A-mer-ica, A-mer-ica …* Her throat quivered as she hit the note hard, then dropped off, holding on, but softly. She remembered an instruction in bold, black type from one of her classical pieces: *Very calm and gently expressive: Tres calme et doucement expressif.*

Several were up from their seats and rocking from side to side. Ruthie opened her eyes and smiled as she sang. Director Williams stood in an aisle singing her overworked heart out. Even Cynthia Washington was up.

Ruthie lowered her eyes to the keyboard, where all ten fingers hammered out slow triplets around the lyrics. Ra-ta-ta, Ra-ta-ta, Ra-ta-ta.

Bootlicker

And crown thy good, with bro-ther-hood …

A fresh burst of applause rose from her new fans. Ruthie felt a presence beside her, then heard a deep, off-key voice nearly singing in her ear. She caught a whiff of something like gum or mouthwash—spearmint, peppermint? Ike pecked her cheek, then moved in front of the piano and waded into the crowd, attempting to embrace or shake the hand of every man, woman and child. Ruthie went around one more time. *A-mer-ica, A-mer-ica* … Out of the corner of her eye, she noticed tiny yellow and blue flames bending nearly sideways in the silver Sterno lamps beneath the casserole trays.

The ovation lasted more than a minute. Ike moved back up front, clapping wildly and looking from the crowd to Ruthie, and back again. She worried this might become part of every campaign appearance. Every few moments, Ike stopped applauding, held an open hand out toward Ruthie, then started anew. "Wheeww," he said as order returned. He mopped his forehead with a fresh, white handkerchief. "I don't believe *Mr. Ray Charles* could do it any better." That started another ovation. Ruthie stood and bowed to the audience, then to Ike.

Agnes took her hand, squeezed it, and held on a long time. "Girlfriend," she said, "you in the wrong bizness!"

Ruthie bowed one more time, laughed as the applause continued and curtsied like a little girl. She giggled and put a finger to her mouth, warning her sweetly naive Sumter friends that they'd better hush up so Ike, now center stage, could begin. They were here for him, after all, not her. And he was ready. He cradled the mike with both hands.

"My friends, I would like to talk a few minutes tonight about justice. No, wait." Ike let one hand drop to his side and circled away from the audience. He rubbed his cheek as if trying to decide whether he needed a shave. "What I mean more precisely is not justice, but *fairness*. This morning, my friend Agnes Stono." He and the crowd looked to Agnes, who placed one hand on the other and bowed to indicate she was their friend and servant. "My friend Agnes took me to a part of Sumter I've never seen before."

"Where's that, Big Ike?" the man with the brown hat asked.

"Tell you 'xactly where. Crayesville."

A murmur rose. Everyone knew the problem in Crayesville. The city sewer lines didn't reach, and septic tanks wouldn't work because the ground was too soft. Which meant no toilets and the indignity of doing one's business the way it was done before modern plumbing.

"My friend Agnes took me to a sweet, elderly woman's home in Crayesville, and it was there that I learned that no one—not the city, county, state or federal government—has been able to find the money needed to connect those folks to the city sewers." Ike started another slow circle. His voice got soft. Several shifted forward to hear better.

"So those folks—are there any with us tonight?" Ike waited, no one answered. "Well, those folks have got to use outhouses. *Privies.* In 1992, in George Bush's America, in our great state of South Carolina, some people are still forced to use outhouses. I ask ... Is that right?"

"No!"

"Is it fair?"

"No!"

"It ... is ... humiliating," he said quietly.

Heads nodded in assent.

"It needs to change," Ike said.

"Got that right."

An old man stood. Ruthie recognized him as one of the men who spoke to her earlier, the one who asked about her father. "You gonna change it?" he challenged Ike.

"*Cyrus.*" The woman next to the man was mortified. Necks craned toward Ike. The crowd wanted an answer.

"That's fine, it's a fair question." Ike got a chair and placed it near the front row, seat backward. He straddled it with surprising grace and sat with his thick elbows hanging off the back. The mike was in his right hand as he faced the people, the *voters*. "I can't promise to get the money," he said. "What you get with me is someone who cares enough to try."

"Can't do more than try," someone said.

"And I am already trying, sister," Ike said. "Let me explain, and tell you more about myself at the same time. Some of you know that besides being mayor of Kilgo, I've worked a long time for Senator Lander Mc-Cauley."

Ruthie studied the crowd. By this stage of the campaign, both she and Ike knew that his working for McCauley brought mixed reviews from black audiences. Ike had developed a way of imparting the information almost as an afterthought, a throwaway clause that was rarely the main subject of any sentence. Then he pressed on quick as possible.

"Senator McCauley was not always one with us, but he's a different man in 1992 than he was thirty years ago. I've just today spoken to him on this matter, and he agrees Sumter should get the money needed to extend sewer service to the people of Crayesville."

Ruthie was glad that Ike took a moment to let his words register. When Ike said *us*, the message was that he was nothing more than another humble black man. But *he* made the call to McCauley. McCauley was taking *his* advice. It was *he*, Ike, who had the clout and know-how to make this happen. "The senator wants to help, but of course he's got a hundred other things he's working on. So I'm doing the digging. I'm looking at every possibility—grants, discretionary funds, public-private partnerships—you name it. I'm working with someone from the senator's staff to find the right people at the right agencies to help get that money from Washington to Sumter."

It was working. He could almost feel people deciding to vote for him as he spoke. The faces had become friendlier as the night wore on. Big Ike's sincerity and intensity were appealing, and his connections would actually get things done. Plus, he was mayor of Kilgo. Kilgo wasn't Columbia or Charleston, but being a mayor was probably still good practice for being a congressman.

At least that's what the expressions on these pleasant, serious faces seemed to be saying.

Ruthie had come to think of him as an accident victim. Ike never planned on being there when McCauley and Tyler Hawke murdered Ezra James in the woods. His presence was an accident. Fate. Ike didn't decide to stay when they prepared to hang that poor boy, he froze. She imagined the terror that chained him to his hiding place: Run. *No.* Run. *Can't.* Run. *Too late.*

In the years after, Ike never planned to ride McCauley's bloody coattails, he just got tangled up and hauled along, she believed. Ruthie thought of her own father, who had marched and learned what it meant to spend a night in jail during the Sixties. But her father was a man of God and believed in forgiveness. Pastor Baines, she felt, would approve and agree with Dr. King, who said that the man who couldn't forgive also lacked the capacity to love. As a congressman, Ruthie knew, Ike would work hard to balance the ledger, to help hundreds and thousands more than he ever hurt. He would be driven, and she wanted to be part of the good works that would result.

But these people? All they saw was a husky, good-natured man who wanted a job so badly, he would hustle down any road that got him closer to his goal, even one that led through an old woman's broken bathroom.

Though slightly beyond middle age, he had not lost his idealism or enthusiasm. Ruthie made a mental note. After the election, she would check Ike's returns from Sumter. Between tonight's performance, possible grant money for Crayesville, and the stubborn determination of Agnes Stono, Ruthie guessed Ike would snatch eighty-five percent of the local vote, maybe more.

The candidate had finished and was back in the audience shaking hands. Some bee-lined for the food. Agnes squeezed her knee. "He did good. *You* did good. Now, make sure you eat. And don't forget my snap beans."

Ruthie soon found herself in the center of a growing circle of new fans. They wanted to know if she played and sang professionally. She was that good, they said, and certainly pretty enough. They asked if she sang in her church choir, if she worked with a group, and if they'd made any albums.

"Albums?" She laughed and shook her head. "No, no, you nice people have it all wrong. I'm in politics, not entertainment. It may seem like the same thing sometimes, but it's not."

Ike moved in and joined the fun. He had a paper plate full of chicken, beans and sweet potatoes, but hadn't touched his food. "C'mon, Ruthie, these good folks know it's all show biz. Except when there's a real problem that needs fixin,' that is."

"That's right," she agreed.

The circle broke into little groups, with some talking to Ike and some to Ruthie. At one point, when they were standing nearly back to back, Ike leaned over and said, "I'm staying up here tonight to get another early start tomorrow. I need you to get Cynthia back to Kilgo. You have your car?"

A forty-minute ride alone with the candidate's wife would quickly snuff out the glow of this wonderful night. Still, there was no way to refuse. "Sure, no problem. But didn't Cynthia come with friends?"

"She needs a ride," Ike said in a tone that settled it. "There's one other thing I need to talk to you about. Meet me in the room where they put the piano in about ten minutes."

She got there first. The spinet had been returned and was back up on its dolly on the far wall of the little room. Ruthie walked to the piano and pushed aside its blanket, a heavy, fleece-lined furniture pad. She smoothed her fingers along the slide-down wooden case that covered the keys, then pushed it back and reached for a chord. Why did it feel so awkward? She glanced down and realized the dolly made the piano nearly a foot higher than normal. The doorknob turned and she jumped.

"Sorry," Ike said. "I'll make it quick; we don't want to be missed."

Ruthie slid the keyboard cover down and pulled the blanket in place. Ike walked toward her. "You saved us tonight. Good job."

"Thanks. It did turn out nice."

"Here's the thing, Ruthie. To get Derrick, I had to deal."

"Oh?" she said, her performance and rave reviews suddenly feeling like old news. "What was the deal?"

"Derrick wanted to come to Washington. As legislative director."

"Hold on, that's."

"No, that's not your job, Ruthie. You're going to be chief of staff, he'll be legislative director. Same salaries, same level of responsibility."

"Who's higher?"

"What do you mean, higher?"

She crossed her arms against her chest. "You know what I mean, Ike. Who has the final say?"

"I do."

"Before it gets to you, damn it."

Ike reached out and cleared a wrinkle in the piano blanket. "You do. On close calls, you make the decision."

Ruthie put a hand on his shoulder and made him turn so she could see his face. "Have you told Derrick that?"

"I will."

"Okay, then, I think Derrick is good. I can work with him. But Ike." She backed up a step, stared him down. "You should have told me first. This was a major decision. I'm supposed to be involved in all major decisions."

The candidate held out his hands. "I would have called you, Ruthie. I wanted to. They had me on the spot. Agnes set it up—she's his aunt, you know. They were all there and the deal was too good. I didn't want to take a chance on messing it up. Are we okay, you and me?"

She turned and made him wait. Four-alligator, five alligator. At eight, she turned back. "Just make sure he knows who's in charge."

•••••

"Your car is very bumpy," Cynthia Washington said, patting her hair as if she were going to a party instead of coming from one. She was a small, stately woman who looked out of place in the old *Beetle*. Each rattle made her shift in the vinyl seat.

Ruthie had felt friction from Mrs. Washington since the day they met. At first, she didn't understand the resentment. She'd been friendly and respectful while explaining that to win the race, Ike would have to put in a lot of time on the road. Using a map of the state, she explained that the district—highlighted in blue marker—was huge, much larger than the state's other five seats, and that it wouldn't be possible for Ike to return home every night.

While the state of South Carolina looked like a triangle drawn by a preschooler or a drunk, the revised Sixth District did not match any known geometric shape. Like other Southern districts drawn to satisfy Justice Department orders to remedy past discrimination, it spread throughout the fabric of white South Carolina like black ink on a beige blazer. The awkward lines journeyed north to south in dozens of odd jogs and zigzags that wound up divvying up communities and even small neighborhoods into different congressional districts. All was done to create a seat that would probably be won by an African American who would become the first black congressman since Reconstruction.

Ruthie felt she was clear and objective in how she explained things, and diplomatic in asking that Mrs. Washington be present at as many events as possible. Ruthie and Ike also wanted her to campaign by herself. A second team of assistants would be assembled, and she would cover additional territory, doubling Ike's exposure. Mrs. Washington turned them down. She would stand by her husband's side, but he was the politician, not her.

"Give speeches, talk to reporters? Not me."

Tonight, Mrs. Washington made her wait, talking to friends and hanging around Ike well past the time they could have made a graceful exit. Now she was complaining as they puttered down the dark, two-lane highway that led back to Kilgo.

"This car's a classic," Ruthie said, patting the dash. "'75 *Bug*, champagne silver."

"I liked our *Town Car*. When Ike is elected, we'll get another."

Ruthie wasn't going to fight that battle now. She turned the radio on and found a Beethoven sonata that drowned out much of the road noise.

"Can you lower it?" Cynthia said. "That music gives me a headache."

Ruthie pretended to turn the dial. They drove the next ten minutes without speaking. The night was still warm, but the sky was clear and filled with a bold, luminous moon that nearly made up for the lack of highway lights in rural Sumter County.

When they reached a stop sign in Sardinia, Ruthie tried again. "Mrs. Washington, are you going to move to D.C. after the election or stay here?"

"Oh, my, I would never leave South Carolina. This is my home. Ike can get an apartment in Washington and come back on weekends. That's what most of them do."

"You don't want to go to State Dinners at the White House, meet ambassadors, party at foreign embassies?"

"Heavens, no."

"Don't you want to make friends with the other spouses, like Mrs. McCauley?"

Mrs. Washington folded her hands in her lap. Her wedding ring alone was probably worth more than the Bug. "Ruthie, dear, I have all the friends I need in Kilgo."

Ruthie kept her eyes forward. The answer seemed to confirm what Ike had told her—that not even his wife knew the history of his tie to Lander McCauley. How could it be? How could you live with a man all these years and not know about something that important? Surely Cynthia knew there was something troubling in her husband's past.

The fact that she knew and Cynthia didn't gave her new insight on Mrs. Washington, and on how she must view her husband's top aide. Some things were obvious—Ruthie knew she was younger, prettier, better educated, and more savvy about politics, for instance. But now she'd learned that Ike had confessed his secret to her and not his wife. Was it possible he tried to tell her and she didn't want to know? She almost certainly knew there was *something* ugly in Ike's past. Just like she probably suspected Ike had unburdened himself to her. As a wife, Ruthie felt she wouldn't be able to bear it if her husband could not confide in her.

"Next left," Cynthia said.

They were on Union Street in downtown Kilgo. Ruthie knew the way; she'd picked Ike up at home dozens of times.

Cynthia gave no more instructions and Ruthie made her way to the Washingtons' two-bedroom colonial on St. James Street. Most of the houses looked alike. She knew Ike's by its old porch swing and the cedar clapboards he'd painted white. "Here we are," she said, easing the Bug's long shift handle into neutral.

"Thank you very much." Cynthia unexpectedly touched her hand. "You did well tonight. I didn't know you had such talent."

Ruthie felt a surge of warmth toward Ike's wife. "I'm glad you were there. When this is over, maybe we can spend more time together."

Cynthia Washington nodded, then fumbled for the VW's small, recessed door handle. She found it, maneuvered herself around and out, and pushed the door closed. It didn't click. Ruthie waited until Cynthia was inside the empty house before closing the car door properly.

······

It was nearly eleven-thirty when she pulled into Shemp's Landing. The streets were empty. The lake was quiet, the moon still bright. She saw the black Honda before she saw Dan. She scanned the front yard nervously and nearly drove the *Bug* into a pair of metal trash pails.

He was sitting on the front stoop and stood when she parked. She rushed to him without bothering to shut the car door. "How long have you … "

"Shhh."

He held her and they necked like teenagers. She caressed his back, let her hands drop, marveled at her own audacity. "Ever do it outside?" she said.

"Once. Her parents caught us."

"*Her* parents aren't around tonight."

Dan cupped her face in his hands. "You serious?"

Their privacy was interrupted by the sound of a neighbor's front door. Either somebody was going to walk his dog, or the light from inside the car had attracted attention. Ruthie shut the champagne silver door and got her keys. "Let's get inside."

"Chicken."

She gave him the middle finger of both hands and ran inside, laughing wildly. He locked the front door and chased her into the bedroom. They reached a stand-off at the bed, she on one side, he on the other. He dove across, but she easily dodged him and ran to the other side. He stood and paced a few steps. "I'm going to get you sooner or later."

She looked at him and her face got serious. "Sooner," she said, climbing onto the bed and sitting on her knees. He matched her movements. She reached for his tie—the same tie he'd worn earlier in the day for his interview with Mac McCauley—and pulled it loose.

"Wait," he said.

"Wait?"

"We need to talk first."

"You pregnant?" she mocked.

"Funny."

He pecked her forehead and turned around, sitting and facing away. "I thought I could talk about this later, but it wouldn't be fair. It's my boss. He figured it out, that we're seeing each other."

"So? He has something against sisters?"

"I'm serious."

Ruthie walked around and got on her knees in front of him. He looked to the side and she pulled his chin back around. "I can guess. Conflict of interest, right? Can't be dating anyone with the campaign because then you're not objective anymore."

"How do you know so much?"

"I know plenty." She stood and walked to the window. The neighbor and his dog were done with their walk. The street was quiet again. She touched her necklace and wondered how everything could be so still and moving so fast at the same time.

"I'm not insulted," she said. "I don't want to screw up your job, and I'm not going to do anything to hurt Ike."

"Tell me something I *don't* know."

She looked at him sharply, wondering if he'd somehow learned part of Ike's secret past, but it was just a joke. "So what do you want to do? Stop seeing each other until after the election?"

He joined her at the window and put his hands on her smooth shoulders. "What do I want to do? Or what do I think we *should* do?"

She turned and kissed his mouth. "I already know what you want to do," she said, pressing her cheek against his and stepping back.

"Tell me your plans. Are you going to stay at the paper? Is that your goal, to run that place someday? Become king of Charleston?"

"I want to go to Washington, just like you. I want to work for the *Post* and never have to think about South Carolina again."

"Oh."

"With one important exception," he said.

She put a hand on his face and slid her fingertips along his cheek whiskers. "I can see us both in Washington, me running Ike's shop, you breaking stories about Marion Barry and his sleazy coke buddies."

He moved up to her, nudging her with his chest. "I can see us under those covers over there."

"That's your idea of not seeing each other 'til after the election?"

"Our agreement," he said, "begins tomorrow."

Bootlicker

She leaned back, found the bed, pulled him on top of her. "Yeah. Tomorrow."

19 *Dan*

He woke with his knees pressed into the back of her thighs. Her body was so warm, he lifted off the summer blanket and slid away a few inches toward the night table. A sheen of sweat had risen in the night while his bare chest was against her naked back. He rubbed his forehead; there was sweat there, too.

Guilt was on him like a hangover. Last night made him a liar. He lied to Butcher and to himself. Still, he wanted her. Right now, even at ... where was the damn clock? His eyes roamed until he found it on the dresser by the light switch; at 6:40 a.m., the time of crusty eyes, stale breath and full bladders. Wanting her made him angry. Feeling guilty made him angry.

He swung his legs around and sat up, feet on the floor. He rubbed his eyes, cursed God for making things so complicated, then thanked Him for sending her in the first place. She stirred and he covered her with the blanket. He loved how her hair lay tangled and wild against the pillow. It smelled like fresh coconut. He wanted terribly to wind his fingers through it right now and whisper something that would make her smile in her sleep.

Instead, he got up and went to the bathroom. He brushed his teeth—just in case she woke up frisky—and got mad all over. Did he have a bargain with Butcher or not? He returned to the bed, got in, and lay on his back, not touching her.

Ruthie rolled over and put her head on his chest. "It's early."

"I woke up. Once I'm up, I'm up."

She kissed his stomach once and ran her long nails down his chest and along his thigh. "So I see."

He lifted her hand—too abruptly, he realized as he saw surprise, then hurt in her eyes—and went for the newspaper on the front doorstep. She took her turn in the bathroom and joined him in the kitchen. She wore a black mesh football jersey with blue trim that was long as a short dress. *Panthers*, number 24. It worked. Anything she wore looked good. The number didn't seem to have significance, so he didn't ask. He didn't look at her and didn't talk. He didn't feel like it, even though she'd done nothing to offend.

He measured his new guilt against the old, saw them as two weights in his upturned palms, found he felt worse about lying to Butcher than mistreating Ruth. That surprised him. That was mean. He'd never thought of himself as mean.

He had the paper folded to a story about a surgeon in Pittsburgh who'd transplanted a baboon's liver into a 35-year-old man dying of hepatitis B. A breakthrough operation, they were calling it. He thought of mentioning it to her.

She poked around the fridge. "Want breakfast? There's eggs."

"Not hungry," he said, not taking his eyes from the article. That did it. She shut the door too hard and something fell over inside. He expected her to pull it open—even anticipated the sucking sound the door would make. Instead, she stood with her arms crossed, one knee forward, bottom teeth pressed into her upper lip. They both heard a dripping sound.

"Ruth."

"Fuck you."

He'd never heard her curse. It snapped his spell of self-indulgence. "Why do you feel guilty? Because you came here last night? Because you broke your little deal with your boss?"

"It's not that simple."

Their eyes went to the refrigerator. Milk—he knew it was the 2 percent she liked—began to drip from the bottom of the door. It fell to the rawhide-colored tiles with a soft, *pop, pop,* the sound that comes out of a kid when he tries to do a goldfish talking. When Ruthie opened the door, the rest of the quart flooded out.

"I'm sorry."

"Shit." She righted the container. He went for paper towels, but she didn't want help. "Just go," she said.

He was suddenly conscious of still being in his shorts and T-shirt. His legs seemed ridiculously hairy. He was a reporter going nowhere, with weeks invested and no story, with a smart and fair editor whom he'd betrayed, and a warm, beautiful woman who wanted him to leave. He bent and helped mop up the milk.

"I'm sorry," he said. "I know I was shitty. I know it's not your fault."

"You don't know anything."

They were both crouched on the floor. He took her hands in one of his, made her stop mopping. "What does *that* mean?"

"Nothing."

He stood and threw away the wet paper towels. His anger was back, along with the guilt. Together, they made a poison that sloshed through his blood. "No, back up. You mean, I don't know anything about you? About relationships? About black people? About *Ike*?"

The anger uprooted his worst fear and yanked it through his mouth. "Have you and him been playing me all along?"

She shrank back. "You just called me a whore."

His heart was thumping. "That's not what I meant."

She threw her towels away and faced the sink. "Get out."

"Ruthie."

"Ruthie? What happened to 'Ruth?'" She mocked what he'd said when they'd met: "Everyone calls you Ruthie. I want to call you Ruth."

"Ruth, I'm sorry."

She went to the guest room. The blue 24 on the back of her jersey was the last thing he saw before she closed the door. He got his clothes from the bedroom and left.

On the street in the Honda, half-dressed, unshaven, hungry, angry, and embarrassed, he put his forehead on the steering wheel. He thought of last night, how happy she was when she got home and found him waiting, and what a bastard he'd been this morning. He'd hurt her twice in less than an hour, turning her down in bed, then calling her a whore. A *whore!* What did it matter that he didn't say the word? She heard it, that's what mattered.

He lifted his head a few inches, let it bounce back onto the padded wheel. He should go back right now, force his way if necessary, not leave until she understood. It was the story. The Ike Washington—Lander McCauley story had to be special, but all he had was routine ingredients. The deadline was close and his watch was beginning to feel like an hourglass.

He sat and scratched his arm. Peering over the wheel, he saw that the automatic sprinklers of Shemp's Landing were going strong, trying to fortify lawns and shrubs and flowers against a sun that was already making steam rise from the wet streets.

What did he have for the most important story of his career? What did he *need?* He opened the window and thought back to his first meeting with Ike, at the diner, the country-boy crap, then the civil rights lecture. The Masons' incident, where they called him McCauley's toady. Okay, he could cover that in his piece, but it was nothing new, nothing with real impact.

"You alright in there, son?"

It was the guy from last night with his dog, a little Schnauzer. He carried a small baggie to pick up the evidence once the dog took care of business.

"Fine, thanks."

The dog jumped up to the window and barked in his face. Small dog, big bark. It scared the crap out of him.

"Fritzy, *down*."

Dan watched as they walked up the block. When the dog did his thing, the guy only pretended to pick it up. As he bent over, he kicked it in the street. The dog-shit patrol. That should be my beat, Dan thought. *Joe Smith failed Monday to clean up after his dog. Neighbors were astonished. A small boy stepped in the ...* He reached for his briefcase and pulled out the seven notebooks he'd filled since taking on the Washington-McCauley story. Each was dated and labeled: *Interview, Ike's Diner; Masons' Forum; Kilgo Cop; McCauley Interview in D.C.; Notes on Cady County; Man on Street—Kilgo;* and, *Other Candidates.*

His handwriting was neat for a reporter. He stayed in the lines of the narrow notebook and rarely wrote on the backs of pages. He'd long ago developed the habit of jotting a few words about the room or atmosphere where the interview or press conference was taking place. He also dashed off notes about facial tics, muscles, height, voice, hair, ears, accents, clothes, jewelry, smoking habits, anything that might make his story more insightful or interesting. Secretly, he hoped the addition of such details would make people think *he* was insightful and interesting.

He fished for his keys and started the car. He still wasn't ready to leave; he just wanted some Sinatra while he rummaged through the notebooks. He turned the key left instead of right, firing up the battery. Sinatra at the Sands, 1961, live, with a swagger. So cocky, he would interrupt his own song to joust with the horn players in Count Basie's orchestra. Just the way he wanted to write, with a swagger.

He picked up the notebook with yesterday's McCauley interview and began thumbing through the pages. The old man knew how to dodge a question, or answer one that wasn't asked, or change the subject so smoothly, you didn't notice. Not to mention how he'd left Dan waiting half the day, or ignored him while he made deals on the phone. Where did it come from, that arrogance? Dan remembered how he jumped when McCauley stepped up behind him. He'd been looking at the poster-sized black and white of the senator's old man in front of the drugstore. Maybe that's what he needed to do—figure out how McCauley became McCauley. He was old now, but what was McCauley's childhood? What did that stern-faced, small-town businessman in the picture teach his son? What did Old Man McCauley think when the senator made Ike part of the team?

He put down the notebook. It wasn't much, but it was a new direction, something to lead him away from this dead-end feeling. He riffled through the other notebooks. There was one other thing he wanted to check. The cop from Kilgo mentioned someone who'd known Ike. No, that wasn't it. It was a woman who was related to one of young Ike's friends. He flipped through several pages until he found it: Jenny Bishop, Ricky Lee's mother. His notes said she made sweetgrass baskets in Charleston. He would check around the market. There weren't that many women who made those baskets. Maybe one would know Jenny Bishop.

He took a last look at Ruthie's house and thought he saw movement, but the urge to go back had faded. He was hot now to get the morning back on track. He wanted to run his ideas by Bernie and get to the newsroom. He wanted to be in the middle of the swirl—editors yelling, reporters grilling people on the phone, budget meetings, coffee room flirting, police radio blaring, copy kids running for clips from the morgue.

All that noise made for an odd kind of quiet he badly needed right now.

20   *Ike*

The Denny's off I-95 in Sumter was packed like they were grilling up free omelets.

Ike pulled the Taurus around three tractor-trailers with Georgia tags and Confederate flag mud-flaps and parked at the far end of the crowded lot. He hoped Ruthie, Derrick Maussipant and Agnes Stono were already inside. He locked the car and checked his watch—11 a.m., plenty of time before the 4 o'clock candidates' debate at Butcher Academy in Florence.

He paused as usual to check his reflection in the driver's side window. His white collar was neatly pressed, starched to two neat points that framed an elegant burgundy tie drawn into a perfect Windsor. He was so pleased, so full of sudden energy, he opened the door and grabbed a small satchel of campaign buttons. Those waiting for a table would probably welcome the distraction, he figured. And why squander a chance to meet new voters?

He left his suit jacket in the car and walked to the restaurant, where the first prospects turned out to be the three truckers. One stood out. He wore a faded denim railroad conductor's cap and held a wet cigar stump in one hairy, sunburned hand. Ike waved and skipped ahead. Truckers were unpredictable. Last thing they wanted to hear before coffee was some political BS. Plus, they were riding Georgia rigs and couldn't vote for him even if they wanted. Next was a clutch of elderly ladies in summer pastels and a few mothers with squawking kiddies. The youngest children put on starving orphan faces and stared longingly at the dozens already seated and eating. Their mothers did not object. Their mothers, Ike laughed to himself, may have suggested it.

He settled on the old ladies. "Morning, ma'am, just wanted to say hello," Ike said, singling out a woman with puffy, stark white hair and pearl earrings. "I'm Ike Washington, running for Congress in this district."

She turned her head, but not her shoulders, and squinted at him through thick, tear-drop glasses. As Ike waited for her smile, the seconds began to bunch up and his own, stupid grin grew big enough for the old woman to count his teeth.

"That so."

"Yes, ma'am. I'd like to give you a campaign button and one of my pamphlets, if you don't mind. And I'd appreciate your consideration on Election Day."

She looked at him a long time, like she was trying to focus and couldn't quite get it, then put a hand on her cheek. Ike couldn't help but stare. Time had turned the white skin pale and thin. There was some freckling, but what he noticed most were the purple veins that crept like vines just below the surface, and her fingers. When she took them from her cheek, they were stained with flesh-colored powder.

She looked back at her friend and spoke like he wasn't there. "Mary, you want to vote for this boy?"

Mary didn't look up. "No thank you." The woman made a stop sign of her palm, indicating Ike could keep his button and campaign literature.

A rush of anger coursed through him, the kind of round-house anger he hadn't felt in a long time, the kind Tyler Hawke once made him feel. But Tyler got his. Oh, yes, that night was burned forever in his memory chest. Ike thanked the ladies for their time and turned to one of the young mothers.

The woman maneuvered the child squirming on her knee so she could take a campaign button. "When's the election?" she said, reaching out suddenly to keep the kid from sliding off. The movement made her bangs fall in her eyes. She used the other hand to brush them aside.

Ike smiled, mostly to cover the fact that he'd forgotten the date. He knew it was soon, that there wasn't much time left. He knew it was in August, on a Tuesday. The polls would be open from 7 a.m. to 7 p.m. There would be live TV coverage. But he couldn't think of the date.

He was still thinking of Tyler Hawke and his boozy sarcasm. Of the way he tried to sing like Elvis. Of the way he died, and how he, Ike, had let him.

·····

It happened during Lander McCauley's first campaign for the U.S. Senate. By then, Ike was fairly well known as McCauley's ambassador to black South Carolina. They knew him in larger cities like Orangeburg and Florence, and in one-drugstore towns like Estill, Denmark, and Harleyville. Ike got around; his network was growing. He made deals and returned favors. A pedestrian bridge here, a new school bus there. When worst came to worst, when black leaders in some town refused to put aside the old hatred they had for Lander McCauley—they knew that crew-cut cracker was a Klansman, didn't matter what he said now, tiger don't change his stripes, they'd say—Ike would work to sand the edge off their anger. And he'd deal. Don't vote for McCauley, just don't organize against him, he'd say. Lay off, and there'll be something for the church building fund, or new playground equipment for the park.

And what about for me, some would ask?

Ike would snap his fingers, close an eye like he was taking aim, and fire the gun he'd made of his hand. The gesture implied a reasonable bribe would be no problem. He was so practiced, his gun move came off fast as a reflex. Usually, something could be worked out. History would record no widespread black opposition to the future Sen. Lander McCauley. Not ever.

Tyler Hawke, once the muscle in McCauley's gang, had turned into the wheels. He complained about going to black towns, said he didn't like the way he was ignored or had to wait in the car while Ike did his business. McCauley said he could hit the highway one way or another—drive Ike to his special jobs around the state or get out. He drove, but was either silent and sullen, or drunk and insulting. At least once each trip, he made some crack about Ike's first night in McCauley's basement.

Such intimidation was unnecessary. Ike could never forget Hawke's powerful grip around his chest, the whiskey smell on his breath, his insane voice as the mallet landed.

They had nearly changed places over the years. Hawke remained the illiterate, red-headed gofer who was never consulted on campaign or legislative strategy. As McCauley grew in stature, he hired smarter, more sophisticated men. While McCauley still gave the orders, he often sought Ike's advice on racial issues. When students at State staged a lunch counter sit-in to protest segregation in 1968, it was Ike who convinced McCauley to show up and make sure the cops didn't beat everyone to pieces. Ike's rewards over the years included a bank account that made him the wealthiest black man in Cady County and a small house of his own in Kilgo.

And yet, nothing meant as much to Ike as the pride he felt when McCauley asked his opinion. When Ike and Cynthia's son was born, McCauley stopped by the house with a check for five hundred bucks. Later, when Ike's mother passed, McCauley was among the first at the funeral.

Bootlicker

Ike would never forget the look on his guests' faces when United States Senator Lander McCauley dropped to one knee in front of the casket to pay his respects.

As Ike climbed in stature, Hawke slipped so far down, his tobacco-stained fingernails barely reached the boss' behind. The biceps Tyler once showed off by cutting the sleeves from his checkered shirt had melted to flabby meatballs; his big chest now roomed with his belly. For all his bluster, he was single and seemed shy and lonely. To get noticed, he grew a moustache that came in thick as a third eyebrow. All three were the color of a pumpkin left out a week past Halloween.

Tyler's best friends these days were his silver flask and a half-pint bottle of Red Eagle bourbon that he stashed in the glove compartment of his '59 Chevy.

"Boss," he overheard Hawke complain to McCauley one day, "can't the nigger drive hisself to Allendale? Spooks me goin' to all them spook towns. 'specially at night."

Ike, standing outside Bunk Meacham's barn, heard the slap that answered Hawke's question. *Crack.* "Anything else, Tyler?" he heard McCauley say.

Allendale, down by the Georgia border, was a long haul, but the problem was simple. Two county councilmen with dimwitted daughters wanted their girls enrolled in USC in the fall. In return, they would ensure a good turnout for McCauley. Ike could have done the deal by phone, but wanted to negotiate in person for something more than a "good" turnout.

Tyler was moody on the way down. He kept the radio loud and his flask between his knees. When they reached Ulmer, about twenty minutes north of Allendale, he turned down the music. "Don't be takin' too long once we get there."

Ike shrugged. "Be out soon as the job's done."

Tyler had been driving right-handed. His other elbow rested on the open window, and his head was propped against his left hand. He looked like a night student trying to stay awake in algebra. As he picked up speed along 321, he changed posture, steering with his knees and using his hands to twist off the top of the flask.

"Want a shot, boy?"

"No, and I wish you wouldn't get drunk when we're going to be driving half the night."

"What're you, my mammy?" Hawke laughed at his joke and took a long pull.

The job turned out to be trickier than he'd expected. The men were brassy and demanding. They wanted scholarships as well as admission for their future *Lady Gamecocks*. That wasn't going to happen, but Ike sealed things by promising "a reasonable amount of personal financial aid."

On his way out, he treated them to his gun move.

Back on the street, he saw Tyler had pushed the front bench seat way back. His legs were up, and he used his belly as a shelf for the flask. He was playing a kind of game where he would balance the flask, jiggle his belly, and catch the silver container before it toppled.

"What in Christ's name took so long?" he said as Ike touched the door handle. "You runnin' on CPT again?"

Hawke was drunk. Ike ignored the "colored people's time" slur and waited for him to move his legs. Hawke took his time. "One more hoozle," he said, tilting the flask back to his thin, wet lips. He swallowed, muttered, "Aaahhh," wiped his orange moustache.

"I should drive," Ike said.

"You should what, boy? Get in the car 'fore I kick your ass up and down Main Street." Ike got in. Hawke coughed and spit viciously out the window. "You drive my baby. That'll be the fuckin' day." Hawke shook his head like a wet dog. "Goddammit, I don't even want you up front. Get in back. You ride in the back of the bus where you belong."

Ike didn't move.

Hawke threw the flask and it hit Ike hard on his ear. "Get back there, boy, I mean it." Ike was angry enough to fight, but didn't. He looked into his heart and found that after all this time, he was still afraid of Tyler Hawke. That hadn't changed. The realization made him nauseous. His ear throbbed. When Hawke ordered him to return the flask, he didn't hesitate.

It was dark when they pulled out of town, Ike huddled in the right corner of the backseat, the yellow legal pad he used for note-taking beside him, Hawke returned to his one-handed driving position.

They had only been driving a few minutes when Tyler blew past the sign for 321.

"You missed the turn."

"Takin' 278."

"That's going south to go north."

Tyler threw a warning glance in the mirror. He took a hit from his flask and pressed a little harder on the gas. Ike resigned himself to a long night—he figured Tyler was headed for I-95, about thirty-two miles down 278. He looked out his window. It was a gray, misty night with no stars, and he could barely make out anything once they passed Allendale city limits. A sign bid them good-bye and announced the speed limit was back to fifty-five. Ike checked the speedometer and saw they were already doing seventy.

He never saw what triggered the crash. No car or truck brushed near them from the other direction. No one was behind them. Maybe Tyler swerved to avoid a raccoon. Ike found himself watching from the backseat like a spectator. He heard the tires crunching gravel and stole a look at the rearview mirror. Tyler's eyes and mouth were opened wide in tense concentration. The car bounced and fought as he jammed on the brake and gripped the wheel. Ike looked through the windshield and saw an abandoned fruit and vegetable stand in their path. Before the crash, the headlamps lit up a hand-painted sign that said, "Fresh peaches—$3." The wood was nearly rotted through and did not slow their momentum.

Beyond the stand was tall grass already slick with evening dew; they might as well have skidded onto a frozen pond. Ike saw Tyler turn the wheel desperately, but he was no longer setting their course. They flew by what looked like an orange grove and plowed into an old oak that had claimed this patch of Allendale County when the only consequence of driving drunk was falling off a horse. As metal met bark, Ike noticed long strands of Spanish Moss hanging on the tree like Christmas garlands.

He woke to silence, save for the pounding in his head. His left eye hurt. When he touched it gingerly, his fingers came away bloody. He tried to focus, realized the car was upright and not on fire. He pressed the door handle. Jammed. He kicked hard and it groaned open. The sound made him realize it was a quiet night. The crickets were on watch, but there were no sirens and no people coming to help. No one had seen them crash. He turned, lost his balance, leaned on the rear fender and looked around. No houses nearby, and they had traveled about seventy-five yards from the highway in a downhill direction that made it hard to see the road.

"Ohhh."

Ike circled behind the car and walked to the driver's side. The tree had won its battle with the baby-blue Chevy. The old bark was cut and bruised. The front of the car was crushed. The force of the collision made the steering column buckle and twist as it pinned Tyler Hawke. As Ike peered into the open window, he saw that Tyler was still trapped, and that the bottom of his shirt was soaked with blood. Ike tried to open the crumpled door. It moved only enough for an interior light to come on. What it revealed made him suck in his breath. The directional signal, an eight-inch spoke of silver chrome, was buried in Tyler's left side; less than an inch showed. The space between the steering wheel and the silver stiletto was so tight, Tyler could not get his fingers on it. He pushed manically on the steering wheel. Frozen. Finally, his hands slumped to his sides and his head relaxed against the seat. His frightened eyes darted around until they found Ike outside the window.

"God's sake, hep me, boy," he whispered.

Ike leaned in a little. The light from within the car made Tyler's flesh look yellow. His shirt was a mess, but the wound was not spurting blood. His eyes, so wild a moment ago, now looked dreamy. Ike was amazed at how the steering wheel was bent sideways. He rubbed his hand against the hard plastic surface. It had a nice, worn-in feel, and yet would not turn left or right.

Ike hurried around the side and grabbed his legal pad from the back seat. *Hurry*, he told himself. He shut the door and propped the pad against the trunk, where the metal was smooth and undamaged. He took his pen from his shirt pocket, tested it to make sure the ink flowed, and returned to Hawke.

"You write what I tell you," he said in a tone so fierce, Hawke looked at him instead of the pad. *"Write."*

Tyler Hawke wrote. It came to two lines.

"Now sign it," Ike said, and Hawke complied.

Ike ripped the page from the pad. Though it looked odd—so few lines on a page so long—the sound of the clean tear gave him a certain satisfaction. He tried to fold the page into quarters but misjudged, and the job was uneven. He didn't bother to try again. He ran his thumb along the folds to flatten the paper and slipped it into the pocket near his heart.

Both men started at a far-off sound that seemed to be coming toward them. Ike stepped back and looked out at the dark horizon. Two small lights were cutting a path through the fog. From his vantage point, Ike could see a bend in 278, and that the lights belonged to a tractor-trailer that was still a good quarter-mile away.

"Truck coming," he said.

Tyler turned his head with great effort. The movement heightened his pain, and he clutched at his side. "Go flag him," he said.

Ike didn't move. Tyler's hand shot out toward the window, toward Ike's neck. He could not reach. The move caused the small spear in his side to twist and tear through new tissue. He screamed. It was a shrill sound that didn't sound much like Tyler's voice.

Ike looked in one more time, took a step in the direction of the on-coming truck, and sat down with his back against the side of the car. His hands were shaking so badly, his bad pinky for once did not stick out. He touched his bruised forehead. It was sore and swollen, bad enough so that the cops and anyone else would believe he'd been knocked out.

When the truck drove by, he watched until its red tail lights disappeared into the night, then waited patiently until he was sure Tyler Hawke was dead. *Order in the court.*

•••••

"Ike, over here."

Agnes, Ruthie and Derrick were in a corner table at the far end of the restaurant. He waved and caught Ruthie's eye, summoning her to the waiting area. He took her aside and said so only she could hear, "The young woman behind me in the green top." Ruthie tried to see, but he moved her chin so she remained looking at him. "Don't look yet. I want you to go over, tell her the date of the primary and give her a brochure."

"Sure, Ike. You okay?"

"Yeah. The primary, it's August … "

"Twenty-fifth."

"Right."

He nodded and joined Derrick and Agnes. Ruthie arrived a few minutes later. They ordered—Ike, suddenly famished, chose pancakes, scrambled eggs, sausage and orange juice—and began to discuss the rest of the day.

Derrick was headed east and appearing for Ike in Dillon. He was to assure tobacco growers they would not be abandoned no matter how strong the anti-smoking movement grew. Agnes had organized a strategy meeting of campaign chairs from Sumter, Richland, Florence, Clarendon, Calhoun, Orangeburg, Williamsburg and Kershaw counties. Ruthie would accompany Ike to the candidates' debate in Florence.

As their food arrived, a young man Ike recognized from somewhere walked up to their table. He looked like a young professional—white, button-down shirt, dark tie. His face was wet with perspiration.

"Excuse me."

"Robert," Derrick answered. "Everyone, this is Robert Bocci, one of my—I mean, Ike's—assistants who came to the campaign with me. I told him where we'd be."

Ike remembered the young man from Agnes' house.

"Sorry to interrupt. Something's happened. I just heard on the radio that Cady Owens had a heart attack."

"Is he?"

"Dead," Robert said. "Keeled over right in his own funeral home."

Ike suddenly saw the playing field as if from a low-flying plane. It was now him versus Dianna Harley in the Democratic primary. That wasn't quite it; there was a white, conservative Republican running in the general election. But given the district's black majority, the primary winner would almost certainly become the new congressman.

Robert Bocci was still standing beside the table awaiting orders. Ruthie gave Ike half a minute to speak. When he didn't, she said, "Ike, I'm canceling our appearance at the debate out of respect for Cady Owens. I'll set up interviews so you can say what an important man he was. Talk about his role in our history, how he was a key figure in the Movement, and so on. Derrick, Agnes, you continue with your plans. Make sure no one connected with our campaign says anything negative about Owens, or about the political impact on Ike and Dianna Harley. And you, Robert, sit down and wipe your face. Have some juice. You did good."

21 *Dan*

It was nearly eleven by the time Dan showered and got to the *Herald-Leader*.

The building had a different feel when something big was up. A New York edge in the air choked off the usual chit-chat. Everyone moved more briskly, even in non-news departments like advertising and personnel.

Dan felt it as soon as he pushed through the heavy glass doors. "Hey, Lawman," he called to Lawrence, the old security guard whose back was curved like half a hula hoop. "How's things?" Lawrence wrinkled his nose in reply.

He took the elevator to the second floor and walked into the newsroom. Several reporters were working quietly at their desks; there were no editors around. The feeling struck again. Joanne the intern looked up from her stack of obituary files. "They want you," she said, pointing to the meeting room.

He started for his desk, intending to check his phone messages.

"Butcher said as soon as you come in."

He weighed which way to go. "Sounded serious," Joanne said, eyebrows indicating he'd better get his ass to the meeting pronto. He picked up a small, gold-framed picture on her desk. "Boyfriend?"

"For now."

She was cute, much better than messing with editors. "Trouble in paradise?"

"Aren't *you* nosy?"

But she was smiling beneath her short-cut blonde hair. Not like the editors. Some of the older ones were stone-faced and bored as clerks at the motor vehicle bureau.

He leaned toward her a little. "I'm paid to be nosy, Joanne."

"Overpaid, probably."

He went to the meeting. He turned the doorknob quietly as possible, intending to slip in unnoticed. Lem Butcher looked up from the head of the long table.

"Patragno, nice of you to join us," he said.

"I ... "

"Cady Owens just croaked."

Dan, halfway in, started to back out so he could get to work on the story. Butcher stopped him. "No, come in, I've got someone else working it."

He felt the eyes of the other six editors. They were rubbernecking, waiting to see if he'd explode because Butcher had given away a piece of his turf.

"I can do it," Dan said evenly, still half in, half out.

"Maybe you can help later. Right now I want to hear about what happened with McCauley in D.C. We're just finishing here." Butcher turned back to the editors. "Anyone got anything else?" No one did. Dan moved aside so they could pass. None looked at him or said a word. Lee Cohen, the night editor, gave him a secret pat on the shoulder.

"Couple of things," Butcher said when they were alone. "First, the *Statesman* had this today."

Dan took the Columbia paper. The lower right-hand corner of the front page had a Leigh Sanderson story on how Ike and McCauley were teaming up to get federal funds for an unusual sewer project in Sumter.

"Shit, McCauley told me about this yesterday. How'd she get it?"

"Ike Washington talked about it at a community center last night. The day you were gone, she had a story about him trading in that fancy *Lincoln* for some blue-collar car."

Dan kept looking at the paper, but he wasn't reading. He could have written the *Taurus* story, and, if Ruthie told him Ike let on about the sewer thing, he could've written that one, too.

"What's going to keep your Northern ass out of trouble here is all the good stuff you got out of McCauley," Butcher said. He tapped the table. "Start enlightening me."

Dan could feel the sweat leaking under his arms. His ideas about the mysterious past suddenly seemed ridiculous. McCauley's father? Secrets held by an old lady making straw baskets somewhere in Charleston?

"McCauley's a little slippery."

Butcher's voice got softer. Bad sign. "We tried to get you last night. No answer. We left a message. You didn't call in. That by itself is irresponsible."

He grabbed the back of a chair to steady himself.

"Were you with her? Did you break our agreement?"

Such loud quiet.

"Answer me."

Caught. Trapped.

"I'm waiting."

"Yeah," he said. "I was with her." He thought about trying to explain, to say he really went to Ruthie to call time out, that things got out of hand. But he couldn't stand the idea of sounding lame again.

"Go home, Patragno. Don't come in the rest of the week. I don't want you here."

Butcher walked out. Dan went straight to the elevator. He did not say good-bye to Lawrence. The bright sun hurt his eyes. He slapped his pockets, looking for sunglasses, remembered they were in the car, a small, final straw that made his shoulders slump. What a mess he'd made. What big newspaper would want him now? Even this little paper, a bastion of Southern charm and hospitality, had thrown him out. He crossed the street to a small park. It was empty; the day was too hot for swings and slides. He thought of his father, who pleaded for him to stay in New York and go into the family moving business. And how proud his parents were when he mailed them his first by-lined article. A dumb story about a six-car pile-up on I-26—no fatalities, no drunk drivers, just lots of traffic—but it sat in a beveled glass frame on their living room wall in Valley Stream. His mother pointed it out to everyone who visited, she'd told him. He was a professional writer, famous in the old neighborhood and among his relatives.

He sat on a bench, felt the hot bolts in the wooden slats. Now what? He looked toward the newspaper, saw *Herald-Leader* written on the side of the building in recently re-painted, black, old English lettering. They'd been nice to him here, and it wasn't such a bad place to be a reporter. Butcher (God, Butcher was so *mad* just now) was a good editor. He could learn a lot from Lem Butcher. He got up and turned in the direction of the Market. It was a couple of miles, but the thought of getting in his broiling car made him sick. So he walked, squinting in the blazing sunlight.

He turned left on King Street. The stores had awnings that created a narrow column of shade, and he tried to stay within. He took off his tie and dropped it into a litter basket. Further down, the stores would yield to stately brick houses with fancy ironwork and two-tiered porticos. Vendors sold everything from fresh fruit to phony parchment copies of the Confederates' Articles of Secession at the Market, which ran about a mile between Meeting and Concord. Every day at ten, the garage-like wooden doors were pulled back and the immense, red-brick barns came to life. It was there, between two of the buildings toward East Bay Street, that he remembered seeing the old basket makers.

He walked with exaggerated purpose, as if his long strides might make up for the doubt he felt. What made him think she would be there today? Was he really arrogant enough to think she'd just be waiting for him? That she'd even talk to him, a reporter *and* a stranger? And even if he got past those hurdles, what could she tell him anyway? Yet he had to do something. Butcher banned him from the newsroom. He couldn't sit in the park all day.

He was sweating and nearly breathless when he arrived at the busy pedestrians-only edge of the Market. Some tourists were handling a bird cage basket and asking questions of its creator. Dan tried to barge into their conversation and the old artisan shut him up with a glance. He realized too late she was trying to make a sale, and that he'd thrown off her timing. At least she wasn't the one he wanted. Her name tag said *Dellaweese*; he was looking for a Jenny.

Dellaweese was one of two basket makers out early, skilled enough to talk as she worked, stitching with hands that were dark brown on back and lighter, almost tan, underneath. She sat at a table shaded from the sun by a canvas beach umbrella.

A young couple watched her fashion a medium-sized basket. She sighed, as if annoyed her trade required telling a bit of its history, as if she felt it was enough that she practiced her craft in public. A patient smile crossed her face. "This basket making, it's the oldest kind of African art being practiced in the United States today," she said.

Dan saw her peek at the couple to make sure they appreciated the significance of her practiced remark. "Brought to Charleston 300 years ago by slaves from West Africa," she said. "Used 'em back then for vegetables, cotton, fish, clothes, everything. Used 'em on these very streets where we're standin'." The other basket maker stayed quiet throughout the ritual. She claimed another patch of shade with her flat-topped cart and was starting a new piece. Several completed baskets in various sizes sat on tables and on the ground. The man picked one up and casually tested its heft, as if the handsome piece had just spun off an assembly line. "Little steep," he said after turning over the price tag. Dellaweese worked a moment longer and put down her materials.

Long strands of straw-like sweet-grass dangled in the still air. "We make everything by hand," she said, massaging the taut muscles in her slender forearms. "I been making baskets since I was a girl, and it still takes twelve hours to finish a medium basket. But you know what? These baskets will last longer than you, me *and our impatient friend over here*."

Dan blushed. "Sorry, I didn't mean to interrupt."

"Well, thank you," the man said, leading his wife away, crushing the basket maker's hope of a sale.

"Damn," she said.

Dan now had what he'd been waiting for, her attention.

"What do *you* want?" she said. "You gon' buy somethin'? I'm guessin' not."

Dan picked up the smallest basket in the bunch. Fourteen bucks. He put it back. "Your work is really nice."

"Yeah, yeah." She returned to her stitching.

"Look," he said, "I'm trying to find a woman named Jenny Bishop. She does what you do. Makes these baskets."

"Don't know no Jenny."

She was blowing him off because she was mad. He was sure of it.

How many basket makers could there be around here? "You're certain? Jenny Bishop?"

"Sure as shootin'."

He gazed up the block. A forest-green carriage loaded with tourists was beginning a run. It didn't seem possible that a single horse could pull that heavy a load, but the huge wood and metal wheels turned easily as the driver gave the animal a gentle rap on its hindquarters.

"I'm sorry I messed up your sale."

Dellaweese pointed at him with one of her needles. "I'm not lyin' to you, young man. I never heard 'a your friend."

He didn't answer. They looked each other up and down. He was the one to cave.

"Sorry, I didn't mean to suggest you were lying."

"Look," she said, "I been doing this for years, but I've only been at the Market since last January. I worked in Summerville 'fore that. Maybe that's why I don't know your friend."

"Thanks for your time," he said. "Sorry I ruined your deal."

She nodded. He was hoping for more. A smile would have been nice, or, a "good luck, young man." He turned to go and paused. He didn't know where he was going. He couldn't go back to the paper. He didn't want to go home. He couldn't call Ruth. He didn't want to go to Bernie's.

"I knew Jenny Bishop."

The other basket maker. She sat behind her card table and was mostly hidden by the work piled around her. A yellow scarf with black tigers held her hair back.

"What?"

"I knew her."

"She makes baskets like you, right?"

"Not no more."

God, don't let her be dead.

"Jenny stopped 'bout a year ago."

"She's alive?"

"What's so important 'bout Jenny Bishop?"

"It's hard to explain. I work for the *Herald-Leader*. I need to talk to her about Ike Washington."

"Ike Washington. He the one running for the Congress? I like him. Stopped by here one time, bought a medium basket for sixty-five dollars."

The basket makers exchanged a knowing look. There are buyers and browsers, the look said; players and fools. Big Ike was a player. This boy, not so much.

Dan nodded. "Jenny. Where I can find her?"

"You ask a lot of questions for someone I don't know."

"Or who ain't buyin' nothin'," added her friend.

"Sorry. I'm Dan. Dan Patragno." He held out his hand.

She studied his face, calling on whatever instinct she used to judge strangers. "I'm Alma Berry," she said, shaking firmly.

"Alma, I'm sorry, it's been a terrible week and I'm in a little trouble. I have to find this woman."

She pulled two long strands through a loop and started to braid. The two new pieces were different shades of brown, which created a checkerboard effect that would run the length of the new basket's handle. "Jenny 'n me worked together some. Nice gal, quiet, minded her business. She got sick. Last I heard, she was at a nursin' home in Mount Pleasant."

"Do you know the name?"

"Don't remember." She looked up thoughtfully. "Wait, yes I do. Ow!" She'd stuck herself. She laid her work down carefully and put her finger in her mouth.

He waited, barely breathing. Unaccountably, he flashed on a night from junior year in high school. The *First Time.* They were in the back-seat of his mother's car. Mia Frazier was going to let him do it. Except her jeans were so tight, she couldn't get them off in the backseat. *Hurry.*

Alma withdrew her finger and squeezed it experimentally. No blood. She reached in a large purse and pulled out a Band-Aid. "It was Magnolia something," she said. "Like everything else in this blame town."

That stopped him. There was a Magnolia's restaurant, a Magnolia Street, Magnolias that bloomed in magnificent pinks and whites each spring. Maybe she had a point. He touched her elbow. "This works out, Alma, I'll be back for the biggest basket you've got."

"Hah."

·····

He found it in a city phone book.

"Magnolia Arms," a sunny voice answered.

"Good morning, ma'am." Dan gave his name and asked if they had a Jenny Bishop at the home.

"Yes, Jenny Bishop lives here."

"May I speak with her?"

"I'm sorry, she's sleeping."

"May I come later and visit?"

A beat. "Hold on."

He held. He was at an outside phone booth on East Bay Street. He wiped sweat from his forehead and temples, cursed himself for not tak-ing the car. Now he'd have to walk all the way back to the paper. Across the street, at the northern end of the Market, dozens of people were mill-ing around, checking out the souvenirs, eating shaved ice, pretending they wouldn't be happier back in their air-conditioned hotel rooms. A different woman came on the line.

"This is Betty Adams, the administrator. You want to visit Jenny

Bishop?"

"Yes, ma'am. I'm Dan Patragno, with the *Herald-Leader*."

"Do you know her?"

"No."

"Why, then?"

"Ma'am, I'm working on a story and I think she can help me."

Another pause. "You couldn't upset her, not in any way."

"No, no, I wouldn't do that."

"Jenny doesn't get any visitors," the administrator said. "She has no family. She's been with us about a year. I'd have to ask her."

"Could you? Now?"

"She's asleep."

Wake her, for Christ's sake. "Do you know when she'll be up?"

"She likes to nap and doesn't sleep long. Why don't you try back in half an hour?"

It would take that long to walk back to his car. "Okay."

A block from the newspaper, he placed the call from another phone booth. Jenny Bishop was up and she would welcome a visit.

"But you can't upset her," Administrator Adams warned.

"I promise."

"Someone will have to be with you the whole time."

"Fine."

"No more than fifteen minutes."

"Fifteen's plenty."

"You upset her, you'll be on your way."

"Agreed."

He heard her breathe. "Okay, then, 2:00 until 2:15."

"I'll be there."

"Mr. Patragno, I'm warning you, you'll need to be patient. Jenny has dementia and very poor circulation in her legs. It's not been an especially good month for her."

Dementia! How was she going to remember anything that happened thirty years ago if she couldn't remember what happened yesterday? "I understand, Miss Adams. See you at two."

•••••

There was a circular driveway for easy front-door access. He parked in the lot.

The sliding glass doors led to a large waiting area with a mix of leather sofas, large wooden chairs with padded seats, and lots of neutral, furniture store-style plants and paintings. It occurred to him that the lobby was set up like three different living rooms so visitors could meet with relatives in something resembling a family setting.

The one-story building was H-shaped and also had a well-shaded courtyard with several wrought-iron tables. That is where he was taken to meet Jenny Bishop. He'd cautioned himself to smile no matter what she looked like—and did. The old woman couldn't have weighed more than 80 pounds. Her wheelchair looked to weigh twice that, as did the husky woman who did the pushing.

"Mr. Patragno? I'm Ms. Adams. I'm going to sit in. This is Jenny Bishop. Jenny? This man is Dan Patragno from the Charleston newspaper. He wants to visit with you."

Jenny Bishop had a light blanket wrapped around her legs despite the heat. She touched her short, white hair like a girl on her first date, and searched his face with teary, hazel eyes that she closed almost three-quarters of the way, he guessed, to pull him into focus. She moved the blanket suddenly. Her legs were thin, knobby twigs that looked like they would snap if she tried to stand.

"Legs are bad t'day," she said, her voice oddly tinged more with mischief than complaint. Was she flirting?

"Now, Jenny," Ms. Adams said, pushing the blanket back in place.

"Hello, Jenny," Dan said, taking the woman's hand. It was frail and slight, and stirred within his gentle grasp like a baby bird.

"Jenny, I'm writing about Ike Washington. Do you know Ike? Do you remember him?"

She fixed her gaze somewhere beyond him. "Fella's supposed to bring a gal flowers. You shoulda brought some flowers. Yella roses. That's my favorite."

"I was going to."

"Where's Ricky Lee? Why ain't he with you?"

"Jenny," Administrator Adams said firmly. "You know your son passed. He died years ago."

"Wait," Dan interrupted. "Ricky Lee was her son. He and Ike were friends. Is that what you mean, Jenny?"

She looked at the woman, eyes darting like minnows. "Why's this boy so 'citable?"

Ms. Adams glared. *I warned you.* "Jenny," she said as if the interview had just begun, "this is Dan from the newspaper. He wants to know if you remember Ike. Ike and Ricky Lee played together when they were boys. Do you remember that?"

Jenny Bishop looked down at her lap and began miming the actions of a basket-maker. She pulled and stitched and snipped. She held up her imaginary basket, appraised it, and went back to work. Minutes passed. Dan looked at the administrator and she shrugged. More of his precious time slipped away. He began to lose hope. The Patragno family furniture business loomed.

"He's the one put me here, that boy Ike," Jenny said, suddenly lucid as an accountant.

"What?"

But she was back at her work.

Ms. Adams jumped in. "Financial matters are of course confidential, but since she sort of told you, I guess it's okay. Ike Washington pays Jenny's bills here. In fact, he was the one who first contacted us."

Jenny began humming. Her head moved slowly from side to side as her fingers moved along invisible strands of sweetgrass. "Don't wanna' leave the Lord no more," she sang in a surprising, rich baritone. "Gonna stay in His hands, Gonna follow His law."

Dan stopped listening. He was trying to gauge the importance of his new information. At first, it had seemed like a breakthrough. After thinking about it, Ike footing the nursing home bills of his old buddy's mother wasn't news that would win the *Pulitzer*. He got up.

Jenny stopped singing. "Why don't Ricky Lee come no more?"

"Jenny," Ms. Adams said, apparently ready to explain again that Ricky Lee was dead and buried.

Dan stepped forward. He took the old woman's tired hands and said, "If I see him, I'll let him know you're looking for him."

Jenny Bishop's eyes opened as wide as they could. Her face got pale and she squeezed his fingers so hard, he almost had to pull away. "Two-a-them knew what they did to that poor boy," she said, her voice a harsh whisper. Dan sat back down. Administrator Adams shook her head as if Jenny had over-exerted herself and would be trouble the rest of the day.

"What do you mean, Jenny?" he said, evenly as possible. "Who knew? Ike and Ricky Lee? What do you mean?"

But her lids had dropped down again. She moved the blanket and ran a bony finger along a dark vein that snaked from her calf to the back of her thigh. She looked up and caught him staring. She smiled and her old eyes sparkled. "Ain't my legs pretty?" she said.

22 *Dan*

"Lem."

"Patragno, I told you before."

"This is huge."

"It's close to midnight! I'm half out the door."

Silence. Dan imagined Lem Butcher, phone to his ear, hand on his side, wrinkled shirt sticking out the back of his pants, an annoyed glance at his watch.

"I know how bad I messed up, how much I disappointed you, Lem. I wouldn't even try if … "

"Alright, I'll wait. This better be worth it."

•••••

The tape recorder sat between them on an oval, smoked glass coffee table. "What you'll hear, Lem, is me, Ike and Ruth Baines, the campaign manager, a couple of hours ago at Ike's diner," Dan said. Butcher leaned forward as they listened to Ike tell the story. Dan jotted notes. At one point, Butcher got up and paced. When Ike finished his long, emotionless monologue, they heard:

Dan: "You're saying Lander McCauley—United States Senator Lander McCauley—and someone named Tyler Hawke lynched a young black man named Ezra James in 1959?"

Ike: "Yes."

Dan: "And that you witnessed it?"

Ike: "I saw what they did. They beat him and looped the rope around his neck. I ran away at the end. But they did it, no question."

Dan: "And they beat *you* up to make sure you wouldn't tell; threatened to kill you if you didn't go to work for them."

Ike: "That is God's truth. See this finger? McCauley smashed my hand with a wood mallet while Tyler Hawke had me pinned."

Dan: "In Lander McCauley's basement."

Ike: "Yes."

Dan: "Judge Lander McCauley. He was county judge then."

Ike: "Yes."

Dan: "A county judge who then became a state legislator and then a United States senator—you're saying he committed murder."

Ike: "I am."

Ruthie: "Almighty God."

Dan: "And he was never charged? What happened when the body was discovered?"

Ike: "No one was charged. It went down as an unsolved murder."

Dan: "Was there an investigation?"

Ike: "The *investigation* lasted five minutes."

Dan: "What happened to this Tyler Hawke?"

Ike: "Died in a car accident."

Dan: "And this kid, what was his name—Lionel, the one they were really after instead of Ezra James?"

Ike: "He disappeared; no one ever heard from him again."

Dan: "And your house and car, being mayor, being one of the state's most powerful black politicians, they forced all that on you too?"

Ike: "Can we go off the record a minute?"

Dan: "No."

Ruthie: "Why the hell not?"

Dan: "He's gone too far, I can't let him off the record now. Everything's fair game, and that includes anything *you* say, too."

Ike: "I see, just doing your job."

Tense moments passed. Butcher looked at the ceiling. Dan remembered how Ike rubbed his forehead while trying to decide whether to go on. Then they heard his voice, a mix of sadness and resignation: "Okay, okay."

Ruthie: "Ike, you don't have to."

Ike: "I've come this far. My family's already going to be hurt. All the people backing me, Agnes, Derrick, the voters. Sorry, I'm rambling, I don't mean to. Jesus. Yes, I liked the power. It's very addictive. And the money. We didn't have much when I was growing up. You probably wouldn't understand. Where you from, Dan, New York, wasn't it? You grow up with money?"

Dan: "What's McCauley going to say when we ask him about this?"

Ike: "He'll deny it. And there aren't any records. His friends ran the police department."

Five more seconds of silence.

Dan: That big picture McCauley has in his office, the one of his father's old store. I was looking at it the day I interviewed him. There are two black … "

" … Ezra and Lionel," Ike said. "McCauley passes by it every day. Doesn't give it a second thought."

The tape went silent. "That the end?" Butcher said. Dan put a finger to his lips. They heard his voice again.

"Mayor Washington, this story could cost you the election. Why are you telling it now? Why didn't you pick 1965 or '75 or some other year to tell it?"

More quiet. On and on it stretched. Butcher and Dan edged closer to hear Ike's answer. No one spoke on the tape; they heard a chair groan as someone shifted. There was also a low, steady buzz. The noisy office air conditioner. He thought of how Ike studied his hands before he answered.

"I don't know why I'm telling now," Ike told the recorder. "Conscience? I know it sounds bad. Where was my conscience all these years, right? I don't know. I thought about telling a hundred times, I swear."

Dan shut the recorder. He and Lem Butcher sat a full minute without speaking.

"No fucking way."

"No way what?"

"No way we're running that story in this newspaper based on that tape alone."

Dan took the micro-cassette from the recorder and held it between his thumb and middle finger. The tape was his future, his ticket to the majors. He felt his anger well up, knew it would spill into his voice if he spoke, that it would ignite a shouting match he couldn't win. *Don't piss him off.* He turned away and looked out at the newsroom. Hardly anyone around. Still holding the tiny tape, he said, reasonably as possible, "Lem, this is the biggest story the *Herald-Leader* has ever had." He spun back to Butcher. "Lander McCauley? A lynching? Come on."

"You don't have that story. Not yet. All you've got is some small-town politician making wild charges. I wouldn't even take this to the lawyer yet."

The *lawyer* was Pierre Devereaux, an in-house, First Amendment specialist summoned to review sensitive stories before they went in the paper. The white-domed Devereaux's record was perfect—during his twenty-six-year tenure, the *Herald-Leader* had been sued eight times and never paid out a cent.

Dan knew there was a price attached to that record. Several promising reporters had quit over the years after their pieces were spiked in the name of prudence, community relations, or other niceties that had little to do with investigative journalism.

Butcher took the tape, tapped it on his desk. "It's crazy. He lives with this all his life, no problem. Then you show up one night with a question about some old basket maker and he spills his guts? C'mon."

"It's not so crazy, Lem. The guilt has been eating him up. I mentioned Jenny Bishop and the floodgates opened. He's been wanting to tell; he needed someone to ask."

Butcher shook the tape at him, said, "Listen, kid, if this stuff is true, Ike Washington or someone else has proof. You get your ass back up there, get him out of bed; tell him you want it. Otherwise, no story. We're not accusing a sitting U.S. senator, a guy who's won three elections by landslide margins, of a thirty-year-old murder without more than this. What'd you get from the police report?"

"Haven't checked yet."

Butcher sighed and slid the tape back across the table. Dan caught it as it went over the edge. He put it back in the recorder and looked at his watch. "It's 1 a.m."

Butcher checked his own watch. "So it is. I'm going home."

•••••

It was nearly two when Dan pulled up to the mayor's house in Kilgo. He knew the address; he'd driven by and taken notes for his first Ike Washington profile, the one Butcher threw out, the "wet kiss." Dan peered up and down the block. All dark and still. He counted the steps from curb to front door to quell his nervousness. Twenty-seven. He considered getting back in his car, doing this tomorrow. He felt like some tabloid hack. Real reporters didn't show up on people's doorsteps in the middle of the night. But what if he waited and Ike changed his mind? The story would die before it ever lived.

There was a glass storm door. He reached for the handle, pressed in with his thumb, felt the levers move and the catch release. In the moment between pulling the glass door back and trying to decide whether to knock or ring, the front door opened. The light made him squint.

"Didn't I give enough at the office?" It was Ike, stripped down to his dress slacks and undershirt. His belt was open and he had a half-gallon of milk in one hand.

"Ike, I'm sorry. They're not going to run it. They want more."

Ike turned his head. His face was hidden in the shadows. Dan waited. Ike pulled the door open wider. It creaked like a warped casket lid. "Come in."

Dan followed him to a den that looked like a larger version of the diner office. Leather couch, blonde wood paneling, a sputtering wall-unit AC and a pair of crowded, side-by-side bookshelves. He stole a glance and saw novels by Steinbeck, Angelou and Ellison, and a few family photos crammed in front of the books. The TV was off, the clicker tossed on a coffee table littered with magazines. On top were *Sports Illustrated, Government Executive, Newsweek,* and a plate of pancake-sized chocolate chip cookies. Ike motioned for him to sit and lowered the music, a slow blues that sounded different from the usual fare. Piano, bass, drums and vibes. Dan imagined Ike sitting here a few minutes ago, listening to music and slugging back milk and cookies.

"Looks like this night wasn't made for sleepin'. Make yourself at home," he said, turning down a hallway. Dan glanced at the black leather couch and saw a large dimple at one end: Ike's place. He sat at the other end, leaned back and closed his eyes, knew he would trade his paycheck for a few drops of *Visine* if someone walked in right now and made the offer. Minutes passed. The quiet, the hour, being alone in a strange house—it began to feel eerie. Where the hell was his host? He rose stiffly and walked to the rows of neatly aligned books. The mayor of Kilgo was either an avid reader or a good collector. He picked up *America in Search of Itself* by Theodore H. White and looked at the cover.

"Classic," Ike said, startling him.

"Haven't read it. What's that?"

Ike had an old alligator suitcase. He cleared some magazines, laid it on the table and worked the rusted metal snaps. One shot up, the other stuck; he had to wedge it open with the black-ringed *Ford* key from his key chain. Inside was the smell of must and one large manila envelope. Ike undid the clasp and shook out the contents.

There were two sets of papers, one on yellow legal paper, the other, on smaller, white paper that seemed to be torn from a child's composition book.

Ike studied the yellow paper and passed it to him. The long sheet was faded and creased. There were several colorless stains—impossible to tell what caused them—and two lines of writing. The cursive letters that made the words wavered as if they'd been written in a moving car. But Dan could read them. They said simply:

"Me and Mac McCauley hung Ezra James.

Mac gave the order."

It was signed by Tyler Hawke and dated June 9, 1979.

"He wrote that right before he died in the car crash I told you about," Ike said. "I was with him." There was no further explanation. He stared at the other papers and passed them on.

Dan sat down to read. The handwriting was sloppy, but again, he could make out the words. *"Last week at Lake Marion Forest, I saw Judge*

McCauley and Tyler Hawke." it began. Dan realized what he was reading and stopped.

"This is you telling the same story you told me tonight in your office," he said.

Ike nodded. "That's the original. About a week after it happened, I wrote down everything I could remember. Saved it all these years. Look at the date."

Dan flipped to the last page. It was signed," Ike Washington, Jr., August, 1959."

"Why didn't you give me this stuff before?"

Ike rubbed his hand along the top of the alligator suitcase. Dust stuck to his fingers. He wiped them on his pants, leaving a trail of gray streaks. "No one has ever seen these papers. I never wanted anyone to see them. They've been locked away a long time. But I guess there's no choice now."

"Not if you want this story told."

Ike got quiet. Dan thought up quick arguments in case the mayor changed his mind. It wasn't necessary.

"It's time," he said, snapping the suitcase closed. "Take them. Take them and go."

·····

The next morning, Dan, Lem Butcher, and executive editor Marshall Ryder were already in the second-floor meeting room when Pierre Devereaux breezed in.

"Gentlemen," he said. "Mr. Ryder has explained the story. May I see the documents?"

Dan, eyes and hair a sleepless mess, leaned back. Devereaux was all business, a pink-faced, Polo-drenched man always rushing to his next appointment. He took off the jacket of his seersucker suit and extended a plump hand with clean, clear-polished fingernails. Butcher handed him the papers.

Devereaux's analysis took less than two minutes. "This," he said, holding up the three white pages in young Ike's handwriting, "is what the system calls 'hearsay.' It would not be admissible in any court. I recommend against even mentioning it in any story."

Dan shot up. "But."

"Young man," Devereaux cut him off, "I'm not here to debate. The newspaper pays me for my legal opinion. That's what I'm prepared to deliver, if you'll so allow."

Dan felt Butcher's hand on his shoulder and shook it off. "He wants to kill it. He doesn't want to help. "

The lawyer ignored him and continued. "This other document is a horse of a different color." Devereaux held up the yellow papers as if suspicious of their authenticity. He put the thumb of his other hand beneath his navy-and-white suspender and tugged it forward. "Crass, audacious and ungrammatical as this is, the courts will allow introduction of a 'dying declaration.' If sued, we would be pressed to make the case that Mr."—he lifted his pewter-rimmed glasses and looked again at the paper—"*Mr. Hawke* knew he was dying and chose to write this confession. If you're wondering, the legal theory is that those who know they're about to die have little incentive to lie about such things. Now, if there's nothing else."

"Hold on, Pierre," Ryder said. "Are you saying that yellow paper protects us if we write this story?"

Devereaux clasped his hands and smiled as he searched for the lowest common denominator for the three baboons before him. "Mr. Ryder, gentlemen. To me, this story is preposterous. If you decide to go forward and we are sued for libel, as I expect we would be, Mr. Washington's boyhood scribbles would be inadmissible in court. They are hearsay. Senator McCauley's attorneys would also argue against allowing Mr. Hawke's deathbed confession into evidence, but I believe we could prevail in that instance. Where would things proceed from there? That would be up to the jury."

"Thanks, Pierre." Ryder took back the papers. Devereaux slung his jacket over his shoulder. "Good day," he said.

"Needle-nosed prick," Butcher said once the door clicked shut. "Who the hell's side is he on?"

"Easy, Lem. As hard as he is to like, Devereaux's a good lawyer. Besides, that's not the issue. I've made a decision."

Dan sat up. This was his story and they were ignoring him. He saw where Ryder was going and desperately wanted to make him reconsider. But the head of news pressed on.

"Dan," he said, "you've done good work, but we don't have enough. Unless you get me more, we can't go with this story."

"I agree," Butcher said.

"Shit." Dan shot up. His chair fell and crashed into the wall. He left it. "I've got the tape. I've got Jenny Bishop in a nursing home with Ike paying the bills. I've got Ike's account the week after they hung that kid. On paper and in his own handwriting. I've got a confession from the accomplice. What else do you people need?"

"We're all on the same team, son," Ryder said.

"Doesn't feel like it."

"That's enough, Patragno. Marshall, would you excuse us?"

"Sure. Listen, Dan," Ryder said, "you put the last piece in this puzzle, we'll run it. My promise."

Dan didn't answer. Ryder nodded his sympathies and left.

"Sit back down," Butcher said. Dan ignored him and gazed out at the newsroom. "Look, you want to figure this out or let it end right here?"

He sat.

"Think. What else does this need before we can put it in the paper?"

"McCauley."

"What else?"

"I don't know. More documentation, records?"

"Yes, but from where?"

Dan pushed down his anger and considered. "Kilgo cops, Cady County Sheriff's Office, maybe the state NAACP has some stats or records on racial murders that were never cleared."

"Good. That's your next move. Now quit feeling sorry for yourself and get to work. I want this story in the Sunday paper."

•••••

The Cady County Sheriff's Department had nothing. The state NAACP had a half-page summary and no new details. Ezra James was a Kilgo local who was lynched in 1959. He had no family, and no one was ever charged.

The Kilgo cops had a file with a picture. Dan wanted to retch when he saw the grainy, yellow-eared eight-by-ten. Poor bastard, he thought, looking at the bloated face and open eyes. The body cooked in the sun all day before it was discovered. Dan stared at the vacant eyes. *Tell me something, Ezra, point the way. Was it McCauley?*

"You done over there?"

No one was happy twenty minutes earlier when he announced himself at the Kilgo Police Department. *Department* was a stretch. There were two cops and three rooms—one for visitors, one for the cops on duty, and a holding cell—all in a dimly-lit building the size of a two-car garage. But they gave him the file. It took some digging through a trio of old, wood and metal filing cabinets. No one remembered the case, predictable since the two guys on duty both looked under forty—but they found it. Besides the photo, there was a one-page report that consisted of several single-spaced lines with a lot of typos and no new information. It was signed in blue ballpoint by Officers Hale Sissler and E. Bishop.

Dan looked hard at the last name. E. Bishop: Eddie Bishop. Jenny's brother. Ricky Lee's uncle. The old cop he ran into a few weeks ago. The guy who let him off with a warning.

"Thanks," he said, handing the file back to one of the Kilgo cops. He forced himself to sound casual. "Know when Officer Hale will be in?"

"Hale's dead five years."

"Sorry," Dan said. "How about Bishop?"

The cop looked annoyed as he turned to his partner. "Gil, when's Eddie on?" Gil looked at the wall clock. "Noon to 8:30. But he's going straight out on patrol."

"Thanks," Dan said.

"Sure. Anything to help the press."

On the street, walking to the car, he remembered it was late morning the day Officer Bishop nearly gave him a ticket for littering near the quiet intersection at the heart of downtown Kilgo. Dan drove back, parked in the same illegal spot as last time, and looked for a pay phone to call Detective Stan LeTourge back in Charleston.

"Stan," he said.

"Hey, buddy, ball this week?"

"Don't know. Listen, Stan, couple of cop questions for you. First, is there a statute of limitations on murder? Can a guy be charged today for killing someone, say, twenty-five, thirty years ago?"

"Who'd you kill, Dan?"

"I'm serious."

"No statute of limitations on murder. But there'd have to be damned good evidence."

"Yeah. Tell me about filing systems in small police departments. Are they thorough? Does stuff get lost or thrown out over the years?"

"Like anything else," Stan said. "Some are better than others. Computers have helped, but if you're talking about something thirty years old, shit, everything was done by hand back then. The more something gets passed around, the more likely it gets lost."

"Thanks."

"Hold on, what are you up to?"

"Tell you later. The guy I've been trying to find just showed up."

Dan hung up without saying good-bye and ran to his car. Officer Eddie Bishop already had his ticket book out and was writing down his license plate number.

Dan raced up, stopping ten feet short of the cop's green and white cruiser. "Whoa, I'm here."

"Sorry, this is an illegal spot. Once I start writin' 'em, I never ... " The cop looked up. "Hey, I know you."

"Right. Dan Patragno, *Herald-Leader*."

"Yup. I let you go last time, can't do it again. Sorry."

"That's okay. I parked here because I was hoping to find you."

"That so."

"I have to ask you about a case you handled a long time ago. A lynching. Lake Marion Forest. Never cleared. Guy's name was Ezra James."

Officer Eddie Bishop's eyes rose from the ticket book. "Ezra James." He said it as if he'd never heard the name.

Dan walked closer. "Listen, I know the whole thing. Ike—Mayor Washington—told me. He wants the story out. So, please. I saw your name on the investigation report."

Officer Bishop leaned his pen against his pad. He looked at the little ticket book as if it were a family photo album. "I'm retiring in less than a month."

"Good for you."

"Ike told you about EJ?"

"Call him if you want."

"You bet I will." He reached in his glove compartment and pulled out a navy, soft-covered address book.

"I'll wait," Dan said.

"No, you move your car to one of those metered spots," Bishop said, pointing to a row of spaces a block down Union Street and ripping up the ticket.

Dan moved his car. The cop made his call. When they hooked back up, the fight was gone from Eddie Bishop. He looked pale. "Meet me back here at dusk."

Several hours later, Dan drove back to the assigned spot. Officer Bishop pulled in a moment later. Bishop looked in all directions, then signaled Dan to the green and white.

"Where we going?"

Bishop reached for the door handle and spoke over the roof of the car. "Big Ike said tell you everything I know about EJ. I know about something that got buried. Even Ike don't know about this. I'll give it to you, but there's a condition. You agree, you get what I got. You don't, this something stays between me 'n the Good Lord Jesus."

"What's the condition?"

"My name stays out."

He didn't need the cop's name in the story, but didn't want to give in too easily. "What do you have, some kind of evidence?"

"First tell me we got a deal."

Dan agreed. They doubled back past the station, turned north on 28 for half a mile, then took a left on a street called McGrory that led to a busy neighborhood with small, modest houses and lots of kids clamoring around an ice cream truck. They took a right on Liles and had to wait for a break in the action of a street hockey game. The rollerbladers seemed used to seeing a cop car in the neighborhood and took their time clearing a path. Eddie Bishop waved as they passed through. A few waved back. He drove another half-block and pulled into a driveway.

"This your house?"

"Wait here."

Dan looked around. He'd never been alone in a cop car. He wanted to play with the police radio, to send out a message to someone—anyone—that his luck had changed, he was getting close. He put out a finger and turned the AC vent. The cool air blew on his face and made his front teeth tingle.

Bishop returned quickly with a small knapsack. He closed the door, looked around, and dumped the contents between them on the front seat. There were two items, both in industrial strength plastic bags tagged with two-inch strips of masking tape. "James—8/59" was written on the tape in faded black marker. Bishop picked up one of the bags.

"This was the belt Ezra James was wearing the day he died."

The belt looked like any other except for a silver buckle. Time had done its work, but Dan could still see the worn-down initials engraved in the silver: *EJ*.

"These," Bishop said, holding out the second bag, "are prints lifted from that buckle. I did that myself day after the hanging. Sergeant said, 'Good job, Eddie, we'll take it from here.' Course nothing came of it. He stashed 'em."

"How did you … "

"That Sarge died a few years later. Fell off a boat while he was fishing, drunk as shit. I was first to hear about it at the station. I went through his stuff, found this. He touched the two bags. And took it back. It's been here ever since."

Dan felt the AC on his neck. "Whose fingerprints are on these cards?"

"Never found out. They closed the investigation fast, blamed 'outside agitators,' and took my evidence. But I have my ideas."

"McCauley, Tyler Hawke?" Dan said.

Bishop took his time answering. He picked up the bag with the cards. "I did a good job; these prints are clean. Whoever they belong to is still walking around with 'em. Person's fingerprints never change."

Dan took the bag and studied the dozens of squiggly lines on the two cards inside. It was true. The ink that made the fingerprints was still dark and clear. "Now what?" he said.

"Now you take that stuff and I go back to waiting for my retirement in peace. Without no publicity." Bishop checked his rearview mirror. "If someone wanted to see justice done—find out who those prints belong to, re-open the investigation—he'd probably pass it on to the state attorney general."

"You ever think of doing that?"

Eddie Bishop slipped his cruiser into reverse. "No more questions," he said. "Don't forget your promise."

Back in town, he called Lem Butcher from the same phone Eddie Bishop had called Ike. While waiting for his boss to answer, Dan studied the phone's metal number plate and plastic receiver. How hard would it be to secretly snag someone's fingerprints? Happened all the time in the movies. He considered calling Stan back after he was done with Butcher. After relaying the latest developments, he posed the fingerprint question to his boss.

"Forget it," Butcher said angrily. "That's not your job. You build facts for stories; you don't collect evidence to charge someone with a crime."

"I was just thinking out loud."

"Alright," Butcher said. "This story's got me jumpy."

"You agree we've got enough to go to McCauley."

"Damn right. Get going."

Jane Peeples' fast shuffle into the waiting area told him she wasn't pleased. He didn't blame her. It was nearly dinner time and he had no appointment.

"You can't show up unannounced and expect time with the Senator," she said, producing a seven-inch card cut narrow enough to fit in the inner breast pocket of a suit jacket. McCauley's daily schedule. "He's been going since a 7 a.m. breakfast and won't be done until a private reception tonight that doesn't even begin until 8:30." She turned the card face down before he could pick out the next event on the itinerary.

"I'm going to see him today, Jane." He wondered if anyone had ever said that to her before. He could imagine what McCauley's press aide was thinking. He hadn't showered; his hair was mashed down on the right side. He felt her sneaking looks at his bed head. Was he scaring her? He touched his tie. It was knotted, but the knot hung three inches below his open shirt collar. "If I have to tackle him in the hall, I'm going to see him."

"People have spent a night in jail for saying less, you know, Dan."

"Fine, put me in jail. We'll write a story that'll get you plenty of publicity."

She looked again at McCauley's dance card. "You won't tell me what it's about?"

"Can't. I need spontaneous answers. I won't get that if you brief him."

She looked doubtful, like she didn't even want to tell McCauley he was here, like the old bastard might dock her pay for throwing something new into the packed schedule.

He forced a tired smile. "It's really important, Jane."

She put her hands in her lap, studied the ceiling. "Wait here."

There were handouts about the Capitol and other Washington attractions piled on a bookcase near the front door. He browsed until he caught one of the secretaries staring at him from behind her computer screen. He winked. He was dangerous, a troublemaker who scoffed at the rules that governed official Washington.

"Would you like to sign our guest book?" she said sweetly, surprising him.

"Sure." He flipped back a few pages to see if he recognized the names of any visitors. He didn't, but people from towns throughout South Carolina had been to see Lander McCauley over the past few days. "Always get this many visitors?"

"Oh my, yes. We get dozens each day during the summer months when the kids are out of school. Why, yesterday … "

"Dan, Jane Peeples here. I don't know how, but he was expecting you. He'll see you in the Capitol office in twenty. Remember how to get there?"

"Fine." He left without saying thanks or goodbye, and walked down three flights of stairs to the basement of the Russell Building. His legs felt light, almost disconnected from the rest of him. He held on to the steel gray railing near the last step and rested, forcing himself to remember all that happened in a day that was both a train wreck and the payoff for all his work. He needed to get things ordered, to clear his mind before he took on McCauley.

He sat on the step and thought back on his night: Butcher's office until 1 a.m., then back to Kilgo to see Ike. The return trip to Charleston, the painful session with Devereaux. NAACP headquarters in Columbia, Kilgo again with Eddie Bishop. Now, Washington.

No wonder he was wobbly. A guard on duty by the entrance to the subway did not ask him for credentials. Dan boarded the single, open-topped car, greeted the driver, and stepped off after the quick ride. Good, he was now in the basement of the Capitol. From there, he hit a small coffee shop, grabbed a cup, medium and black, and made his way through throngs of summer tourists to McCauley's second-floor office.

Auralee, the bassoon-playing, rose-scented guardian of McCauley's hideaway was on duty. "They're ready, go on in," she said, more serious than he remembered her. He went through the door that led to the inner office and found himself face to face with McCauley and two other men. Pinstripes everywhere, not a smile in the room. All but McCauley wore three piece, button-downs with white shirts and gold tie bars. Enough American flag lapel pins for a miniature parade.

"Mr. Patragno, I'm Carter Strickland, the Senator's administrative assistant. This is Jeremy Broadnax, his personal attorney."

He shook hands with the assembled firepower. When he got to McCauley, the Senator pushed his chair back, folded his arms, and left him hanging. Fine. The chairs had been arranged so that it was three on one. He took the single and faced the evil axis. He could feel the hatred radiating from McCauley. The others were cold; he knew they were sizing him up.

"Um, could you spell Broadnax for me, sir?" Dan said.

"Jesus H," McCauley said.

Broadnax spelled his name and there was silence. Dan hadn't quite anticipated this moment, the time when he'd have to ask a U.S. Senator if he was a murderer. McCauley leaned back on his chair and let the front legs down gently. He looked at his watch and slid it back into his vest pocket. The others waited patiently. Strickland had a gold fountain pen that he began tapping lightly on the pad within his leather binder.

Broadnax sat with closed lips and eyes that seemed trained not to blink.

When the quiet became unbearable, Dan heard himself say, "Senator, Mayor Ike Washington of Kilgo has accused you and a man named Tyler … "

McCauley charged up from his chair with a ferocity that halted him mid-sentence. Carter Strickland and Jeremy Broadnax rose and took one of the old man's arms. McCauley shook them off and stepped forward, his voice pure rage. "The nerve, comin' in here with this shit. I will beat the livin' crap … "

"Senator," Strickland said. McCauley nodded, brushed off the front of his shirt with his hands, and let himself be guided back to his chair.

"I'm sorry Senator," Dan said, fighting to stay composed. "I'm trying to do the fair thing here. We want your response."

"This is our response," Broadnax interrupted, handing Dan a one-page statement. "The Senator won't be answering any questions."

Dan read the statement. In it, McCauley denied any role in the death of Ezra James. Tyler Hawke was a long-time employee, but he, McCauley, had no knowledge of Hawke's involvement in Mr. James' death. McCauley, it said, was a respected county judge in 1959. He then won a seat in the state legislature and served until he was elected to the U.S. Senate.

"Are you calling Ike Washington a liar?" Dan asked McCauley.

"You have our statement," Broadnax said.

"Senator, several fingerprints were taken from Ezra James' belt buckle the day after he was hung. Would you be willing to give police your prints to prove you never touched that belt?"

McCauley glared at him a moment, then swiveled his chair so that he was looking out the back window, toward the Washington Monument.

"You have our statement, Mr. Patragno," Broadnax said. "The interview is over. Your newspaper has been informed that if you print these absurd accusations, we will be forced to take legal action. Now if you'll excuse us, the Senator is a busy man."

23 *Ike*

The story ran in Sunday's *Herald-Leader*.

Ike knew it was coming, Patragno alerted him. Now the secret story that had shaped his life was out on the porch, scrunched into a plastic bag, one pebble amid a mountain of state, national, international, and business stories. The ads were stuffed in too: *Super-K*, *Sears*, *Piggly Wiggly*, and the rest: sports, the TV listings, the comics, the magazine, the book reviews. It was just like every other Sunday paper, except he was afraid to go out and get it.

He rolled over, then back toward Cynthia. She had listened quietly last night when he told her what would appear in the morning paper. He remembered bowing his head, and the feel of her hand on the back of his neck. "You've suffered enough," she'd said as his tears flowed freely. "You go now and become the congressman. Make things better for people. And for yourself." Her strength surprised him. Not a word about how his scandal would affect her life. No hurtful probing about why he kept his secret from her. His quiet, accepting wife was a proud woman and, he now knew, a lot tougher than him.

He closed his eyes against the morning and moved his leg so it touched hers. Her flesh was warm and familiar. The feeling of their bodies together beneath the light blanket helped him relax. But there would be no more sleep this morning. He settled on his back and scratched his belly. Was it on the front page? Were there photos?

Minutes later, he stepped onto the porch, checked side to side to see if any neighbors were out, and casually picked up the paper. Scrounging through the bag as he walked back through the narrow foyer made him forget Cynthia's wicker magazine basket, and he cracked his shin. The pain nearly stopped him. He hopped to the kitchen, where he turned the plastic bag upside down and dumped it. He found the front section, held it open as if appraising a piece of art, and saw the paper twitch in his trembling hands. He was big news this Sunday. He sat and read quietly, barely breathing as he went from line to line, paragraph to paragraph. After a time, he stopped to get a ruler from the laundry closet. The report not only claimed the upper third of the front page, it filled two inside pages and took a good chunk of a fourth. He put the ruler down. The story of his checkered life measured one hundred, six-and-a-half inches. He wondered idly what it would cost to buy that much space in a daily newspaper. He turned back to the front page and stared at the block-lettered headline: *McCauley Accused of 1959 Lynching*. The smaller sub-hed just below said: *Veteran Senator Proclaims Innocence*. The newspaper used side-by-side thumbnail photos of himself and McCauley on the front page and the police photo of Ezra James' body inside with the story jump. The paper also ran a photograph of fingerprints allegedly taken from Ezra's belt buckle. It did not say how the prints were obtained, or speculate on the owner's identity. They were provided by "a credible source who requested anonymity," according to the story, written by Dan Patragno.

Agnes Stono and her little dog J.R. were at his door before the church bell at Kilgo First Baptist struck seven. Derrick Maussipant arrived soon after. An avalanche of calls followed. County campaign leaders frustrated by the constant busy signal began showing up in person. By eight, Ike and Cynthia had a full house.

And yet he didn't realize the magnitude of what he'd done until later, when he tuned in the early morning news, and, when the trademark fanfare of horns and kettledrums faded, one of the network shows began: "From South Carolina, a published report linking U.S. Senator Lander McCauley to an alleged lynching that took place in 1959."

He flipped to another channel, where an on-scene reporter was camped (along with half a dozen other TV reporters and their camera crews) outside the senator's apartment building in downtown Washington. "McCauley has strongly denied the allegations, which were made by congressional candidate Ike Washington and printed by the *Herald-Leader* newspaper in Charleston, South Carolina," the reporter said. The station switched to footage of McCauley entering the building and pausing to chat with the raucous horde. "I don't know what to say, boys," he told the media. "Life's short and fulla' blisters. Ike Washington worked for me thirty years. Tell me why he'd do that if I was guilty a'this terrible thing." When reporters pressed, he held his hands out and shook his head. "Can't discuss details, boys. We're fixin' to sue that so-called paper 'inta a pile of sawdust."

By 10 a.m., Derrick, Ruthie, most of the county chairmen, the campaign's chief fundraisers, and several other key supporters were camped in Ike's living room. TV crews, radio reporters and print journalists were beginning to gather on the front lawn as the news spread and reporters plotted their follow-ups to the *Herald-Leader* bombshell. Cynthia, somber as a new widow, made pot after pot of coffee and shooed away any reporter who dared approach the front door. "This is private property," she said.

Ike, barefoot and wearing Bermuda shorts and a white *Ike's for You in '92* campaign T-shirt, took one of the metal folding chairs Cynthia brought from the garage and sat in a corner. His supporters left him alone. As the room filled and the voices grew louder, he began to feel small and inconsequential. He chuckled at the notion of Big Ike shrinking and quickly cleared his throat, lest someone think he was laughing. Eventually, people began to argue as if he weren't there. The core of his campaign seemed to be splitting into two camps, the angry and judgmental, and those who believed young Ike had no choice but to go along with McCauley. He wondered if he were looking at a microcosm of the electorate. Final arguments over, he'd somehow wound up an invisible spectator in the jury room.

"Shoulda' told us," he heard.

"Wouldn't have made a difference to me."

"Gonna make a difference to the voters."

"Why? He didn't do the crime, McCauley did."

"A young man was hung. He knew and didn't tell. Saw it all and kept it to himself."

Someone picked up the *Herald-Leader* and waved it impatiently. "Did too. Told it all right here."

"Took thirty years."

"Put yourself in his spot," challenged Jeremy Akin, Ike's chairman in Clarendon County. "What would you have done?"

Silence.

"Well?"

Nothing. Akin turned his shoulder and addressed the crowd. "All of you—*any* of you—put yourself in Ike's place," he repeated. "What would you have done?"

Again, silence.

Ike looked up. Was there hope in the quiet? *What would you have done?* Forget the campaign, he thought. What person *anywhere* could say, "I would've told and lived or died with the consequences?" He became excited. How many households were condemning him this morning? How many were defending him? How many voters had dropped him for Dianna Harley? How many were upset, but willing to stick with him?

He rose, smoothing his shorts in the manner he routinely patted down his suit pants. "Excuse me," he said. The room hushed. He felt their eyes, as if they were seeing him for the first time. "You've all read the story," he said. "The reporter did a good job. It reflects the truth as best as I can recall." He looked again at Ruthie, who nodded for him to continue. He swiveled until he found Cynthia. Had she changed her mind? Eyes on his wife, he said, "I need to know how many of you think I should drop out, and how many think I should stay in the race. I won't take it personal. Who wants me out?"

People looked at one another. Cynthia came to his side. A few hands went up slowly. Then a few more. Ike counted less than one in four. But one was Sparkle Westbrook of Kilgo, his hometown chairwoman.

"Sparkle, you want me to give up?" Sparkle Westbrook was a small-faced woman with a tight, white bun who was known until middle age by her given name of Charlene. When her eyes began to fail in her early fifties, she browsed through and rejected dozens of pairs of glasses until she came upon a pair of diamond-shaped harlequins. A friend agreed they suited her, said aloud that they made her face sparkle.

Charlene Westbrook—"Sparkle" for the past twenty-five years—put her hands on her knees as if she were going to stand, but instead exhaled softly. "I was here in this town the day they found that boy Ezra. Coloreds were scared. We thought it was the start of something, payback for us wanting to vote. Lot of us wondered who would be next. *What* would be next. We knew no one would be punished for what happened to that boy.

Ezra James. You were in a hard spot, Ike. I'm not sayin' you weren't. But we need to remember that boy was a human being."

It was as if the old woman had reached in and plucked her words from his conscience. He pulled a chair in front of her and took her hand in his. "I need you to stay, Sparkle. I've put my worst secret out for everyone to see. Said I'm sorry. I've lived alone with this burden all these years. Even my wife didn't know. Please, don't leave us now."

Everyone looked at the old woman with the funny glasses. It seemed that Ike's future suddenly hinged on her verdict. Sparkle Westbrook spoke quietly. "I wasn't ever going to walk out, Ike. I just don't want anyone to forget what happened to that poor boy."

There was a murmur of agreement. Ike kissed her hand, stood, and again asked if anyone present could no longer support him. Like before, one hand went up, then another. Ike smiled when he saw Sparkle with her arms in her lap.

"You seven," he said to the detractors, "I apologize, wish I'd handled things better. Thank you for your past help, thank you for coming today." He went to the door and held it open, an unmistakable invitation for the seven to leave. In the time it took for the first to reach the door, he added, "I understand how you feel, but I've decided to stick it out. I'm not quitting."

"*Alright!*"

Ike whirled around, knowing before he saw her that the voice belonged to Agnes Stono. "Ike's for You in '92," she chanted softly, clapping on each word. Others joined in. Ike smiled as J.R. Stono used the diversion to snatch half a banana muffin from the coffee table.

As the last of the seven stepped into the media circus outside, Cynthia again joined him and circled her arm around his waist, hooking a thumb into one of his empty belt loops.

"Thank you, Cyn."

"You poor man," she whispered back. "All these years … " She leaned back and looked at him again, then pressed her face into his big shoulder.

When the room calmed, Ruthie spoke. "Today is Sunday, August 16th. The primary is August 25th. That leaves eight full days. We've had a setback; we have to work double-time to get back on track. Dianna Harley and her people are going to come hard. Be ready. If you get called by reporters, make it clear you still believe in Ike. What happened in the past was terrible, but it wasn't Ike's fault. He's sorry he didn't come forward sooner. You can say the same thing."

"Ruthie," said Jeremy Akin, "what do we say if they ask if Ike will be able to work with McCauley when he gets to Washington?"

Ike left Cynthia's side. "Tell 'em I'll work with anyone who wants to help the Sixth District of South Carolina, including Mac McCauley. If he doesn't want to work with me, there's nothing I can do about it."

"Maybe McCauley's time's coming to an end," Derrick said.

Ruthie shook her head. "He's not up for reelection until '94."

"I didn't mean that." Derrick's lanky, basketball frame unfolded like a hydraulic crane as he stood. "If the state wants, it can re-open the Ezra James case. McCauley could get indicted, go on trial. The old man could wind up in jail."

"Your words to God's ear, son," someone said.

Ike moved in. "That's out of our hands. We've all got to concentrate on things we can control. First up is this gang outside." He moved to the window, peeked past the white curtains with pale yellow sunflowers. "There's more than a dozen reporters out there."

"Go feed the beasts, Ike," Jeremy Akin laughed.

Ruthie huddled with Derrick. They broke and she tapped her glass with a spoon. "Listen up, everyone."

Minutes later, Ike, shorts and T-shirt traded for beige dress slacks and a sea-green, short-sleeved dress shirt, stepped onto the porch. As he and Cynthia walked forward and the reporters snapped to attention, twenty-eight men and women began to file out of the house and line up beside their candidate. When Ike took his place at a makeshift microphone stand, his supporters formed three neat rows behind him. When he spoke, they stood erect as soldiers. When he opened deadpan with, "Anyone have a question?" they smiled, but did not break formation.

"Dianna Harley says the decent thing for you is to drop out, Ike."

He tried to put his hands on the podium, but it was crowded with tape recorders. Just beyond, a half-dozen TV cameras waited for his response. He chose one and looked straight into the lens. "You can call me a lot of things. I'm not adding 'quitter' to the list."

"She says you're a disgrace."

"That's up to the voters."

"Ike," pressed Leigh Sanderson of the *Statesman*, "Seven people came out a few minutes ago. They were your supporters, but they said they don't believe in you anymore."

"You know, Leigh … "

"Excuse me, I didn't ask my question yet."

Ike put up a hand in apology.

"My question is, if your own supporters can't believe in you, why should anyone else?"

Ike felt his troops stir behind him, but hostile questions never shook him. Strange that it was McCauley who taught him how to deal with an aggressive reporter. *Don't make it worse by blowin' up. That's just what they want.* "Leigh," he said, "I've apologized publicly and privately. Those seven were very important to me. Did I want them to stay on? Course. Am I sorry they couldn't find it within to forgive me? Sure. But if you look behind me, you'll see twenty-eight others who are still on this team. Twenty-eight who still believe in Ike Washington."

Another voice from the side. "Why'd it take thirty years to tell your story, Ike?" That was the one he was waiting for. He glanced over his shoulder, drew strength from his small army, felt Cynthia give his hand a gentle squeeze. He took a breath, turned to the reporter, said, "I don't really know. Part of it was being scared, part was getting caught up in politics. I'm not proud of having waited. I'm ashamed and I live with that each day. As you pass judgment, though, I'd ask you to consider something." He looked past the scribbling writers into another camera lens, imagined it as a living room with mom, dad, grandma and grandpa waiting, weighing, struggling—as he did so long ago. And said, "What would *you* have done?"

"Isn't that kind of a cop-out, Ike?"

Christ, Sanderson again, ruining the moment. "Not to me, Leigh," he said patiently. "I want the voters to remember I wasn't an experienced 50-year-old mayor back then, I was a 17-year-old kid who'd never been out of Kilgo. Isn't it fair for me to ask the voters to consider that?"

Leigh Sanderson scribbled in her notebook, but let it go at that. No one attempted a follow-up.

Back inside, the campaign soldiers shucked their straight faces and pounced on him. Nicely done, they said. Look out now, Dianna Harley, they said. Cynthia put up more coffee and brought out just about everything left in the refrigerator and closets: plums, milk, tuna salad, a pitcher of iced tea, half a chocolate cake, white bread and peanut butter. The phone rang and he picked it up before the message machine could answer.

"Ike?"

"Speaking."

"Carter Strickland. The Senator would like to see you."

Ike turned away from his friends, leaned his forehead against the wall. Had he really thought he wouldn't have to face McCauley? He licked his lips. "What for? What's the point?"

"He didn't explain to me, Ike. He just wants to see you. Tonight, at Bunk's place. Ten o'clock."

"I ... "

"He's asking, not telling, Ike. It's not an order. He just wants to talk."

Ike looked at his wife. She was serving quartered up pieces of his jumbo chocolate chip cookies like they were hors d'oeuvres. "Why ten? Why there?"

"It'll be quiet," Carter said. "Guess the Senator doesn't need any more attention right now. You can understand that."

Ten at night, in that old, suffocating barn north of town. The place where McCauley and Bunk Meacham taught him their brand of politics. He was suddenly seventeen again, scared and taking orders without question. His pinky began to throb.

He could think of twenty reasons to say no.

"I'll be there."

"Good, I'll tell him."

"Carter," he said quickly, afraid the aide had hang up.

"Yes?"

"It's over." His voice was trembling; he knew Carter could tell. But he forced the rest out. "I'm done taking orders. Not from him or anyone who works for him. Make sure he knows."

"Right, Ike, I'll mention it. See you later."

•••••

His hands were dry and steady as he turned left at the wood-post mailbox that said *Meacham* and continued down the dark, unpaved road that led to Bunk's barn and farmhouse. Bunk was dead a long time, but his widow still lived at the old place. McCauley must have cleared the meeting with her, he thought, steering toward the dimly lit barn three hundred yards ahead. A shiver plunged down his neck as he pulled up and parked on the wide ring of gravel in front of the barn.

He got out and stopped, the old smells strong around him: cows, horses, manure, the adjacent forest of pines, the ancient barn itself. He whiffed as he neared the door, his nose wrinkling at the stench of rotted wood beside the almost sweet smell of curing tobacco leaves. The last was a leftover; he knew the tobacco operation died with Bunk.

He stepped inside and checked left and right quickly in case of an ambush. He heard McCauley's voice: "Look who's here, Carter."

One bare light bulb lit the inside. His eyes were drawn to the harsh light, turned on and off by pulling a length of twine that swung back and forth in wind blown by a noisy box fan.

McCauley sat at a table that had once been a giant spool of telephone wire, butt on one chair, feet crossed and up on another. He was casual— beige golf pants and a white polo, looked like he'd just finished eighteen holes at Crosscreek Golf and Country. There was a bottle of *Jack* on the table and two stubby glasses. "Leave the briefcase and wait outside," he told his aide. Strickland nodded to Ike as he passed.

When they were alone, McCauley put his feet down and took his time. "Drink?" Ike accepted. He drained his shot and helped himself to another. He waited a moment for McCauley to say whatever was on his mind. The Senator didn't say anything, just picked up the bottle and stared at its label. Ike walked to a corner of the barn and paused before the cracked mirror he used to admire himself in once McCauley started buying him nice clothes back in the early days. He looked at himself now and didn't like how the jagged crack cut his image in half at the chest.

Odd that it never bothered him when he was young. He moved slowly around the barn, stopping every few feet to touch things—a brown, scarred-up dog collar, a rusted pitchfork, a ball of gray twine. There'd been grand and terrible moments in this place. It looked smaller now, too small for all his memories.

He remembered how the man before him scratched out the first campaign with a stick on the dirt floor. How he insisted Ike explain it back. How he looked at Bunk and said, *Jesus H, that's it 'xactly.* How surprised they were when it turned out he was a smart kid.

McCauley was seventy-one now, an old man, nothing like the Klansman who once killed a man and enslaved another in the same day. He remembered McCauley's crew cut, an inch of straw-colored, pomaded hair that stuck up straight as comb points; how his cool blue eyes closed a fraction when he laid out the deal—*you can join him or join me*—the feeling of the warm breath on his neck as Tyler Hawke readied the mallet. *Know what insurance is, Ike?*

The rage spilled out before he even felt it bubbling up. He walked briskly to the table, made a move as if he were going to choke McCauley. Stopped before his fingers reached the white cotton collar. "I should kill you, same as Tyler."

McCauley's eyes were big, bigger than he'd ever seen them. But he was calm, didn't even flinch when Ike charged. "Tyler?" he said. "That boy died in a car crash."

"I could've saved him. I let him die. I'd let you die, too."

McCauley put a foot back on the table, winced as if the motion hurt his knee. He seemed to be working over the information about Tyler. He tossed back another shot and shrugged. "You're a weakling, Ike. Weak and greedy. That's why I stuck with you so long."

"What?"

McCauley coughed and spat. "That's right. You're a weakling, always have been. We did some rough things back then—maybe I don't agree with them now—but we did 'em cause we believed in something, values, a way of life. You did what you did for yourself. For Ike Washington. You sold out, son, sold out your own folks."

The words snuffed his fire. "You forced me."

McCauley snorted and banged his shot glass on the table. "Ain't that a hoot. Day you got fitted for that suit by Benny Lee was the day we knew we didn't have to force you no more. You liked lookin' good and havin' money. Try and deny it."

Ike stood with his mouth open. McCauley shook his head. Case closed. "We—me, Bunk, even Tyler—we all knew. We laughed about it. You liked being on the inside, makin' deals, playin' 'Big Ike.' That's why I kept you on so long. Knew you were too greedy to ever make trouble."

"Not true."

"It's true. Even that boy me and Tyler used to teach a lesson to the niggers had more guts than you. Went down fightin', that one did. Why, that boy kept fightin' even when he was starin' at the noose."

Ike knew what he meant. He flashed to the forest, saw Ezra, rope around his neck, yank his head up suddenly and spit in McCauley's face. "And now,"—McCauley stood stiffly and summoned the voice he used on the floor of the United States Senate. "Now you think you can make it right by telling your story to the papers. You're too dirty to come clean, Ike. Your stain don't come out."

Ike slumped against a wooden beam gray and splintery with age. McCauley pulled an unblemished eight-by-ten envelope from his brief-case and brought it to him.

"This here's for you, son."

Ike took the envelope and kept his eyes on McCauley. They were a foot apart. He could smell the liquor on the Senator's breath. Maybe it was his own breath. "What's this?"

McCauley walked back to the table and closed his bottle. "That's your election, Ike."

The envelope contained a half-inch file marked "Opposition Research—Dianna Harley." As Ike leafed through the pages, McCauley said, "Didn't I tell you back at the Capitol we were going to dig up some dirt on that woman?"

Ike nodded.

"That there's enough dirt to bury her."

Ike stopped reading and let the report rest against his leg. "Why would you do this now, after what I've done to you?"

McCauley laughed again. "Nothing gonna happen to me, Ike. Few bad stories in the press, maybe a protest by the N-Double-ACP. We hit back by suin' that newspaper, holler a little about irresponsible journalism. In the end, it all goes away. Hell, publicity'll probably help in *my* next election. Yep, won't be long before you and me are working together in Congress. One of the first things you learn up there is you don't take nothin' personal."

"They have your fingerprints."

"Hah. First, it's fifty-fifty those prints belong to Tyler. Second, prints on a belt buckle don't mean I killed a person. Jesus H, no jury in my great state of South Carolina would convict me on that. It wouldn't even get to trial."

Ike put his back to the wooden beam and let himself slide to the floor. His right hand landed in the sticky web of a trap-door spider. He brushed the silky mess off on his pants and watched the spider scurry away. It seemed impossible that no justice would come from all he'd revealed. The only one he hurt was himself. And now he would again owe

Lander McCauley. He could hand back the report, but there was a critical debate approaching. Dianna Harley would be ferocious. He could take his chances or stop her with the new ammunition.

"So long, Mr. Congressman," McCauley chuckled as he picked up his bottle and briefcase and walked out.

Ike didn't answer. He pulled himself up and brushed dirt and dust from the seat of his pants. He adjusted his shirt, put the report under his arm, and followed McCauley out the door without looking back at Bunk Meacham's barn.

24   *Ike*

"We need a new commercial right away," Ruthie said.

They were returning to Kilgo from an early-evening barbecue and rally in Cameron on the western side of Lake Marion in Calhoun County. The sun was nearly down, and drivers headed the opposite way on I-26 were already using their lights. Ike, pleased by the big turnout in such a little town, relaxed for the first time in two days. He drove with his seat tilted so far back, he looked ready for a nap.

Ruthie was morning fresh, poring over several pages of notes she'd taken during the day. "You're starting to come off flat. It's natural—you've answered the same questions hundreds of times the last few days. Let's do a TV spot where you address the Ezra stuff one last time. End it by saying you're not taking any more questions on the subject."

He poked his tongue around the inside of his cheek.

"C'mon," Ruthie said, jabbing his thigh. "It'll be perfect," she said. "You make a passionate statement that sums it up once and for all. Then say you're done talking about it. People will respect that. Plus, it lets us move to other subjects."

An overnight poll by the Columbia *Statesman* showed voters were stunned by the story. Ike's negative rating soared from eighteen to forty-nine percent. But there was good news too—eighty-two percent said they would still consider him. If the election were tomorrow, Ike would edge

Dianna Harley by four percentage points. Either of them would trounce Orrin Baxter, the lone Republican running in the general election.

Baxter, an insurance salesman and first-time office seeker from Florence, was positioning himself as the choice for voters who didn't want a black congressman. He campaigned lazily on an anti-Washington, anti-welfare, anti-abortion platform, but most knew his game. When Baxter declared that voters should pick the best candidate "regardless of skin color," the message was that it was okay for the district's majority black voters to choose him instead of Ike or Dianna Harley. Even a small percentage of black votes combined with total white support would make him competitive.

The poll confirmed what insiders already knew—Baxter was not a factor and the primary, now six days away, was the real election.

"Set it up," Ike told Ruthie. "But it's not going to stop the questions."

"It'll help. We should do one more piece of mail, too. Nice family shot of you on the cover, quotes inside from officials people would recognize, your accomplishments as mayor, five items you'll tackle as a freshman congressman."

Ike started to wonder how long she could go without air.

"On the back panel, a homey touch: a thumbnail of Agnes with her recipe for snap beans with hot sauce and fatback."

She was right. The TV ad would hit hard, the mailing would be soft and fuzzy. "How much do we have left?"

"After the commercial and direct mail, probably six thousand."

They had raised four hundred thousand for the campaign. Now they were down to six. If he won, though, campaign funds would never again be an issue. Businessmen fell over themselves giving to incumbents. He would build a war chest so huge, no one would dare run against him in '94.

"Do it."

The jazz station they were listening to crackled. Ike leaned over to play with the fine-tune button and the *Taurus* lurched to the right. He moved them back to their lane. "How long will it take to get a new ad on TV?"

"We've already got air-time," she shrugged. "We'll tape the ad—just a head and shoulders shot, thirty seconds—and sub it for one of the other spots." When Ruthie tried to jot some notes, her pen was dry. She licked the tip and scribbled a line of circles on her legal pad that showed up as round dents. "Got a pen?" He reached in his pocket. "Tomorrow's Thursday," she said. "If we shoot in Columbia tomorrow morning, we can get it all over the district by Friday."

"Friday's the debate," Ike said.

"No problem. Tomorrow's open. We'll do the ad and spend the rest of the day getting ready."

The radio squawked again. Ike played with it a moment, found the station, lost it, and gave up. "I miss the *Lincoln*. These seats hurt and the radio stinks."

"Focus, Ike."

•••••

Murray College in Columbia was founded four years after the end of the Civil War to teach former slaves the skills—mostly agricultural and mechanical skills—needed to survive as free men and women. Over the decades, particularly during the 1960s, Murray grew into a home for seven thousand students. It was now among the state's most important historically black colleges and boasted dozens of prestigious alumni, including the first black to serve on the federal bench in South Carolina, an NFL quarterback, and an internationally-renowned sculptor.

Four years earlier, in 1988, three million federal, state and private dollars were collected for a new concert hall. Samuel Hammond Auditorium was built to dazzle with state-of-the-art acoustics and unobstructed viewing from all eleven hundred and fifty thickly-padded seats.

On the night of August twenty-first, at precisely 7:30, Ike Washington and Dianna Harley strode crisply on stage, shook hands, turned, and paced off the steps to their podiums. Before any debating could begin, white-bearded college president Henry Carpenter, Jr. made a surprise visit to Ike's microphone.

"We were built to accommodate eleven-fifty and have more than thirteen hundred this evening," Carpenter said with a nervous laugh. He held the smile and adjusted his bifocals. "Everyone can stay; just please find a seat in the aisles or stand in back." Peering up the aisles and toward the front doors, he shouted, "Ushers!" Several young men and women in burgundy sports coats and gold-stitched crests spun around. "No one else comes in unless someone leaves." They nodded and he ambled off.

"Alright then, thank you Mr. President. Guess we're ready to go." Veteran news anchor Ron McPherson from Channel Ten grinned at the overflow crowd and pressed a finger to his thick, walnut hair. It yielded like foam rubber, accepting his digit and quickly rebounding to its previous shape.

"Welcome, ladies and gentlemen, to the hottest ticket of the political season—a debate between the candidates for the Democratic primary for South Carolina Congressional District Six." Ike snuck a look at his rival. Dianna must have picked the quietest ensemble in her closet: shipyard gray, double-breasted suit with pearl buttons, small-ribbed rose shirt peeking through the jacket, glossy black shoes with a medium heel. The outfit was set off by a gold link necklace and triangular teak earrings in the shape of small African masks that stood out nicely against her new, toned down hairstyle. She could be executive vice president of some rental car company, or admissions director of the college, or—*he had it!*—his future congressional office manager. He smiled as he opened the top button of his favorite navy pinstripe and tugged down his vest.

McPherson was droning on about the rules: two minutes for opening and closing statements; the candidates would be permitted to question each other; and to the audience—*Please, we know you have a favorite*—be respectful of both candidates. Ike shifted his weight from left to right. Dianna was going down. Tonight. "Mrs. Harley won a coin toss backstage and has decided to go first," McPherson announced. He held out a sweeping hand as if asking her to dance. His nails shone with clear polish. "Mrs. Harley," he said.

The crowd stilled. Harley and Washington signs and banners stopped waving. The ushers crossed their arms and blocked all doors. In the media section, pens hovered like sniper rifles. Ike scanned the front few rows. Squinting against the stage lights, he picked out Cynthia, Ruthie, Derrick, Dan Patragno, and Dianna Harley's New York wanna-be husband, proctologist Abe Harley.

Dianna did not smile, clear her throat or say good evening. "Several weeks ago, I told a Rotary Club luncheon that this seat was too important to go to just anyone." Ike shook his head. *When would she learn to behave?* The audience got quieter still. "But it turns out it's worse than that," Dianna said.

Ike didn't know whether to look at her, the crowd, or his short stack of index cards. He prayed people were watching his new campaign ad on TV tonight instead of this shrill woman. He'd done well in the ad, he thought—contrite, a bit sad, yet strong and forthright as well.

"It turns out my opponent"—she pointed his way—"made his fortune by keeping silent about the murder of a young man named Ezra James. For more than thirty years, Ike Washington held his tongue and collected his check from one of the men he says did the killing. This is not my interpretation of the facts. Mr. Washington has admitted all to the *Herald-Leader* newspaper in Charleston." She held up a copy of the article.

A thin-shouldered old man in the audience could not contain himself. Eyes turned as he lurched up and shouted, "'At's the truth, Mizz Harley. Righteous truth!"

"Shut-up and sit down," someone yelled.

"Please," Ron McPherson warned, flashing his best six-o'clock-news smile. "We don't want to have to remove anyone. Mrs. Harley?"

Dianna roared on. "Ike Washington is a criminal. If not in the eyes of the law, then in the eyes of God. "You—she spoke directly to the audience, then to the TV camera behind Ike-and all of you watching tonight, cannot reward his behavior. It would be a mockery." She paused. Even Ike felt himself lean forward. He saw her lightly bite her lower lip and felt his pressure rise. It was as if she were going to pass sentence. She did. "*He should go to prison*," she said, "*not to Congress.*"

Samuel Hammond Auditorium erupted in a fit of cheers and hissing. Dianna could not go on and the rest of her time was lost. She didn't seem to care. Ron McPherson pleaded for quiet. "We are being carried live on public access," he said, italicizing each word like a parent scolding naughty children in front of company.

Ike could not respond, the din was too loud. He tried to smile, to be interested in his index cards, to appear anything but shaken. He scanned the front row and saw Cynthia with a hand over her mouth. He forced a deep breath that didn't help; Dianna had given voice to his worst misgivings. He thought of the first hundred he took from Lander McCauley, of the ripple of pleasure when he slipped on his first custom-made suit. How he preened in front of that cracked mirror in Bunk's barn! McCauley's words tortured him. *You liked playin' Big Ike.*

McPherson failed to settle the crowd. The moment swelled to more than a minute. Ike cut his eyes to Dianna, so smug, and then watched as the moderator left his desk and approached the edge of the stage. President Carpenter joined him. A TV cameraman with a ratty ponytail positioned himself in the ten-foot gulf between the audience and the two men, and then began pivoting back and forth to get shots of the unruly crowd as well as the pleading officials. A scuffle broke out between two women several rows back. One lost the butterfly clip that held her hair and the stiff, tangled mess now swung in her face, hiding her left eye. The other glared and kept up her fists. She wore a row of silver bracelets on each wrist that flashed in the light from the TV cameras. Both women were escorted out by two Murray College football *Cougars* in burgundy sports coats with gold-stitched crests.

"If I cannot get quiet," McPherson warned in the sudden break that followed, "we will clear the hall and continue with no audience."

"Last warning," Carpenter threw in.

Order returned slowly. McPherson, pink-skinned part ruined by a platoon of walnut locks that broke ranks during the melee, returned to his stage desk. He did not fuss with his hair. "Mr. Washington," he said, clearly disgusted with the whole affair.

Ike felt the heat from his detractors. It sizzled and seemed to consume the encouragement of his supporters. He wanted to loosen his tie, but kept his hands on the podium and fiddled with his cards. These Harley people weren't indifferent; they hated him. He sipped his water and waited for a full thirty seconds of silence.

"Mr. Washington?" Ike looked up and couldn't help but stare. McPherson looked like he was melting. The bottom strands of his hair were wet and sweat leaked through his make-up. When the anchorman wiped his forehead, he smeared a line of flesh-colored paste along his dark eyebrows. He looked grotesque. Ike wanted to tell him. "Mr. Washington, your opening statement."

Someone in the audience shouted, "Nothing to say, Ike?"

"Yes, I have something to say." The calmness of his voice surprised him. "I am not perfect, I've admitted that."

"Damn straight," came from somewhere in the crowd. McPherson turned. Ike spoke before the anchor could chastise the crowd. "But she, my opponent, is not without sin either."

Dianna spun toward him. "You're ridiculous."

He hammered his fist onto the podium and shouted at McPherson: "She allowed to step on my time?"

"Mrs. Harley, please," McPherson said. "You'll have a chance to respond." She crossed her arms and twitched her head to the right, away from both men, as if they were now ganged up against her. Ike waited to make sure he had the floor and pulled a sheaf of papers from a short shelf inside his podium. He cleared his throat. And waited some more. Then he said, "Mrs. Harley has misused her position as chair of the NAACP. She has used NAACP funds for personal use."

"*What?* He can stand there and say any lie that comes in his fool head?" she demanded of McPherson.

"She and her husband have vacationed on NAACP money," Ike continued. "New York, Detroit, Puerto Rico."

"Those were conventions. NAACP business."

"They have bought personal items on their trips and charged the association. Wine, luggage." He scrutinized one of his papers though he knew just what it said. "*Private massages each day for a week at the Hyatt Regency in New York City: seven hundred, seventy dollars.*"

"That is an outright lie," Dianna yelled to the reporters scribbling frantically down front. She grasped the sides of her podium, reloaded, took aim. "You desperate, bootlicking bastard." He ignored her and held up the rest of his papers. Cameras flashed. "These are copies of receipts. They'll be available to the media after the debate."

President Carpenter rushed on stage and whispered something to McPherson.

"The debate is over," the anchorman reported.

"In that case, these"—he brandished the evidence McCauley had provided like a weapon—"are available right now."

Reporters mobbed the stage. Campaign aides rushed to their candidates. "Cut the feed," McPherson yelled to his producer. President Carpenter grabbed a mike and ordered his ushers to clear the auditorium. McPherson kicked his stage desk over and walked out. Dan Patragno and Ruthie Baines arrived by Ike's side at nearly the same moment. "This stuff true? Where'd you get it?" Dan asked Ike.

He didn't answer. He was busy searching through the mob for—shit, where was he? Ike shifted left and right, making himself small to see around all the people on stage, then standing on his tip-toes to see over the top. At last, he glanced to his right and saw what he'd been half-expecting. Abe Harley was by his wife's side, urging her to be quiet and ushering her out of the media spotlight toward a room backstage.

Ike balled his fingers into a tight fist and whispered a terse, "Yesss." He and Ruthie exchanged winks. "Okay, I'm ready," he joked with the reporters, "How can I help you guys? Don't you have enough news for one night?"

25   *Ike and Ezra*

He is back in the barn, before the cracked mirror in a new, shark-skin suit that clashes badly with the humble farm tools and dusty furniture. The stifling air is soaked with the odor of peat and tobacco. His eye is drawn to the mirror. It is a good-looking suit, a shiny, slate gray job flecked with black. His shirt is creamy white with French cuffs and pewter links that bear his initials, *IW*. The tie is half gray, half black, bisected by a thin white line that runs from knot to bottom. *Armani*. He does not remember getting the suit. Or returning to Bunk Meacham's barn. In the corner, a point of light skips off the stud of a dog's collar. Cody! But Bunk's old coonhound's been dead thirty years. He approaches the panting dog, makes to pat his back. Its eager tail beats the dirt floor, just like the old days. As Ike reaches out, the dog's head pivots. Instead of eyes, it has two black, wormy holes. He recoils and trips on a rake, goes tumbling around like an off-balance skater, lands on a rusty, three-foot lantern and tears a hole in his pants. Mocking laughter makes him look up.

Gotcha.

Ezra!

This our last visit. Thanks for dressin' up.

What do you mean?

Last time I'll be calling.

Why?

You came clean as you're able. I guess you got some good in you and some bad. Like most.

Ike fits the flap of his torn pants back in place, smearing the blood on his scraped leg.

McCauley's the one who did it. McCauley and that Tyler Hawke. I've told my part. Put it all on the line. I'm sorry. Sayin' it again to you right now, sorry I didn't try to help. Sorry I ran. Sorry I let you die. Sorry I didn't tell sooner.

Listen, Ike. You listen hard, boy. I'm done visitin'. Your problem ain't with me no more, you hear? 'Gonna get harder now, lot harder. You just remember, your problem ain't with me no more. I'm forgivin' you.

26 *Dan*

"Great piece, kid. Pass me a sugar."

Dan fished a white packet out of the dolphin holder and flipped it to Bernie Weinstock. He glanced around, acting like a celebrity who didn't want to be bothered, even though he knew no one at Bernie's Broad Street Cafe had the slightest idea who he was. Still, several in the sleepy-eyed shorts and T-shirt crowd were reading the paper, and his story was hogging the front page. He kept his ears open for any snatch of conversation about McCauley and Auralee, hoping secretly for the big payoff: A guy freezes with his cup halfway to his mouth, looks up, says, "Hey, Steffie, *get a load of this ... "*

This morning—two days before the election—voters focused on Ike Washington and Dianna Harley woke to his second big scoop in as many weeks: Senator Lander McCauley's Washington staff includes a twenty-nine-year-old, bassoon-playing secretary who, by her own admission, did not type, make appointments, or perform any of the other duties typically assigned to the secretarial pool.

When asked by the *Herald-Leader* what she *did* do, Auralee DeMossier brushed the dirty blonde bangs from her blue eyes and said she served the senator's personal needs. "When he's not here, I practice my instrument," she added without guile. McCauley declined to comment. The Clerk of the Senate listed Ms. DeMossier's annual salary at forty-nine thousand dollars.

Bernie tore open the sugar and dumped half into his coffee. "What's next?"

"Not sure. Probably an investigation by the Senate Ethics Committee. No movement yet. Fuckers probably all have their own Auralees.

"Ha."

"Rumor's also floating that Mrs. McCauley developed a sudden urge to visit friends in Europe." He smiled. "She's not due back anytime soon."

Bernie picked up the paper and re-read his lead. "Your paper might not have run this story a couple of years ago. Too afraid of offending a big shot pol. This go through the lawyer?"

"Devereaux's in deep shit. We all knew he was old friends with McCauley, but Butcher figured out he's the one who told him I was headed for D.C. on the Ezra James story. That accounts for how they were waiting for me in McCauley's private office."

"Did they fire him?"

"Not yet. He crossed the line, though. Butcher said he'll never ask Devereaux to review another story before we publish. Ryder feels the same."

They both looked up as a horse-drawn carriage clip-clopped up Broad. A woman with piles of brown curls stuffed into a pale yellow golf cap pointed a camera at the cafe. Bernie looked at his hands. Dan waved. "Maybe you should try TV."

"Listen, Bern, the wires have picked up my stories. I'm starting to get calls."

"Yeah, who?"

"City editors at the *Charlotte Observer* and *Tampa Daily News* want me to interview."

"*Observer's* a good paper. Part of Knight-Ridder. The *Daily News* also does nice work."

"I know. I'm not so sure what I want anymore. Ever since I got here, I've been trying to work my way to a bigger paper." He laced his fingers through the handle of the jumbo mug. "Now I don't know. Lem Butcher's a good editor. I'm learning a lot at the *Leader,* and you couldn't ask for a better beat."

"How 'bout if it was the *Post* instead of the *Observer?*"

"Guess I'd go." He thought about that a second, then looked up and saw Detective Stan LeTourge's black *Marquis* turn the corner and pull within shouting distance. Stan push-buttoned the passenger window down, caught Dan's eye, wagged his head.

"Patragno, I'm about to ruin your day off. Right back."

Stan drove half a block and began a parallel park. "What's *that* about?" Bernie said. Dan kept his eyes on the car. Stan was breathing a little heavy. He sat down in one of the high-backed cafe chairs, put his elbows on the table and lowered his chin. "You didn't get this from me."

Dan rolled his eyes. They'd been through this before. Stan had given him half-a-dozen tips and he'd never mentioned the detective by name.

"Say it," LeTourge insisted.

"I didn't get it from you."

Stan turned to the third member of their Sunday-morning bull sessions. "I can trust him, no?"

"He's alright," Bernie said.

"Okay." Stan signaled to a waiter for coffee and his usual banana muffin. "People in Columbia—people who know this for a fact—tell me McCauley's about to become the target of a grand jury investigation. Jury's going to be empanelled tomorrow. AG's been burning to do it since you broke that story."

South Carolina's attorney general was Bryce Salaby. Young, good-looking, connected, and very ambitious. No surprise that he'd seize a chance to nail McCauley. Still, a grand jury was going to look at the possibility of indicting a sitting senator for a thirty-year-old murder. Awesome. "Anything else, Stan?"

"Yeah, the feds are looking at it too. If this crime happened the way you said, it took place on land owned by the federal government. That'd make it a federal civil rights case."

"Never thought of that," Dan said, already envisioning his lead for the Monday paper. "Shit, I have to get in, start making calls. Where can I find you later?"

"That's all I've got."

"If I come up with more new stuff, where you going to be?"

"Home. Leave a message if I'm out."

"Thanks, Stan, owe you."

LeTourge winked. "Never liked that old bastard McCauley. Checkers?" he said to Bernie. "Set 'em up."

Dan dropped a twenty on the table. "Coffee's on me. Checker champ keeps the change."

As he left, he passed a table where a couple was poring over the Sunday paper. The man had a foot up on the wrought-iron table and his nose buried in the sports section. The woman had the front page.

"I'll bet she's playin' a lot more than that bassoon," Dan heard as he bounded off to the newsroom.

27 *Ike*

The polls closed at 7 p.m. The Associated Press called it at 7:01.

Ike Washington, assuming a near-certain win over Orrin Baxter in the general election in November, would become South Carolina's first black congressman since George W. Murray joined the opening session of the fifty-third Congress on March 4, 1893. Murray, the media were fond of repeating, was born a slave in Sumter County in 1853.

Ike, Ruthie, Agnes Stono, and dozens of top-level supporters watched the early returns at Ike's Place in Kilgo. Those who couldn't squeeze in the small diner spilled outside, sharing sidewalk space with the unshaven, jobless gang that convened each day and contemplated USC football and what they would do if they ever got their hands on one of those cute *Gamecock* cheerleaders. Sigh.

Ike knew the bums had little use for politics. They were friendly because he let them hang in front of the diner, and because he sometimes sent Yvonne or one of the other waitresses out with a pot of coffee. Earlier, they piled in a rented school bus that took them to Shady Ridge Elementary, where they happily punched a hole on their ballots for Ike Washington, Jr. When the TV news began flashing vote totals, they joined in the cheers.

Ike was thrashing Dianna Harley everywhere, piling up four-to-one margins in big counties like Florence, Orangeburg and Charleston, and doubling Dianna's totals in the small, rural corners of the district, in counties like Clarendon and Calhoun.

"Got your speech?" Ruthie whispered so only Ike and Cynthia could hear.

Ike tapped his pocket. "What time should I do it?"

"We'll give Dianna until 10. If she doesn't concede, we'll declare victory at 10:05."

Ike agreed and returned to studying the numbers on TV. Exit polls revealed that most in the black-majority district felt he was victimized by Lander McCauley. Voters said they believed young Ike had no choice, and that, as an adult, he deserved credit for coming clean, even if it did take three decades.

McCauley's approval rating nose-dived from the high sixties to single digits in the wake of the Ezra James, Auralee DeMossier and grand jury investigation stories broken by Dan Patragno. Voters said they expected McCauley to be indicted, which lent credence to Ike's claim that the old senator was once a hell-raising Klansman capable of murder.

"Sickening what happened to that young boy Ezra James," one businessman told a TV reporter. "I don't think Ike could've stopped it, no matter what he did. For me, the election came down to who'd do better in Congress. I picked Ike. He's been tested." The same exit polls found that voters were unnerved by the NAACP scandal touched off by Abe Harley and his homosexual lover, a 34-year-old Latino stockbroker named Pedro Serrano. After the uproarious debate at Murray College, Dianna's husband confessed, first to her, then at an emotional press conference a day later in Columbia. He and Pete met by accident in New York City, he said. They never planned to have an affair, and it was the first homosexual experience for both men, he swore.

What did *that* have to do with ripping off NAACP funds, the press demanded?

Abe wiped his forehead with the inside crook of his elbow. "Nothing," he said. "That was wrong—inexcusable—and I swear I'll pay back every cent." The public airing did little to help Dianna. *Pete's Meat* jokes were rampant. Abe Harley, critics snickered, had retooled the organization into the *N-Double-A-C-Pee-Pee*. Outraged board members ordered an independent investigation and audit. Reporters scoured several cities for Pedro Serrano and found he was on extended leave in his native Brazil. It was Abe, not Dianna, who had helped himself to the NAACP credit card. Dianna tried to make voters see the distinction in the days before the election. Ike fought to keep the line blurry. Every time Dianna stamped out a fire, he stroked a match somewhere else. The exit poll found most voters didn't know if Dianna or Abe were guilty. Some didn't care.

"Don't want no part of that mess, honey," one grandmother told the TV cameras after voting at First Jerusalem Baptist Church in Greeleyville. "I'm for Mr. Ike Washington *Junior*."

By 9 p.m., anchors on all the local stations had declared a landslide. "Looks like Ike Washington will top 50,000 votes to less than 10,000 for Harley," Ron McPherson told his viewers. The top-rated anchorman wagged his head; his hair moved like a shiny helmet. "One week ago," he marveled, "this race was too close to call."

The phone rang in Ike's private office just after 9. Ruthie answered, said, "I'll get him," and put her hand over the mouthpiece. "It's *her*." Ike stepped from the diner to his back office and took the phone. He knew TV cameras were probably trained on Dianna. The concession call was high drama, and his vanquished foe was unlikely to ban the cameras and risk being called a sore loser.

Ruthie waved in Dan Patragno and two of the TV guys covering things at Ike's end. The camera jockeys scrambled for position—one at Ike's feet, shooting up, the other, across the small office for a tight shot of him leaning forward in his leather chair, elbow on desk, phone to ear. They flicked on their lights and the room brightened. Ike shielded his eyes until a pair of second, small red lights signaled that the cameras were recording.

When it was time to talk, he pressed a gray button that put Dianna on speaker. After gently hanging up the receiver, he clasped his hands behind his head, leaned back, and said, "This is Ike Washington."

"Hello, Ike. It's Dianna."

He imagined her: fangs retracted into a sweet smile, long, pearly nails digging into her palms as she forced herself to be nice.

"Hi, Dianna." He wasn't going to help. A slight pause. He grinned with his lips closed. The cameras rolled.

"I wanted to congratulate you," Dianna said. "It was a hard campaign. Maybe we both said things we'd take back."

He hesitated. Should he agree? He looked to Ruthie, who warned him off.

"Anyway," Dianna said, "Congratulations. Be a good congressman."

"Thank you, Dianna, I promise you, those who voted for me, and those who didn't, that I will do my best for this district."

Ruthie slid an index finger across her throat. *Cut!*

"Bye, Ike. Best of luck."

But he couldn't let her off that easy. "Dianna," he said, "Can we count on your help in the general election? Will you ask your supporters to join us?"

Silence. Had he gone too far? The cameras' red lights glowed like cigarettes. Ike saw Dan Patragno write in his notebook. "Absolutely," Dianna said softly. "I want this seat to go to you, not Orrin Baxter."

Bootlicker

A cheer went up in the diner and out on the sidewalk. Ike pumped his fist. Ruthie squeezed Dan's forearm, jarring his pen. "Thanks a lot," Patragno said, holding out his pad to show a snaky line of blue ink that cut across his notes.

"Sorry," she said and burst out laughing. It was a contagious giggle, far more than was warranted by the dumb scribble or the annoyed look on Patragno's face. Ike joined and laughed until tears appeared in his deep brown eyes.

·····

When, then, did his mood turn?

He stood at a white pine in the misty, early-morning light and scratched at a piece of bark as he thought back and tried to pinpoint the moment he began to spiral downward. He gave his little speech and then yielded to the post-victory clamor—reporters demanding private interviews, then racing to get fresh quotes in their final edition or late-night broadcast. He remembered trying to think up new ways to say the same old garbage, to be confident without sounding conceited, to appear eager for work even though he was dog-tired and wanted only to feel a cool pillow against his cheek. He felt as though he could sleep for two days, yet knew somehow he would not shut his eyes this night.

After the press left, the party charged into overdrive. Three cases of champagne appeared. Bums clinked glasses with corporate execs and small business owners. He laughed when Timmy Jefferson, a street-corner regular who hadn't worked in ten years, cornered Boston Ames, a loan executive at *NationsBank*. "We're like stockholders in the same company now, right Bro?" Joe said, lighting one of the celebratory cigars that came with the champagne.

Western Union delivered a telegram from his son and daughter-in-law in Charlotte that said, "Way to go, Mr. Congressman. We'll be down soon to help celebrate." His blood felt hot as he pressed a fifty into the driver's hand.

Dozens more showed up. The celebration blossomed into a block party that stretched nearly a quarter-mile to Union Street. Someone got hold of a gargantuan boom-box, and bodies were soon gyrating in alcoholic abandon to the Best of James Brown. Officer Eddie Bishop of the Kilgo Police Department was dispatched to lower the noise, and the two of them wound up slugging down plastic tumblers of champagne in the back office.

"How long before you retire, Eddie?" Bishop lifted his tumbler, gave it a shake, watched the bubbly wine swirl around and around. "Less than a month."

"You've been loyal to me, Eddie. I don't forget. I've got a way for you to boost your pension if you're interested."

"Yeah?"

"I need someone to keep an eye on Cynthia when I'm in Washington. Nothing hard, just check the neighborhood, be there if she needs someone."

"Shoot, Ike, I'd do that free."

"I can give you twenty-eight thousand a year."

Eddie's eyes popped. "Sold," he said, and they laughed together. He remembered looking at his watch after his old friend left to join the dancing. At one a.m., he was still in high spirits. So when did the ache begin? When was he overcome by the urge to return here?

Ruthie was drunk. Nothing obvious, yet he could tell. Her eyes were different, narrower, like she was squinting slightly to keep the night in focus. He watched from afar, proud as a father. She laughed and danced, and never forgot who she was and about to become. Ruthie Baines was going to Washington. She would enjoy herself and never slip. No scandalous behavior would ever cause her to lose her position to Derrick Maussipant.

"You stay with us tonight," he ordered when she wandered in for a pit stop. "I don't want you driving."

"I'm fine." She put a hand to her ear and made a show of listening to the music blasting outside. She bounced and shimmied. *"I feel good."*

"It's not a request."

She crossed her arms and stepped back, then seemed to have a change of heart and kissed his cheek. Her breath smelled of champagne and popcorn. "Fine, I'll sleep on the couch. Want to dance?"

He danced with Ruthie, then Agnes, then Cynthia. The night was warm, so he tossed off his jacket and slipped his tie around Cynthia's waist to draw her close. He was surprised when she whispered, "Why do you look sad? This is your night. Be happy."

"I'm happy, don't be silly," he said, heart sinking.

She was right. He felt like he was being sucked into the muck, that the more he fought, the more it closed around him. Why? He'd confessed, taken his punishment, hadn't complained when people stared as though he'd been partner to the lynching. He'd laid it all out, and the voters still wanted him for their congressman. Cyn was right; he should be feeling good.

He dropped his tie to the street and held her closer, making sure to keep his right hand on her back so she wouldn't feel the twitch in his left pinky.

Now, deep in the woods, his sad eyes widened. The thick bushes. The trees, some ramrod straight, some shooting off at bizarre angles. The small clearing. The place of his rebirth.

He looked around, aching, trying to take it in, to re-create the scene as it was that summer day in 1959. An owl hooted; cicadas buzzed. Over there, he thought, moving to a stand of enormous pines that must have been saplings thirty-three years ago. He touched one of the trees, imagined himself and Ricky Lee in their hiding place. He shifted and sank to a knee, ignoring the wet dirt that stuck to his suit pant. He wanted to see the clearing from the same vantage point he did that day. He found the spot and waited in a crouch, as if something might happen.

He remembered Ricky Lee racing off once McCauley and Tyler Hawke dragged Ezra from the truck. He turned his head in the direction Ricky Lee ran, wondering for the millionth time why he, too, didn't run before they saw him.

•••••

It was 2:30 a.m. when the block party ran out of gas, nearly 3 a.m. when he pulled into his driveway and opened the door for Cynthia. Ruthie was still giggly. "Put a light on. I'll get her settled," Cyn said. He stepped on the porch and glanced down, even though he knew the newspaper wouldn't arrive for a few more hours. He went inside and saw the message machine blinking. Eighteen calls. He listened to three and shut it off. They were all the same: Congratulations. Knew you'd do it. Knock 'em dead in Washington. *My Man.*

My ass, he thought. He went to the kitchen and poured a glass of milk.

"*You're hungry?*"

Cynthia's voice startled him and he nearly dropped the glass. "I really didn't eat much all night."

"Well, don't fill your stomach. You'll never sleep."

"Sure, Cyn."

"Ruthie's sleeping on the couch. I'm going up."

"There in a minute," he said.

"You okay?"

"Fine, fine," he smiled.

She studied him a moment and turned for the stairs. He sipped some milk and put the glass down more than half full. His impulse was to follow his wife. Instead, he took a step toward the garage. He reached for the doorknob. Ruthie's voice stopped him. "Ike?"

He hurried to the living room, switched on the lamp, and sat on the coffee table next to the couch. His knees made the sound of knuckles cracking. "Right here, Ruthie. You sick?"

"Nah," she said sleepily. "We did it, huh, Ike? Showed Dianna good, showed everyone."

Even drunk and drowsy, she was beautiful. Fresh, oozing with energy and ideas and idealism. Had he taken her innocence? He touched the row of turquoise beads in her hair. "Get some sleep."

She struggled to lift her head. She looked dazed and yet spoke with clarity. "When we get up there, we'll make it all right, huh Ike? Both of us? We're going to get it done? Help a lot of people back here?"

He wanted badly to hold her, to beg her forgiveness, to return to the time when they first met and tell her, *Thanks anyway, but you're a little young, Miss Baines, I already have a campaign manager.* He put a hand on her cheek and said, "Lay down. Get your rest."

Her eyes closed before he got up and walked creakily back to the garage, where, without bothering to put on a light, he pulled out an old alligator suitcase, forced the sticky latches, smoothed his hand along the crushed gold velvet inside, and withdrew a thick, carefully-coiled eighteen-foot length of rope.

•••••

Ezra screamed they had the wrong man. He remembered that. They were after Lionel. Lionel was the agitator, trying to get everyone registered to vote. Ezra's voice quaked with fear. "Lionel's the one went to the lunch counter sit-in, talked back to Old Man McCauley at the drugstore, not me," he pleaded. "Wasn't me!"

For a second, Hawke looked at McCauley as if to say, *What if the nigger's telling the truth?* The moment passed. Mac McCauley was bent on sending a message. Didn't matter if the boy's name was Ezra, Lionel, or Mickey Mantle.

Ezra begged. He remembered that as well. They beat him for begging. Tied his hands, then threw him in the dirt right there and kicked him with their pointed country boots until he couldn't beg anymore. They waited while he caught his breath. Ike walked to the spot and grabbed a handful of dirt, crushed it against his chest. His eyes were wet, his breath ragged. He wanted to run. A raven shrieked.

Ezra fought them. Anyone could see the change when they yanked him to his knees. His face was caked with dirt and grass, but his eyes were open. That was the last and only way left to fight, with his eyes. When McCauley pulled off his white hood and screamed, "Look at me," Ezra's gaze rose from the ground. He met McCauley's eyes and spit fast and hard, then crumpled forward as Hawke kicked him viciously in the spine. Ezra never saw McCauley's smile as he wiped the spit from his face and ordered Hawke to get the rope.

That was when he, Ike, moved from his hiding place. The twigs snapped, loud as a bomb in the still forest. McCauley turned and saw him. He ran, a boy reborn.

Lionel? He took off, too. The day after they found Ezra. No one knew where, and no one ever heard from him again.

Years later—long after Ike had been pressed into service, long past the time they stopped threatening him because he now worked willingly for McCauley—Eddie Bishop brought him the rope. Eddie was the first black Kilgo cop, sent as part of the team to investigate Ezra James' death.

Or at least to make it *seem* that Ezra's death was properly investigated.

What better way to make the inquiry credible than send along a black cop? Ike knew it was Eddie's fear and ambition that kept him quiet when the crime went down as unsolved. Eddie Bishop was just like him: guilty.

When the sergeant who stashed the Ezra James evidence croaked four years after the crime, Eddie stole it from a locker in the police station. He didn't say why, but Ike knew. Eddie, like himself, wanted a shot at future redemption. He remembered the day Eddie delivered the rope. It still had the slip-knot McCauley and Hawke used on Ezra.

Using his elbow and the space between his thumb and first finger, he re-wound it into a new coil and placed it in the alligator suitcase with his handwritten account of what happened to Ezra. Later, he added the paper he forced Tyler to sign the night he died. He'd given those papers to Dan Patragno, but kept the rope. He didn't know why.

Now he knew.

Holding one end, he tossed the heavy cord rodeo-style into the clearing. It fired out smoothly and landed with a soft thud in the dirt. The noise scared some night birds, who streaked from their bush to a branch high above. He followed their flight. That's the tree, he thought. He stood and studied the giant oak carefully. That's the tree, and that must have been the branch.

The limb, about nine feet high, seemed sturdy. It slanted slightly skyward, which meant the rope would not slip off the end of the branch. He tried it. The first toss fell short. The second missed altogether. On the fifth try, the rope looped around the branch. Ike pulled the slip-knot end until both sides were equal. Wrapping an end around each fist, he tried to lift himself off the ground and found he wasn't strong enough. It was evident, though, that the branch would support his weight.

He let the rope dangle and ran his hands along the bark. Rough enough to climb. He looked for footholds for his black loafers and tried to plot a course that would take him high enough. Logistical problems arose that he hadn't anticipated. Should he put the slip-knot around his neck, climb, then jump? Or climb first with the rope in his hand, put it on, then let himself drop? Did he want to strangle to death or snap his neck? He thought of prisoners who hung themselves in their cells. That was easier. They had a chair and a lower perch.

A mosquito bit his neck. He slapped at it and realized he still wore his dress shirt. He took it off and threw it aside. His sleeveless undershirt was soaked with sweat. There was another problem—how to anchor the rope. It was too short to fasten around the base of the thick tree. He circled around like a contractor contemplating a new project. There was another branch around back that was lower down and which looked solid enough for the job.

He tied the rope around the lower branch and triple knotted it. Then he stood and pulled with all his might. It held.

He took the rest, threw again until it landed on the high branch, and saw that the slip-knot end was at least seven feet from the ground. He was five-ten. The rope was high enough. Solving the problem gave him a degree of pleasure.

Everything was ready. He sat in the dirt on his knees and prayed. He asked forgiveness for not helping Ezra, for putting himself before God and his family, for serving a man he knew to be a murderer, and for the sin he was about to commit. He asked God to watch over his granddaughter.

He prayed his body would not be ravaged by birds and forest animals, and that he would be found by someone who didn't know him.

His eyes opened suddenly. He hadn't left a note. He considered returning to his car. The *Taurus* was less than a hundred yards away.

Ruthie's pen and pad were in the glove compartment. He decided against it. What would he write? Dianna had said it all. *Bootlicking bastard.* McCauley, too. *We didn't have to force you ... You liked playin' Big Ike ...* He rose. The morning mist had already coated the rope with moisture. He took a breath and put it on, sliding the noose down until it was snug as a Sunday tie.

He tested the lower branch again and snapped around at the sound of a car. Impossible. No one else knew about this place. No one except McCauley, and the papers said he was hiding out in D.C. Ike peered into the mist. The car was getting closer; he could see headlights bobbing and hear the tires churning up earth. A camper? Tourist? No, the car seemed to be going too fast. He could almost feel the driver's sense of urgency. He removed the noose and tossed it behind the tree. The rest of the rope was still out in the open.

The first thing he saw was the headlights stop bouncing. Then colors, green and white. Then the letters, Kilgo P.D. Then Eddie Bishop was walking straight toward him. He had his plastic-brimmed police hat in his hand.

"Park's closed, Ike."

He tried to see himself through Eddie's eyes. The mayor and soon-to-be-congressman wore mud-spattered pants and a filthy undershirt, and stood in the forest before dawn beside a tree with a long rope that swung with the breeze.

"Get in your car and drive away, Eddie."

"Can't do it."

He found a tree stump and brushed off some fire ants. "How'd you find me?"

"Women heard you leave. Cynthia called, real worried. Didn't know where you were headed. I took a guess. I've been here before too, you know."

The two exchanged glances. He saw Eddie's eyes cut to the rope. He felt ashamed and sank to the ground. He squeezed up a mound of dirt and let it sift through his fingers. He stared into the dark bushes. "Can't live with it no more, Eddie."

Eddie dropped to the wet dirt with him so they were face to face and dug his fingers into Ike's shoulders. "We both sinned, Ike. I should'a come out when they hung that boy and the Northern papers were down here nosin' all around. I should've led 'em right to this spot. I kept quiet, just like you." Eddie touched the nametag on his khaki uniform. "I was the first colored man on the police force. Couldn't screw that up. Man, that was history."

"Was your Mom proud of you, Eddie? I thought Mama was proud, but she never trusted me being with McCauley." He drew in the dirt with his finger. "She hid it, but knew something wasn't right. When she was dying, she made me tell. She turned her face away from me, Eddie. Closed her eyes and turned away. Made me promise I'd tell the police what happened to Ezra. I swore on her deathbed, and never did it."

"Times were different when she died, Ike. She'd understand now. She'd be proud."

He shook his head. "I'm hurtin', Eddie. Can't make it stop. Thought by telling the truth, it'd clean me inside." He snuck a look at the rope.

Eddie saw him and grabbed his shoulders. "That ain't the way. Listen to me, Chrissakes. Maybe what we did was so bad, we don't deserve no forgiveness. But—listen, damn it—maybe we just ain't earned it yet. Maybe we got to keep tryin'." Eddie shook a fist like he was getting ready to roll dice. He seemed to be struggling for what to say next, but when he looked up, it was clear he'd known all along.

"Only one thing I know for sure."

Bootlicker

Ike waited, barely breathing.

"To save *me*," Eddie said, "I gotta save *you*."

Epilogue

Everyone wanted a piece of the little girl in the pale yellow dress with white lace trim.

An older guy from the Associated Press hitched up his trousers and got on his knees. Pen to pad, he said, "How old are you, little lady?"

She held up a hand and four fingers that wriggled like she was waving bye-bye.

"And what's your name?"

"Marva."

"Can you spell that for me, Marvelous?"

She looked at him cock-eyed. "M-A-R-V-A."

"Monster," Ruthie whispered to Dan in a corner away from the crowd.

Other reporters pressed in on the little girl. "Where do you live, Marva? What grade are you in? Do you like your teacher? Do you have any pets? Aren't you proud of Grandpa?"

Dan slouched against the wall." This is Washington journalism?"

"Slow news day," Ruthie said.

Cameras flashed. Marva put one small hand to her tightly coiled braids and slid off the leather couch. She shucked off her white, patent-leather shoes, leapt back onto the couch, and started bouncing. Little jumps at first, then higher and higher. "Wheee," she yelled, her mouth curled into a devilish grin. Her tongue rolled out to reveal a cherry Life-saver. She plucked it off with two fingers, studied it a moment and put it back in her mouth.

"Ugh," Ruthie said.

More flashes. TV camera lights bathed the office in white light. A young woman ran out of an inner office, nearly tripping over a pile of electrical cords. "*Marva Rainey-Washington*," she said in a voice that about froze the child mid-jump.

Little Marva pulled her legs in and executed a nice seated landing. Except that the back of one thigh caught the arm of the couch. "Owww. My *tush*," she said, giggling.

Everyone laughed with her, save for Mrs. Washington, who grabbed one of the girl's stick-thin elbows and marched her off for a crash course on proper behavior in the office of a United States congressman.

"That child," Ruthie said.

"Where's her father? More important, where's Gramps?"

"Jerome went with Ike."

Dan led Ruthie to the seventh floor hallway of the Longworth House Office Building. "I'll be glad when this day is over and all the families go back home," she said. "This place is like a nursery."

He looked back to the office. An eight-foot South Carolina state flag—blue, with silver crescent and lone palmetto tree—stood beside the open door. A wooden nameplate had already been tacked to the wall: "Rep. Ike Washington, 6th District, S.C."

"Where did they go?"

"Meeting of the new Democratic Caucus. They'll be back in." She checked her watch and scanned the corridor. "Well, they should have been here by now."

They reached a window that overlooked a large park with concrete benches arranged horseshoe style. There was a playground set and a full-body marble statue of someone in a navy cape that Dan didn't recognize. The park was empty; it had begun to snow. Ruthie put her hand on the window and shivered.

"Going to have to get used to the weather," she said. "This is only January."

He rubbed her shoulder and pulled back, afraid he'd offended her. "Want my jacket?"

She shook her head and put a hand on his cheek. He smelled the perfume on the inside of her wrist. It reminded him of waking up beside her.

"Ruthie, I'm sorry ... how it worked out and all."

"Me, too."

"I'm better than the way I behaved. I've thought about it a lot. I've wanted to call you."

"You came instead. That's better."

"This? This is work. I'm leaving tomorrow. They just wanted me to cover the swearing-in ceremony."

"Oh."

"But I knew I'd see you. I was hoping we'd get time to talk."

She lifted one eyebrow.

"Just talk," he assured her.

She walked a few steps and turned back. The movement made the bottom of her brown skirt swirl. "I wanted to call you, too," she said softly. "We went too fast, Dan."

"Maybe."

Both of them turned as Marva Rainey-Washington, four-year-old eyes red and puffy, shot out of the office and tore past them, patent-leather shoes clacking with each step. "I wuh,wuh-want my Da-Da-Daddy," she cried without slowing.

Ruthie smothered her laugh until Marva turned a corner. "That child."

"Listen, have dinner with me tonight. I want to tell you about my new job."

"You got a job with the *Post*?"

"Nope."

"*New York Times*?"

"No."

She rubbed her chin. "*L.A. Times? Miami Herald*?"

"Close," he said. "You're looking at the new Washington Correspondent for the *Tampa Daily News*."

"Very nice, Mr. Patragno."

Ike and Jerome Washington emerged from the corner where Marva had disappeared. She walked between them, demure as a ballerina. The three held hands. When they were halfway to the office, Marva burst forward, then cackled in delight when Ike and Jerome lifted her from the ground, swung her back and forth, and set her down. She tried again and they hauled her in.

Ike was puffing by the time he reached the office. "Patragno, hi. Met the family?"

"That one's hard to miss," he said, nodding toward Marva. "Hey, Jerome, how's things in Charlotte?"

"Busy, though I wouldn't miss this."

His wife—Ike's daughter-in-law—sidled up. Marva slipped away.

"Dan Patragno," Jerome said, "my wife, Hester Rainey-Washington."

"Nice to ..." Her eyes met his, then scanned around like she'd dropped something important. "Marva?" No answer. "Excuse me," she said.

Ruthie laughed. "Hope you're not expecting her to give you another grandchild soon, Ike. That woman's got her hands full with *one*."

"Amen," Jerome sighed.

Dan nodded and allowed himself a long look at Jerome. Probably a portrait of Ike twenty-five years ago. Medium height, stocky build, thick linebacker's neck. He—they—were handsome men, with deep-set, nearly black eyes, easy smiles, smooth complexions, and one flaw—too-small ears that screamed for longer haircuts.

As they crowded back into the office, Dan touched Ruthie's elbow. "So, tonight?"

She smiled. He remembered the feel of her lips. Yearned for it. "We'll see," she said.

•••••

At mid-morning, Ike's entourage of friends, staff, family, and reporters left for the Capitol. Since it was snowing, they took the indoor route: members-only elevators to the basement, then a maze of underground tunnels to another set of elevators that let them off on the second floor of the Capitol, just outside the House floor.

Dan saw that he and his reporter colleagues had a choice: watch through a door from a lobby just off the historic chamber, or hustle up to the third-floor press gallery that overlooked the floor of the House. He chose the door and cursed when an usher with white gloves closed it in his face.

He flashed on Butcher bitching at the six hundred bucks it cost to send him to Washington. The only point of coming up was to see Ike get sworn in. He had to see it to be able to describe it. He started to elbow his way out, got stuck in a crush of reporters, barely noticed a row of multi-tiered, crystal chandeliers that lit up the lobby with its antique tables and hardwood floors. Besides press, the room outside the chamber was mobbed with family and friends of the new 104th Congress. Each representative was allowed to bring one guest inside; the rest had to watch from the visitors' gallery one floor above, or wait in the ornate lobby.

Dan raced out, considered the "media only" elevator to his right, and opted for the wide, gray marble staircase dead ahead. He took the steps two at a time. They felt flat, worn and a little slippery beneath his feet. How many reporters had chased congressmen up and down these hallowed steps? He passed a mural of some great moment in American history and promised himself to come back and read the inscription when there was time.

He raced to the press gallery, not quite sure where to find the entrance to the media seats that overlooked the House floor, not really wanting to ask anyone and look like a hick. The gallery was like a long, rectangular newsroom. Moving through was like going from car to car on a train. Larger news organizations had their own work spaces, tiny cubicles with two or three desks jammed in. Other reporters sat with laptops at desks that were first come, first served.

Certain the ceremony had begun, he raced past a line of seven phone booths—all occupied—and saw the entrance he needed. He raced for the door, only to be stopped by a bald, bored-looking guy in navy coat and tie and lapel badge that said: "Roger Gaylord—House Press."

"Sorry buddy, no more seats."

"I'll stand," Dan said, breathless.

"No can do."

He gathered himself and spoke quietly. "Roger," he said, close enough now to see a tiny wart on the guy's neck, "I've come all the way from Charleston, South Carolina, to watch the local congressman get sworn in. This is a big thing for us and I'm going in there. Try to stop me and there's going to be a scene. You want that?"

Roger rolled his eyes and stepped aside. "Stay in back."

Dan swung open the door and stopped. He remembered stepping

from the dark concrete ramps as a child into the magnificence of Yankee Stadium. This was the political equal. He moved forward, drank in the flavor, felt proud to be an American, then embarrassed at being so sappy. His colleagues sat in several rows of dark wooden benches and seemed oblivious to the setting.

He continued down several steps toward a brass guardrail that circled the cavernous room. Beyond and on both sides were the visitors' galleries; directly below was the rostrum, province of the Speaker. A wall-length American flag hung behind his chair—the same flag shown during State of the Union addresses, he realized. There was a clock above the flag. He wrote down the time and date: three past noon, January 5, 1993.

A familiar voice below snapped him back to attention. Washington Democrat Tom Foley, Speaker of the House since 1989. The ceremony was underway.

"Welcome to you, the new members of the 103rd Congress," Foley said. "I salute you. Please stand and repeat after me." He waited and they stood. "I do solemnly swear that I will support and defend the Constitution of the United States."

Dan scanned the floor below, remembered reading there were four hundred, forty-eight seats altogether. Members were not assigned specific chairs; instead, they sat with their parties. Something made him glance up. Ruthie was on the right side of the visitors' gallery, sitting beside Cynthia Washington, Derrick Maussipant, Agnes Stono, Jerome, Hesther and Eddie Bishop, who wore a beige suit instead of his khaki police uniform.

Ruthie had seen Dan's problem and was pointing down to the far right corner of the House floor. He gave her a thumbs-up and shifted position.

Bootlicker

There, in the corner was Ike, erect as a first-year military cadet, right hand pressed over his heart. Dan watched intently, jotting notes without looking at his pad. Standing on the seat beside Ike was Marva Rainey-Washington, who seemed to realize in the midst of the oath that no one was paying attention to her, and that the oversized leather cushion beneath her feet was very bouncy. She tested the spring in her seat, flexing her knees like a diver.

Ike must have sensed what was coming. He put his left hand on her slight shoulder and prevented the take-off. Marva looked up at him sharply, lips pursed, hands on her hips. He gave her a hard stare that said, *Just try it.*

Maybe I will, her bright eyes answered. But she didn't. After a time, the little girl sighed and seemed to decide the only game left was to become a congresswoman.

She turned to Speaker Foley, smacked her right hand to her chest, and never saw Ike's smile as she—and he—recited the remainder of the oath.

- the end -

Discussion Questions:

1 – Is Dan good or lucky as a reporter?

2 – Why aren't reporters supposed to get personally involved with their sources? Wouldn't close relationships produce more inside information?

3 – The story takes place in 1992. How have newspapers changed since then, for better or worse?

4 – Why did Judge McCauley think young Ike would be a good liaison to the black communities of South Carolina, and thus be able to help him politically?

5 – What qualities does Ike demonstrate that will make him a good congressman?

6 – Ezra forgives Ike, but Ike can't forgive himself. Why? How will this affect Ike in the future?

7 – What does the future hold for Senator McCauley?

8 – Does Ruthie have a solid future in politics, or will she move on? Will Dan remain in her life?

9– Name some items that were popular in 1992, the year the story takes place, that have been swept away by time.

Interview with the Author

How much of this story is real?

South Carolina did elect its first black congressman since Reconstruction in 1992, but that is where reality stops and fiction begins in *Bootlicker*. The rest is simply imagination and literary license, inspired by my time as Washington correspondent for *The Tampa Tribune*, and later, The *Charleston (SC) Post & Courier*.

How do you view Ike?

Ike was a victim of circumstances who came to see his plight as a ticket out of poverty. It was a short-cut, however, one that ultimately caused tremendous guilt. I think in the end, the positive side of Ike will prevail and that he will do more good than harm. I also believe he learned important lessons that will guide his future behavior and make him a valuable mentor to young people just beginning their careers.

Dan has serious lapses in judgment, yet ends up just fine. Is that how it really works in journalism?

Though reporters are supposed to abide by a detailed code of ethics, the field is still more art than science. Dan is pretty raw in *Bootlicker*. He has lots to learn, and will hopefully not make the same mistakes again. Journalists who commit libel are done. Same for those who fabricate facts and stories or embarrass their newspapers or stations in other ways. Those who commit less egregious errors can learn and go on to do important work. That said, no editor I ever worked for would forgive Dan twice for the mistakes he makes while covering Ike's campaign.

Did Sen. McCauley keep getting reelected because he was a savvy politician, or because the voters of his state didn't care enough to run him out of office?

It's probably a combination of the two. Many Southern politicians who thrived by exploiting racial tensions were drummed out when blacks came to political power. Others got old and retired or died. A very few saw change coming and adjusted their actions—if not their hearts—to accommodate the new political landscape. McCauley is clearly reprehensible, an opportunist with no conscience in a position of influence and power. Will he ever be punished? Perhaps that is the cornerstone of another novel.

Do you think your story will touch others or anger them?

All writers want to provoke a reaction. I think some will be touched and some will be angered. Mostly, I hope readers will find an entertaining escape from their daily lives in *Bootlicker*, but also find this a timely story of hope, a tale of guilt and redemption, and real enough to be true.

What else were you shooting for with this book?

In a year of heightened political sensitivities, I wanted *Bootlicker* to go where C-SPAN is never invited—to back rooms where deals are cut, futures are plotted, and where right and wrong are not so easily defined. I wrote this story for women intrigued by powerful men, men intrigued by the path to power, and all who thought they understood politics.

What is your own background?

I'm a native New Yorker who wound up spending 25 years working for Southern newspapers. In 2002, I switched gears and became the speechwriter at a large federal agency in Washington, D.C. I serve there today as deputy communications director. I also teach journalism classes at American University. My wife is a special education administrator in Montgomery County, MD, and we have three adult children, one in public relations, one studying to become an art therapist, and one an engineer. I hold a B.A. in communications from American and a Masters in fiction from Johns Hopkins University.